Any resemblance between the characters in this book and persons living or dead is strictly coincidental.

Copyright @ 1999 by Chameleon Publishing

Printed and bound by J. & M. Reproductions

Cover design by June Hubbard

Library of Congress Catalog number pending

All rights reserved. Printed in the United States of America. No part of this book may be used or reproduced in any manner whatsoever without written permission except in the case of brief quotations embodied in critical articles or reviews. For information address Chameleon Publishing, 3430 Salem Drive, Rochester Hills, Michigan 48306.

ISBN 1-892419-02-5

February, 1999: First edition

Grateful acknowledgement is made for permission to reprint the following works:

"The Veil" by Christine Miller. Copyright @ 1995 by Christine Miller. First published in Taler's Tales No. 2, Fall 1995.

"Welcome Home" by Martha Pound Miller. Copyright @ 1998 by Martha Pound Miller. First published in Haunts Magazine.

"Isle of the Dancing Dead" by Rick Kennett. Copyright 1991 by Rick Kennett. First published in The Fifth Book of After Midnight Stories by Robert Hale, Ltd, U. K.

"The Buried Past" by Phil Locascio. Copyright @ 1997 by Phil Locascio. First published in Issue 7 of White Knuckles magazine – winter/spring 1997 issue.

"The Lovers" by Edo van Belkom. First published in Crossroads Magazine.

"Red Whiskey" by Tina L. Jens. Copyright @ 1994 by Tina L. Jens. First published in South From Midnight, edited by Richard Gilliam, Martin H. Greenberg and Thomas R. Hanlon, published by Southern Fried Press.

"Eight Words" by James Van Pelt. Copyright @ 1995 by James Van Pelt. First published in Pulphouse #19, 1995.

"But None, I Think, Do There Embrace" by Colin W.J. Joss. First published in Whispers.

Acknowledgements

Many dear friends helped bring this book to life and, to all of you, I am ever grateful. Whatever success this venture might attain is due totally to the tremendous help I have received in launching this project.

In creating **Cemetery Sonata** it was my wish to find new talent as well as established authors: the main goal being to put together a good, wholesome, SCARY group of stories. I am impressed at the wonderful talent who helped make this possible.

To all my contributors, thank you. This book would not be but for your talents. And to those I could not fit into this volume, I wish to say that it was not because of lack of talent, but lack of space and resources. For this reason, I hope to create a volume II of **Cemetery Sonata**, a volume III and so on, should there be the demand. Good writing should never be kept in a drawer.

Specifically, I want to thank my husband, David, for enduring my many mood swings, my daughter, Becky, for being so patient, my dear friends Danielle Iserman and Denise Bruchman for keeping me sane and believing in me. And, especially, thank you, Gail Fox and Danielle Wyrecki for your unfailing support. I couldn't have done this without any of you.
And, most of all, I want to thank my darling Shih Tzu and mentor, Max. I couldn't have survived those many long nights without your furry presence at my feet.

To all who have made this book possible, my sincere appreciation and gratitude.

June Hubbard
Editor

Contents

Cemetery Sonata - Danielle Iserman	1
Ashes to Ashes - Steve Eller	12
Before I Sleep - Steve Eller	21
For the Love of Claire - William L. Churchman	29
A Stitch in Time - Denise M. Bruckman	33
Incineration - Daniel Keohane	40
The Veil - Christine Miller	51
The Last Stone - Dianne Buckman	73
Welcome Home - Martha Pound Miller	85
The Cabinet - Gail Sosinsky Wickman	93
The Roots of Evil - Lisa Becker	102
My Dear Companion - Steven Lee Climer	118
Hope is an Inanimate Desire - Trent Zelazny	125
Side by Side - Brad Jeske	140
Helena - Philip Caveney	144
Family Reunion - Catherine Nichols	164
Bring Out Your Dead - Laura Capewell	168
Isle of the Dancing Dead - Rick Kennett	175
Paradise Lost - Carol MacAllister	184
Till Death Do Us Join - James O. Dukes	187
Harold - Gayla D. Bassman	196
Bitter Pills - Deborah Markus	207
Little Voices - Matt Doeden	226
The Buried Past - Phil Locascio	231
The Lovers - Edo van Belkom	245
Summer House - Calvin K. Bricker	248
The Mako Shark Society - Ray Roberts	265
The Grave - K. D. Wentworth	272
Red Whiskey - Tina L. Jens	285
Grounded - Robert Devereaux	300
Better Forget - Liz Holliday	313
I Know What Scares You - Greg Burnham	319
Caretaker of the Ring - Michael C. McPherson	340
Mr. Aberystwyth and the Three Weird Sisters - Robin Lochlann Spriggs	351
When Sparrows Fall - Lisa S. Silverthorne	365
Water this Cold - Terry Campbell	376
Eight Words - James Van Pelt	390
The Man in Black - Carl Hughes	400
Portrait in Graphite - John Urbancik IIII	412
Mending - Cheryl Jessop	432
Epitaph - Fara Moore	448
But None, I Think Do There Embrace – J.W.C. Joss	455

Cemetery Sonata

Cemetery Sonata

Danielle Iserman

Most Southerners expect a few eccentric kinfolk to branch off their family tree - the kind of relatives that made family reunions memorable. Miss Emily was just such a branch in the LeBlanc family lineage.

The townsfolk of Madison, Georgia nodded politely whenever they happened to pass Miss Emily on the sidewalk but could barely refrain from whispering about her until she was safely out of range of their wagging tongues.

Miss Emily was her own worst enemy when it came to fanning the flames of that gossip: she refused to wear anything except long black crepe dresses - out of respect for the "Glorious Dead." She was in perpetual mourning for the Old South the "Late, Great Unpleasantness" - that's how she liked to refer to the War Between the States. Miss Emily denounced the North's victory and considered the whole idea as nothing more than Yankee propaganda. The funny thing was that, even though Miss Emily was considered to be older than dirt, she certainly wasn't old enough to remember the war. However, since her granddaddy, Captain Louis LeBlanc, fought and died for the "Cause" at the Battle of Franklin, Miss Emily had carte blanche to mourn to her heart's content, and her life long membership in the United Daughters of the Confederacy was merely icing on the cake of her obsession. Miss Emily proudly displayed the Captain's blood stained uniform on a dressmaker's mannequin in the parlor near the red portieres where if looked like a decapitated, limbless Confederate soldier lurking in the shadows. Halloween was a year round event at the LeBlanc house.

Poor Miss Emily, besides being a lonely spinster, had the misfortune of resembling the wicked witch in the "Wizard of Oz" – minus the green skin and the wart on her nose. Her beauty betrayed her about the same time her hair turned white, and the big blotch of red rouge on her cheeks just made things worse. And, always...the black crepe dress.

Miss Emily's peculiar behavior was indulged by Madisonians because of her extraordinary gift. She was a pianist with talent that could only have been given her personally by God. Madison society clamored to send their less-than-talented children to her in hopes of musical greatness. It was no secret that, even more than the Old South, Miss Emily loved music and her Steinway piano.

Like Miss Emily, the LaBlanc mansion was a falling-apart Greek Revival testament to a time of chivalry long passed into the abyss of time. A tattered Confederate battle flag snapped noisily from the flagpole adorning the front yard as Amanda Thorne trudged up the mansion's crumbling steps with her sheet music clutched under her arm - George Gershwin's "Rhapsody in Blue" to be exact. Amanda calculated that she'd been to Miss Emily's 880 times - every Saturday morning from the time she was five not including today, one week before her sixteenth birthday.

She rapped the brass knocker sharply against the door. A chill November breeze sent red and gold leaves skipping across the sidewalk. Miss Emily opened the heavy oak door. "Right on time, as usual. I wish all my students were as punctual as you, my dear," said Miss Emily with the cracking voice reserved for old Southern women. She smiled warmly at her favorite student as she motioned for Amanda to come inside.

"How are you today, Miss Emily?" asked Amanda as she took her seat on the green tufted piano bench that was long enough to seat three people. She propped "Rhapsody in Blue" up on the music stand and waited for Miss Emily to take her place beside her. Amanda's fingers stretched to reach the difficult opening chords as pianist and piano paid homage to George Gershwin's genius.

An hour later Miss Emily's thin arm reached to stop the ticking metronome on the Steinway.

"Amanda, you've worked very hard this week and I believe that George Gershwin would be pleased with your rendition of "Rhapsody in Blue." It's not perfect, mind you, but if you concentrate on the finale, you'll be proud of your performance. The recital is next week and, if my memory doesn't fail me, it's on the same day as your sixteenth birthday," she said as she patted Amanda's hand.

Miss Emily stumbled as she walked Amanda to the front door. "Miss Emily, are all right?" cried Amanda as she caught her teacher just before she fell. The old woman rubbed her left arm. Her face was pinched with pain.

"I'm fine, child. Don't you worry about me," she said as she brushed a stray blonde hair away from Amanda's frightened face. "As long as I have my music, I'll be fine. Who knows, maybe I'll play even after I'm dead and gone." She continued to rub her arm, but offered a weak smile to Amanda as a token of reassurance.

Amanda Thorne didn't play "Rhapsody in Blue" at the Madison Recital the following Saturday - the sheet music ended up in the trash. She understood how it felt to mourn the loss of someone you loved. Miss Emily dropped dead on Amanda's sixteenth birthday.

The LeBlanc family crypt loomed in the far corner of the Madison Cemetery just past the railroad tracks. Ancient, twisted cedar trees surrounded the huge burial ground of what was home to hundreds of restless souls.

A litany of four-letter words permeated the air as the two piano movers hired by Miss Emily's attorney pushed and pulled the black Steinway into the middle of the crypt. Lucky for them, Miss Emily had the courtesy to die during the fall instead of the murderous Georgia summer. Despite the cool breeze, sweat trickled down the burly men's backs.

"Crazy old woman."

"Crazy old rich woman, ya mean?"

Preston "Digger" Williams, Madison's mortician, thought Miss Emily's final request was a joke - until her lawyer assured him it wasn't. He'd never heard of anything so bizarre. Except for the time when the vet had to put Joe Cunningham's pet Collie to sleep so it could be buried with him after old Joe died from choking on a ham sandwich. He had quite a time getting them both in the coffin. That was weird, but Miss Emily's request won the blue ribbon at the county fair of weird. It was certainly a challenge though, and something the folks in town would talk about for years. Digger drifted in a fantasy of accolades as he dialed the number to the welder's shop. "Hey, Jeff. Is that brace ready yet? I'm gonna need it Thursday mornin'." He turned to look at Emily LeBlanc's corpse laid out on the stainless steel table - he had just finished embalming her. Yes, he would be famous. People would come from all over Georgia, maybe from all over the United States, to seek his expertise for their dearly departed loved ones. Maybe he could advertise on the local television stations. He'd be able to buy that new Caddy hearse before next summer. He was sure of it. "It's done – great! I'll be right over." He untied his rubber apron and tossed it onto the counter. "I'll be back in a few minutes, Miss Emily. Don't go nowhere, ya hear?" He patted the dead woman's cold arm as he walked out the door.

Late Thursday afternoon, Pastor Bernard Simons followed Digger Williams through the cemetery toward the LeBlanc family crypt. The mourners had returned to the land of the living, and all that was left to do was to escort Miss Emily to her final resting place. The key to open the crypt jingled with the change in his right pants pocket. He double-checked just to make sure the key was still there. He didn't want to get all the way out in the cemetery with Miss Emily's corpse and not have the key to open the door. Pastor Simons was very uncomfortable about the whole macabre ordeal and wanted it over with as quickly as possible. Seeing Miss Emily's body sitting on the piano bench gave him the creeps. He knew it would be good for a week's worth of nightmares. How did Digger Williams get her propped up on that bench anyway? Maybe he didn't want to know, and he certainly wasn't going to ask.

Amanda watched Jasper Herron and Buddy Taylor push the dolly holding Miss Emily's corpse down the narrow cobblestone path with the Pastor and Digger Williams following in solemn funeral-march fashion.

"Let's be careful, boys. I've got her strapped on the bench pretty tight, but I didn't think we'd want to pick her up off the ground now, would we?" said Digger in a voice loud enough for Amanda to hear.

"No, Sir, I surely wouldn't want to do that," agreed Buddy Taylor.

Amanda didn't think Miss Emily's request was so strange really. People wanted to be near the things they loved, and the only thing she loved in her life was her music and the Old South. This wasn't any stranger than scattering someone's ashes on the beach or off the top of a mountain. No....it really wasn't that strange.

The sun slipped slowly behind a wall of Georgia pine trees and the woods changed from deep green to black. The tombstones cast long shadows throughout the cemetery. Jasper and Buddy lifted the piano bench and carried Miss Emily into her eternal home and placed her body in front of the Steinway just as she requested in her will. Digger Williams smoothed her black dress and pushed a stray hair pin back into place before he placed her hands on the keyboard...just as she specified in his will. Jasper Herron had a coughing fit from all the exertion.

"Jasper, you don't give up those damn cigarettes, you'll be taking a dirt nap right next to Miss Emily," scolded Buddy Taylor. "Say, you play the guitar some, don't you? After you kick the bucket from lung cancer or emphysema, Ole digger here can prop you up next to Miss Emily and you can play a duet." Everyone laughed except Jasper.

"Come on, Digger, let's lock this hotel for the dead up and get the hell outta here. I don't want to be here after dark," confessed Buddy.

Pastor Simons closed the door after mumbling an obligatory prayer. "Good—we're done. Now, let's go home."

How did Digger Williams get her to sit up so straight?

The following Thursday evening, Pastor Simons was practicing Sunday's sermon on the evils of alcohol. He liked the way his voice boomed in the empty church sanctuary. A wicked little smile crept across his lips as he pictured his napping flock jumping out of their pews when he pounded on the pulpit during the sermon's high point. That's what they get for not paying attention.

It was warm in the church and he'd worked himself into quite a preaching frenzy. Sweat snaked down his back and wet circles ringed his armpits. He pulled his rumpled handkerchief from his pants pocket and dabbed at the perspiration crowning his forehead. He'd been at church for more than two hours and was ready to call it a night. Thoughts of the fresh apple pie his wife baked that afternoon made his mouth water and he couldn't wait to get home and eat a big slice of it – with a scoop of vanilla ice cream on the side just for good measure.

The piano music was so faint Pastor Simons thought he imagined it. He pried open a side window next the choir loft and listened closely. He recognized the tune as "Moonlight Sonata" - he'd never heard anything so beautiful. Yes...something was wrong. The music was coming from the cemetery. Chills raced up and down his spine as the image of Miss Emily's corpse strapped to the piano bench invaded his mind. His skin crawled. It was impossible. He didn't believe in ghosts. He scrambled out of the church, leaving his notes for Sunday's sermon scattered on the carpet next to the pulpit. Gravel sprayed the side of the church as Simons sped away. When he got home, he wasn't hungry for pie.

The posthumous midnight concerts emanated from the LeBlanc crypt and the ethereal mist swirled around the spirits as they danced in their dark realm to the music that touched their souls' memory.

Amanda Thorne sat under a big oak tree next to the Confederate grave down by the tracks. She didn't believe all the rumors running rampant in town about what was or wasn't, going on in the Madison Cemetery. It was a fact, though, that Pastor Simons had a nervous breakdown six months ago and was in a sanitarium somewhere in Alabama. And, it was another fact that his nervous breakdown came on shortly after Miss Emily died. But, it was still just circumstantial as far as she was concerned.

The warm Georgia night felt like silk against her skin and the scent of honeysuckle tickled her nose. Amanda didn't have to wait long for "Moonlight Sonata's" melody to drift through the darkness. She remembered that Miss Emily told her she'd find a way to play after she was dead. Amanda knew now she wasn't kidding and death was merely an inconvenience. She closed her eyes and listened to the most beautiful music she had ever heard. She imagined she was seated at the fine old Steinway as she played in unison with her teacher. After the last note fell silent, the crickets and cicadas continued with the night's encore.

Six weeks later, "Moonlight Sonata" was no longer recognizable. All you could hear was the sound of someone pounding on the piano keyboard. Amanda's nightmares started about the same time the music changed.

The nightmare always began with Amanda trapped in fetid darkness - not alone, but unable to see who or what was in the darkness with her. She'd awake soaked in sweat, her heart pounding in her chest and grateful that it was only a dream.

Tonight, as the nightmare faded, reality became worse. Amanda knew she wasn't alone as she slowly pulled the blanket from her face. A chill raced down her spine. Her body suddenly paralyzed by fear. Miss Emily's ghost floated at the foot of her bed. The spirit's skeletal hands stretched before her trying to show Amanda...something.

An icy mist swirled around Amanda's room. She could see her breath come in short staccato bursts. The specter cried softly as it retreated to the dark recesses of the room and vanished.

"Help...me...Amanda. Help...me."

Amanda fumbled with the light switch next to her bed, praying for the safety the light offered. She fell out of bed and staggered to the open window for fresh air. She inhaled the cool night air deeply into her lungs. The thudding in her chest was quieter, but her hands still trembled.

She heard someone pounding on a piano keyboard...it was coming from the cemetery.

"Amanda, help me."

Her instincts begged her to stay away, but Amanda tiptoed down the stairs and into the indigo night. She was powerless against the force pleading with her. Miss Emily needed her. She grabbed a lantern and a crow bar from her daddy's tool shed and ran down the block toward the cemetery. Her thin nightgown fluttered against her bare legs.

Amanda wriggled through two bent bars on the cemetery's black iron gate. A terrifying thought crossed her mind: was someone trying to get in...or get out? She picked up the lantern and stumbled toward the LeBlanc crypt. The pounding on the piano grew louder.

Amanda wedged the crowbar between the crypt's iron doors and pulled with all her strength. Again...again...again. Finally, the lock surrendered and the door creaked open.

The smell of rotting flesh escaped into the night. Bile swelled in Amanda's throat. She wheeled around and vomited her mother's supper onto the ground. Something ran across her bare feet and scampered into the night.

"Amanda, please help me."

She covered her nose with the sleeve of her nightgown as she forced herself into the crypt. The yellow lantern light fell upon the dust covered Steinway. A scream rushed from the pit of her stomach.

Bone jutted from what was left of Miss Emily's hands as a fat gray rat gnawed on the blackened flesh. The rodent stared defiantly at Amanda before it ran into the darkness.

"Amanda, please help me..."

"It's all right now, Miss Emily. I'm here." Amanda staggered to the piano bench and took her place beside Miss Emily's corpse. She gently placed Miss Emily's half-eaten hands in the folds of her black dress. Her sanity dissolved.

"Amanda...please...play...for...me."

The lantern light dimmed and the crypt's heavy iron door creaked shut and the world that Amanda once knew disappeared...

Mist swirled in the ethereal realm as spirits danced in the darkness to the haunting melody of "Moonlight Sonata."

* * * *

MISSING: Amanda Thorne, age 16

Height: 5'6" Weight 127

Long Blonde hair/Blue eyes

Disappeared from her home January 3, 1997. If you have any Knowledge of this child's location, please contact the Morgan County Sheriff's Dept.

"It sure is a shame about the Thorne girl. I feel so sorry for her parents. She's been missing about six months now, hasn't she? Say, you know, I could have sworn I heard someone pounding on a keyboard late last night...but it sounded like it was coming from the cemetery. But that's impossible."

Ashes to Ashes

Steve Eller

"Ashes to ashes."

He cradled the silver urn in his hands. Its sides were smooth, etched in flowing filigree. The lid rose in ornate leaf patterns, tangling to a thorny crest. He set it atop the mantle.

"Dust to dust."

He took another sip of wine, staring in silence at the urn above the fireplace. The evening was warm, but he'd started a fire in the hearth. He found the flames strangely comforting, as if the popping and sizzling of logs might somehow soothe his pain. Billows of smoke rose from the fire, ashes tumbling within gray clouds. Flecks of ash burned brilliantly, yellow and orange, but only for a moment. Then they lost their light and fell back into the fire. Black and cold. Dead.

His wineglass was empty. Again. He lifted the crystal decanter to refill it but only dark drops swirled in the bottom, dregs staining the glittering glass. Sullen, he placed the decanter back on the table. A glint of silver caught his eye. There on the tabletop, next to the decanter, stood the urn. His eyes throbbed from too much smoke and too much wine. He rubbed them with his thumbs as he tried to recall moving the urn from its place on the mantle. He couldn't. Reflections of flame danced across the shining silver. Shards of color, orange, red, yellow. But when he touched the urn with his fingers, it was cold. Only the illusion of warmth.

Stinging tears welled in his eyes, hot as they traced down his cheeks. A soft sound, like sighing laughter, fluttered in his throat. It'd been a full day that he hadn't cried, and imagined he'd finally run out of tears. But more came. He didn't try to stop them or wipe them away. His emotions swept through him like tides, and he let himself be borne as they ebbed and flowed.

Squinting away tears, he looked past the urn. On the other side of the narrow table, her chair was empty. His eyes drank in each tiny detail, the thick curls of dark wood, the ox-blood leather. It was the twin of his own. Both chairs faced the fire, but the other was turned slightly to the right, toward the table between, while his was angled to the left.

His heart ached as he saw the faint marks on the arms where her warm, soft hands had rested. Memories drifted through his mind like ghosts. Of spirited conversations, and times of profound silence. Of days spent in sadness or intimate amusement. Hours, sitting, watching the fire in the solace of togetherness. The leather seat held a shallow imprint, as if one of the ghosts had come to rest.

The fire felt warm on his face, as warm as the wine within him. But not as warm as the tears streaking down his cheeks. He closed his eyes, and let the memories singe his heart to ash.

He heard the surgeon leaving, the wheels of his carriage clicking over the cobblestone way. The bowl on the nightstand was empty, dull red smudges criss-crossing the white porcelain. In his mind's eye he saw a ghost-image of the glistening leeches that had writhed in the bowl, each one filled with her precious blood.

He cooled her sweltering forehead with a silk handkerchief soaked in water. Her skin was pale and withered, so thin he could see a tapestry of veins beneath. Brushstrokes of shadow shrouded her eyes. He traced his fingertips over her delicate face. It was so heartbreakingly small, nearly lost in drifts of silk sheet and ruffled pillowcase. Like the face of a fragile doll.

Droplets of water fell from his fingers, tracing her cracked lips. As her eyes opened, he brushed back the dark, wet ringlets of hair from her burning cheeks. Her splintered lips, so thin and blue, smiled. He wished the smile was for him, but imagined it born in the haze of her fever. From the darkness behind her sunken eyes, her lids rose, and her eyes closed again.

Her hand tightened around his, fingers still strong for nothing but slender bone beneath a veil of skin. Her lips parted and she whispered a single word. It faded before he could hear. He lowered his cheek to hers.

Her fever had vanished in the space of a heartbeat, the fire now dead beneath her ashen skin. Her face felt as bitterly cold as a winter rain. He kissed her icy forehead, hoping it would numb his lips so he might never feel again. And he prayed it would do the same to his soul. As he drew away, she whispered again, tatters of words.

"See you - together - again."

"When," he whispered, "when, my love?"

"See you – "

His heart shattered the pieces sharp and cutting. The pain brought fresh tears to his eyes. He cried out, and the sound brought the nurse rushing into the room, breathless. She withdrew quickly as he hurled the bloodstained bowl against the door. The porcelain shattered into slender shards, like his heart, like his love.

He gazed down at the fragile face of his beloved as a delicate sigh drifted over her lips. His ruined heart swelled and his mouth fell open. But instead of blood, words spilled out. He begged her to stay, pleaded with her to never leave him.

"When," he cried, "when will I see you again? In the name of God, when will we be together again in love?"

Her last, sweet breath carried a single word to his ear. Soft, fading

"Soon."

The world crumbled, consumed in roaring flame. Her funeral pyre. All the fires of hell as he cursed God for taking her. For taking his love. The village priest drifted up behind him rested a warm hand on his shoulder.

"Grieve, my son, but be strong. Have faith in God. Hold onto the words from my sermon, that you mustn't think of your loved one as gone, but merely as reaching Heaven first!"

The priest's words crawled up his spine like a venomous spider looking for a tender place to bite. He thought his skull might shatter from the violent whirlwind of his thoughts. He turned, knocking the priest's hand from his shoulder. His eyes filled with malice and madness, his voice brimmed with poison.

"How can you say that to me? How can there be a God that does such things as this? That could even allow them to happen? There is no God! For if there was, he would have to be a cruel and heartless monster. Mocking love! God is only a dream, a nightmare!"

"Please, son. You don't know what you're saying. It is the grief, the pain, speaking. God will forgive."

"Forgive! Forgive me? I need no forgiveness, I ask for none! Better to ask me if I'll ever forgive Him! For I won't! There can't be a God. Not one that could permit such tragedy, such pain."

"The will of the Lord is unimaginable, son. Our minds can't begin to comprehend his plan."

"Liar! I won't let you say that to me! Make him explain! I've got a mind! He's God, he could MAKE me understand. If he really wished to. If they're truly was a God."

Somber faces turned away. Mourners, shrouded in black, departed slowly over the damp grass. The sky was a dull slate-gray, threatening another storm with whispers of distant thunder. A pale imitation of the rumbling funeral fire.

The priest, shocked into silence, joined the mourners. Heads shook slowly, veiled eyes exchanged knowing glances. Pity. Tongues clicked behind teeth. The priest turned back, holy duty unfulfilled.

"Please try and make peace with this, son. And with the Lord. You know this isn't how the dearly departed would've wanted you to remember – "

"How dare you! How dare you say that to me! Did you know she prayed? Did you know she begged your heartless God for help? Help that never came! I hope she cursed him at the end, I know I would have. And I'll tell you this. If there is a Heaven, when I get there I'll have some questions for your precious God! And if he doesn't have some damn good answers, I'll spit in his eye. At least that will win me the favor of the Devil when I get to Hell!"

He listened to the fire. Not Hell at all, just the crackling of the fireplace. A charred log split and fell, tumbling down into ash. A cloud of dust rose.

The urn still stood on the table. Sighing, he reached out for it. For her. His fingers touched the metal. It was so cold. His hand trembled and closed around nothing. The urn suddenly slid across the glimmering tabletop and fell to the floor.

He froze in silent horror, each second endless, each heartbeat an eternity. The crested lid came free, clattering on the wooden floorboards. The tiny bell tone echoed in his ears. The dark ashes within flew, spiraling in the air. He heard a soft hiss as they swept across the floor. The crash of the hollow urn striking wood was deafening.

A fresh spring of pain bubbled up in his chest and he flung himself from his chair, crying out. His palms struck the floor, his quivering fingers sifting through the drifts of ash. Wisps of dust rose around his face. Each mote a piece of her. He gasped, the taste of her ashes bitter in his mouth. He thought he might go insane from the sting of the loss. He had lost her again. He stared at the ashes through a shimmering glaze of tears. His hands were gray and smudged. He wondered how he would ever bring himself to wash them again.

A heartbeat later, a single flake of ash rose, fluttering in the air like a shadowy snowflake. It glittered darkly in the light from the fireplace. His mind was lost, he knew, for this could only be a madman's dream. Then a second sliver of ash rose, circling the first. They tumbled together, drifting. He smiled at his fantasy. Not such a horrible way to lose his mind, he decided.

The scattered pile of dust and ash rose slowly, swirling into a spiral. He watched, laughing. The spinning cloud darkened, its center growing more solid with each turn. He reached out his hand to touch it. The dust danced over his skin, twisting between his fingers. Soft, warm, it brushed him.

The sound of the whirling dust was like a gentle wind through a patch of reeds. He listened, lost in the beauty of it. He closed his eyes, straining to hear more.

Sssssoooonnnn

His eyes shot open. It had sounded like a whispered word, from within the turning cloud.

Sssooo sssoooooonnn

His chin fell. He stared into the whirlwind, deeper into its darkened center.

And he saw her. Her outline was faint at first, a shadowed hand, a dark line of cheek. But as dust and ash spun, she grew distinct, solid. Her eyes shined in the darkness like stars in the night sky. Together again, he thought. Together again in love. The shimmering voice answered him.

Ssssooo ssoooonnn   Sssooonnn

He rose to his knees and reached out for the shadowy image of his lover. In his shattered heart he didn't care if she was real or ghost, as long as they were together once more. Her ashen eyes seemed full of love and hope. But she shook her head slowly, curls bouncing, as she had done in life. A playful scold, when he didn't understand something she'd said, or something she'd meant. A wan smile traced her lips.

He reached out for her hand, but she moved it away before he could touch the skin. She raised her finger, pointing to the table. His eyes followed. The table was except for the crystal decanter.

"What, my love, what is it you want me to do?"

Her smile widened. She cocked her head to one side, her gray curls jumbling over her shoulders. The finger pointed again. He looked once more, and saw the drawer in the front of the table.

He crawled across the floorboards and opened the drawer. Inside was a golden letter opener. He lifted it out, turning it in his hand. The flames in the hearth sent shimmers of orange and red over its sharp point. He held it out to his beloved.

"Is this what you want, my love? Take it. Take it from me."

He glanced up, trying to read her eyes. Her head shook. She pointed at him. He opened his mouth to speak, but before he could make a sound it came to him like a vision. In his broken mind, he understood. They could never be together, like this. Not while he was flesh, and she was ash. He knew what he had to do. Her eyes glittered in the firelight. She nodded.

He leapt to his feet and took the shovel from beside the fireplace. He filled it, again and again, with glowing embers then dashed them over the velvet curtains and swept them across the Persian rugs. When the hearth was empty, he dropped the shovel and turned to consider his labors, sweating and breathless. Tendrils of smoke curled up from the shadowed corners of the room. Tiny tongues of flame licked at the fabric of the curtains. He smiled.

He knelt again before his ghostly lover. She smiled at him, the love in her eyes warming his soul. As the flames crept closer, he lifted the golden letter opener and pressed the sharp tip against his heart. She nodded.

"Then will we be together, my beloved? Together in love?"

He heard a faint, dry whisper.

Ssoooo ssoooonnn

Through curling wisps of smoke he saw flame tracing intricate patterns over the Persian rugs, wandering closer to the place he knelt. He would soon be ash, like his lover, after the fire had claimed his dead body. Ashes to ashes.

Gripping the handle with both hands, he drove the letter opener between his ribs. The pain was harsh, but no harsher than the pain of his grief. Gouts of blood, warmed by love, cascaded over his fingers. His vision swirled in tears and heat-haze, and he fell. The handle of the letter opener struck the wooden floor. His body drifted above it for a heartbeat, then slid slowly down. The heartbeat ended.

Within the tempest of dust, the image changed. The lips splintered as the smile broadened the mouth opening wide over rows of jagged teeth. The nose flattened into a ripple of ashen skin. Dark cunning filled eyes that had once showed only love, the pupils slicing to slender slits. Pillars of dust spiraled around the misshapen head, forming into twisted horns. The body swelled into a bloated travesty of bubbling flesh. Laughter, evil and black filled the room as the flames closed in.

He felt himself descending, silently falling. He heard the raging fires of Hell, and knew they were real this time. And so very close. From some place far away, above him, he heard the precious voice of his lover. She was crying, saying the word *no* again and again, like a mournful litany. He envisioned her tiny hand, so distant, reaching out to him. It grew smaller, farther, as he fell.

He felt the first brush of flame, tracing tapestries of agony over his flesh. But he did not burn. He drew in a hot, ragged breath and prayed to be ash.

Before I Sleep

Steve Eller

Seeing so many people by her graveside brought an old Italian proverb to mind. *The dead are no longer lonely.*

The priest closed his eyes after finishing his prayers. Folding his hands across his chest, he clutched his holy book close to his heart. He bowed his head, and I couldn't help but wonder if he was granting a final blessing to her soul, or checking his watch.

Mourners in somber dress ringed the open grave, but my place wasn't among them. I mourned, but kept a distance away, just as I always had. Surely, surrounded by so many loved ones, she wasn't lonely. It helped me to think so, although I had no reason to believe such a thing.

I was lonely.

At a distance from the mourners as discreet as mine, others waited. Photographers, and journalists. The horrified and morbidly fascinated. Some of these spectators wrung their hands, weeping as if they'd known my wife. I wondered what this vicarious sorrow did for them. What need it fulfilled in their hearts?

I could tell them a thing about sorrow. About anger, and regret. Even madness. I could tell them many things. But then again, I couldn't tell them anything. And even if I could share my story, would they learn the lesson I should've? Would they look to the bindings of love? To the simple brush of flesh against flesh? Or would they just return to weep at the burial of the next butchered lamb? While their own ties unravel.

But in the end, their lives and their needs made no difference to me. I was no guardian angel. I was neither. And it was time to be about my work.

The phone call came as I was shutting down my computer for the evening. I snatched up the phone angrily, wondering what she wanted this time. For me to pick up something at the store, on my way home from work. To see how I was doing, and when I might be coming home. Just because. Maybe to make sure I was actually still at my desk, instead of off with some other woman. I stared into the darkness beyond my slitted blinds, sighing in preparation.

But a strange man's voice answered my flustered hello, calling me by my full name. Asking me if I was my wife's husband. Asking me if I was sitting down. Telling me she was dead. Murdered. Just that simply.

Sometime later, moments or hours, I discovered myself behind the wheel of my car, careening down the highway with no regard for anything in my path. Living, or otherwise. I couldn't recall if I'd said anything to the voice on the phone, or silently hung up. I couldn't remember leaving my office, or getting into my car. The passing minutes were no more meaningful than the insects spattering my windshield, and left less of an impression. Absently, I squirted blue fluid onto the glass, then watched as the wipers smeared the guts away. I wished the knot in my guts was as easily swept aside.

I sped down residential streets, ignoring traffic lights and signs, ignoring car horns and curses. No police cars pursued me, because they were all parked zigzag in front of my house. Spinning lights illuminated my lawn in blue and yellow and red like bizarre holiday decorations. I wondered, as I screeched to a stop and jolted out of my seat, if an officer would be waiting to slap a pair of handcuffs on me, glaring at me in certain knowledge that such suburban murders were always the work of a loved one. But no one even took special notice of me, and I finally had to approach an officer and introduce myself.

Unreal as the scene was, with strangers trampling through my house, stuffing items into plastic bags, things spiraled further out of control. The killer was already in custody, I was told, and was waiting not twenty yards away from me. Cuffed in the back seat of a police cruiser. The officer I spoke with pointed the man out with two hands. Then used those same hands to restrain me as I dove at the car.

Ancient instincts were now in control, guiding my heart and hands. I struggled against the officer's grasp, but my rage was diluted with sadness. There wasn't enough strength in me to break his grip. There wasn't strength enough to keep my heart from breaking.

Speaking nonsense in soothing tones, the officer led me into my house, past the shadowed outlines of my neighbors. Although I should've known every face, they seemed like strangers etched out of the darkness. Their eyes flashed like a cat's in the colored light. The officer sat me on my couch.

So things could get worse.

Tragedy, like water, sought its own level. I tried feebly to throw barriers in its way, but it kept rising to meet me.

"No," the officer said. "There was no forced entry. Your wife let him in."

Distancing myself emotionally didn't work. My wife and I had been having problems. For a long time. At least I'd been. But I couldn't find solace in the walls we'd put between us. That I'd put between us.

"In fact," he continued. "We have reason to believe they returned here together from a second location."

Hardening my heart did no good. If she'd tried to soothe her pain by turning to another man, it came as little surprise. The closest we'd come to touching in months had been pointing a finger in the other's face. The only exchange of fluids, spittle from nose-to-nose shouting.

"We don't know it yet for certain. But we think he's done this before. There are several unsolved murders across the state similar to this one. We're still looking into it."

Finding absurdity was of no use. She'd finally decided to make other arrangements for her life. And ended up throwing herself into the arms of a serial killer. Beginner's luck.

"It was just luck that a cruiser spotted him running down the street. Bloodstained clothes, and all."

Yeah, I thought. Just luck.

In hard times, there's no substitute for hard liquor.

As I drank alone in my motel room, I thought it all through. There was no way I could sleep in that house tonight, even with all the blood cleaned away. Maybe not tomorrow. Maybe never again. Surprising, how lucid my mind was. With each passing moment, and each swallowed mouthful of scotch, it became clearer what needed to be done.

He had to die.

I just couldn't get my mind around the scenario the cops had drawn. That my wife had gone to some tavern and picked up a stranger. Then brought him back to our bed for a sweaty hump. She knew I tended to work late, but that I could still drive up at any moment. And even more than that, she wasn't one for casual sex. Not even when we first got together. My guess was that she'd needed someone to talk to. And had met him somewhere. Either that or the bastard had been going door to door, looking for lone women, under the guise of selling bibles or something.

Yeah, my alcohol-fueled anger answered. That's it. She let him in, and instead of a bible, he whipped out a blade. Probably his pecker, too.

I threw my drained glass against the floor, and it bounced over the carpet. It would've been nice to hear it shatter. Grabbing the half-empty bottle of Dewar's White Label by the neck, I did shots. Timed to my breaths.

The cops didn't know anything for sure. And they always liked to concoct sensational yarns to feed their egos. Lurid stories of sex and murder. Tall tales to tell over tall, cold beers. My wife wasn't like that. She wouldn't screw a stranger. She wasn't even particularly interested in screwing. Not with me, anyway. My brain couldn't sketch a scene of her allowing another man to put his hands on her.

But my anger spoke again. Assuring me that the killer had put his hands on her. All over her, his fingers slick with blood and fear-sweat. Oblivious to whether she was still alive or not. So much blood would keep her skin warm and supple.

He had to die.

He was in my house. With my wife. Touching her. Killing her.

He was on TV.

I dropped the bottle, ignoring the scotch that splashed my legs. Groping for the remote, I turned up the sound. But the words the newsreader recited made no sense. They were nothing more than background noise for the images. Of the man who'd sliced up my wife like a sausage walking a gauntlet of reporters. Even with an officer holding each arm, and his shoulders wrenched to his ears, he was a tiny thing. His face was bland, the kind forgotten a moment after being seen. But I wouldn't forget it. The dark eyes that skittered like frightened insects. The jagged, receding hairline. The button nose. All burned into my brain. He wore a vest over his orange jumpsuit. To stop any bullet intended for him. I wondered if it would've stopped the blade he used on my wife. Or if he would've just found someplace else to carve.

The camera zoomed in on him. But instead of sharpening, his features blurred. The tears welling in my eyes melted his face into a pale smear. My anger had already claimed his life, but my sorrow softened his appearance. Almost like absolution. Because I'd created him. And now, like in some bad movie, I had to destroy the horror I'd brought down on myself. And my wife.

We'd married right out of high school, two stupid eighteen-year-olds. Defying our families, certain of the truth that love smoothed all the sharp edges out of life. Then, almost twenty years later, waking to wonder what time had done with the people we'd promised to love forever. Another old proverb said that a man wanted his wife to stay the same as on his wedding night, but that same night was when a wife wanted her man to start changing. On both counts, it didn't work out for us. She changed, and I remained a boy, only changing in ways she didn't like. Now it all seemed so petty. The little irritations. The dinginess when I needed room. The distance when I needed a touch. My inability, or refusal, to recognize the same times in her. She was the only woman I'd ever loved, even if it had begun as a childish love. She was the only woman I'd ever been with, despite her accusations of infidelity at my perpetual late nights at work. I'd created her murder, scripting the scene. I'd created his necessity

But sorrow and guilt were no match for denial and anger. Nor was fuel. I promised the little man with the blurry face he would die. Somehow, some way, I'd get to him. He'd feel my hands on him. My face, stark as death, would be the last he'd see before he went straight to Hell.

Senses clarified with intent, I studied the TV screen. Something was wrong. Two words buzzed in the upper left corner of the screen. *Earlier today.* This was old footage. The newsreader's voice was hurried, as if he needed to tell his tale before anyone else could. The words finally made sense, and I lashed out, kicking the bottle at my feet. It flew across the room, splintering against the wall.

Hanged himself in his cell, the unseen voice repeated.

Tragedy, like water, like always, sought its own level. And like water, he'd slipped through my fingers.

He'd robbed me of my home. Of my wife, and any chance to bridge the distance between us. He'd robbed me of my normalcy. At least, with nothing left to lose, I'd had my revenge to cling onto. Now he'd taken that away.

Overwhelmed by the cosmic unfairness of it all, the staggering injustice, I looked away from the TV. To where a puddle of scotch soaked the filthy carpet, jagged splashes painting the peeling wallpaper. Just like my wife's blood had painted the walls. My walls, my home. A subhuman growl rose in my throat and I ran across the floor, kicking at the stains. But instead of making the blemishes disappear, I added to them.

Broken glass sliced my bare feet, puncturing my soles, cutting the skin. My blood swirled in the pool of scotch, the alcohol stinging in my open wounds. It burned, but I craved the fire. An icy void had opened in my heart, and was spreading through me. I needed something to force it back, to keep my anger from cooling to despair. Certainty flooded me as my blood flooded the carpet. Beneath the flood was purpose.

Reaching down, I picked up the largest shard of glass. It twinkled in the light as I turned it in my fingers, staring at the long streaks of red. My blood, staining the glass. Stained glass. Something holy.

Instead of anger, purpose spoke to me. Reminding me I'd made promises. And nothing so simple as his death was going to make me a liar.

"I've promises to keep," I whispered to myself. The blood exploded from the diagonal slash across my wrist. "And miles to go, before I sleep."

Grinning, I changed hands.

The priest dropped a handful of soil into her grave, then turned away. Some of the others did the same, or tossed solitary flowers. Most did nothing. Only left. If the dead were no longer lonely, now was the time for her to learn.

The strangers took longer in departing, and I wondered if perhaps some of them had known tragedy in their own lives. With the bodies of their children never found. Or worse, found with the history of their suffering etched into their flesh. Maybe some of them had lost loved ones to the same man who'd murdered my wife.

Sadly, I doubted they'd find what they sought at her open grave. I hadn't.

I'd thought I might see her. Rising like an angel. Or perhaps bound to the Earth as I was, work undone. But there was no sign of her. It helped me to think she'd gone on to somewhere better, if there was such a place. But it saddened me to think she had nothing more to settle with me. Whatever business there'd been between us, to her it was finished. It was enough.

I'd thought I might see him. The killer returning to bask in the carnage of his crime.

But there was no sign of him, either. Surely he wouldn't leave so easily. His life's work, in his mind, would never be finished.

It made no difference to me. If his ghost was still here, I'd find it. I'd travel to the fringes of the world. And I'd keep my promises. Miles to go. I'd make him pay. Before I sleep.

And if I couldn't find him here, I'd keep searching. There would always be one last place to look.

For The Love of Claire

William L. Churchman

As I open my eyes, the cold, hard light of dawn glares through the lace curtains rendering a net-like shadow on the patchwork quilt. I immediately wonder as I do every morning - is my beloved wife dead?

I throw back the covers and the room's icy grip engulfs me. It had undoubtedly snowed again last night. I hurry to use the chamber pot, find my slippers, and slip my heavy woolen robe over my night shirt before pouring water from the pitcher into the pan I use to wash my face.

The hour is later than usual. There's no time to get dressed before I see to Claire's needs, and go downstairs to build a fire and make her breakfast. Do I hear movement in the next room, or is it just the cold north wind causing the house to creak? After taking care of my dear Claire for all of these months, my ears are finely tuned to detect any sounds of her distress.

I pray daily for guidance. Each morning I wake empty with the fear that she has passed on, but the way she suffers, sometimes I wonder if it would be a blessing. I hesitate before the oak-framed mirror to brush the gray hair back from my forehead. I must not fool myself into believing that a woman of her years can be so sick for so long and not eventually succumb. My dark, determined eyes stare back at me and I swear by all that's holy that I will ease her pain to the best of my ability, always putting her needs before my own until that day comes.

The ancient wooden floor creaks as I make my way into the hall. I blink and sudden warmth overtakes my body. The faded flowery wallpaper disappears to be replaced by pristine white walls and woodwork that shines as if new. My step falters and when I look again the illusion has passed. This was not the first occurrence and I sometimes fear that perhaps a growth in my brain is causing the hallucinations and will eventually bring about my own demise. But nothing will keep me from attending to the sweet woman I have been married to for fifty-one years.

The hinges protest with a screech, and as I step into her room, my heart jumps into my throat. The bed is made and the room lies empty. Surely she could *not* have moved on her own.

I find myself in the hall. "Claire, where are you?" I wail.

Warmth again overtakes me with the return of the white walls. Over the banister at the bottom of the stairs, I spy the horrified face of a young woman staring up at me. In an instant she disappears and the icy cold returns.

My confusion mounts and I lean back against the wall and hold my head. Could my brain malady have progressed to the point that I could have forgotten Claire's passing?

I open the door to the third, upstairs, empty bedroom. "Oh, Claire," I moan.

I must search the house. Deep inside, a dark depression mounts. The unsettling feeling stays with me as I enter the musty parlor downstairs. "Claire." Suddenly the room is bright and cheery and filled with tantalizing aromas waffling from the kitchen. My senses are assaulted by strange music and I turn to behold an open-mouthed man standing in the library doorway, an open book lying at his feet.

Who can these shades be that have invaded my house? Are they somehow connected with Claire's disappearance? The dark, icy cold of winter returns and I pull my robe closer. There is nothing to do but continue my search.

By the time the day has passed, I have been over the house many times, the fire neglected, but feel compelled by a force greater than my own to continue. I rise from the cellar into the kitchen, a lantern in my hand, for the pale gray winter skies have darkened and night quickly approaches.

Exhausted, I am drawn to the parlor, by what I do not know. To search the room once more? This time seems different.

"Come to us, oh spirit of the house," a woman's voice chants with crystal clarity.

"Claire?" Warmth surrounds me. "Claire, can that be you?" Has this day just been a figment of my imagination and my darling yet waits for me?

Then I hear my name called. "Edwin Boles, come to us," the same voice repeats.

I enter the room which is my parlor, yet not. As in a dream, I move as if predestined and not quite of my own volition.

Sounds of crickets in a summer night reverberate strangely through an open window and six people grasping hands, sit around a table, a candle burning brightly in the center. Two are the young man and woman I saw earlier in the day.

One of the other four, who is the speaker, looks straight at me. "The spirit is among us." She put her head back. "Spirit, are you Edwin Boles?"

I try to speak but words will not form on my lips. My confusion mounts and I can only utter, "Claire." All eyes instantly dart toward me.

"See I told you," the young woman whispered urgently. "It said, 'Claire'. We looked up the history and Edwin and Claire Boles built this house in 1837 and they both died in their sleep on the same night, February 8th 1888."

Bone-chilling cold assaulted me as the six at the table began to fade.

"Hush!" the woman with the intent eyes admonished. "We're losing him." She raised her voice. "Return to us, Edwin. We have a message."

I am torn, feeling compelled to stay, yet overwhelmed with the necessity of finding my lost wife. "Claire," I sigh. I am sure she needs me.

"Return, Edwin. We can help." The woman, who spoke, once again looked straight at me and the warmth returned. "Your time here has passed, Edwin. Your search is over. With our combined might, we now break the spell that has bound you here for all these years. Go and join your lost love."

What is happening to me? I feel light and disconnected. The parlor blurs before my eyes.

"Edwin, I am waiting for you."

What? I am sure I hear the sweet tones of my beloved. I am overcome with relief. My heart abounds with joy and I weep as I float from the house toward the sound of her voice.

Stitch In Time

Denise M. Bruchman

Ethel Grosberg sat in her mother's favorite old recliner and worked on her needlepoint. To say the recliner was worn was an understatement. The sun coming through the windows of her third story walk-up had long ago faded the royal blue corduroy to a dingy denim blue with a gray fuzz peeling off like dead skin. One spring had worked itself free of the musty, moldy padding to poke at Ethel's thin, bony hip and to trouble the arthritis growing there. It hadn't escaped the paper-thin material that still clung to the frame, but it would burst free any day now. That was why Ethel now worked on a new pillow for the seat to protect her from the vagrant metal spring.

Ethel loved to needlepoint and crochet. She looked for any excuse to pick up her instruments of choice and to create a new masterpiece. Pillows, wall hangings, afghans, and such had endeared Ethel to one and all in her building, and even though her eyes were not as clear and her stitch not as true, Ethel's creations continued to be snatched up. Why just last week she'd finished that baby blanket for Mrs. Sanchez's new baby girl. The woman had six children, but each had to have his or her own blanket from Auntie Ethel. It had taken Ethel twice as long to finish this one than it had the last because she kept dropping stitches and losing her count. Her eyes kept blurring the design. They often seemed to play tricks on her anymore. Why just the other day she'd thought she'd seen her dead mother standing over her in bed.

Mrs. Grosberg had worn the same handmade flannel nightgown and lace cap she'd worn every night since Ethel was a child and had had her thin white hair braided into the same skinny white braid Ethel remembered her mother wearing for as long as she could remember. Beatrice Grosberg had appeared to her daughter as clearly as she had in life, along with all of her knick-knacks and things. And then she was gone. Ethel knew she'd been dreaming because her mother had passed on nearly eleven years prior and Ethel had packed away all of her mother's things before moving into her parents' room, just as she had her father's belongings fifteen years before. She was all alone in the stodgy old apartment. Alone with her stitchwork and memories. She'd been an only child who had grown up with her parents and never found a reason to move away. Most of her friends were long ago buried in the city cemetery and she'd never married or had children.

Bounce, bounce, scuff Bounce, bounce, scuff

Ethel smiled to herself. There was Billy Nedermeier playing with his rubber ball just like when they were children.

Bounce, bounce, scuff Bounce, bounce, scuff

She remembered how he'd play with it for hours, bouncing it against the wall, then the floor, and then catching it to start again until one of the adults in the building would yell at him to stop. He'd had curly dark hair and dark eyes with the longest black eye lashes Ethel had ever seen on any boy. His mother had always dressed Billy in a little sailor suit and hat.

Bounce, bounce, scuff

Ethel had been so jealous of his fine little suit and hat and of the black paten shoes that Billy was always scuffing and smudging.

"Ethel. Can you hear me? Ethel," he called.

"I can't come out and play with you, Billy. I must finish my pillow first. Almost done.

Almost done," she called. Ethel hummed a little to herself. Her father had hated it when she'd made any noise. Children were to be seen and not heard, but he'd been dead for more than twenty-five years so she didn't figure it would matter if he heard her or not. He hadn't heard her begging or pleading when she'd wanted to marry Ralf Watkins. He'd ignored her cries as if he hadn't heard them and left her to pine in her room and to dream of running away to elope.

"You didn't hear me then, Papa," Ethel murmured. "You never heard me."

Ethel shifted a little to lessen the contact between the bothersome spring and her hip.

Bounce, bounce, scuff Bounce, bounce, scuff

"I'm coming, Billy. I'm coming. Just be patient. 'Patience is a virtue.'" Or so Mama had always claimed Of course Mama was good at waiting for things. She'd waited all of her life and gotten nothing but a casket for her troubles. Ethel figured that must make her mother one of the most virtuous women in the world.

Ethel's needle pierced her finger, sending a jab of pain up her skinny, shriveled arm. She sucked on the bruised, bleeding digit until the pain ebbed and then returned to her work. She was going to finish the pillow before the chair's spring broke loose and bit any deeper into her flesh.

"'A stitch in time saves nine', Ethel," she chirped, parroting her mother's stern advice. Her mother had ever been handing out advice whether it was asked for or not. And her cup of sayings, proverbs, and bits of wisdom had runneth over. Ethel smirked at her own bit of humor. Her mother would not have appreciated it any more than she had appreciated what she had called Ethel's sense of the dramatic. She had sternly counseled Ethel to forget about Harry Anderson after her father had refused his marriage proposal. He'd sent Ethel to her tiny little room without supper for having even entertained the absurd notion. The Grosbergs would not even consider such a lowly match. He was completely unsuitable and could never be taken seriously as a suitor.

Ethel loosened her grip on the needle and rubbed at a cramp tightening in her hand.

Bounce, bounce, scuff Bounce, bounce, scuff

Billy had been the only boy her mother had tolerated her playing with as Mrs. Grosberg considered his family of the right sort. But alas, Billy had died one hot summer afternoon when they'd been playing hide-and-go-seek down in the basement. They'd often played in the basement because that was where everyone stored their junk and where small children could find ways to entertain themselves for hours. They'd had tea parties and fought pirates, found buried treasure and discovered new lands. She and Billy had always had a grand time playing in the basement until that last time.

Ethel teared up thinking about it. He'd been her only friend in a very lonely world. Her parents had been old and emotionally dead years before Ethel was ever born. They hadn't expected a child to invade their staid comfortable lives and hadn't known what to do with her when she arrived. Looking back on her life with them, Ethel realized that she had probably seemed as foreign and incomprehensible to them as all the new tenants seemed to her now with their thickly accented English and odd customs. The difference was that she ignored the odd and embraced the warmth of their human contact. She listened to their strange sounding words and chose to see their smiles and laughter.

"I'll never get this done if I don't quit daydreaming," she sighed. Ethel rubbed her tired eyes with her gnarled, twisted hands and tried to clear them enough to see the pattern. She'd been promising herself this pillow for years, but had put it off in lieu of other projects. Now she meant to finish it.

Bounce, bounce, scuff

"Not now, Billy," she called. "I'll play with you later." Idly she reflected on the last time she and Billy played together. He'd hidden too well for her to find. She'd searched and searched and searched, but she couldn't find him even hours later. Her mother had come down to the basement to retrieve her. Ethel remembered how angry her mother had been because she'd held up dinner and her father was upstairs fuming. Ethel had protested, but her mother had pulled her upstairs to their stuffy apartment. The summer sun had baked the building all afternoon so that even the occasional gusts of wind didn't bring any relief. She had worried about her friend all through dinner, which had seemed interminably long with her father's brooding silence. 'When Mrs. Nedermeier came to their apartment to inquire about Billy's whereabouts, Ethel's stomach turned over. They'd searched for most of the hot sticky evening with everyone looking accusingly at little Ethel before they finally found him. But it was too late. Billy had chosen an old rusty steam trunk to hide in. The clasp had dropped down to lock in place when he'd closed the lid on top of himself. His little white coffin wasn't much bigger than the trunk.

Ethel's eyes misted over, losing the pillow's pattern once more as she remembered. No one had played with her after that.

Bounce, bounce, scuff. That sound had echoed throughout the basement as she'd searched for him. She'd thought he was teasing her, daring her to find him.

Sniffling, Ethel cleared her eyes and rubbed her nose. Then she resumed her needlepoint. She was close to finishing. She could feel it. Just a little while longer and then she could stuff the pillow with the polyfoam she'd bought just for this. It would completely protect *her* rear end *from* the spring's cruel bite. If she hurried she'd finish before she lost the sun's dimming light. The floor lamp standing next to the chair had quit working just as she'd finished the baby blanket. She hadn't wanted to waste any time trying to get it fixed so had relied on the sunlight streaming through her dusty windows.

Bounce, bounce, scuff Bounce, bounce, scuff

The sound of Billy's ball had grown louder and angrier. He didn't like being kept waiting and always grew impatient with her when she tarried. Ethel felt excitement and anticipation as she finished the pillow's pattern. Her eyes cleared enough so she could see the perfection of the intricate garden scene. Every flower and fern was clearly defined down to the finest detail. Pride swelled within Ethel as she reached into the bag beside her chair and began stuffing the empty pillowcase with the polyfoam. It was perfect. She quickly sewed up the opening and gave the pillow a few good slaps to work out the lumps. Then, carefully levering herself up, Ethel stuck the pillow beneath her bony frame and settled down to enjoy the first comfort she'd felt in years.

Bounce, bounce, scuff Bounce, bounce, scuff Bounce, bounce, scuff Bounce, bounce, scuff

The door crashed open, thrusting Mrs. Sanchez and Mr.Greenley, the superintendent, into Ethel's apartment.

"Do you think she had enough locks," Mr. Greenley asked. "I thought we'd never pry them all loose."

"Whew! That smell," Mrs. Sanchez exclaimed. "It's even worse in here than out in the hall or in my apartment."

They both walked across Ethel's faded threadbare rug to stand in front of the recliner.

"Dios mio," Mrs. Sanchez said, crossing herself furiously as her eyes teared up from the source of the fumes.

"Poor old woman," Mr. Greenley said. "How long you suppose she's been dead?"

"Aahhhh," Mrs. Sanchez moaned. "She ruined the baby blanket," she said She gingerly pulled at one corner of the half-finished blanket and accidentally displaced Ethel's rotting fingers. "I paid good money for that yarn, she cried. "Now look at it. I can't even clean it and finish it. I'd never get the stink out of it."

Mr. Greenley just stared at the disintegrating corpse that had been his oldest and least troublesome tenant in the building. Miss Grosberg had always paid the rent on time without a single complaint, but now she'd never pay him again.

"She doesn't even have any family," he murmured.

"Of course not," Mrs. Sanchez said. "She was crazy. She was always talking to herself and calling the boys Billy. She was loca." Mrs. Sanchez stormed from the room, leaving Mr. Greenley alone with Ethel's remains. He'd already called an ambulance, assuming the worst when Miss Grosberg didn't answer her door or come down to pay the month's rent. As the EMTs struggled to get her body into the bag without it falling apart, he noticed a brand new pillow, stitched with a lovely garden scene resting in the seat of the chair. Miss Grosberg's body fluids hadn't damaged it in the least, and it smelled of her light perfume when he picked it up to take it home. It even felt warm.

Alter the ambulance had left and the residents had all dispersed, Mr. Greenley shuffled down to his apartment. As he walked through the doorway, his foot struck something that scuffed across the warped wooden floor. He locked the door before bending to retrieve the neat crisp envelope his foot had kicked. It smelled faintly of perfume and when he opened it, Mr. Greenley found the rent check from Miss Grosberg, written in her neat handwriting. As he stared owlishly at the rent check, he heard the sound of kids playing ball in the hallway - bounce, bounce, scuff- and then their high pitched giggles. Bounce, bounce, scuff. Bounce, bounce, scuff

"Come on Ethel. Let's play."

Slowly Mr. Greenley unlocked his door and poked his head outside to take a look, but he saw only an empty hallway.

Bounce, bounce, scuff.

Incineration

Daniel Keohane

The top half of the casket's lid stood open, and Patrick, even in his quiet terror, began to calculate how he would maneuver himself beside Mister Benchman's body without touching it. A new wave of nausea rolled over him.

Above the three boys, the remnants of the summer day burned away into evening. A thick humid blackness fell around them. Patrick, Kenney and Kenney's best friend Jacob crouched in the grass. The rectangle of yellow light from the basement window was like a campfire between them. They watched the old man approach the coffin, close the lid and twist the ornate brass latch.

Jacob whispered. "Don't worry. You can still get in. The latch won't lock. Just turn it and lift."

Patrick swallowed, wondering again what he was trying to prove. That the son of the town's Baptist preacher wasn't just another wimpy Jesus-lover? That a wimpy Jesus-lover can die as easily as anyone else? His father would kill him if he found out. Beat his devil-possessed son to death with one of those massive bibles he preached from. Not for the first time, Patrick decided to get up and leave. Tell Jacob and Kenney to find someone else to jerk around with this stupid dare. Someone with more guts. He sighed quietly at this last thought and waited.

The old man stood by the large oven doors, tinkering with a faucet and various switches.

He looked to Patrick like a mad scientist from one of those old black and white movies.

Jacob was moving way too much. He smiled. "OK. Get ready, Bible Boy."

"Don't call me that."

"Once he fires this sucker up, he'll leave the room while it gets cranking. I've seen it a hundred times. He'll be gone for five minutes. Maybe more."

The old man flipped a switch. The darkness beyond the doors exploded in a brilliant flash of light. Patrick closed his eyes. A minute later Jacob slapped him on the back. "OK, he's out. Let's go."

The casket was closed. Behind the windows in the furnace doors, fire danced like a thousand burning fingers. Kenney, who had said nothing since they left on their bikes from Jacob's house, moved his heavy frame into the square of light. He slid a thin piece of aluminum along the edge of the window. Something clicked. He lifted the sash and propped it open with the jimmy.

Patrick looked at Jacob. "You never did this."

Jacob glared back at him. "Damn right, I have. Twice. Don't chicken out on me now, or everyone's gonna hear about it."

"I'm not chickening out. I just don't think you ever did it." Lying facedown on the grass, Patrick shimmied backwards. His legs dangled over nothing for a moment, then his toes touched the concrete floor. The faces of Jacob and Kenney hung ghostlike in the window. Darkness beyond them. Patrick let go of the sill.

The room smelled like the science lab at school. Chemicals, Bunsen burners. Looking around, there wasn't much to see besides a desk, four folding chairs, and the coffin. He'd better get this over with before the old man came back and pushed it into the oven, with him inside.

The thought of being trapped burned alive with the corpse of Mister Benchman, sent a tremor through him. He walked toward the coffin.

The latch turned easily. Patrick lifted the upper lid. The head of Mister Benchman did not turn towards him with an evil grimace, as he half-expected. The face was sunken, covered in too much makeup. The storekeeper didn't look right. Where was the smile? Whenever Patrick and his father came into Selver's Variety the man always had a smile.

The platform was metal mesh wrapped around rollers. He gave the coffin a shove to make sure it wouldn't roll into the furnace doors. It didn't. It sat low to the floor, so Patrick had no problem climbing up beside it. He remembered the last time he saw this man alive. When his father had gone back to the cooler for a forgotten jug of milk, Mister Benchman handed Patrick a Three Musketeers candy bar. The boy immediately had shoved the treat deep into his windbreaker's pocket and prayed his father hadn't seen it. Candy was forbidden in their world; both Patrick and Mister Benchman knew that. The storekeeper simply smiled as usual, never letting on to this dark new secret as the preacher returned with the milk. That was one month ago and Patrick only garnered enough courage to eat the damned Three Musketeers three days ago. That was the day he heard that Mister Benchman was dead.

He worked his left leg into the coffin, wincing in reaction to the stiff, papery feel of the dead man's leg. There was no way he'd get in there without touching the guy.

"Hurry up, you idiot." Jacob's head poked into the room. "He'll be back in three minutes." Patrick wondered how Jacob was keeping such precise time, since none of them wore a watch.

"You just make sure you throw the pebble when a minute's up."

"Two minutes."

"One minute. I'm not getting caught by that old guy."

"Whatever! Just do it."

Patrick sat on the edge and put his other foot inside the coffin. He looked up.

"Show me the pebble."

Jacob was about to say something, thought better of it, then reached into his pants' pocket. He held the pebble between two fingers. Patrick turned away from the window, trying not to look disappointed.

The coffin was uncomfortable. Under the frills and satin sheet was nothing more than the wooden bottom. No cushions, no soft down bedding. Patrick pushed his way over the curls of the sheets. His eyes blinked away sweat.

"Close the lid." From the window, Jacob's voice sounded breathy, like he'd been running. "Close it. Close it."

Patrick slowly reached over the dead man and grabbed the inside of the lid. The move brought his face too close to Mister Benchman. Vomit wormed its way into the boy's throat. He closed the lid as fast as he could, turned his head away and threw up. It splattered across his shoulder. The acidic smell filled the cramped interior, intensified by the increasing heat from the oven. In the complete blackness of the coffin, facing away from the wooden figure beside him, Patrick felt an uncontrollable urge to cry.

Instead, he counted. One. Two. Three. His tongue tasted sour, as if he'd drunk a glass of bad milk. This mental image sent more vomit against the coffin's wall. Patrick spit out a chunk of something caught in his cheek. *Don't think about anything,* he thought. *Just wait for the pebble.*

The sound of the basement door opening was muffled from inside his tomb, but Patrick knew instantly that he had lost. The old man was back.

Moments earlier, Jacob watched Patrick lean over the dead man and close the lid. He tried to swallow, but his mouth couldn't work up any spit. Once the coffin was closed, Jacob shifted his position until he lay belly-down on the grass. He had to. The erection in his jeans made crouching too uncomfortable. Since a few months after his twelfth birthday, this had become a new twist in his life. It was not received, this time, with the terror and embarrassment he'd suffer in the middle of Miss Monroe's Social Studies class. This time it felt right. Jacob's stomach tightened at the thought of Patrick laying alone with the corpse, and the fact that he had no intention of tossing the pebble. He stared at the flames licking each other behind the furnace windows, and his arousal intensified.

"Come on, man," Kenney said, leaning back on his haunches. "This is just too sick. Throw the rock so we can get the hell out of here."

For as long as the two boys were old enough to cross the street, they had been each other's only friend. This may have been because they were the only children their age on that end of Washington Street. More likely it was because their mutual obsession with all things macabre tended to alienate them from the rest of their classmates. Last Thursday, Kenney brought Patrick into their fold. Now, he couldn't help thinking that Jacob concocted this scheme just to scare away the threat Patrick presented to their long-standing twosome.

Jacob continued his vigil and waved away his friend's suggestion. Kenney grabbed his arm. "Throw it, you piss-head."

At that moment the door to the small room swung open.

In a reaction more instinctive than calculated, Jacob slapped at the metal bar. He caught the window at the last moment, closing it silently. His eyes never left the old man. Carefully, like an animal backing away from a threat, he slithered in the grass until he was out of the window's light.

Kenney whispered, "Oh, my God." He was on his feet, pacing behind Jacob. "Oh, my God oh my God oh my -"

"Will you shut up?" Jacob's hiss froze Kenney's hysteria for the moment. Kenney looked down, eyebrows raised in a silent plea.

Jacob whispered, "We do nothing." He scrambled onto his knees. "Just stay put and see if he leaves again."

Kenney shook his head, but did not move.

Benson Laraby shuffled past the coffin. In his peripheral vision he tried to see if the Kinsley boy was still at the window. He had seen someone up there earlier. He knew damned well who it was. *Sick idiot kid,* he thought. This was the third time he'd spied the boy watching him. He turned and faced the window. Nothing but darkness beyond. He sighed. The boy was probably still there but as before, the old man decided to leave him to his devices rather than call Robert Kinsley and get the kid in trouble. Last thing he wanted was a bunch of broken windows to deal with later.

The internal temperature looked good. Laraby released the safety and pulled down hard on the old iron lever. The twin doors leading into the oven screeched open. In seconds the basement room was thick with heat.

Patrick took short, silent breaths. He listened to the old man's footsteps. All but forgotten was the stench and feel of the vomit. Two opposing voices in his head fought for control. One screamed "Open the lid! Open it and climb out the window. He'll see you but might not recognize you! You'll be safe."

The other voice was calm, a soothing unperturbed whisper. "Don't move," it said. "Just stay calm and wait to see what happens. The last thing you want is for Jacob to see you running like a little girl. The old man'll recognize you; don't kid yourself. Then what will your father say?"

This last voice is what Patrick obeyed.

Something shifted beside him. He turned his head in the darkness. With terrifying clarity he realized the only other thing in the coffin was Mister Benchman.

When Kenney pushed past his friend, Jacob grabbed him by the shoulders and pulled him down. In the boy's ear he whispered, "What do you think you're doing?"

"The old man's gonna burn him, we have -"

Jacob covered Kenney's mouth with his hand. "You're right," he said, looking occasionally through the window. "Little Patrick's going to burn. The doors are open. The old man's going to pull another lever and the coffin'll slide in and the doors will slam shut." He smiled and wiped at a string of spit with his free hand. "There's nothing we can do now but watch him die."

Kenney shifted sideways, sending Jacob rolling in front of the window. "You're nuts, man. I'm not letting him die!"

Jacob saw the old man move to put the casket between him and the furnace. The burning in his belly was now an inferno. Kenney crawled towards the window. Jacob jumped on top of him. Kenney dragged himself along the ground. He was seconds away from ruining everything. With both hands Jacob lifted the biggest rock within reach and crashed it onto the back of the other boy's head. Kenney grunted only once. His left arm twitched, as if trying to shake off a bug, then stopped. He lay unmoving just outside the square of yellow light.

Something dark turned in Jacob's stomach. He ignored it, knowing that Kenney would start bawling at any moment. He looked through the window and hoped he hadn't missed anything. He watched with renewed excitement as the old man pulled the final release, sending the casket rolling along the conveyor and into the oven.

For one joyous moment Patrick thought the old man was gone. The footsteps faded behind his head, towards the door. Was he gone? The oven doors must have been opened. The roaring of the furnace muffled most of the outside sounds. He wished he could be sure.

The calm voice returned. "Stay where you are. Don't blow it now."

"Patrick, run!" The other voice, still heard only within his head, sounded different, not his own. It sounded like Mister Benchman. Still half-turned in the darkness towards the body, Patrick pushed himself against the vomit-covered wall. He heard the sound again, the rustling of polyester, cloth rubbing against itself. The coffin shook. Patrick had the sensation of riding on a roller coaster.

The howl of the furnace raced around him. The old man hadn't left. He just rolled them into the oven. Suddenly, it seemed too late to do anything. If he opened the lid, he'd be burned alive. Patrick's mind spun in a chaotic jumble of thoughts. If he didn't do something now he'd burn anyway. What would his father say? He closed his eyes, panicked sobs fighting for release. "Don't make a sound," the calm voice said. "Shhh."

The unmistakable screech of the closing doors. Now he was going to die. Again the sound of rustling beside him. Something grabbed his leg. An arm fell across his chest. Patrick opened his eyes, expecting to see the old man pulling him out. All he saw was darkness. Fingers closed tighter around his leg. Patrick screamed as he'd never screamed before.

The oven doors slammed shut. Immediately the shape of the coffin was lost beyond the windows, wrapped in a savage blanket of fire as the gas jets opened completely. Laraby maintained his grip the release lever. That was a scream he heard; it had to be. There was no longer any sound but the roar of the furnace. He looked around, up to the window. At that moment three thoughts crystallized in his mind: he *had* heard someone, the Kinsley kid was at the window earlier, and now he was gone. The old man looked at the oven door, back at the window.

"Oh, shit."

"Burn," Jacob breathed. "Burn." He saw the vague outline of the coffin in the flames. "Are you screaming?" He almost laughed the words. He rubbed his hands against the front of his jeans. A sudden, shaking release filled every corner of his body. He sighed in ecstasy. A blinding flash of light forced his hand to his eyes. The doors had been opened. Safety valves kicked in, shutting down the oven.

Jacob leaned into the square of light. He shouted, "No! What are you doing?" The old man pulled the burning husk of coffin through the doors with a grappling hook.

Laraby thought he heard shouts behind him, but knew they had to be from inside. The top of the coffin was engulfed completely in flames. The layers of polish had melted, leaving the wood along the sides to blacken and pop. Once the majority of the box was free of the doors the old man grabbed the burning lid. The pain in his hands was instant and immense. He let go and grabbed once more for the grappling hook. His palms sizzled against its handle. He allowed himself a short high-pitched scream. Then he noticed the coffin's latch was open. Why the hell hadn't he seen that before? Above him, fire and smoke licked at the cement roof. The sprinklers did not react, but the fire alarms screamed in panic.

"Come on, oh God this is insane." The coffin just kept burning. Heart smashing in his chest, he maneuvered the hook under the edge of the lid and pulled. The melted hinges fought him for every inch. Laraby howled with the effort and the constant pain. The burning lid raised completely.

What he saw in the coffin made him stop. Benchman's body lay sprawled atop a young boy. It wasn't Kinsley. The fire spread to the coffin's lining. Cursing, he flung the dead man away. An arm landed in the fire; the dark jacket's sleeve glowed with red burning spots then ignited.

The kid was heavy, dead weight. Laraby worked his arms under the shoulders and pulled. The side of the coffin was as hot as coals, searing his knees. The boy's legs caught on the lower lid. Laraby slipped and fell onto the floor. He clambered back to his feet, reached into the burning coffin and gripped the boy by the shirt. Beside him, the corpse itself was lighting up. Chemicals pumped through veins to replace blood now burned like gasoline. Laraby pulled the boy from the coffin headfirst. Together they crashed to the floor.

Black smoke filled the room halfway to the floor. Laraby leaned closer to the boy, but heard no breathing. His fingers were too blistered to look for a pulse. He opened Patrick's mouth and exhaled into it. Once, it seemed, was enough. The boy gasped in the burning air, then coughed with such violence his body twisted on the floor like an epileptic's.

The old man crawled to the door and opened it, hand disappearing into the smoke when he reached for the knob. He pulled the twisting body of the boy out of the room.

Smoke drifted under the window; black clouds obscured everything beyond. Jacob wobbled side to side, searching for a break through which to see what was happening. Useless. He found the metal bar; held his breath and propped open the window. Smoke poured into his face. He flattened himself against the ground, coughing once out of reflex. As soon as the cloud beyond the window was spent enough, he raised his head and looked inside.

The wood of the coffin was a blackened, burning log. Within, the crackling bones of Mister Benchman separated from each other as the final licks of flame disintegrated tendons and muscle. Freed of restraint, the skull turned sideways. Jacob stared into two pillars of smoke drifting from the eye sockets. He gripped the tall, neglected grass below the window in an attempt to control his fear. "Where is he?" he whispered. "What did you do with him?" As if to answer, the skeleton's jaw dropped open in a flaming mockery of laughter.

Jacob scurried backwards without taking his eyes from the window. "Come on, Kenney. Let's get the hell out of here."

The other boy did not respond. He lay face down; the rock still rested against his head.

"Kenney?"

The first fire truck screamed into the yard. In the hellish red glow of the emergency lights, Jacob knelt beside his friend and howled into the night.

The Veil

Christine DeLong Miller

Shannon stared up at the house as she stood on the snow-covered walk.

It wasn't the ankle-deep snow on the ground that made her shiver. It was the house. It glared down at her, it's windows as dark and black as a cave. Devoid of life.

She hugged herself.

"If you think the outside is impressive, wait until you see the inside," Jacob said. The look of happiness in Jacob's eyes twinkled brighter than the snow. He honestly thought that she liked it. If it had been any other house, she would have been dying to get inside. Old things thrilled her. She loved finding out about their history.

But, there was something wrong with this house.

Shannon smiled up at Jacob. She'd never let him think that she didn't like the house. Jacob had been so excited when he had found the big, old Victorian. She didn't want to burst his bubble.

Jacob slid his arm around her shoulders. "Come on. I can't wait for you to see," he said, leading her toward the huge porch that wrapped itself around the house like the forbidding moat of a castle. That's what the house reminded Shannon of, a misplaced castle, totally out of its element with its deep red sandstone in sharp contrast to the white two-story houses that lined the street.

It belonged on the side of a wind-blown, rocky cliff.

The front door was massive. It was made of dark mahogany, the color of dried blood, and when Jacob opened it, it creaked with age. A breath of cold air rushed from the interior.

Shannon shivered again.

"Shall we?" Jacob asked. He made a grand gesture, allowing her to be the first inside.

Shannon took a deep breath and stepped across the threshold.

The entry hall was wide with a glossy hard wood floor. At the far end was the staircase leading up into the darkness of the second floor.

The front door closed behind her and she jumped.

Jacob draped his arm over her shoulder and led her deeper into the house. "Just look at these floors. Aren't they beautiful? What do you think? Isn't this what we've always talked about?" he asked, hugging her close.

"You just can't find houses like this anymore," he whispered against her ear.

Shannon smiled tightly. "No. You sure can't."

Jacob stopped in front of a set of paneled doors. "Wait until you see this room. You'll love it."

He slid the doors open. The doors slid neatly into each side of the wall. "Pocket doors," Jacob said, grinning.

Shannon walked into the room.

It was dark. She could make out a fireplace at one end. Two windows on the far wall reached from the floor to the ceiling, but heavy velvet drapes held back the sunlight. She heard a switch click behind her.

Sconces lined the walls, their light bulbs shaped like candles. They glowed dimly, casting little light into the room which Shannon could now see was a library. Bookshelves lined the dark paneled walls and both sides of the fireplace. The first twinge of pleasure touched Shannon.

She had always wanted a library.

All ready, she could picture the room, the shelves lined with leather bound books, oxblood leather furniture situated around the room, candles burning, a fire burning in the fireplace, an Irish Setter curled up in front of it. A smile warmed her cold face. She turned to Jacob.

"I love it," she said.

"I knew you would."

Shannon looked around the room again. Maybe the house wasn't so eerie after all. It just needed some decorating. She could get over the chilling feeling that she had felt about it, couldn't she? She walked around the room, her hands grazing the shelves where she would place her books. She didn't have enough to fill them yet, but she would. She would fill them with classics, leather bound, unique editions. She'd have to start haunting antique store, garage sales, and bookstores.

She couldn't wait to get started.

She made a full circle of the room and ended up back in front of her husband.

Shannon put her arms around his neck and pulled him close for a kiss. When they parted, she looked deeply into his eyes. His eyes glimmered in the light. "I love you, Jacob," she said.

"I love you, too."

An hour later, the furniture arrived and Shannon's work began.

"I'm so glad that we didn't buy modern when we furnished the apartment," she said to Jacob as she watched the movers struggle up the staircase with the massive headboard of their four-poster bed. One of the movers almost dropped his end. It scraped sickeningly against the banister.

"Be careful," Jacob warned, "I'd better go help them." He squeezed Shannon's arm and went up the staircase to help the men with their load.

As they lay beside each other in the huge bed that night, Shannon let her mind wander. The bed fit the room perfectly. The bed was so high off of the floor that Shannon had to use a tiny footstool to get up onto it. The floral wallpaper in the room had faded with age, but it was perfect. She wondered vaguely if she could ever find the same pattern now. She doubted if any of the wallpaper stores carried it. She rolled over and laid her head on Jacob's chest.

"When do you have to go to the office?" she asked softly.

"Monday. So, I've only got tomorrow to help you, then it's back to work."

"Well, at least you can help me put the right pieces in the right rooms." She trailed a finger across his chest.

"Are you glad that we moved here?" he asked.

Shannon hesitated for a moment. "I think so."

"You like the house don't you?"

"It'll be wonderful, as soon as I can get started on it. You know, make it mine."

"I almost forgot," Jacob said, leaning up on his elbow, "The former owners said something about leaving some things in the attic. They said that there was some stuff that was left by the old lady that lived here before them. You might want to look up there. Some of the stuff is probably pretty old."

Shannon grinned. "A treasure hunt. I can't wait."

"We'd better get some sleep. We've got an awful lot to do tomorrow," Jacob said. He turned off the light.

Shannon lay beside him, letting the house close around her in the night.

A chill passed over her.

She snuggled up against Jacob, who was all ready snoring. This house is sure drafty, she thought. Of course, any house this old was bound to be. Shannon wondered how much it was going to cost to heat the place. They might have to close off some of the rooms in the winter months. She'd discuss it with Jacob in the morning.

She closed her eyes.

An hour later, something woke her.

A sound.

Creaking.

Shannon opened her eyes in the dark. She couldn't see a thing. Jacob slept soundly beside her, no longer snoring. Shannon held her breath and listened.

There it was again.

It sounded as if someone was walking in the attic.

Shannon sat up in bed and waited.

Another creak.

Whatever it was, it was moving.

She shook Jacob's shoulder.

"Hmm?" he mumbled.

"Jacob. Jacob, wake up. Someone's in the house," she whispered, shaking him harder.

"What's going on?" he asked sleepily.

"Listen."

Another creak.

Jacob rolled back over. "Your imagination. Go back to sleep, Shan."

"There's someone up there."

"It's just the house settling. Go to sleep." Jacob put his pillow over his head and turned away from her.

Shannon lay back on her own pillow. She'd never sleep now. Living in the apartment, you heard noises, televisions, stereos, people talking. She wasn't used to hearing a house settle.

If that's what it is, she thought.

She listened intently until Jacob's snoring drowned out every other sound.

After a while, she fell asleep, her dreams filled with creaking doors and floorboards.

It was only ten o'clock in the morning and Shannon was tired.

She opened another box that she had pulled from the stack in the bedroom. She hadn't slept well, not well at all. It's just the new house, she told herself, as she pulled clothes out of the box. She draped five of Jacob's shirts over her arm and walked into the huge walk-in closet.

It was more like a dressing room.

Odd, she thought, usually you didn't find closets like this in houses this old. They usually had large wardrobe cabinets in the bedrooms. Maybe the most recent owner had turned this into a closet. She wondered what the room had been before becoming a closet. She slid the hangers across the rail.

"What in the - ?"

Shannon ran her hand over a small door that was set in the back wall of the closet.

The door was only about four feet tall, but it was as wide as a regular door. It had a cut glass door knob that was absolutely beautiful. She wondered where it led. She giggled at the thought of a secret passage. She had read about houses of the same period that had secret passages all through them.

She opened the door.

She felt along the wall on the other side of the door for a light switch. There was none. She put her hands on her hips. She needed a light.

She ran to the kitchen and searched through the boxes there until she found a flashlight that worked and raced back upstairs.

"That's funny," she said when she entered the closet.

The tiny door was closed.

She had left it open, she could swear. Maybe, a draft blew it shut, she thought.

She opened it again. She shined the flashlight beam into the doorway.

The doorway was four feet tall, but the ceiling lifted just on the other side. The flashlight illuminated a staircase, going up.

The attic, she thought, as she started to climb, shining the flashlight on the steps in front of her. They were covered with a thin layer of dust. Every step that she took caused a puff of dust to drift up to her nose. The inside of her nose tickled. She sneezed.

When she reached the top of the staircase, it opened into a huge room.

Shannon played the flashlight around the cavernous space. She sucked in her breath.

The attic was humongous. It spanned the whole upper story of the house. The flashlight beam illuminated all sort of antique trappings, from trunks and baby prams to actual pieces of furniture. It was a dream come true for Shannon. There was enough stuff up here to keep her busy for months. She had studied antiques in the city. Jacob had even gone out to the suburbs with her on weekends, but this -- nothing could match the treasure that the attic held.

She ventured carefully into the attic, her light making wide sweeps across the floor in front of her. The light swung across an old trunk.

Shannon knelt down in front of it. She ran her hand over its humped back. A smile crossed her face when she realized that the straps that crossed over the trunk were made of leather. It was a real find. She could picture it in the library. She shined the flashlight onto the front of it.

An old lock dangled from the hasp.

What could be in there, she thought, weighing the lock in her hand.

A cold draft blasted down on her, blowing her hair across her face.

"Go baccckkk....."

Shannon whirled around and landed on her backside. The hair rose on the back of her neck. She shot the light into the darkness. She heard a rustle. She jerked the light around. The light caught a human form. Shannon gasped and scrambled back, away from the intruder. She moved the light back to what she thought was a person.

It was an old dress form, wearing a satin dress.

Shannon gulped for air.

Just an old dress form, she thought.

She got up from the floor and walked over to it. It was covered with a film of dust. The color must have been a beautiful emerald green at one time, but now it was faded to the color of a dim reflection in a stagnant pool. She ran her hand tenderly down the material. It felt dry and crackly to the touch. She drew her hand back, afraid that she would damage it.

She'd have to take this downstairs. It would look great in the corner of the bedroom.

"Shan?" Jacob called from the bedroom below.

Shannon jumped.

"Up here. I'll be right down," she called back. Shannon took one more look around the expanse and started back down the stairs. When she reached the door that led back into the closet, a chill blasted her from behind again.

She rushed through the door and bumped smack into Jacob's chest.

"Hey," he said, catching her before she tripped over him.

Shannon shivered.

Jacob turned from her and stuck his head through the doorway. "What's up there?"

Shannon placed her hand on his shoulder. "It's just the attic. Let's go have some coffee."

"The attic?" He turned back to her. "The door to the attic is in the hall. I didn't know that it had another entrance." Jacob scratched his head.

Shannon pulled on his arm. "Come on." She didn't want him going up there. Not yet. She wanted the attic all to herself.

After Shannon and Jacob had coffee and a sandwich, Jacob went back outside to finish with something in the garage and Shannon searched through boxes to try to find some kind of light that she could take up into the attic with her. She found one of Jacob's shop lights and an extension cord and headed upstairs.

She turned on the shop light after hanging it from a nail she found on a post. It shed more light than the flashlight, but it still left most of the attic in shadow. Shannon brushed her hands on the legs of her jeans. Where to start?

She decided to move the trunk and the dress form first.

She circled the trunk, trying to judge its weight. It was old and cumbersome. She brushed at the dust on the top. It came up in a cloud. Shannon coughed. It's going to take a lot of loving care to clean this stuff, she thought. She checked out the handles on the side. They were made of some kind of metal. They looked sturdy enough. She wrapped her hand around one and gave it a tug. It would hold. She started to drag the trunk toward the stairs.

"LEAVE IT BE ..."

Shannon's head jerked up.

"Who's in here? "Who was that?" she said, frozen.

It had been a woman's voice. An old woman. She remembered the creaking that she had heard the night before. Was someone really up here?

"Hello?" Shannon said, softly and a bit scared.

'Leave it.'

Shannon lowered the trunk. It was heavy.

"Is - is someone here?"

'Leave the trunk. You're not meant to know,' the voice whispered.

"Not meant to know what? Who are you?" Shannon started to back toward the stairs. The hair was raised on the backs of her arms. Quickly, she grabbed the handle on the trunk and jerked. She pulled the trunk as fast as she could toward the stairs.

It thudded on the risers all the way down.

Shannon dragged it away from the door to the attic and slammed the door shut. She leaned against it, breathing hard.

She stared at the trunk.

There was something inside that someone didn't want her to see.

But, who was that someone? And why was she here?

Jacob came down from the attic covered in spiderwebs.

"There's no one up there. Are you sure that you aren't just hearing things?" he asked, trying to brush himself off.

"Someone was up there." Shannon moved to help him brush off the grime.

"The only thing that I saw up there were your footprints and where you dragged that trunk across the floor. Nothing else."

"All I know is that someone spoke to me. And I heard someone walking around up there last night."

The look in Jacob's eyes said it all.

"You think I'm nuts, don't you?" Shannon asked.

"No, I don't think you're nuts. I think that maybe you're having trouble adjusting to the move, that's all." Jacob threw the towel he had been using to wipe at the spider webs into the sink.

"Maybe we have a ghost," Shannon said, crossing her arms across her chest.

"Now you're being nuts," Jacob said with a chuckle.

"Why? This house is ancient. We could have a ghost." Shannon pouted.

Jacob put his arms around her in a bear hug. "Why don't I help you open your treasure chest that you brought down from the ghost's lair? Then, you can spend the rest of the day going through the musty old junk in it," he said.

Shannon stuck out her lower lip. "Okay."

The trunk sat in the middle of the library where Jacob had left it after bringing it the rest of the way down stairs. Shannon looked at Jacob. "What do you think?" she said, lifting the lock in her hand.

Jacob crouched beside her. "I'm going to have to break it."

"That's a shame," Shannon said.

"Do you want to know what's inside?"

"Of course."

"Then, give me some room."

Shannon moved back.

Jacob placed a screwdriver where the hasp connected. He brought the hammer down on the end. The lock disintegrated. "Boy, this must be old," Jacob said, picking up the pieces from the floor. "There you go. Open it."

Shannon scrambled across the floor to the trunk.

She slowly lifted the lid of the trunk.

"Good God, that's smells," Jacob said, backing away as the lid fell back.

A clinging, musty odor rose from the trunk. Shannon took a breath and put her hand over her mouth.

"What the hell is in there?" Jacob asked, leaning over her shoulder.

Shannon peered into the trunk.

"Books. Old books," she said, lifting one volume out of the trunk. The book smelled moldy and damp.

Aged.

Shannon was almost afraid to open the book's cover, afraid that it would fall apart in her hands.

"I hope that you're not planning on putting those on the shelves in here," Jacob said, backing toward the door, "I've got work to do outside."

Shannon cradled the book in her lap. She waved Jacob on, totally absorbed in her find.

Shannon felt a draft at her back. She turned toward the door. Jacob was gone. She sat cross-legged on the floor and turned the book over in her hands. There was no title on the cover or the spine. It was bound in leather with scrollwork stamped into it. I'll bet it was beautiful when it was new, she thought as she ran her fingernail along the swirling design in the leather. She leaned over the edge of the trunk. All the other books inside matched this volume. A set. Why would someone want to lock them up? Especially with this library lined with shelves. The books would look great lined up in a row. She ran her hands over the cover of the book in her lap again.

How in the world was she going to get rid of the odor? She definitely planned on adding these volumes to her collection.

Carefully, she opened the cover of the book.

An unbidden wind blew into the room, whipping Shannon's hair up and around her face. She let out a scream. The trunk lid slammed shut. Shannon clutched the book to her and crawled across the floor to the door. She made it to the entry hall. The wind was blasting through the house, coming from the staircase. Shannon raised her hand, shielding her eyes from the assault. This is no draft, she thought. She looked toward the staircase.

Shannon couldn't even scream. What she saw coming down the stairs robbed her of her voice. She stared as the apparition floated down the stairs, its hands held out before it, reaching.

Shannon started to shake. What did it want? It was a wispy form of a woman, dressed in tattered satin dress the color of algae. Shannon scooted across the floor toward the kitchen door, away from the ghostly woman. She reached the kitchen door just as the apparition stopped at the bottom of the stairs.

'You mustn't, you mustn't know. You aren't meant to know,' the ghost whispered, its arms still reaching.

Shannon looked down at the book, still clutched against her chest. The ghost wanted the book. Shannon looked back to the ghost. It wasn't there anymore.

The wind died down, disappearing as quickly as the ghostly woman had.

Shannon found her voice.

"Jacob!!!!"

Outside, the cold, crisp air snapped Shannon back to reality.

Jacob held her by the arms, shaking her. "What is wrong with you? What happened?"

Shannon grabbed at his shirt, tears burning her eyes. "Jacob, I-I saw a ghost."

"Come on, Shan, your imagination is getting the better of you," Jacob said.

Shannon backed away from him. "You don't believe me." She could see it in his eyes. They held a look of sarcastic superiority.

"No, I just think that after finding all of these antiques, that your mind is making up stories about them, that's all."

Shannon backed away another step and crossed her arms over her chest, still holding the book. "I can't stay in that house. Not tonight. Not any night."

Jacob ran a hand through his hair. "Now you're being ridiculous."

Shannon raised her chin. "You think so? Well, you didn't see what I saw or hear what I heard." She was starting to shiver, but she wasn't sure whether it was the cold or her anger causing it.

Jacob walked over to her and put his arms around her. "I'm sorry. Tell you what. Let's go inside and I'll go through the house with you from top to bottom. Every room, every nook and cranny. I'll show you that there's nothing to be scared about."

Shannon looked down at the book. "I don't know - "

"Come on," Jacob said, leading her back toward the house, "besides, it's cold out here and you don't have a coat."

Jacob succeeded in talking Shannon into spending the night in the house. She had made him go through all the rooms, the basement, and most importantly - the attic.

The dress form was still in place, undisturbed. Just as she had left it.

Shannon suffered under Jacob's watchful eye the rest of the evening.

The book now lay next to the lamp on the bedside table.

Shannon lay next to Jacob and wondered about the origins of the book. She hadn't felt any more unearthly drafts, but she hadn't opened the cover of the book again either. Curiosity gnawed at her insides. The vision had said that she wasn't meant to know.

Meant to know what?

Shannon chewed her fingernail in the dark. She wanted to read the book. There was something in the book that someone didn't want her to know. Maybe, the ghost wouldn't appear with Jacob right beside her.

Shannon lay in the bed feeling the warmth of Jacob beside her, comforting and safe. She made up her mind. If the woman did appear, at least Jacob would see her and then he would know that it wasn't her imagination.

Shannon reached out into the dark for the light switch. The fringe on the lampshade brushed against the back of her hand. She jerked her hand back, then chided herself for being so jumpy. She reached back over and turned on the lamp. It cast a soothing glow onto her side of the bed. She glanced over her shoulder at Jacob. The light barely reached him. He slept soundly. She pulled the book toward her and braced it on the bed, keeping her back turned to Jacob.

Her eyes drifted around the room.

No drafts. No ghostly images.

Shannon opened the cover of the book.

There was no title page. She turned a couple of blank pages, then found the page where the text began.

She began to read.

The book read like a bible. It was about the notion of heaven and hell. Shannon chewed at her thumbnail as she read the faded words, trying to understand. The print was faded with age. She had no idea how old the book was. The pages weren't even numbered.

The book was depressing. It was about the process of death. Spiritual and physical. Shannon pulled at her lip. Memories of her mother, who had passed away a year ago, drifted through her mind. But what was it about the subject that the ghost did not want her to find out? That there is no heaven?

"There is no heaven. Nor hell."

Shannon slowly lifted her eyes from the page to find the swirling, shifting form of the woman standing directly in front of her, not three feet from the edge of the bed. Cool air drifted over her, not a breeze this time, but like standing in front of an open refrigerator door.

Shannon rested her hand on the book.

"Who are you?" Shannon whispered.

The ghost floated forward a bit.

Shannon watched its face shift and thought that she detected a slight, demure smile.

'I am no one ... and everyone.'

"I don't understand," Shannon said.

The ghost moved toward the bed. Shannon slid back a little, not sure of just what the ghost would do.

The woman-ghost raised a wispy hand and touched the book. "You are not meant to understand. Not yet," she said.

"Why don't you want me to read this? Where did it come from? What are all the others about?" Shannon had so many questions. She felt no fear of the ghost now, who it seemed would not hurt her. Shannon wanted to touch her, put her hand into the wispy haze of the woman's body, but she wasn't sure just how far she should go.

"Do not read the tome. Insanity is not a comfortable frame of mind," the ghost said, shaking her head, "You must do as I ask. Lock these tomes away."

Shannon pulled the book toward her chest protectively. She narrowed her eyes. "Tell me why."

Shannon saw exasperation in the ghost's face. The ghost took a step back.

"You are being difficult," the ghost said.

Shannon felt the cold increase. Jacob shivered beside her and pulled the cover up over his shoulder. The light coming from the lamp dimmed, making the ghostly image of the woman glow eerily. "You must tell me why I shouldn't read these or I will take them from this house," Shannon dared the woman.

The ghost raised her hand. "No. You mustn't. You must lock them away so that no one sees."

"Then, tell me."

The ghost lowered her eyes. She considered Shannon's request then came to a decision. She looked back at Shannon. "Insanity suits you then?"

Shannon didn't say a word. She waited, her hands closed around the book.

The ghost approached the bed and sat on the edge. She folded her hands primly in her lap.

Shannon watched the woman staring at her hands. Shannon could tell that the pale image didn't want to reveal what was in the books. Shannon couldn't let this find pass her by. She had to know. Shannon reached out gingerly to touch the dainty hand.

When her fingers grazed the ghost's vaporous hand, she felt little resistance and passed on through it to rest on the bed.

The woman turned her gaze on Shannon.

"Tell me," Shannon whispered.

"You must promise to place the volumes under lock and key, never to let anyone see them again."

Shannon nodded.

"Well, then, I shall begin."

Shannon laid her head back on the pillow and listened.

"The process of death is not an easy one," the woman began, "It is extremely hard. I know that you have lost someone close to you recently. I can feel her, here with me. As I said, I am no one and every one. These books were written ages ago. By whom, I am not sure. My husband came across them in his travels abroad. He brought them here and read them.

'Within the time that it took him to finish every last volume, he was insane. He would try to explain the process to me, but by then, he made no sense to those of us living.

"He passed on to this side wrapped in that insanity. Or so I thought then. Now I understand."

The woman looked back down at her hands.

Shannon saw silvery tears glittering in her glowing eyes. Shannon wanted to reach out to her, but knew it would do no good. She waited while the old woman collected herself.

"You see, there is a thin veil between where you are and where we are. A very thin veil. It can be torn to shreds easily.

"There is no heaven, no hell. We are here and we are here forever. Everyone who ever lived is still here. On the other side of the veil.

"When the veil is ripped by someone, someone who somehow has got a glimpse of us on the other side, insanity is the usual result."

Shannon frowned. "I don't understand. Insanity? Why wouldn't someone feel comforted that their loved ones who have gone before are really still nearby?"

The ghost sighed.

"Do you realize how many of us are here? Millions. I know that you cannot see it, but this room is filled with them. The only reason that you can see me is that I believe strongly enough that you should not know about the veil. I only tell you now because I know that you are one that I will not be able to stop, one that will find out at any cost.

"You see, finding out that there is nothing else, no beautiful heaven, no pearly gates, leaves people with nothing to believe in. Nothing to comfort them about the process of leaving the existence that they have come to know.

"Everyone is afraid of death. It is the only thing that you must go through absolutely by yourself. Alone. You don't know what is happening; you don't know where you're going. You are scared. I was. And if you don't have something, some God, some religion, to believe in while you are on the other side of the veil, all you do is wait for the time to come when you pass through.

"You have no hope. To live without hope is not to live at all.

"It drives you insane with despair."

Shannon thought about all the beliefs of her childhood. She thought about how her mother had been so sure that there was a heaven and how that had sustained her through the illness as she slowly withered away.

Shannon shuddered. "Oh my God." How lonely, how disappointed her mother must be.

The ghost's eyes softened. "I am so sorry. I should not have told you. I should have found another way. I can see that the insanity has already begun in you." The ghost raised her hand as if to stroke Shannon's hair, but stopped. The ghost rose from the bed and stood. "Remember your promise." The ghost pointed a finger at the book that was clutched to Shannon's chest. "Lock them away from curious eyes."

Shannon shook. She watched as the ghost faded into the darkness and disappeared.

Shannon had a fever in her mind now. Knowing that there was nothing to hope for, no place where there was no pain and no hunger, no abuse. Nothing waiting on the other side except for more of this world, but a much lonelier world filled with wandering souls that had not found the peace that they so believed in.

The shaking grew until she could not stop.

The summer heat swarmed around Shannon as she sat in her wheel chair and looked out the bedroom window to the lawn below. There was something going on down there.

Things were placed all over the lawn. Furniture, lamps, knick-knacks. And there were people down there, picking up things, handing money to Jacob and taking the things with them and leaving.

"Nurse," Shannon croaked.

The nurse came up to stand beside Shannon. "Yes, what can I get you?"

"What are they doing down there? Those are my things," Shannon said, still looking down on the people.

The nurse leaned over Shannon's shoulder and looked out the window. "Oh, that. Your husband is having a yard sale. I guess your care has gotten so expensive that he thought it best to sell a few things. You won't need them when we move back to the city anyway." The nurse patted Shannon's shoulder and moved away.

Shannon frowned. She watched as her things, her personal collection was slowly being taken from her.

Suddenly, Jacob came into view, dragging something with him.

Shannon leaned forward in the wheel chair.

Her heart hitched.

It was the trunk.

The trunk that held the secret of the veil.

Shannon watched in horror as a mother and a little girl talked to Jacob as he stood over the trunk. She saw Jacob raise a hammer.

Shannon opened her mouth to scream.

The hammer came down on the lock that she had placed there months ago. It fell away in slow motion. Jacob lifted the lid of the trunk.

Shannon tried to stand up.

The little girl reached inside the trunk and pulled out a book.

The wheel chair rolled away from Shannon as she stood and braced herself against the glass of the window. She raised her hand and hit the window feebly.

The little girl opened the cover of the book. The mother said something to the little girl. The little girl nodded her head and smiled.

Shannon heard the squeak of the nurse's shoes racing toward her from behind as she raised her hand to hit the window again.

The mother handed some money to Jacob.

Shannon's hand crashed through the glass.

She felt the nurse's fingers graze the back of her nightgown as her head shattered the window completely. Her body followed the arc of her hand.

She fell, seeming to float, to the ground, landing in a heap on top of the open trunk, her back broken.

"Shannon!!" Jacob cried. He tried to raise her up.

Shannon struggled not to fade into the veil. Pain filled her being. She couldn't let it stop her. She looked at the little girl with the horrified eyes. Shannon reached out a shaking hand toward her. "The- the b-book," Shannon whispered.

The little girl took a step away and whimpered.

Shannon coughed. She tasted something salty. "Please," she said. She looked up into Jacob's eyes. "She - she mustn't know. N-Not one so - "

Shannon could hear the sound of something tearing.

Her eyelids fluttered shut.

Shannon forced her eyes open again and peered through the gauzy veil of death. She watched the little girl walk away, the book cradled in her small arms, her mother comforting her.

Shannon screamed in despair.

She knew that no one on the other side of the veil would hear her.

The Last Stone

Dianne Buckman

"What are we doing here?" Derek asked, a nervous look crossing over his face. Mike ignored the question as he pulled his battered work Ute over by the barbed wire fence that surrounded the ruins. He rested his chin on the steering wheel and stared straight ahead. So you coming?"

"What do you mean am I coming?"

"Are you going to help me get some blocks?" Mike already had the driver's side door open and was starting to get out.

"Like hell... you wanna take something from in there you do it yourself."

Mike tapped the top of the cab, "Come on, no one's going to miss a few bluestone blocks. We're out in the middle of nowhere. No one will see us.

"I ah - "

"Honestly Derek, do you see any cars? Did we pass any on the way out here?"

"It's not the living I'm worried about."

Mike slammed his hands on top of the cab then lowered his head into the car. "Oh please, don't tell me you believe those stupid stories we used to tell as kids."

"Old Mrs. Horton reckoned she saw them out here once."

"Superstitions... stupid, ludicrous, unintelligent superstitions."

"Say what you like, insult me if it makes you feel better but I do believe and if I were you I'd stay well away from that prison. "Well stay here then, I'll be back soon. That is if the spooks don't get me first."

Mike climbed through the fence still shaking his head in disbelief. How could a grown man still believe in childhood ghost stories? Derek could be such a sook at times that made working with him all the more frustrating. Unfortunately Mike didn't have much choice in that matter, he was Sharon's brother and as Sharon so often pointed out to him one had to help one's family. Mike dragged a crowbar behind him, he figured he'd need it to help dislodge the heavy blocks. Especially now that he was all alone.

As he approached the crumbling bluestone walls of Wrightsville prison he smiled. He needed the bluestone so he could give his home a historic feel. Young wattles and gum trees were now growing in the interior of what once was a building. Limbs reaching in through the cracks in the wall had caused some of the blocks to fall into a pile at the base of their trunks. Nature was so good at claiming what was it's own and so good a helping him out. No one would miss the ones that had fallen to the ground. Anyway he figured he was doing the environment a favor. That was all the justification he needed for stealing from a historical site. Besides it seemed more of a crime to leave the blocks here unused. Neither ghosts nor law were going to scare him off.

Mike started prying the blocks away from the base of the tree with his crowbar. His landscaper's mind was running riot with all sorts of plans, so at first he didn't notice the gap in the wall but when he did he was intrigued. Beyond the wall some white stones caught his eye. They seemed to glow from beneath the shadows of the tangled bush that hung low forming a canopy above them.

Curiosity invaded him and he decided to go take a look. As he stepped through the gap in the wall he felt a chill breeze swamped the warm Spring air. Mike shivered as goosebumps formed on his exposed skin.

"Must be ghosts," he said, laughing nervously. "Yeah right," he continued as if trying to reassure himself

Mike moved between the rows, the stones were numbered. Suddenly he realized what they were - gravestones. That was the only explanation he could think of A smile curled up the corner of his mouth as his imagination began to soar. He pictured the arch shaped stones lining his driveway. They would be perfect and definitely unique and unique was what he wanted. After all, he had to encourage clients. Without any further thought he started pulling up the stones and started carrying them to the back to the Ute.

Derek was leaning on the bonnet of the Ute when he came back with the first lot of stones.

"Aren't you frightened the ghost's will get you?"

Derek screwed his face up into a smart smile. "I'm not the one stealing from them. What are they anyway?" He asked, pointing to the stones Mike carried.

"I think they're gravestones." Mike piled them into the Ute.

"What? Are you crazy? What about the bluestone?"

"These are much better." Mike said brushing his hands together.

"You can't take headstones from peoples graves. That's desecration. Aren't you even a little scared?"

"What of? Ghosts? Oooooh..." Mike raised his arms in the air and made his hands like claws and towered over Derek. "Anyway you can't call them headstones there just a series of whites stones with numbers on them. No names, they were only criminals for Christ sakes. No one cares.

Derek shrugged his shoulders. "Well I think you're just asking for trouble now." Mike smiled defiantly at Derek and went back to score some more of the stones.

"Let 'em come get me." Mike said as he walked away toward the ruins his arms outstretched. "I don't think they mind at all." Alter collecting over a hundred stones Mike decided to call it a day.

"Jeez, you sure there's any left?"

"Plenty. They sure killed a few crims in there. I'll come back tomorrow and get some more."

"Yeah well you can leave me at home."

"Don't worry I was planning too."

Mike felt relieved when he dropped Derek at home. He hadn't given him a moment's peace on the way home. His constant nagging of rights and wrongs had almost driven him crazy. At least he'd managed to extract a promise not to tell Sharon where he got the stones. The last thing Mike wanted was his wife as well as his brother in law whining at him. That was a fate worse than the wrath of any would be ghosts.

Mike loved entering his driveway. He couldn't help but admire his new home. He felt so proud of himself and Sharon. Together they had created a beautiful home. To think only a year ago the house had been virtually unlivable. They had spent every free minute, renovating the old weatherboard until it resembled a home not just a square box of rotted wood.

Mike jumped out of the car and started unloading the stones. He laid some of them where they would be permanently set then stood back to take in the effect. They looked great even better than he had imagined, only he would need a lot more. He would have to go back tomorrow and round up some more. He picked up all the stones and carried them around to the side of the house, so Sharon wouldn't see them when she got home. He wanted to surprise her with the finished job.

Strange noises disturbed Mike's sleep later that night. They seemed to be coming from the lounge room. Carefully he slipped out of bed so as not to disturb Sharon, he padded across the plush style carpet that lined the entire house until he reached the lounge room. He stepped boldly out into the open doorway but no one was there.

And the noises had suddenly stopped. He started to believe it had only been his imagination when he noticed that things were indeed missing. Yet as he investigated a little further he realized the burglar's hadn't taken anything important. All they had stolen was junk, like the revolting silver tea set Sharon had inherited from her great Aunt. That was no great loss, both he and Sharon had spent many laughter filled evenings inventing ways of ridding themselves of the thing without offending anyone. Well at least that was one problem solved.

Mike checked the doors and windows but everything was secure. Except for the missing things you wouldn't believe anyone had been in there. He wondered if he should ring the police but considering nothing important was missing, he decided against it.

Mike was glad to be surrounded by the solitude of his car after Sharon's yelling this morning. Apparently she really loved that damn tea set after all and wanted Mike to call the police. Which he promised to do some time today but first he had some stealing of his own to do.

He stepped through the fence and weaved his way through the ruins until he reached the thick bush that covered the stones. Again Mike felt a chilled wind caress him like an ice-cold whisper on a hot day. Mike shrugged off the shiver, he had never believed ghost stories and he wasn't going to start now.

As he neared the cemetery he was blinded by a strong light. The sunlight had been captured and reflected sharply back into his eyes. He walked closer shading his eyes, and as he stepped out of the sharp light he gasped. It was the silver tea set purposefully arranged with the rest of his missing belongings on the stoneless graves. A feeling of dread gripped him. Nausea turned his stomach as he looked around nervously, wondering who had put his things here. Someone knew, but who? Mike scanned the surrounding bush he couldn't shake the feeling he was being watched. A mood of disquiet had settled within him, he peered in the jigsaw of tangled bush. Sometimes he thought he caught a glimpse of a glowing face that appeared then disappeared as he set his full gaze upon it. "It couldn't be," he assured himself trying to ignore the tingle of fear that played throughout his body. "Anyone there?" No answer came forth only that now familiar chilly breeze drifted over him. A breeze that seemed to come from nowhere, carrying with it a stench. Foul like the smell of something rotting.

With carefully plotted steps Mike moved toward his possessions. He felt something tap him on the shoulder, he turned quickly only to find nothing but an overhanging branch. Something slithered around his ankle he jumped but only long blades of grass motioned beneath him dancing to the breeze. Did the earth move as well? His heart was now thumping heavily. He stopped so he could calm himself taking deep breaths hoping that would help. "Oh now I'm being paranoid. Derek and his damn ghosts." A smile formed on his face for the first time this morning. "Derek," he said aloud. It was the only rational explanation. He was the only one who knew about him taking the stones, he was also the only one, besides Sharon and himself, who had a key to the house. That would explain the absence of signs of forced entry. And hadn't he said that Mike would be asking for trouble. Obviously Derek was out to teach him a lesson. It all made sense, well Mike would show Derek that he wasn't the only one capable of practical jokes. Mike laughed, "to think he had me convinced he was terrified of ghosts. Well Derek, we'll see who's asking for trouble when I get hold of you." Mike said with a laugh in his voice.

Mike walked with newfound confidence; any fear he had refused to believe he felt had vanished. He reached down to pick up the teapot. A hand or something that resembled a hand shot up from the ground, grabbing his wrist. A head followed. A head empty of eyes, a head the flopped to one side and rolled without the support of it's neck. A head where the only living part of it were the maggots that wriggled over it like a continually moving skin.

"Ah tea time," it gurgled as a bundle of maggots fell from the cavity of its mouth. "One lumps or two." Mike screamed pulling his wrist from its bony grasp, a finger detached itself from the corpse and hung from the cuff of his shirt. Mike frantically shook his arm until it fell. His heart was racing again, nausea swirled within his stomach. He walked backwards away from the corpse that was now playing with the tea set.

The bush crackled with movement and Mike looked up to see more corpses emerging from within the twisted wood. Most of them with heads rolling from shoulder to shoulder as they walked toward him. Others had knives sticking out of them somewhere, and some with gaping holes in their rotted torsos. Great fleshy windows through which one could see the landscape beyond. Slowly they walked forward encircling him. Mike stared in disbelief but kept his backward pace almost stumbling over rocks. His mouth as dry as the flesh that flaked from the dead fiends that were approaching him. Making it so he couldn't scream even if he wanted too. When the distance between him and the gruesome chain gang had widened he turned and ran toward his car. Let them have the bloody tea set, forget the unique stones, he was out of there. He jumped in the car turned on the ignition, took one look back to make sure they hadn't gained on him then gunned the engine sped off leaving clouds of dust behind him.

Mike lay awake that night; visions of the ghoulish criminals wouldn't leave his head. He still felt sick with fear, he told no one of his horrific experience, preferring to keep it to himself. Sharon was still angry with him and hadn't even noticed his silence she was too busy yelling at him. Even if he had tried to explain why the tea set had disappeared she'd never believe him. She was the exact opposite of her brother.

Sleep finally won but not for long. A loud noise woke him. He opened his eyes and gasped. A deathly white face was staring back at him from the doorway. Fire searing out of the holes that once held eyes.

"101 arsonist," it said as it floated away back down the hallway holding what looked to be a petrol can in it's fleshless hands. Mike swallowed hard forcing the sickness back down. He looked across at Sharon who was still, thankfully asleep. Slowly he got up the courage to get out of bed and tiptoed back down the hall.

He pressed his body hard up against the wall just before the lounge room door. Sweat slithered down his body. He inhaled deeply then one, two, three he jumped into the open doorway. "What do you want?" he asked, his voice shaking.

The pale disfigured face of the arsonist turned to him, eyes still ablaze. "You took our stones."

Another transparent ghoul with a lopsided head was going through his cupboards pulling things out on to the floor.

"152 burglar." He stopped what he was doing and looked at Mike an evil toothless smile on his rolling 'lead. "You're one of us now."

"Please stop this!" Mike cried.

The floating arsonist laughed viscously as it poured the contents of the can all over the house, the flames that burned from its eyes blazed out igniting the fuel.

Mike howled with horror, he felt powerless against this unearthly attack. "Sharon quick get out of the house," he yelled just before an explosion of flames knocked him to the floor. Dazed and choking on the smoke he scrambled to his feet and managed to get to the bedroom.

Flames following close behind him. Sharon was already out of bed.

"What the hell's going on? Where's all the smoke coming from?"

"Quick, get out the window. The house is on fire." Mike frantically tried to open the window but it wouldn't budge. "Shit'." He looked around the room and spied the chair by the dressing table. He grabbed the chair and broke the window with it. Quickly he cleared away the jagged pieces of glass and helped Sharon get out before the flames surged forward toward the window. They engulfed Mike, he tried to get free but rotting arms reached out from the flames held him. There was no way he could escape the inferno.

Derek pushed through the crowd that surrounded the burning house and was relieved when he saw Sharon being treated by some ambulance men.

"Sharon, thank God you're all right." He said as he rushed toward her. "Where's Mike?"

"Oh Derek, he's still in the house - they can't get to him. He must be dead." She said sobbing into his shoulder.

A sudden shiver spiraled down Derek's spine, as he watched the fire take hold, mesmerized by the grotesque beauty of the sight. Suddenly above the house, hovering in the billowing black clouds of smoke Mike's face appeared. Derek glanced around the crowd; no one seemed to notice the unearthly presence.

"The stones, take back the stones." Mike's hollow voice echoed in his ears as his face disappeared. Derek shuddered again as he watched as a group of ghosts claimed Mike and carried him away in the direction of Wrightsville Prison.

"Oh I told you, you were asking for trouble."

"What did you say? Are you all right?" Sharon asked between sobs.

"Yes fine."

Sharon spent most of the following day with the police. They informed her the fire had been deliberately lit. Their chief suspect was Mike who had tragically lost his life in the incident. Sharon was horrified as they asked so many personal questions. She was glad to see Derek when they finally let her go. "Oh Derek am I glad to see you. You have no idea what they've been asking? They wanted to know if we were in financial trouble. If either of us were having affairs. Even implying that I may have done this on purpose myself" Derek put his arm around her rubbing her shoulders, "I think what happened had something to do with the stones."

"Stones?" Sharon looked up at Derek quizzically. "What stones'?"

"You know the white ones Mike brought home for the driveway." "He never told me about any stones for the driveway."

"He got them from Wrightsville Prison. Sharon, they're gravestones. I think he's offended some of the old spirits or something and they've taken their revenge."

"Hang on a minute." Sharon stood back from Derek shaking her head. "You're trying to tell me ghosts, set my house on fire and murdered Mike because he took their gravestones."

"Yes."

"That's just wonderful and here I was thinking the police were insane."

"Sharon on the night of the fire I saw Mike hovering in the clouds of smoke. He asked me to take the stones back."

"Oh Derek I know you're distraught over Mike's death, so am I but honestly this is just too far fetched."

"Distraught or not I'm putting the stones back. I have to do it for Mike."

"Okay if it'll make you feel better. They must be somewhere in the rubble of the house. I'll help you if you like."

"No Sharon, this is something I want to do on my own."

Derek located the stones beneath the ash remains of the house. He piled them into Mike's Ute and started the slow journey out to the prison. He was in no real hurry to get there. He wanted to conquer his fear and do the right thing for Mike and try to somehow make amends for not trying harder to stop him from taking the stones in the first place.

Derek swallowed hard as he got out of the Ute. He stared for a long time at the ruins, wanting to make sure no one or nothing was there. His shaking hands made it nearly impossible for him to cut the wire fence but eventually he managed it. He piled the stones into a wheelbarrow and wheeled them through the ruins until he found the graveyard. His head constantly turning making sure no one was about. Quickly he surveyed the stones and realized they were in numeric order and that Mike had only taken the first hundred or so.

Once he had them in order he placed them on the graves as quickly as he could, his mouth dry with fear, nothing would make him stay here longer than he had too.

An hour later he was left with just one stone without a number. He was just about to throw it away when a chilled breeze encircled him. Nervously Derek turned around, nothing. Next he felt a cold pat on the shoulder, he turned again to see Mike's charred face starring back at him.

"Oh Jesus," he said stumbling backwards. Mike appeared to smile but as he did deep cracks opened up on his leathery looking face, slimy liquid oozed out of them. Derek lost his footing and fell backwards watching as Mike's hideous form floated away, beckoning to him. Derek got up from the ground and followed somewhat reluctantly. Mike stopped at the end of the last row, hovering above a space. He pointed down to the ground and said, " I'm one of them now. 1004 - Grave robber."

Derek laid the last stone down. A sad smiled formed on Mike's hideously burned face. His white teeth gleamed from within the frame of charcoaled lips. He gave Derek one last wave then slipped down into the earth beneath the last stone.

Welcome Home

Martha Pound Miller

Some say you can never go home. But I can. Granny told me so. She said, "Mattie honey, stop your crying now and go with your Mama and Papa. But don't ever forget that Granny and her house are waiting for you. You come home any time you want."

I was six years old, sitting on the stairs in Granny's front room, crying my eyes out because Mother and Father were moving away from the town where Granny lived. Moving west. I begged them to let me stay with her. Granny's lap was warm, her arms always ready to cradle me while she rocked, singing, "Sweetest little angel, everybody knows, ain't nobody like her for she's mighty like a rose."

Mother, tight lipped and disapproving of my emotional excesses uttered a steely, "No, Mattie. You are going with us."

Now I'm wondering, was it all a dream? But I'm here, walking the long moonlit lane to Granny's house, the night all silver and black like a picture negative held to the light. The house sits atop a sloping hill at the end of the road, gabled roof a dark peaked cap. Four columns punctuate the long porch; tall narrow windows let out not a pinprick of light. Next to the house, the big cherry tree where Father hung my swing tosses restlessly in the wind. I can hear the wind moaning and sighing from right here where I stand.

I remember the oversized furniture, deep mysterious basement, the hot cobwebby attic where Granny hung hams to cure, the tiny pantry where she baked bread and fried chicken, perspiration gleaming on her face. I roamed the house freely, poking into corners, surprising a mouse occasionally, experiencing the contentment of acceptance, of being myself with no explanations or apologies. Granny took me the way I was.

Mother and Father, on the other hand, had great expectations. I was to be tidy, well mannered, and above all, no trouble to them. I was to listen when spoken to, come when called, recite when nodded at, and act like a lady at all times. It was far too much to live up to, and the childish joy of visiting Granny where I could shriek with laughter, cry with frustration and sleep until noon was such a sweet contrast that I loathed to go back to Mother and Father's house with its hot rooms, mothball odor, and immaculate kitchen presided over by a succession of women who cooked for us.

I remember vividly that morning we left Granny's for the last time. Still crying, I clung to the staircase banister, looking down into the parlor at her grand piano and dishes of African violets in the window. Mother and Father argued behind closed doors in an upstairs bedroom.

How could he leave this house where he grew up, I wondered? Or forget this village and daily walks to the post office to pick up his mail? What will he do when he can no longer hear the distant horn of the diesel train sliding through the farmland on its way from Kansas City?

I would not forget, I whispered. And I would not leave until I put something here that belonged to me, something with the power to bring me back. I would do it quickly before Mother and Father finished packing and came out of that bedroom.

I removed the pin holding my sun suit straps together and began scratching my name in the pink flowered wallpaper.

M-A-T-T-l-E. I scratched it where the carved banister met the wall just above my head.

Now, I stand in the moonlit lane. The house waits. I am tired from my long journey, and wearing a dress with no jacket so I am cold. I shiver in the wind that shakes the cherry tree until it undulates like kelp under the sea.

Mother and Father moved away without a backward glance. We drove west for three days to the heat and dust of Phoenix. I never forgot the damp mists of Granny's town, the flowing green lawns surrounding her house, her singing, and her acceptance.

I tried to be the person Mother and Father wanted, but I seemed always to fall short. They bought a big modern house on the desert and contributed to the arts by hosting parties and serving on committees. As their only child I was expected to follow in their footsteps. I finished grade and high school, attended a good private college in California and came home ready to make a suitable marriage, or so they thought.

One day I received a letter from a college friend in Los Angeles. "A friend of mine, Hans Schneider, has begun a brilliant singing career," she wrote. "He will soon be coming to Phoenix to sing with your symphony. Try to meet him," she urged in her letter.

"It just so happens," I wrote back, "that Mother and Father are hosting the reception after the concert where Hans Schneider sings. I will most certainly meet him."

The concert was held on a blustery December night. Just before leaving the house, I glanced around at the red poinsettias; soft lamplight and black-garbed caterers arranging silver on the table. Mother and Father did everything just right. I arrived at Symphony Hall and took my seat in time to see Hans enter the stage to polite applause. He walked briskly in spite of the cane he carried, looking splendid in a dark suit of tails with shining white shirt. He took his place in front of the musicians. The music began a Brahms piece, according to the program I stole a look at, and Hans sang in a tenor voice that gave me chills. He sang to me alone, I thought, then told myself every woman in the hall probably felt the same way.

When Hans and I were introduced at the reception afterwards, he offered me his elbow and when I slipped my arm through his, I felt strength and masculinity. In spite of his cane, he moved like a swimmer, slowly, languorously. He did not leave my side all evening and I kept my arm boldly linked through his. As we talked I learned with a momentary surge of disappointment that he was married, but he made me forget my concern by engulfing me in words and attention. He stayed until two in the morning. After the other guests left, Hans and I sat in the living room while the caterers cleaned up, talking by the dying fire about our dreams.

"Someday I'll go home to my Granny's to see if my name is still scratched in the staircase."

"I will take you," he whispered, "and I will kiss your eyes and ears and sing you to sleep."

I was so excited that after he left that I did not fall asleep until the sky glowed with dawn.

Hans called me every day until I agreed to join him in Boston. I made up a story for my parents and flew away to meet him. He asked me to finish the tour with him. I was ecstatic, falling deeper in love every day. I refused to miss any of his performances and watched anxiously the adoring women who flocked around him afterwards. He would break through the throng to take my hand and hold it until they drifted away.

I worried that he worked too hard, or that he would fall prey to some germ in one of the many hotel rooms where we stayed. Throughout our travels, I carried a large bottle of potent, caustic disinfectant, carefully cleaning the tub and sink in each hotel bathroom, knowing that I was protecting my adored Hans' health.

I asked him about his wife several times but he said only that they were separated, and I should not worry or ask him any more. Then we learned that I would bear Hans' child. I wept with joy. Hans held me close as I cried. "I must take very good care of you, Mattie my darling," he said. "I have always feared my own life will be short, but now because of you, I will live two lifetimes."

Mother and Father were horrified at my situation. When I called them with the news of my pregnancy, Mother asked, "Aren't you getting married?"

"Hans is already married, Mother."

She asked no more questions and I saw her only once after that.

Hans was called to Munich for a concert and I agreed to stay home. We knew the baby would be born in the next few weeks and Hans worried that the trip would be too hard on me. "Why not call your Granny and see if she can come visit?" he asked to assuage my disappointment over being left behind.

"Or I could go there," I agreed. "Kansas City isn't far. It wouldn't hurt me to travel there."

Before I could make the arrangements, little Johan was born suddenly in the middle of the night while Hans flew over the Atlantic enroute to Germany.

Soon afterwards Mother called to tell me that Granny had died. "There is no need to go to Missouri. She has already been cremated and the service held. The local doctor bought her house."

"Why didn't you contact me?" I cried. "I can't believe you didn't let me know."

The last time I saw Mother was after Father died a few months later. I flew to Phoenix for the service. Mother was too stricken to talk before the service and took to her bed afterwards, wailing, "He was the only one who understood me."

Little Johan grew fast and required much of my attention. We traveled with a tutor who was also his nanny, but I wanted to spend as much time with him as possible since Hans was often busy day and night. I wanted Johan to have as much of a family life as possible. I still carried the caustic disinfectant with me and now had two reasons to sterilize everything.

I stare at Granny's house. It is much closer now. The moon is under a cloud; shadows race across the blank windows. Chilly wind pulls and lifts my skirt. I am cold, anxious for the warmth of the house. Yet I move slowly, savoring the moment.

I hear a piano somewhere and remember how fluidly Johan played Granny's piano, which I insisted, would be mine. Hans' musical ability was transposed to Johan's long, slender fingers that could reach octaves by the time he was eight. He loved to sit in a darkened room playing Schumann, his hands searching out the notes infallibly, eyes closed, body leaning into the music. His touch was so unerring, so tender, that I sometimes felt tears sting and slide down my cheeks. When he played for Hans to sing my pride was boundless.

Now I stand in front of the house. It looms above me, dark and silent. It is very important to me that my name be visible on the wallpaper, that the power of my name has brought me home.

"Mattie," Hans had said to me that day. "My wife Angeline is very ill and I must go to Los Angeles to tend to some legal matters that affect Johan and you." His face was expressionless except for the tight line of his lips. "I want to take Johan with me."

I was too frightened to argue. I clung to both of them before they got into the cab that would take them to the airport. "Please come back to me," I whispered in Hans' ear.

I hugged Johan, who squirmed away in his excitement to be on an airplane again.

"Please," I said to Hans as he squeezed my hands before dropping them to pick up their small bags. "Hurry back."

"Please," I whispered as I watched the cab pull away from the curb in the rain, "be careful."

It was still raining three days later when I buried Hans and Johan. The accident involved their cab and a bus on the freeway, slippery with rain, on the way to the Boston airport.

I walk up the steps to Granny's house. I still cannot believe that I am home. I have dreamed of this moment.

"Please," I had said to the officer who came to tell me about the accident, "tell me it isn't true." He had been kind but harried. So many bad things happen to good people, he had said. Do you have any family you can call, he asked? A person needs family at a time like this.

The lawyer was brief and impersonal. Hans' estate was totally tied up in a trust in Angeline's name. He was sorry but there was nothing he could do.

I open the unlocked door to Granny's house. It swings wide into the dark living room. Someone is in the kitchen pantry, clinking dishes. I smell bread baking, chicken frying. Somehow I must explain my presence to this new owner. But first I go to the staircase and climb, one step at a time. "Please," I whisper. "Let my name still be there."

After Hans and Johan were buried I lay on my bed and stared at the rain blurring the window. When night came, I kept staring at the darkened window, wondering what to do with Granny's piano. It wasn't good for a piano to sit without someone to play it.

I stared at the window all night.

In the morning when gray light streaked the window I still hadn't figured it out, so I went into the bathroom and drank long and deep from the bottle of caustic disinfectant.

I climb the stairs now. It is dark and I sit on a step, leaning against the banister. I reach to touch the wallpaper, sliding my fingertips around, close my eyes. I touch something rough and trace my fingers along the familiar path.

M-A-T-T-l-E.

I stand, walk slowly down the stairs, across the front room and into the dark hall. Light gleams ahead of me from the pantry. Someone is there, cooking dinner. Chicken sizzles noisily, the aroma drifts my way, awakens old memories. I step into the brilliance of the pantry, light halloing the white haired woman working at the stove, her back to me. She turns slowly, sees me.

Granny. My God, Granny!

"Mattie, my dear" she says, extending her dimpled hands speckled with flour. "We've been waiting for you. Welcome home."

The Cabinet

Gail Sosinsky Wickinan

Joe loved wood - the smell, the feel, the swirl of the grain. He loved the way tools and time could turn a few boards into something beautiful. When he was laid off at the brewery, he began taking small cabinetry jobs, and eventually, his business grew enough that he hired Ralph, an unhappily retired family friend, to help out.

As his reputation spread, Joe began working regularly with local contractors; however, he still occasionally built cabinets for people who were remodeling. Elsa White hired him to make new cabinets in cherry. Joe had just finished installing them when the trouble started.

"Lovely," Elsa said, tracing her hand along the rich red wood in an uncharacteristic show of emotion. "Absolutely lovely."

"I'm glad you like them," Joe said, slipping the check Elsa had given him into his wallet. What Elsa lacked in personal warmth, she made up for in quick payment and decisiveness. She knew exactly what she wanted, which made her easy to work with. "If there's ever anything else I can do for you, let me know."

"Actually, there is," Elsa said. She pointed to the one empty corner in the kitchen. "I'd like a corner hutch."

"I'm afraid the door to the cabinet would open into your doorway."

"That's all right. I won't be in it often. I want it to have a glass door so that I can display my mother's carnival glass. She died last year. It's where I got the money to remodel. I guess I feel I owe her, somehow."

Joe measured the corner, and they discussed the cabinet's height and hardware. He didn't have another order due for two weeks, and that was well in hand. One corner hutch shouldn't take long to complete.

"I'll have it to you in a month," he promised, giving himself some leeway.

But that night, Joe received a rush order from Harlow Mack, the best general contractor in the area, a man Joe had dreamed of working with. Harlow was building a house for the Parade of Homes barely a month away, and his regular cabinet guy had just skipped to Mexico with Harlow's secretary, Nancy. Joe jumped at the chance. Not only could he connect with a top echelon builder, but his presence in the Parade of Homes would get his work and name seen by all sorts of potential customers.

In the flurry of work, Elsa's cabinet fell by the way. It wasn't that Joe forgot it -- he even got as far as ripping and jointing the wood -- but his business had reached a crossroads, and it was time for him to leave the gravel lanes behind.

After the first month, Elsa began making polite phone calls once a week to find out when her cabinet would arrive. Joe would take the calls in his shop, assuring her he'd get it to her as soon as the Parade of Homes was over, watching Ralph and Tim, the new guy he'd hired, as they worked to finish orders he owed to his other contractors. He himself worked on Harlow's cabinets.

Joe and his wife, Susan, celebrated the day the Parade started. They strapped the kids into the car and drove from home to home. By the time they'd completed the circuit, their two year old had fallen asleep, and their four year old was having exhaustion tantrums, but he saw in Susan's proud face what he already knew: his were the finest cabinets on display.

After he helped Susan get the kids to bed, Joe headed out to the workshop. He had pulled out the plans for Elsa's cabinet when the phone rang.

"Joe, son, you did us proud," Harlow said. "Pulled through when I needed you."

"Glad I could help."

"Well, I was wondering if you could help me out again. I've got a home on Windsor that needs cabinets."

Windsor Drive! One mile of new construction built with city-bred managers in mind. Those homes started at $500,000. Joe could feel his breath quicken.

"I was wondering if your could come measure it tonight," Harlow continued. "I'd ask you to come in the morning, but I have to talk to a lawyer. Nancy's using the business credit card to pay for Jacuzzis in Chihuahua, and somehow she convinced the credit card company that I don't have the right to cut her off."

"You're kidding."

"Wish I were, son. Vindictive is what she is. Never can tell who's going to turn nasty on you. Tell the truth, I half wish Frank had taken my wife. I can't find a damn thing in this office." Joe could hear paper shuffling and a muttered curse as something large hit the floor. "It's 608 Windsor, son. You with me?"

"Sure thing. I'll be there in half an hour." Joe hung up, shut off the lights, and left Elsa's plans in the dark.

The second month passed in a haze. His presence in the Parade of Homes and Harlow's good word had orders flowing in. Joe hired another worker, but he still was out so often that Susan ended up taking Elsa's calls.

"You're going to have to get back to her," Susan told him on a rare night when the kids were asleep before he'd dropped from exhaustion. "I told her you're out of the house by six every morning, but I think she's getting mad."

It was eight-thirty, but as Joe reached for the phone, he noticed the way Susan's long, black hair slipped along her back as she stooped for a toy. And the kids were asleep.

The next morning, Elsa called. At 5:30.

"I wanted to catch you before you left. Will you be bringing my hutch today?"

He promised her it would be soon.

Thus began the morning ritual. Every morning, Elsa called, and he gave her a new excuse or recycled an old one. Every morning, he vowed that *tonight,* as soon as he got done with the work on the big orders that paid the bills, he'd finish the cabinet. But every night, after sanding or staining or dragging home from an installation, he could barely crawl to bed, and the cabinet, and Elsa, waited.

Joe stopped setting his alarm. Elsa's 5:30 call was more reliable. Susan begged him to let Ralph, or even one of the new guys, finish the hutch. Ralph, who was tired of ducking Elsa as church, pestered Joe for the time to do it. But Joe was new to management and couldn't bring himself to delegate what he considered a personal promise.

One Friday night, after a particularly late installation, he and Ralph were headed back to the workshop when they came upon an accident. Police cars blocked the road, lights flashing, and Joe watched as the Jaws of Life pried off a door and a mangled body was lifted out. In the flashing light, he saw the paramedics pull a blanket over Elsa White's face.

A weight of emotion struck so hard it crushed the breath out of him. He felt the horror that anyone feels when violent, sudden death points out one's own mortality. He felt a stab of pain for Elsa's granddaughter, who was in his daughter's preschool. Unbidden, relief flooded through him when he realized the 5:30 calls would stop. Revulsion followed when he realized he could feel any kind of happiness over Elsa's death.

Joe made a solemn, silent vow that the next job he did would be Elsa's cabinet. He'd finish it and give it to the family, his parting gift to Elsa.

Ralph silently smoked his pipe all the way to the shop, and Joe began to believe the old man hadn't noticed how shook up he was, but Ralph, instead of getting into his own truck to head home, stopped Joe in front of the van.

"You ok?" Ralph asked.

Joe hoped the moonlight wasn't bright enough to show his sudden flush. "Yeah. That was quite some accident, wasn't it?"

"Son," Ralph said, pulling his beat up Packer cap more tightly over his gray crew cut, "you and I both know you wronged that woman. You can't make it right, but have you figured how to live with it?"

Joe looked toward the house, seeing the lawn that needed mowing, the half-constructed swing set, the broken railing on the front porch. He'd neglected a lot to build his business and wronged his family as much as Elsa. At least he had time to make that right.

"I'll work it out," Joe said, starting for the workshop. Ralph's hand clamped on his shoulder.

"Head to bed, son. I'll make sure everything's in order inside."

Joe nodded. "See you Monday," he said and walked to the house. He collapsed on his bed, unshowered. Despite the hot August night, he shivered under the covers and didn't fall asleep until the small hours of the morning. At 5:30 a.m. he sat up in bed, fully awake. When he realized he was waiting for the phone to ring, he laughed at himself and huddled under the covers, eventually falling back into his fitful sleep.

When Joe finally got out to the workshop Saturday morning, he couldn't believe what he saw. There was Elsa's cabinet, flawlessly finished. Even the glass sparkled. Ralph must have needed to say his own good-byes, but he couldn't believe that during his troubled night, he hadn't heard Ralph out here working. His own course, now, was easy.

Joe carefully loaded the hutch into the van. He'd drop it off at Elsa's house on the way to a 10 o'clock meeting with Harlow. He expected one of Elsa's kids would be at the house, and if not, he still knew where Elsa had hidden her key outside. He'd leave the cabinet and a receipt that said paid in full. He drove off with a light heart.

He was about to exit the divided highway when his left front tire blew. He spun across the two lanes into the median strip, fighting to control the van as other drivers slammed on their brakes or swerved to avoid him.

The police were there almost immediately. One officer kept shaking her head, confused that a tire with so little wear could have failed so completely, especially when it hadn't hit a pothole or debris on the road.

Joe put on his spare, glad that it was a real tire. If he hurried, he could still make it to his meeting. He expected he'd have to do some repair on Elsa's cabinet, but amazingly, it hadn't a scratch. He thanked his lucky stars he'd packed it so carefully. He could drop it off later in the day.

Harlow's meeting included all his subcontractors. He unveiled a plan to build luxury homes on a lake close enough to three major metropolitan areas that the commute would only be annoying in the winter. The planning and anticipation carried through lunch and on into supper, so that it was 8 o'clock before Joe could get away. He headed for Elsa's, his elation from the meeting tempered by his tension at being behind the wheel again after the blowout.

The tension was what saved him. He sensed the deer's presence even before it sprang in front of the van. He hit the brakes, feeling them pulse beneath his foot, seeing only a flash of hooves, antlers and the deer's summer red coat.

The van landed in the ditch, thankfully upright. Joe hugged the wheel as he caught his breath and fought the shaking that convulsed his hands. How could antlers in velvet look so sharp and menacing? He got out. The van wasn't too far off the road, and the ground was solid. The police who had been so quick this morning were absent. He hoped he'd be able to drive out without help.

The left front fender was crumpled, and the windshield had a small spider web of broken glass. He couldn't find any blood or hair on the van, but he knew the buck had to be hurt. He walked along the road for a hundred yards in each direction, but he couldn't find the body or even tracks. It was as though the deer had never been there. Joe shivered in the cool of the falling night.

The van rolled back on the road without trouble, and Joe headed home. Two accidents in one day was strange enough, but he was disturbed by the fact that Elsa's cabinet hadn't suffered damage in either of them. No scratch in the wood, no crack in the glass. Still he shouldn't question his good fortune. He just needed to get home, to see his children sleeping, to sit in the familiarity of his cluttered family room, to put his arms around Susan and remember his own strength.

Joe backed the van up to the workshop and grabbed the plans from his meeting. He had just stepped into the workroom when Susan came running.

"Joe, I'm so glad you're home." She gave him a quick hug. "One of Ralph's neighbors called. Ralph had a terrible accident on the way home last night. They're not sure he's going to make it."

Joe felt his muscles freeze. Why had the old man stayed so late to finish the cabinet? He'd probably been hit by some drunk who hadn't given up at bar time.

"Where is he?"

"They flew him to the Twin Cities, to one of the burn units. Ralph's neighbor said it took the fire fighters until almost midnight to put out the fire."

"Midnight?" Joe turned to her. "When was the accident?"

"After he left here. Around eleven or so. Joe?"

He was staring at her, seeing his raw fear take root in her puzzled eyes.

"If Ralph left here right away, who finished Elsa's cabinet?"

"Elsa's cabinet? You ignored it for so long, what diff - " She never finished her sentence. A revving engine washed a wave of warning across Joe's fear-heightened senses just as the van crashed through the wall, backing straight for them. He threw Susan into his office, wrapping himself protectively around her as the van splintered the glass and wood of the open office door.

The van rolled past, crashing into a workbench, back doors swinging open. It stood silent, dead, tame.

Joe released Susan and stepped into the workroom. His eyes locked on a point just beyond the van's open back doors. She began softly touching the cuts on his arms and back, making tiny mother sounds. He stopped her hands and said, his voice flat, "Susan, would you make sure the kids are all right?"

She turned to look at what he saw: In the midst of the broken materials and scattered tools, the cabinet stood impossibly unharmed, upright, glowing brightly from within.

"But you never finished it," she whispered. He heard her turn and run.

Joe circled the cabinet, gathering scraps of wood - hickory, walnut, birch. He crumpled some paper -- design plans, contracts -- it really didn't matter -- and tossed it into the cold wood stove. Even as he lit it, he did no more than glance away from the cabinet. He knew where the danger lay.

He grabbed his ax. The first swing shattered the glass, and it was as if a great gust of wind blew the shards at him. He covered his eyes, but he could feel the pieces strike his hands, his lips, his neck. He shrieked in pain and fear and brought the ax down again and again until no piece left was bigger than his palm. He opened the stove door and reached for a piece of the destroyed hutch, but the wood burned his hand like acid, blistering his skin. He filled a dustpan again and again, and by the time the last of the wood was in the stove, the metal pan was a lacework of holes.

The wood hissed as if green, spitting and sparking. Sulfurous smoke rolled out of the opened door, stinging his eyes and lungs, but Joe knelt in front of the stove, needing to see the flames. Only when the last ember winked out did the chill leave his bones and the tears run freely down his bloody cheeks.

He stumbled to the house. Susan begged him to go to the emergency room the whole time she pulled out wood splinters and glass and bathed his wounds. Her harangue comforted him, and he kissed her, and she let him.

He fell into bed, pulling Susan with him, holding close to the comfort of flesh, slowly releasing the conviction that he had killed Elsa a second time. His fear ebbed with each breath, and the peace of the night settled around them.

At 5:30 a.m., the phone rang.

The Roots of Evil

Lisa Becker

In late summer of 1988, I developed an interest in old cemeteries. I know what you're thinking: I've slipped a cog, I'm off my rocker, I'm a few bricks short. But anyone that knew me would've told you I wasn't weird in any way that really mattered. I just enjoyed the quiet, the solitude, the sense of history, that I felt whenever I visited these places of the dead.

On one cloudy Saturday afternoon, I drove to a cemetery about twenty-five miles from my country home The church on the property was built of fieldstone, with a bit of wooden trim that looked like an afterthought. Standing by my car, marveling at the original stained glass windows, I heard a clang from behind the church.

It turned out to be an old guy with a wheelbarrow and a rake. He wore a plaid flannel shirt, open at the neck, to reveal what I was sure was an official old-man undershirt; his suspenders held up what was more a collection of patches than a pair of pants. He was stooped and wiry, but I couldn't tell if he was sixty or eighty; being only twenty-eight myself, it didn't really matter, old was old. When he saw me, he set the wheelbarrow down, took off his straw hat, and wiped his forehead with his shirtsleeve.

"Can I help ya?" he yelled. His voice surprised me; it was young and strong, polite yet firm. My voice, on the other hand, was shaky by comparison.

"No, not really. I just wanted to look around a bit, if it's okay."

"Are ya lookin' for anybody in particular?"

"Well, no. I'm just kind of interested in old cemeteries and that.'

"That's a helluva thing to be interested in." Which I thought was a helluva funny thing for him to say, given his occupation. I started laughing, partly because it was funny, partly because I was nervous. This proved to be the proverbial icebreaker and he began to laugh too.

"Yeah, I get your point," he chuckled. "Name's Walt Foster, but folks mostly call me Red."

That got me going even more, because, although his hair was completely white under his straw hat, his bushy eyebrows were blue-black. He picked that up right away too, and admitted that he didn't know why either. When our laugh-fest finally subsided, I held out my hand.

"Will Griffen. Pleased to meet you Red."

"'Spose folks call ya Grif?"

"Well, no, actually they don't." That got us going again.

That's how I ended up sitting in the tool shed, sharing a bottle with Red, while he shared something I ended up regretting way more than the hangover.

"The church was built in 1806," he began. "It was looked after by a Reverend Lewis. By all accounts, he was all fire an' brimstone, scarin' his flock outta Hell instead of leadin' 'em into Heaven. The first man hired for the caretakin' job was Isiah Foster, my Granddad. He an' Grandma had a small farm, but with four growin' boys to feed, they needed the extra money the job brought in. As well as the diggin', Granddad looked after the church an' the house that used to be here. It was a full-time job, but the boys, my Daddy bein' the youngest, did a lot of the farm work. One spring day, Dad went with Granddad to help. Lewis gave 'em a job that turned out not to be worth all the money in the world. In fact, Granddad ended up bein' the one to pay." Red seemed to be studying the windows of the church which were already reflecting late afternoon sunshine. I decided he needed a little prodding. Besides, I thought I had guessed what had happened.

"Your Dad broke a window and Lewis took it out of your Granddad's pay?"

For a minute, I thought he might cry, and I wondered if the whiskey and memories were too much for him.

"No Grif," he answered softly. "What got broke was my Granddad's life an' he almost paid with his soul."

That did it. I changed my mind about the effects of whiskey and the past on the old man before me. The guy was nuts. Not really scary nuts, mind you, just kind of quietly crazy, probably from loneliness and long hours spent with only the dead for company. I tried to think of a way to get out of this one gracefully; I felt bad for him, but what good would it do either of us to go on with it? I glanced at my watch.

"Jesus, look at the time. I'm really sorry Red, but I've got company coming. I have to get home."

"Yeah, 'tis gettin' awful late. Better pack up before it gets dark" He didn't look surprised and he didn't seem upset. When I thought about it later, I knew why; the bastard knew he had me hooked.

I went back the next Saturday, but Red didn't seem inclined to continue that other conversation. I didn't know if he just didn't want to, or if he'd forgotten about it

Over the course of a month, I pretty much forgot about it too, but I continued to go to the bone-yard once a week, simply because I found I enjoyed Red's company. In him, I didn't find anything as sentimental as a father figure, but rather a damn nice guy who enjoyed good conversation and a good laugh. Then, one day, he held up a bottle of whiskey.

"Got any glasses?" I asked.

"Glasses are for girls, but I think I can find ya one," he grinned. We walked to the shed laughing, and I realized the hair on the back of my neck was standing up; for I knew that today was different, and I knew that Red wasn't crazy.

"As it turned out, Lewis had a special project for Granddad that day. He led 'em to a crate sittin' on the ground, an' handed Granddad a crowbar."

"'*Well!* Open it!' Louis snapped, an' Granddad set to work, Dad watchin' quietly. He was mighty disappointed an' a little puzzled when all the open lid revealed was a stack of steel buckets an' a pile of tree taps. They set to work hammerin' the taps an' hangin' the buckets."

Here Red paused, "Now, Grif, I can see you're kinda confused, an' you can bet they were too, but they knew better than to ask questions," he looked at me pointedly before continuing.

"They worked late, an' it was gettin' dark by the time they finished up. They were just about to head for home when Dad turned to take a look at the cemetery an' saw Lewis, standin' by the last tree," he stopped talking and held out his hand for the bottle; he took a drink but didn't hand it back.

"When my Daddy told me this story years later, he said one of the things he remembered most clearly about that summer was this: when he looked back, Lewis looked up at 'im. He was smilin'," Red grimaced. "Kinda gives ya the willies, don't it Grif?" I nodded and he continued.

"My Dad was an old man when he told me, but he wasn't a liar, an' he wasn't crazy. I tried to tell myself that maybe his mind had slipped, but it just didn't work. I also tried to find a reason why he chose to tell me; I know why now, an' it's the same reason I'm tellin' you. I have no sons, an' I guess I've used you in a way, an' I'm sorry for that But here's the thing, Grif, I'm the old man now an' I'm tired. I don't want to spend whatever time I have left bein' the only one that knows; that, an' I have a responsibility to pass it on - somebody has to know, has to be here, just in case."

He lifted his head and he looked more than tired; he looked like death was waiting for him at the door of that shed. "If ya wanna leave now, Grif, I'll understand. This is somethin' that'll weigh on your heart 'til the day ya die, an' ya didn't bargain for that," he smiled weakly. "You were just in the mood for a drinkin' buddy an' a good story."

Briefly, I thought this may be his way of keeping me interested, but, as his smile faded, I realized it wasn't so. He was serious about giving me a chance to end it right then. Maybe his conscience was bothering him, or maybe he liked me as much as I liked him. On the other hand, I needed to hear the rest and I think he knew that too. It's probably what his Dad told him.

"Red, I want to hear the rest. And you're right, I did come for a story, only it's is gettin' damn cold out here, and the whiskey's gone. If you've no pressing engagements tonight, why don't you come to my place? I'll get a fire going, open a fresh bottle, and we can finish this thing in comfort."

He looked relieved, and it wasn't because he was cold or thirsty.

We sat in two old armchairs, and since we were indoors, decided that glasses were civilized not girlish, and I left the bottle on the table in front of us.

"Well, Granddad kept on with his duties at the church," Red continued. "Sometimes he'd look at the buckets an' shake his head, sometimes he'd look at Lewis an' do the same. But mostly, he was too busy with the job an' the farm to think much about it until the day Lewis told 'im it was time to take the buckets down. The job was planned for Saturday, an' Granddad asked Dad if he wanted to lend a hand. He agreed with a bit of convincin', an' they set off with a coupla sandwiches an' a jar of lemonade. Dad said that's somethin' else he remembered clearly; walkin' to the church with his Dad on that spring day an' thinkin' maybe there was nothin' to be afraid of after all; nothin' bad could happen with the sun shinin' an' his Dad takin' care of 'im." Red looked thoughtful, "It's a hard thing to learn that bad things do happen an' that parents are only human after all. Dad learned both those things that year, but he didn't blame Granddad; he knew that nobody could've stopped what happened, maybe not even God himself." He stopped to pour us a drink while I threw another log on the fire.

"So how did you end up with the caretaker's job, Red?" I sat down and waited.

"Well, the job just seemed to be an inherited kinda thing," he replied.

I thought for a minute, "You said there used to be a house there too. What happened to it?"

"Burnt down," he replied softly. He seemed to force himself to continue.

"They collected all the buckets, but left the taps as Lewis had told 'em. Dad was ready to get some kindlin' for a fire when Lewis spoke, "That will be all Foster, you an' your boy can go now."

I had to interrupt, "But what about the syrup? Lewis didn't make it himself did he?"

"No," Red answered. "No, he had somethin' else in mind. Granddad didn't ask what, but as it turned out, he found out for himself."

I began to speak again, but Red held up his hand, shaking his head. I shut my mouth and he continued.

"Life was good that summer; Granddad kept on with his job, but Dad didn't go with him again. He was too busy playin' an' swimmin' to think about work. Soon he'd be helpin' his brothers more, but for now, he only had a few chores in the mornin' an' the rest of the day was his.

"The fun came to an end when my Dad's oldest brother died. He'd been choppin' wood when the axe slipped an' hit an artery; he bled to death before they found 'im. Dad was hit hard. Robert was old enough that he didn't mind takin' the time to talk to his little brother now an' then. They buried Robert in the hole Granddad had dug the day before."

"He had to dig his own son's grave?" I was shocked.

"Yeah. The neighbors offered, but I think it was somethin' Granddad had to do, to make it seem real, like." We sat in silence for a minute.

"Would ya mind switchin' on that lamp there, Grif?" He pointed to the stained glass lamp beside me; it reminded me of the church windows.

"Dad spent a few days tryin' to take over Robert's share of the farm work Grandma an' Granddad let 'im go 'til it looked like he was gonna run himself ragged, then told 'im to go play. Dad didn't feel like playin', but went for long walks instead. One day, he found himself at the cemetery, standin' by Robert's grave, talkin' to 'im as if tryin' to make up for lost time. He cried for a long time too, but when he finally dried his tears, he saw there was still a tap in the bark of the maple nearest the headstone. He pulled himself up, brushed the grass off his pants, an' not really knowin' why, went to pull the tap out. He didn't hear Lewis come up behind 'im an' clap a hand roughly on his shoulder. Dad barely had a chance to catch his breath before Lewis was yellin'. "Don't you know what happens to bad boys that play with things that are none of their concern?"

"Somethin' in Dad snapped. He shook loose of Lewis' strong grip an' faced 'im with fire in his eyes. "I was visiting my brother's grave, dammit!" he yelled right back. Lewis looked shocked, then spoke through clenched teeth. "You will regret that, boy!"

"Dad said he expected more, but that was it. He took off runnin' an', by the time he got home, he was cryin' again; he looked wild an' scared the hell outta Grandma. After he'd had a drink of water an' a cool cloth for his face, he was able to tell 'em what happened. Grandma started to cry an' held 'im. For Granddad, it was more than that; he slammed his fist on the table an' was out the door before they could ask where he was goin'."

"The late afternoon was chilly, the path through the woods filled with shadows, but Granddad barely noticed, his anger drove 'im on. He was a good, God-fearin' man an' had taken abuse from Lewis good-naturedly, believin' the bad temper was not actual meanness. But this time, by God, he'd gone too far. His son had gone to visit his brother, ready to lay his grief to rest, an' Lewis had destroyed that, Reverend or not, before this day was out, he would answer for his cruelty."

Red took a deep breath and looked at me thoughtfully, "I never thought I'd be repeatin' this if I lived to be a hundred. It's easier than I thought it'd be."

I gazed at his haggard face and thought that it hadn't been easy at all. "Let me grab some more ice, I'll be right back." I went to the kitchen and took the ice from the freezer. We'd drunk a lot, but we weren't getting drunk; I think we both wished we could. In the window over the sink, my reflection looked ghostly; I caught a glimpse of the old man I would become and it scared me. I shook my head and went back to the living room. Red was stoking the fire and smiled when he saw me; he looked like someone's Grandpa, like he should be surrounded by family, instead of trying to get drunk and relive painful memories with a stranger. I sat and had to force myself to smile before he continued.

"Well, Grif. I guess this part of my little tale is the strangest," he paused and shook his head. "If I'd heard it from anybody else, I wouldn't 'ave believed it, but as I've said, I know my Dad wasn't a liar, an' I know he wasn't crazy. I often wish he hadn't told me, but I don't blame 'im; I know he had to, just like I know I have to tell you. I hope in the years to come, you don't blame me either."

I started to protest, but stopped; I knew I would believe anything he said, and I knew the worst was yet to come. "Go on Red, too late to turn back now.

"Yeah," he replied. "I guess it's always been too late. Anyway, Granddad said he didn't really remember gettin' to the church, but the walk hadn't calmed 'im down any. He had to squint to see in the gatherin' dusk, but what he thought he saw turned his blood to ice; he didn't know exactly what it was, but it made 'im feel bad. Not bad like sad, or mad, or sorry. Just sick bad, like he might start pukin' an' never stop."

"What the half-light showed was this: His son's grave, the tree, an' a figure crouched by the tree, almost huggin' it." 'Hey! Get away from there!' he yelled. The figure turned an' stood; there was just enough light to see the wild hair an' the cloak blowin' in the wind. He didn't need the light to see the eyes though, for they were a sick yellow. A moan escaped the hidden lips."

"What do you think you're doing?" The dark figure moaned again, the sound so full of agony that Granddad stopped in his tracks. Maybe it wasn't some lunatic or drunk; maybe it was some poor soul that had come to the church lookin' for help. "What is it friend? Do you need help?" As he waited for an answer, the clouds blew away from the risin' moon, an' he saw the face; it was Lewis. His crazed look sent Granddad stumblin' back a few steps, but that wasn't the worst. The worst came when Lewis, or the thing that had been Lewis, spoke.

"Maybe I can help you, friend," the voice was a snarl, no longer human; the sound of it tried to take Granddad's sanity. He stood completely still, like a dream where you're tryin' to run but your legs won't move. The thing chuckled then, an' the sound seemed to unlock Granddad's legs. He ran for home an' didn't look back, not even when he was sure he heard somethin' on the path behind 'im. He ran in the door, an' Grandma was waitin' for him at the kitchen table, her face all shadows from the glow of the lantern. Granddad looked just as wild as Dad had when he'd come runnin 'in the door earlier in the evenin'."

"'Is it Robert?' she asked quietly." Red stopped and sipped his drink.

"Now Grif, we know it wasn't Robert, not really, but it kinda involved 'im in a way."

"What was it Red? Why Robert?" I whispered. He continued as if he hadn't heard me.

"Granddad didn't answer, but took down his shotgun loaded it. Then, he opened a cupboard, took out ajar of whitelightnin', an' took a big swig before sittin' beside Grandma. Only the tickin' of the clock broke the quiet. He stared at her, an' she stared at the jar, the gun she barely noticed; a fox sometimes got in the hen house. But Granddad had never been a drinkin' man, an' that jar told her somethin' bad was happenin'. Maybe even worse than Robert's death.

"What is it, Isiah? Did you talk to Reverend Lewis?" She couldn't think of anythin' else to say, an' she had to break that awful quiet. "No honey, I never got a chance, but I saw him." She was a good woman, an' a brave one too. She'd stood a fair amount of hardship in her life, an' had been made stronger by it, but, when he looked at her lined face, he still saw the innocent girl he'd married, an' decided that she would never know the truth. "There was a crazy man at the cemetery an' he attacked Lewis.'" She gasped but he ignored her and plunged on before he lost his nerve. "I don't know if Lewis was alive when I left, but I'm goin' back." He put the jar in his pocket an' picked up the gun.

"You have to get Bill Wilkens and Ham Marshall; you can't go alone!" she clutched the front of his shirt.

He put his arms around her an', although he had no intention of bringin' anyone else into it, put her mind at ease, "I'll get them, Janey."

"Walkin' down the path, he noticed that the wind had picked up an' it had grown darker still. There was an occasional clap of thunder, an' lightnin' flashed in the distance. He also noticed he was walkin' slower than he had earlier, but then he had just been mad. Now he was afraid - afraid for more than his life. He didn't know what he'd find, an' he didn't know what he'd do about it what he did know was that his family was not safe until he put an end to it.

When he reached the church, all was quiet but the wind in the trees. For awhile, he thought that if he saw the thing that wore Lewis' flesh, he'd shoot it. Now, he dared to hope that it had just gone away. But deep down he knew better. He approached his son's grave an' bent down.

"'Help me Robbie. Please help me if you can." He felt his eyes fill with tears but didn't let 'em slip down his cheeks. He heard a rumblin' that came, not from the church, but the house. He cocked his gun as he walked, his feet feelin' like lead. When he reached the house an' twisted the doorknob, it wasn't locked; he knew it wouldn't be.

The inside was all dark. Givin' his eyes a minute to adjust, he stood quietly, listenin'. He couldn't hear anythin', but he could feel it; it was evil, just plain evil. It hung around 'im like a wet blanket. It wanted 'im, an' as he stood there in awe, it seemed to have 'im. But, "You'll not have me that easy," he whispered.

He heard an awful laugh from the cellar, an' that laugh seemed intertwined with horrible words; it reached out like ground-fog.

"All right then, come to me. Stop me if you think you can. I have all the time in the world, an eternity. Perhaps I'll let you see your son - " That broke the spell an' Granddad moved; toward the cellar, the demon, perhaps Satan himself.

"The cellar door blew off its hinges, knockin' the gun from his hand, sprayin' 'im with splintered wood. He glanced at the shotgun but didn't pick it up; he almost laughed for thinkin' it would be of any use. He started down' the stairs, his world filled only by a strange, muddy light, an' a rotten meat smell. Shakin' free of both, he looked around; the cellar was bare.

"He started to think he'd been tricked, when somethin' fell from the rough beams of the ceiling. Lookin' up, he thought the floor above was collapsin'; the beams seemed to buckle an' drip, as though it was rainin' inside. Then a huge, dark shape was blockin' his view, movin' like smoke, until he was able to see the face, or rather, the faces; they shifted lazily so that he thought he recognized some of 'em, includin' that of his dead son. When the features were still, it was Lewis' face, but the skin was gray, the lips black; when it smiled, the teeth were the same dirty yellow as the eyes.

"Welcome friend," it whispered. "How good of you to join us."

"Who are you? What are you?" Granddad's voice was a whisper too, for it was all he could manage.

"Ah...We are one but we are many." Now its voice was huge, like the slitherin' of a thousand snakes.

"I don't understand! What have you done with Reverend Lewis an' the others? What have you done with my son?" For that was really why he was here. He knew he may die, but first he had to know.

"Then the ultimate horror, "Its me Daddy, its Robbie. Aren't you happy to see me?" The voice was close, but it was like Robbie was tryin' to speak through a mouthful of gravel, an' as gentle as the face tried to be, it couldn't quite get rid of the other. Although he knew it was a trick, a cruel lie, for a minute he allowed him self to believe there was a chance to change it all, to take the real Robbie home, to tell his wife her son wasn't really dead. He held the hope close an' then it was gone. The demon shifted, returnin' to its own face, which was much easier to bear.

"You know you're going to die here, don't you?" It looked almost thoughtful.

"'Maybe, maybe not,' Granddad said quietly. "But first, I want to know what you are."

His knees were shakin', but he felt kinda calm.

"'Alright then. Perhaps when we split your ribs apart and suck out your soul, it will taste sweeter if you know what's happening. We are old, older than the earth itself, created with the stars. We are the few that have consumed the souls of many; feasting on the good, gorging ourselves on the righteous." The edges of the thing's cloak seemed to reach out, searchin', to all corners of the cellar. The face pulsated, but still looked mostly like Lewis.

"But what about Lewis, he was a man of God. Or was that just another trick?"

The demon laughed. "Yes, he was. That's what's so perfect, don't you see? If we can have the good and the innocent so easily, perhaps we can have the angels themselves! Your god would have nothing!"

"It was so sure of itself that Granddad felt anger in his heart. "No! Nothing can defeat the power of God! You may have gone all this time with nobody to stop you, but someone will. Maybe it ends now!"

"Oh, it's so easy for you to believe that your god is all powerful. Well, he's not, little man. And now, I think we're tired of the game."

"Wait! You still haven't told me, why us? Lewis, Robbie, me?" He was desperate for the truth. The thing sighed, as though bored, then continued. "Lewis was the perfect hiding place. We need fresh souls, and what better place to find them than a cemetery?"

"'But how? They weren't willing, how could you take them?" He refused to believe his son would've given in to the horror before 'im.

"It's so easy to take them just after death, when they're still confused and afraid. You even helped us!"

"How? I couldn't! I wouldn't!" But he thought he'd begun to understand; not understand so he could explain it, but in the back of his mind, an idea was formin'.

"You helped! The day you hammered in the taps, you did all the work!" It laughed so hard, It seemed unable to hold its face still.

"The buckets, the sap; you were - taking the souls through the sap, an' I helped you!" The realization hit 'im like a blow. He clutched his face.

"Oh forget the buckets! Forget the sap!" It was growing impatient. "It's the trees, the roots! The roots that reach into the ground, into the very hearts and souls of the newly dead!"

"'Our souls leave our bodies when we die,'" Granddad whispered. "You can't just keep them!"

The demon answered, still smiling, "Ah ...but not immediately, not without the words of a priest. And everyone buried here has had a funeral mass said for him; it's just that you poor idiots didn't know that the words we spoke weren't Latin! It was a language much older than Latin, much older than your religion. The incantation keeps the souls and the power they hold earthbound, trapped, until we can feed on that power; the power that has grown' stronger with each century. And you think you can beat that, that you can beat us?" It laughed an' laughed.

It was too *much* for Granddad. He howled an' *flung* himself forward. *The demon* stretched out its arms an' held 'im; he felt his breath rush out, his ribs grind together. His vision went black an' his mind grew cloudy, yet he knew this pain was nothin' compared to the torture he would endure if this thing captured his soul.

He had just enough strength to reach out once, not with his mind, but with his spirit, his human spirit an' as his spirit reached, he felt it connect with somethin' bright an' good. He held on to the good an' heard it whisper, 'Vetis'. The word felt right, an' with the last of his hope, he found the breath to scream it.

The demon screamed too an' released its hold on Granddad, who fell back against the stairs, turnin' to look at the thing.

The ground started to shake, the dirt floor began to crumble an' break apart. The demon's attention was on what seemed to be growin' from the floor. The cellar was filled with noise; the thing howlin', a great wind, a thousand voices screamin'.

A large tree limb broke the surface of the floor an' grew up the demon's legs; it twisted an' spiraled upwards, wrapped itself around its neck an' gripped with deadly force. The earth shook so hard it seemed the house would fall down around 'em. The demon's feet disappeared, followed by its waist an' chest, an' finally, mercifully, its face, cutting the scream in half.

The dirt closed around it, leavin' only a puff of dust to mark the spot where it had stood. It was gone an' the voices were gone, all but one, an' it seemed to come from far away.

"Goodbye, Daddy," was all it said.

"Granddad ran up the stairs an' out the door, knowin' what he had to do. He took the jar from his pocket, barely noticin' the crack were it had begun to leak, an' walked around the house, splashin' pure alcohol as he went. He glanced back at his son's grave, struck a match, an' tossed it. The house, bein' made entirely of wood, went up immediately. He stood an' watched the flames for awhile; white, bright an' good.

"Grandma was clutchin' her Bible when he got home. "What happened Isiah?" she asked quietly.

"'Lewis is dead an' the house is burnt down" he said without lookin' at her. She held out her arms an' didn't notice that his black hair had turned completely white.

"He lived another 20 years, an' kept the caretakin' job. Sometimes Dad went with him, not afraid now that Lewis was gone. Folks knew what happened that night, or thought they knew. Only Granddad knew' the truth, but he didn't tell anyone until 2 days before he died, when he told my Dad. When Dad was ready to go, he told me. Well, that's it, that's the end." Red looked like he didn't really believe it, but the hour was late and the whiskey was gone, so I let it go.

"Wow," I took a deep breath. "So how come you're there Red? How come your Dad became caretaker and you after him? Hadn't your family had enough of that place?"

"How come my Daddy an' I took the job, Grif?" He looked a bit puzzled. "Well I thought that woulda been obvious after hearin' the story." I just shook my head.

"Somebody has to be there, somebody that knows. Just in case." We sat silently for a minute, staring into the fire.

"Red, do you...I mean, do you think it was just that one place, that one time? Do you think that's the end?"

"No Grif, it ain't. I know it ain't. I think the only reason Granddad beat it that time was because it bumped up against his firm belief that good always defeats evil. How many people do ya think really believe that today, Grif? How many people do ya think have that kinda faith anymore? Its gone on since before time, an' I bet It just keeps gettin' stronger with nobody to fight it. I think it hasn't come back here because it doesn't want to lose again. That an' somethin' else I've figured out over the years."

"What's that, Red?"

"We know its name."

"Vetis. That was its name?" He nodded. "But what difference does that make?"

"I think that if you know its name, you have power over it. That night, when the power of good told Granddad its name, Vetis was defeated; it lost that round."

"Vetis," I repeated it to myself and then out loud.

"Yeah, Grif. That's why the job's always been passed down, because we know what could happen, an' because we know its name. When I go, Grif, I want to be buried alongside my kin. An' that's the real reason I've told you all this; I want the cemetery to be safe, I want my soul to be guarded. By someone that knows its name.

It wasn't hard to get the caretaker's job after Red died. I think the committee thought it was rather quaint - good friend of Red's and all that

I had him buried here, just like he wanted. I've remembered that name all these years. So now, I watch and I wait. I watch to make sure it doesn't sneak up on me. And I wait for somebody to come along, someone with an interest in old cemeteries maybe.

Someone to share a drink and a story with.

My Dear Companion

Steven Lee Climer

"Mr. Bryant, you want another cup of coffee?"

He lifted his ancient, withered head from the half-empty cup and looked at her pretty smiling face. Norma Jean, the name on her uniform echoed in his brain. He pushed out a quiet laugh, partially wheezing, partially dying.

"Not much left around here, is there?" he finally said.

She gave him a friendly caress on his bony shoulder sheathed in polyester, "you're okay, Mr. Bryant."

"I suppose so, there ain't much else to do."

Norma Jean poured coffee into the stained mug before moving on to the next patron in the diner. She was so friendly and happy, Mr. Bryant liked that in a woman. Too bad, those qualities hadn't always been with her. Mr. Bryant could look into her face, past the makeup and bleach job, and see the real Norma Jean. She was a waitress now, and happy to be one.

Outside on the sidewalk, Mr. Bryant could see little kids playing in the hot summer weather. A fire hydrant had been cracked open, spraying them with water. One of them had a little white dog with only three legs. The dog was so elated to have a little boy to play with. And the child was happy, too. He finally had a dog like he always wanted but could never have. They were the happiest pair he'd seen in such a long time. The puppy jumped into the boy's arms and they got soaked by the hydrant.

Norma Jean was on her way back through the diner to greet more guests at her door. Like a butterfly checking a flower, she hovered near Mr. Bryant's table. "Mr. Bryant, ain't the coffee good today?"

"It's good every day, hon." He smiled at her, "I was just watching the kids and that sweet little dog."

"Yeah, that little boy's been waiting for that dog for as long as I can remember. About as long as you've been sitting in this booth, Mr. Bryant." She grinned that million-dollar grin, but now it was worth much more.

Mr. Bryant returned the smile, "are you happy here, hon?"

"I wish I knew how to tell you how much." She looked out the window as a little girl joined the boy and dog. "Maybe about as happy as that little girl is to see her brother again."

The boy and girl held hands, the dog nipped and jumped playfully at them. "Time for them to move on," Mr. Bryant whispered lonesomely.

"Yeah, time for them to move on." She looked down at him, "are you gonna be okay?"

"Soon, I hope."

"You hang in there," Norma Jean smiled and moved on to a new patron who just entered. Mr. Bryant turned in his booth to see who had come in. It was a nice-looking man, but he seemed all confused. That's a familiar expression, Mr. Bryant thought. Poor boy. Norma Jean was scanning the diner for space for the new customer, but all of the seats were filled. People were lined shoulder to shoulder at the counter and all the booths were full. Waving his hand, Mr. Bryant caught Norma Jean's eye just as she was about to turn the young man away.

"Hon, he can sit with me."

With her beautiful smile lighting the way, Norma Jean led the wary stranger to the empty bench across from the old man. "That's so nice of you, Mr. Bryant."

"I know what it's like to be the new kid in town." The old man gestured to the seat, "Take a load off, son."

"Thanks," while he sat, his eyes roamed the joint.

"You hungry?" Mr. Bryant asked.

"No, thanks."

"Coffee?" Mr. Bryant gestured to Norma Jean who was already heading in their direction with a fresh cup.

"Yeah, that sounds good." He looked across at Mr. Bryant's compassionate face. "Thanks for sharing your booth. I was kind of lost and tired of looking for a place to get out of the sunshine."

"This is as good a place as any, I suppose." Norma Jean silently filled their cups and went away.

"Where are you from?"

"From Detroit." He sipped the coffee. "Mmm, it's good."

"Can't say I've ever been to Detroit," His eyes saddened, "my wife's from Detroit, though. We met a long time ago. Her name was Kathy."

"Is she?" The new man asked.

"She's not with us," Mr. Bryant sighed.

"I'm just so confused lately, "the man replied. "I'm sorry for being so rude, my name's Richard Smith."

"Nice to meet you, Richard," Mr. Bryant extended his hand.

"I'm Mr. Bryant." He looked into the young man's big brown eyes. "It's nice to talk to a fresh face around here."

"Is there a phone?" Richard felt around for some spare change in his pockets.

"No, I'm afraid not." the old man replied. Then, he drew Richard's attention to the street. "Look at all those kids having a good time. I remember when I was that young."

Watching the children made Richard's impatience wane. The kids danced and played in the spray, laughing, skipping and running.

"Whose kids are those?" Richard asked. "It's not safe for them to be playing unattended."

"They're fine, we got our eye on 'em."

Richard studied Mr. Bryant's face as the old man looked out at the children. His age couldn't really be determined. Although his face was like wrinkled tissue paper, his eyes were lively and blue. The more he watched the children, the younger he seemed. But then, he would suddenly stop and his expression would turn solemn.

"This diner is lonely," Mr. Bryant said to Richard. "I hope you eat quick."

"Are you waiting for someone?"

"A long time, I've been waiting a long time." "If they aren't coming why don't you just go home."

"Because I haven't seen her for as long as I can remember."

Richard smiled. He understood that sentiment. "I know how you feel. I miss my Emily right now. That's who I wanted to call."

"Don't call her, son. Just wait for her here."

"Here? She doesn't know where this place is. I don't even know where this place is."

"She'll be able to find you, I've seen it a hundred times." Mr. Bryant's voice was a whisper, "sometimes, sooner than you really want to be found and sometimes it takes too long."

Richard was silent; he didn't know what to say to his companion. Both drank their coffee and Norma Jean came around with warm-ups. She always had a pleasant word of encouragement for Mr. Bryant who seemed ready to give up at any moment. His eyes reflected the loneliness in his heart. Richard felt a tug of his own as he thought of Emily.

Suddenly, as he looked up at the diner's door, Norma Jean was greeting a new customer. Richard's face erupted into the biggest expression of joy and surprise he'd seen in a long time. Turning, Mr. Bryant saw Norma Jean pointing in their direction. The beautiful young girl at the door rushed through the crowded diner. Richard stood, just in time to receive her warm embrace. Mr. Bryant looked up at the young lovers, his eyes happy yet lonely.

"Mr. Bryant, this is my Emily," Richard was overflowing with emotion.

Emily had the same confused expression that was on her husband's face a little while ago, but now it was mixed with genuine rapture. "It's nice to meet you."

"I've heard a lot about you," Mr. Bryant said. "Richard loves you very much."

"I know he does," Emily kissed her husband. "You had me so worried. I couldn't find you and I drove all night."

"Mr. Bryant said you'd find me." Again, they hugged.

Norma Jean then came up behind the couple, "I'm so glad she came for you. It's time for you to go, there's plenty of people waiting for a table."

"Thanks for letting me wait with you," Richard said.

"Your welcome, son." He settled back into his booth, alone again.

He saw Richard and Emily walking out toward the road. They greeted some of the children with hugs and kisses, and a few of them followed as they continued to walk down the sunny street. Mr. Bryant sighed and looked at his coffee. It was nearly empty and what was left was cold. Then, the familiar coffeepot was there to pour for him.

"I'm almost tired of waiting, Norma Jean." He made little circles with his spoon. "I'm starting to forget."

"No, don't ever stop remembering," he heard the waitress say. Only instead of Norma Jean, it was the voice of an old woman. "I didn't." Mr. Bryant slowly raised his head to see the face of the new waitress. He hadn't seen that face for as long as he could remember, but it was her nonetheless. Still beautiful with curly silver hair and warm eyes that twinkled when she smiled.

"Kathy," he cried as he rose to meet her.

They fell into a deep, warm, familiar hug. Mr. Bryant sighed and she took up his weight. He'd been waiting so long for her.

"I waited for you," he whispered.

"I knew you would." Kathy put the coffeepot down on the table.

Norma Jean came up from behind and touched the couple, "see, Mr. Bryant, I told you everything would be okay. Now, I hate to rush you off, but there's people waiting for your table."

"Yes, of course," he touched Kathy's face once again and gave her eyelids a tender kiss.

Norma Jean walked them to the door as a lone busboy cleared the table and wiped it down. She held the door for them. "I'll always remember you, Mr. Bryant. Every time I bring coffee to that table, I'll think of you. It was nice to finally meet you, Mrs. Bryant."

"Please, call me Kathy."

"Okay, bye-bye Kathy." Norma Jean grabbed a menu as a new customer entered the diner. "Hold on, it'll be just a second while we clear the table."

Norma Jean walked through the crowd, smiling and greeting many of her customers that had been there awhile. The new customer followed her to the table and Norma Jean put the menu in *front* of her. The young woman held a newborn in her arms and a toddler was tagging behind.

"Hi "Norma Jean smiled, "would you like some coffee?"

"Oh, that sounds good. I'm waiting here for my husband." She gave her little baby a tender kiss. "We got separated from him and found this place. It's too hot out there for the kids. Is there a phone?"

"Don't worry, he'll find you." Norma Jean tousled the hair of the little girl, "hi, sweetie, would you like some crayons and a coloring book?" The tiny girl nodded. "Okay, I'll be right back." Norma Jean paused and looked back at the table as she walked away, "I didn't forget that coffee either."

Hope is an Inanimate Desire

Trent Zelazny

It had ceased. After what had seemed an eternity, the pain was finally gone. And now there was nothing more for him to do than sit and wait - wait until someone spotted his car, and got some help.

He wouldn't deny that he'd been drinking. If he did, he knew that the only person he'd be lying to would be himself.

It hadn't been his fault. The tire had simply flown from off the wheel. It had been a spare. On his way to the bar, he had run over a nail. Though it wasn't until he'd come out, drunk off his ass, that he'd noticed the flat, and he was forced to change it with blurry eyes, and fuzzy mind. Tye and Frank had tried to stop him. They had told him he was too messed up, piss drunk; but, as usual, Calvin refused to listen. And now it was obvious that he hadn't put the tire on very well, not tight enough. And because he didn't listen he was now stuck, strapped upside-down to the driver's seat of his car.

It was dusk. The sun would soon creep away, and he would be waiting in blackness. The chances of somebody seeing him at night were slim. No one had seen him since he'd crashed two hours before. Why should anyone see him in the dark?

He could not move.

He hadn't been able to move for over two hours now, and he was quite sure that he was paralyzed. So he sat, immobile, upside-down, held up only by the safety belt which had saved his life, or had possibly just decided to ruin it, in which case he would hope for death. But there was no sense in concerning himself with any of this at the moment. It was best, he had said to himself, to just wait. Somebody would come for him. Someone would have to see him eventually.

The sun crept away behind the hills. Night would soon arrive in full bloom. He could feel himself swaying gently, back and forth, back and forth, like a clothesline dancing in a lonely breeze.

His view was little more than a dashboard, a few weeds and stones peeping through a shield of cracked glass. There was blood on the windshield, and he knew it was his, for it couldn't be anyone else's. The upside-down clock told him that it was five of eight. If no one saw him by nine, then he knew that most likely it wouldn't be until daybreak when he was spotted and rescued. If he could make it through the night. In any case it would be best for him to just get some sleep.

There was nothing for him to listen to - nothing except for the sound of his own dying breath. The few parts of his body that he could still feel were tingling; and his head still spun slightly from shock, and from the alcohol he had consumed earlier, along with the amount of blood, which undoubtedly had made its way to his brain.

Why had he been so stupid? What kind of an idiot changes a tire while drunk, only to then go out and drive on it?

It didn't matter. What was done was done. It would do him no good to beat himself up over it. He seemed already to have crippled himself beyond repair. There was no sense in adding the mind into it, if it could by chance be avoided.

It was a long and winding road, up and down a mountainous terrain. He had been in the outside lane - the lane with the twenty-foot drop off on the side. And as he wouldn't deny that he had been drinking too much, he wouldn't deny that he had been speeding. Taking a fast left turn, there was a popping sound from the back, and his car jumped, then spun out of control. Fishtailing, right. Left. Right. Left, then off the side and down - down the rocky slope, round and round. And for a very brief moment he could have sworn that he had seen himself outside the vehicle, watching. Screaming bloody murder. A ghost? It had simply been a dumb move all around. And now he was paying for it; and he would pay for it until he died, be it in five minutes, or in fifty years.

You did it this time, Calvin, he thought to himself. You finally pushed yourself over the edge – literally – over the edge. You knew this would happen some day. Your family and friends had told you that someday you would kill yourself if you didn't stop. But did you listen? No, of course not. Do you ever listen to what other people say? Sometimes it really is a smart thing to do, y'know. Oh well, maybe this will finally teach you.

He told himself to shut up. He didn't want to listen.

And now you won't even listen to yourself.

His head was aching like an avalanche of stones. Hanging upside-down for as long as he had been was really getting to him; and he was starting to feel as though his head might soon explode.

There was a wind picking up, and the dusk weeds began to move a bit more than they had been. The sun was creeping away quickly.

Why hasn't anybody seen me? I think that I even smashed through a side-rail. Yes. I know I did. Someone would see the damage and then look down here and find me, wouldn't they? But why hasn't anybody stopped? I've heard cars go by. I'm sure I've heard cars go by. But that's all that they do. Go by.

Drip, drip, drip. There was a subtle dripping sound below, above his head. And because he couldn't move, he used his mind to probe the parts of his body that he could until he had found its source, where it was coming from.

Well, well, well, my head is bleeding in back.

He looked at the blood-covered windshield.

Front and back, way to go Calvin.

He could only imagine what he looked like.

He sat for a while, listening to the steady rhythm of his own dripping gore. Drip-drop. Drip-drop. Be-bop-a-drip-drop. Be-bop a-drip-drop. Thoughts only, he began to sing songs of no meaning, creating melodies in his head as he went along, trying to think up words. Trying to pass the time - waiting for someone to see him and the carnage he had created all by himself. Many of the words were not words at all, though they began to come together in their own way. The dusk weeds seemed to sway back and forth, as if dancing to his tunes.

Be-Bop-a-drip-drop -

> *I feel something funny in the back of my head.*
> *I hear something that's funny, something funny*
> *Someone said. I turn the clock past zero, but*
> *It still keeps my time. The allegorist hero*
> *Never thinks about time.*
>
> *Be-bop-a-drip-drop . . .*

He sang it through his head, over and over, trying to think up another verse. No other would come.

His body. Though it was almost completely deprived of sensation and motion, he suddenly realized - knew with unpleasant decisiveness that he had to relieve himself. Fluid excretion from the kidneys into the bladder, voided through the urethra. And he was immobile. Would he be able to control it? Or would it just come when it was time? This was, though in some ways it seemed near unimportant, the major priority at the moment. Images of his car seat acting as an upside-down urinal began to enter his mind, refusing to disappear. In reality, he knew that if the unimaginable happened, his own strung up body would be acting as the receptacle for his urine. He was never into golden showers. There were things that he found far less appealing, but this was close to the top of the list, and he had no interest in experimenting. Especially with his own or in this particular situation.

It would not be a pretty sight.

The sun was now entirely gone. There was nothing more than black. He was alone in the dark. He could still hear the slight breeze outside. It served as his only companion, and it brushed across his face through the broken driver's side window.

"Hello wind," he said as best he could, for he was weak and affected with at least temporary paralysis.

"Swooosh, " said the wind.

Calvin thought intensely for a long span of time. Then, with the same weak voice he asked: "Am . . . am I gonna get out of this? Am I gonna live? Survive, I mean? Or is this my time? Is it my time to leave this world I've known for so long? Thirty-two years? Have I really been alive for thirty-two years?"

"Swooosh . . . "

The wind's answer left Calvin filled with drunken hope. And it continued to swoosh and swish its words of comfort, mixing with the rhythm of his dripping head.

Be-boo-a-drip-drop . . .

"It I get out of this," he said to the wind, to himself, or to anyone who might be listening, 'I promise." He paused. "I promise to give all this shit up." His lungs refused him any more words: they felt like wet sponges. Soaked through and through.

I'll give all this shit up. Yes, sir, yes I will. No more drinking. No more driving, no more not listening to people when I know I should be. No more goddamn pride ruling over smarts.

"Calvin, if you'd just listen--"

"No."

"Why do you always have to be such a stubborn jerk?"

"Fuck you! You don't tell me what to do. You don't run my life! So cut it out!"

That's pretty typical of you, Cal. Your standard talk, your standard conversation with any friend or family member. Your standard defense, when defense is unnecessary. You just can't stand to think of someone else being right. Because we all know that you are always right, ain't that the truth of it? Mr.Calvin with the last name I forget, the man who is never wrong and always right . . . What the hell is my last name?

He wanted to shift with discomfort at the realization of not knowing his last name, but he was unable. His body still refused movement. His body simply continued swaying, back and forth. Back and forth, and even the wind seemed to have lost interest, gone silent. He could no longer remember the song he had been singing in his head. Something about heroes, though nothing more could he remember. But the steady dripping of blood continued.

Be-bop-a-drip-drop . . .

Fast rush, train brushes, throw wet on dry and

fly into a cherry pie. Flying notebook, I wanna go home.

I is high if the eye is high. If I had a dollar for every time I puked, that would sure as hell make me puke.

Be-bop-a-drip-drop . . .

With the new song of nothingness running through his head, he began to find that his eyelids were beginning to slip closed. Open, close, open. Close. And then they closed and remained so.

He was at the bar.

The wind sat beside him in near swooshing silence.

Both had beers in front of them. The wind did not have to worry about driving drunk, for it could be anywhere and everywhere all at once. If it so felt the desire.

"Shon't shrive," said the wind. "Shon't shrive shrunk." It told him that if he got into that car, revved up the engine and pulled onto the road, he could kiss his sorry ass good-bye. And though he knew he shouldn't, and he knew that it was too late, he refused to let even the wind tell him what to do. 'What is this? Some kinda fucking public service announcement?" Flinging his beer off to the side, he stood up and half stumbled, half stormed out of the bar - out into the sky and its preparation for evening.

"Goddamn wind." He inserted the key into the ignition, turned it.

The car started.

Calvin woke up, still upside down, swaying gently, back and forth, back and forth, the blood still dripping from his head, though much slower than before. He figured that it was because he was still upside-down, the blood would still not cease to flow. Drip, drip, drip. The difference between now and before was that he could now feel pain crawling through his body, but only through specific areas, through his head, and dripping from somewhere near his brain. Drip, drip, drip.

Outside the night was blacker than Death. He wondered what time it was. He couldn't tell. It was too dark to see the clock. The wind blew through the trees outside singing silent songs with their swaying branches. There was no moon out this night. If there was, it was sure doing a great job of hiding. Then, he noticed. What he'd hoped wouldn't happen had happened while he was asleep. He had wet himself. His crotch. And shirt, all the way up his back, and front and sides, as the shirt pressed against his stomach and chest and back, he realized that it was damp. And that he now smelled of urine. It was uncomfortable. However, it wasn't nearly as bad as he would have thought. Maybe it was because he had been fighting with the wind when he had done it, and he hadn't been anywhere around for the experience. Didn't matter. There was nothing he could do about it at the moment. It would dry up. If nothing else. His bladder felt better, relieved. Plus, he had more important things to consider. As he thought about his bladder, his stomach entered into his mind. He was hungry. Though it was not audible, he could sense growling sounds coming from within. He did his best to forget about it; but the more he tried to forget it, the more he thought about forgetting it, which caused him to think about it more.

Sing another, son, he told himself, think of another song that can help you to take your mind off of your belly.

No song would come to him and he realized that the dripping sound had stopped. There was no more beat to follow. No more drip. Drip. No more rhythm. He knew that it would be best if could simply sleep - sleep and leave all his troubles behind until morning. For all he knew, morning may only be an hour or so away. It would be preferable to just slip into a deep slumber until he was discovered: or better yet, just sleep for a while, and wake up to find that nothing had really happened - that the situation he was in was really nothing more than a bad dream, and that he would wake up in his own bed. For the moment, though, he knew that all he could do was hope. Hope is a word that should always be used in quotes, he thought. Hope is a desire accompanied by expectation and anticipation; and what if…what if no one found him until it was too late? The hope would all be for nothing. To him, at that moment, hope seemed the most trivial thing in the world, inanimate, pointless, though he found that he could not expel it from within himself. There was nothing more for him to do than this very human thing - perform the trivial, inanimate, mind bending desire that is "hope."

He heard another car pass by, up high above him, without even slowing down as it passed by the unseen wreckage. Yes, he knew that in the night, he was invisible. No one was going to find him until daybreak, maybe not even then.
Of course they would find him.

There were enough people in town who knew his regular routine, who would notice when he didn't show up here or there. They would start asking around and then, there would be a search. The search would not take long, for it was a small town, and he had driven his car oft the road - the road which led to his home. They would most certainly check. And when they found the broken side rail. They would stop, and they would see him and rescue him. Maybe it would be later in the afternoon, or even in the evening, but he would be found. He was certain of that. He would be found, rescued, and taken to the hospital. It would be a two-hour drive to get there, and he would be lying in the back of an ambulance the entire way, with paramedics staring at him, poking him. But he would most likely hear his last name, and he would be safe. The doctors would help him. They would rid of the small pains, and give him back his movement.

If only he could move.

If he could move, it would be as simple as bringing his right hand to the buckle of his seat belt. Pressing the little red button, with the word "PRESS" embossed on it, and he would drop down. Maybe then he could, if nothing else, climb out of the car, and lay in a patch of dead weeds and hard stones. Anything would be better than swaying back and forth, upside-down, with most all of his blood pooling in his head.

I've gotta get down. He told himself. Gotta get down climb outta the car. However. He knew that it was impossible. He could not move. The few parts of his body, which he could feel, were filled with nothing more than weak, numbing pain.

There was nothing for his eyes to see. Nothing but black lay before him, a dark cover wrapped around his world - nothing but a void - his only company being the wind, which had grown sleepy. He felt, in some ways, as he did when he was six or seven years old, back a quarter of a mile behind his house: and he had climbed down into a pit: a pit too steep and deep for him to climb back out of. His brother had been witness and fortunately ran back to the house and fetched his father. In that fifteen minutes of waiting, however, he had never felt so alone, so scared, so helpless. This time, however, he knew that his father would not be coming to his aide.

No.

His father had been dead eight years now. Aneurysm while in bed. Apparently he had awakened his wife - Calvin's mother - in the middle of the night and told her that his head hurt really badly, then he simply dropped down onto his pillow. If only now it was that simple for Calvin, to have just one quick moment of pain, then have it all end. There was a chance that it would be that simple, and he wanted it to be so. He hoped, though he didn't want to hope.

Hope is an inanimate desire

Nearly without movement, he still felt himself swaying, swaying like the sleepy breeze outside. Through the silence and darkness. He heard the sound of footsteps. Too quick to be human, they made their way around the car and halted at the driver's side window. He could only see to the side what his eyes would allow, for he could not turn his head. What he could make out in the darkness was a pair of pointed ears. And the sound of panting breath. Then he heard its eerie howl, ripping through his ears. It was a coyote inquiring about him, discovering him. And all Calvin could think was that he wanted it to go away - go away and leave him alone. Far off in the distance he heard a return call, and then the loud, ripping howl pierced his ears once again. He wasn't sure how, but Calvin suddenly knew that the coyote's eyes were fixed upon him, and the wild dog began to growl and snarl. Go away was all Calvin could think. Just go away. Leave me alone. Remembering the first time he had ever been bitten by a dog – he must have been four - he thought of the blood, the pain, and how he now had no interest in reliving such a situation, especially at such a disadvantage as this. He just wanted all of this to end. There was a great moment of silence, then the dog simply turned away, walked to the back of the car, and then his world was quiet, still. After the calming momentary pause, he could hear the animal gnawing on something: a juicy old bone, possibly, a recent kill. With his heart easing up a bit tension was still there, though now that the animal was not directly before him, he felt better, calmer. What was the animal gnawing on? Maybe when his car had come crashing down - through the small trees and rocks - some poor animal had been in the way, and was now the midnight snack of this lonely coyote.

The gnawing was not too loud, but with little else to hear, it began flooding into his ears. Reiterating. Reverberating. Now, more than ever, he wanted to get out, to go home. There was a crunching sound and the dog's breath deepened. The sounds grew more and more violent, then quieted down again, continuing on as before.

It was the thought of what he may be like if no one were to find him soon. Could he be one of the coyote's next meals? Even if he were to die, strung upside-down in his car, smelling of urine, covered in blood, it was likely that, at some point he would become a beast and bugger banquet. It was a natural part of the decomposition process. And what happens when you die? he wondered.

Where do you go? Is there a real Heaven and Hell? Or is it nothing like what we've all been told about? What if, when you die, you simply stay in your body? What if you can feel certain things? Feel things like your body decomposing, cremating? What if you don't go anywhere. And all that happens is you simply lose control of your body, you stiffen up. But you are still there, aware?

The lazy breeze washed over him again.

His mind snapped back to reality when he heard the sound of the coyote's footsteps. The animal was coming back his way. Heart tensing up. He saw the wild dog simply pass by, trotting along happily with something in its mouth. He only saw it for a brief moment as it passed by and vanished into the blackness, but a rush of horror hit him. He wasn't sure it what he thought he saw was really indeed what be had seen. He'd thought that he had seen an arm - a human arm, in the clutching jaws of the wild animal. No, that couldn't be right, could it? Surely he would have seen, even in the chaos, that there was someone down the slope. Surely he would have seen a man or woman, as his car slammed into them, ran over them. He would have heard a scream. No. That couldn't be right. There hadn't been anyone there. He was sure that his imagination was beginning to run away with him. If it was a limb, it was probably from a dead animal: something he had possibly hit and run over as his car descended the rocky slope. That was how it happened, right? The memory now seemed fuzzy. Almost like in a dream. Five minutes ago he would have been sure, but now, he didn't quite know.

Yes, that's right, his car had. . . . What had happened to his car? All recollection of the event was quickly vanishing, obscuring into nothing.

It didn't matter.

All the memories in the world weren't going to change the fact that he was still stuck in his car strung up by a seat belt, unable to move, caught in pitch black darkness. The only thing that mattered was getting out. It didn't matter how it happened. He just needed to get out - he needed to get out or have someone find him soon

How many hours remained in the night? He wasn't sure. There was no way of telling how long he had been asleep, or how time was moving. The dashboard clock was invisible in the dark. It might be minutes, it might be hours before the sky would begin to lighten and bring forth the day. It might be an eternity, or several of them before anyone found him. And he was helpless to do anything about it. Even the dull pains he had been having were gone now. His entire body was without sensation. All he had was slow movement of his eyes and weak maneuvering of his tongue and jaw.

I'll give all this shit up, he said to himself. Yes, sir, no more drinking, no more drivin'. I just wanna get out of this and be okay. Please, make this all end. Just kill me, if that's what's going to happen. Just kill me, get it over with. Why am I being punished so severely? What have I done? Just kill me, rid of me. Let me go. I can't take this! Can't take this any longer! More than anything he wanted to twist and turn, throw a tantrum of some kind but his body wouldn't allow it. Stop! Stop it! Just kill me! Let me go! I don't deserve this! I don't want it, this way! I was always right, yeah, ain't that the truth of it? Mr. Man with the name...He could no longer remember his name. Didn't it start with a "B" or maybe a 'D?

Suddenly he felt calm. Everything that had been running through his head had stopped, and he was sleepy, so sleepy. His eyes began to close. His mind felt at rest, at peace. It was time he decided to go into eternal sleep. All was quiet.

A loud sound startled him into wakefulness. The sun was up. The birds were singing. He was still in the car. He hadn't died, and now he heard voices.

"I can't believe this " one voice said. It sounded familiar as an old friend. "Frank, it's him." It was Tee's voice. With his slow moving eyes, he focused them on the rear view mirror at his left. It was Tye, and after a moment, Frank entered into the reflection.

"Man," Frank said, then he turned and called up the hill: "Yeah, it's Calvin Sawyer alright."

Calvin? Was that his name'? Yes, but somehow it didn't seem quite right. He didn't feel like a Calvin at all. But what other name could he have? No, his name couldn't be Calvin. If they were talking about him, they would be standing before his car, looking at him, trying to figure how to get him out. What were they looking at, back behind his car? He had to be Calvin, so what did they find? Why weren't they coming over to help him?

"Looks like some dog got at him in the middle of the night." "Let's get him out. He's long dead."

Dead? No, I'm still here! I'm over here! What are you guys doing? Come get me out! Help me!

He continued to watch the reflection. The two guys were busying themselves. Just out of the small mirror's view. There were a few huffs and puffs from the two men, followed the sound of something dropping.

"Let's get him out," one of them said. The two men entered back into the reflection, this time dragging something...Someone.

Who is that?

The familiarity was amazing. It took him a moment to realize that it was he, or rather his body, the left arm gone, ripped apart. Bitten off. It had been a human arm he saw last night. It was the remains of Mr. Calvin Sawyer.

But it can't be me! I'm over here! Why am I over there when I'm here? What the hell is going on? He watched the two men ascend the hill, carrying Calvin's body with them. There was nothing for him to do but wait.

About an hour passed and he heard the sound of a tow truck. In the mirror he saw his car, only briefly and only a part of it as it slowly climbed the hill. Once the car was towed up, there was nothing left and the world was still. The wind blew through the window causing him to sway back and forth, back and forth.

Side by Side

Brad Jeske

Staring out the window at the fading light of day, Sara closed her eyes and prayed softly. The large pail of cold water was becoming heavy, and she needed to get to her husband. Softly walking down the wooden hallway, she quietly entered the dimly lit room.

She lighted the small kerosene lantern, and kneeled down beside him. His once strong face had faded into a pale glow, and his bright eyes had become dark circles filled with an impending death. His hair was matted with sweat, as was her own long dark hair.

Sara pulled back the remnant strands of hair that hung down onto her husband's face; she dipped the washcloth into the pail, wrung it out and rubbed it across his heated forehead.

His response to the cold water seemed weaker. She knew he was fading away.

"Is he dead?" a voice asked from the dark corner.

Sara jumped; she had forgotten the horrible man who sat behind her like a vulture in the shadows, watching and waiting. And her husband was dying. She knew that.

"How is he?" the man repeated

"He's doin' fine!" Sara snapped uncontrollably, but then she quickly turned around to see the man's reaction.

"Won't be long," the man said, ignoring her outburst.

She hovered over her husband, carefully blocking the man's view from behind. "Please, husband, please," she pleaded gently to the nearly motionless man on the bed. She placed her hands on his face.

"Please. . . you can do it."

Sara's heart raced. It pounded so hard she could feel her head pulsating with each terrifying beat.

She wrung the cloth again and ran it across his forehead, this time drawing a response. His eyes open slightly, his lips moved and he spoke softly. Sara bent over, nearly touching her ear to his lips.

"Are they here?" he whispered dryly.

Sara nodded. She said nothing

He closed his eyes before he spoke again.

"I'd never thought this would happen," he said. He slowly opened his hand, and Sara placed her hand in his.

"You will be there?" he asked

Sara nodded her head.

His breathing had become more laborious. He closed his eyes and for a moment Sara held her breath. She lightly grabbed his shoulder and shook it trying not to arouse the man behind her.

He opened his eyes again.

"Please," she said. "You know you mustn't leave." He said nothing. "Please. *Please!*"

He closed his eyes again and said nothing. Sara pulled away and watched for a long moment. He didn't move, and she knew his time had come. But why so soon?

"It is done," the man said simply.

Sara didn't answer. She only slumped back on the chair at the bedside, and that was enough to give him his answer. She did not hear the man leave the room, but she heard the bell from outside the house ringing harshly, cutting the night sky. The man came back into the room and led Sara out the front door.

A chill ran down through her spine and the core of her soul, as she saw the lanterns appear in the distance. First, as a faint glow of one light, but soon the glow split into two, then four, then eight and more. She couldn't even count them all when they reached the house.

Dark figures in the night. Silent, motionless faces. The women approached.

One woman, silently wrapped a shawl around Sara's shoulders to help cut the chill of the night air. Just as they had done to all the others.

She knew every face that was here because there were the times when she carried the light through the fog to a darkened house in the night.

Tonight the house was hers.

They took Sara down a rutted dirt road, in a winding procession that led them to the cemetery. Men scurried around the cemetery as they neared and she saw the dark hole that soon was to be her husband's place. How quickly they worked, she thought.

Next to the grave was a simple pine coffin, and inside she saw her husband lying motionless.

The procession grew in a tight circle around the coffin; the lanterns filled the night sky with a yellowish glow that left the leaves on the surrounding oak trees glimmering in eerie silence, witnesses to many similar nights from the past.

No words were said. Sara felt faint, but she fought off the feeling. All eyes followed as Sara was led to the coffin. She peered inside. Her husband lay in a quiet peacefulness. Sara was lifted, and as they placed her next to him, they told her that it was right; she'd been taught that it was their way of life. And they had provided a good life for her and her husband. They were there for them when so many others weren't.

They had taught and preached the lifestyle as the only one they would ever have to know and believe. But now at this last instance, Sara felt something wrong. This wasn't right.

She screamed. A scream that sliced the night like a sword, breaking the ritual silence.

Sara fought the men, kicking, scratching, biting at their arms as they lifted her and placed her next to her husband. One of the men held her inside the coffin. Reaching out she raked her nails down his forearm, raising a thin line of blood. They slammed the lid down on top of her.

Sara kicked the sides, as she felt the box being lifted, and then slowly lowered, the coffin bouncing off the sides of the grave into the gaping hole in the earth.

The sound of the rocks and dirt hitting the top made Sara scream louder. She kicked wildly at the sides of the coffin.

The screams grew faint as the hole filled slowly up. A man moved forward. His face glowed in the light of the lanterns. He rubbed his graying beard.

"We must keep our community together. We provide for one another, we help one another, and in marriage we live with our partner and die with our partner. This is our way. Our community is perfect."

Once finished they headed back to their quiet homes, cutting through the cemetery that was full of tombstones. The rows were neat, the grounds well maintained. And deep within the earth the bodies lay still.

Side by side, two by two.

Forever.

Helena

Philip Caveney

I wish I could enjoy the festive season as other men do. I wish I could rid myself of certain memories that linger at the back of my conscious mind like vultures waiting to descend from the skies. I wish I had never heard the name of Victor Lawson, nor visited his house on that fateful Christmas Eve of 1873; but what use is wishing now, so many long years after the event.

These days I can put a brave enough face on it as I sit beside the fire with my Grandchildren at my feet, watching as the chestnuts roast in the glowing embers. But I was a young man then, young and impressionable, totally unexposed to the horrors of the world.

And always, at this time of year, when the Christmas festivities begin, I find my mind going back into the past, to recall the events that have haunted me for so long; that no doubt will haunt me to my dying day. In remembering, I am drawn to retelling the story; and my eager young wards, thinking the tale nothing more than a fanciful piece of fiction, crowd around me, shivering in delicious anticipation.

I close my eyes and I am back there in the jolting, shuddering coach as it clatters up the stony path to Rowton Moor. At the best of times, the Moor is a grim inhospitable place, but that chill Christmas Eve, it had the appearance of some strange dreamlike landscape. A harsh wind came howling in from the crags that bordered the horizon to my left and the poor coachman was doubtless shivering in his very boots.

It was late afternoon and the sun was declining in the West, staining the sky with crimson. I sat hunched in the swaying interior of the coach, a scarf around my face in a vain attempt to ward off the icy blasts of air that kept gusting in through the glassless window. For perhaps the fiftieth time that day, I cursed my bad fortune.

It was a miserable imposition to be expected to work at a time when most other men were preparing for some merry family gathering, but when Mr. Lawson's letter had arrived at the solicitor's office in which I was then employed, I had known immediately that the task would fall to me. The letter was an urgent appeal for the services of a solicitor. The wording of the communication made it quite clear that the work must be undertaken before Christmas. Mr. Lawson was a well-respected customer of the firm and there was no contemplation of delaying his request even though the letter did not arrive at our offices until the twenty-third.

As the most junior of the employees at Lovett and Sheridan's, I was prevailed upon to undertake the journey the following day. As my employer Mr. Lovett was quick to point out, I was unencumbered with a wife or family and thus my absence would be less sorely missed than any of my fellow workers. The instructions in the letter were brief, but pointedly urgent. Mr. Lawson's will was to be made up without the slightest delay. Presumably, he was in poor health and was not expected to live to see out the New Year. So resigned to my fate, I made the necessary arrangements and the following morning, set off on the uncomfortable and interminable journey to Rowton Moor.

And now, here I was; chilled and aching in every bone, with the prospect of a dull Christmas away from my own lodgings. Little wonder my mood was such a disagreeable one.

The horses lunged up a steep incline and ahead of us lay a vast, barren stretch of moorland, devoid of vegetation and lit only by the lurid glow of the dying sunlight. Away in the distance, I caught my first glimpse of Lawson's house, a great rambling dwelling of black stone, standing up gaunt and ugly in the midst of desolation.

At that very moment, my eye was drawn to a figure, walking slowly alongside the coach. It appeared to be a young woman, travelling in the same direction as I and moving with some difficulty against the force of the wind. She was wrapped in a heavy velvet cloak, with a large hood that covered her face and the garment flapped behind her as she walked. I leaned out of the coach window to shout to the driver to halt for a moment, intending to offer the woman the relative comfort of my carriage. The coachman brought the horses to a halt and then stared down at me and demanded to know what was the matter.

I turned back to point out the woman and was astonished to find that she was no longer anywhere to be seen. I glanced this way and that, convinced that she had momentarily passed into some deep gully and that at any moment, she would reappear, struggling valiantly on her way. But after a few seconds, it became clear that there was nobody about. Apart from myself and the coachman, the Moor was completely deserted.

I could only turn back to the impatient coachman and mutter some feeble apology. With a barely disguised sneer, he whipped up the horses and the coach lurched onwards once more. I was mystified and rather disturbed by the incident. I had always prided myself on possessing excellent eyesight and was not of that fanciful nature that allows some men's imaginations to get the better of their rational judgment.

And yet, I had seen the woman, as plain as day. Eventually, I could put it down to no more than a trick of the light and I had to dismiss the matter from my mind as the coach drew nearer to Mr. Lawson's residence.

As we approached, I could see that the house was in a bad state of repair. The guttering was hanging loose in some places, tiles were missing from the roof and several windowpanes were broken. In this wild location, the services of a handyman must have been in constant demand, but perhaps there were few tradesmen willing to make that long journey across the Moor.

The coach halted for a second time and I clambered out of the carriage, glad of the opportunity to stretch my legs. The coachman handed down my case and I arranged with him that he should return for me at his earliest convenience, which he claimed, would not be until the afternoon of Boxing Day. Then, with a curt good night, he lashed the horses and wheeled the coach around in a reckless circle. He set off in the direction of home, anxious no doubt to be back with his own family.

With a sigh of resignation, I made my way along the weed-ridden path that led up to the front porch. The vast oak door had a bell pull that was fashioned in the shape of an eagle's head. I stared at it forlornly for a moment and then reached out to pull the cord. The clanging of the bell seemed to echo throughout the house. I stood shivering beneath the stone lintel of the porch as the wind howled an eerie welcome.

After what seemed an eternity of waiting, the door creaked heavily open and a woman stood in the entrance, eyeing me disdainfully. She was a tall thin woman with a dark complexion and long black hair that was tied in a severe bun at the back of her neck. She had tiny glittering eyes that seemed to stare knowingly into my own and she had a thin hook of a nose that put me in mind of a crafty bird of prey. At length, she demanded to know my name and my business at the house. I explained that I had come to make up Mr. Lawson's will and at that, she nodded and ushered me inside.

I found myself in a great, dimly lit hallway. There was no furniture and the place was badly in need of cleaning. As I moved forward, my footsteps echoed hollowly and it was barely any warmer here than it was outside. The woman announced that her name was Mrs. Meachum and that she was the housekeeper in this grim place. Glancing about, I could only conclude that she was desperately poor at her work, since every surface in sight was grimy with dust.

I smiled, in what I hoped was a good natured manner and asked if I might see Mr. Lawson directly, for I was anxious to conclude the business as soon as possible. Mrs. Meachum escorted me to a place she called "the library"; and indeed, as I entered, I could see that it had once been a grand place. But now it had fallen into decay. There were countless shelves of books along each wall, but every one of them was festooned with mildew and cobwebs.

In an armchair, before a slumbering fire, sat Mr. Lawson. He turned his head to look at me and I was taken with an abrupt sense of surprise. I had been led to believe that Victor Lawson's age was some two score years at most; but the fellow who sat before me was surely much older than that. He was a stooped, frail figure of a man, with an untidy shock of silvered hair and a gaunt, almost cadaverous face. His sunken eyes were rimmed with red and his white cheeks were thick with stubble, as though he had not picked up a razor in days.

"So, you are here at last," he said, in a dry croak of a voice.

Considering the personal sacrifices I had made to keep this appointment, I considered this a rather churlish remark; but then, he seemed to soften a little and asked me if I should like to partake of some mulled wine. "It is a foul night, " he observed. " The wine will doubtless warm your bones."

I confessed that the idea seemed an agreeable one and he dispatched Mrs. Meachum to fetch two tankards of the brew. He bid me sit in the other chair and warm myself at his meager fire. "This is not a propitious time to be travelling," he murmured, staring thoughtfully into the grate.

Thinking that he referred to the season of goodwill, I agreed most heartily with him and inquired if he would be indulging in any celebrations. He stared at me scornfully.

"We do not celebrate Christmas in this house," he said. He went on to explain that he had merely been referring to the inclemency of the weather. "It's a hardy creature who can travel out on those moors at this time of year," he observed.

"Without a doubt, Sir, " I replied. " But would you credit it, that only a short while ago, I saw a young woman travelling on foot - on foot mark you! - Across those very moors of which you speak."

No sooner had these words left my lips than I sensed a change in Victor Lawson. He turned to look at me, his eyes seeming to burn with a curious expression that contained elements of both rage and fear.

"You're a fool Sir!" he snapped rudely. "Nobody could survive out there in that cold, nobody! "

"I would have thought so too Sir, I assure you. And yet - "

But he had turned away with a dismissive wave of his hand. A terrible silence descended. I sat, waiting patiently for him to recover his good humor. Presently, Mrs. Meachum returned with the tankards of wine and taking mine from her, I sipped at it gratefully, feeling the warm brew restoring a little of my sapped vitality. As for Mr. Lawson, he seemed to have fallen to musing silently over the embers of the fire, his head nodding rhythmically, his lips moving as though he was muttering to himself beneath his breath. Mrs. Meachum went out of the room, closing the door behind her.

Again I resigned myself to wait until Mr. Lawson was ready to issue some instructions, but now he seemed to have fallen into some silent contemplation. At last, I grew tired of waiting and myself suggested that we should proceed with the task in hand. He lifted his head to look at me again, a curious searching expression in his eyes.

"The - woman you saw - " he murmured. "Did you - see her face? "

" I shook my head. "No Sir, for she was well wrapped and hooded against the cold."

He frowned. "Hooded," he echoed softly. "Yes, of course. She would be."

Then he seemed to make a conscious effort to put the matter out of his mind.

"Let us begin," he said. He got up from his chair and led me over to a small desk, where writing materials had been laid out ready for me. As we went through the contents of his will, I was surprised to discover that Mr. Lawson was, in spite of the shabbiness of his surroundings, an extremely wealthy man. There were various small amounts to be left to old family retainers, considerable sums to be set-aside for various nephews and nieces and there was a handsome payment of fifty pounds to be made to Mrs. Meachum for her years of faithful service.

But the lion's share of the money and the house and surrounding land was to be left, to use Lawson's own term of endearment, "to my dear wife Helena." Again, this was something of a surprise to me. It being the usual custom for a wife to greet any visitor to her husband's household, I had made the assumption that Mr. Lawson was a bachelor. But no. Evidently his wife was as lax in the ways of etiquette as he was himself. At last, it seemed that all the points were covered and I deemed it necessary that the will be signed. I indicated to Mr. Lawson that a witness to the signature would be needed and he immediately announced that he would ring for Mrs. Meachum.

"Your wife might make a more appropriate witness," I told him. I confess that I was curious about her, but his reply puzzled me.

"That would not be possible," he said; and he smiled, an odd, disconcerting smile that for some unaccountable reason sent a cold chill through my heart. He picked up a brass bell from the desk and rang it, the shrill tone cutting like a knife through the oppressive silence of the house. After an interval, Mrs. Meachum came gliding into the room and she stood by as Mr. Lawson inked his signature at the foot of the last page. This accomplished, Mr. Lawson seemed to relax a little. He sank back into his armchair with a sigh. Once again, I was struck by how old he looked. The age he had given me for the purposes of the will was forty-six years. I fell to wondering what kind of life it was that could age a man so prematurely.

"You must be tired," he said suddenly. "Mrs. Meachum will show you to your room." It was said, not as an invitation but as a dismissal. He clearly wished to be alone and though the last thing I wanted was to be obliged to bed down in some forsaken corner of this disagreeable place, I could do nothing but collect my case and trudge resignedly along in Mrs. Meachum's wake. On the way out of the room, she took up a candlestick to light me to my bedchamber. In the doorway, I glanced back at Mr. Lawson. His head was bowed and he was gazing abstractedly into the fireplace as though willing it to go on burning a while longer.

The hallway was dark and draughty and Mrs. Meachum was obliged to place one hand around the guttering candle flame in order to prevent it from being extinguished. She led the way up the wide sweep of the staircase and I followed.

"He has made up his mind then? " she observed aloud. It was such a patently obvious remark that I declined to answer it; but she continued unabashed. "I suppose I can guess who will inherit his fortune."

I was astonished by what I took to be a shameless bout of snooping on her part. "Madam," I replied. " The contents of that will are Mr. Lawson's business and not for anything would I divulge them to you."

She turned to survey me, a sardonic smile on her face. In the flickering light of the candle, her pale countenance looked quite disconcerting.

"You foolish man! D'you think I'm fishing for sprats? I have no care in the world if the poor devil had provided for me, though I dare say he will see that I'm comfortable. Oh, I know only too well who will receive all the treasures that he can bestow. Helena. Poor sweet Helena." There was sarcasm in her voice and outright malice too. I thought it most impudent that a mere servant should be so outspoken about her employer.

"Whether or not that is the case," I told her angrily, "it really is no concern of yours, Madam."

She laughed again. "And this whole business is nothing that she should be concerned with," she retorted. "Helena is surely beyond such considerations."

"What do you mean?" I demanded.

" There is something you evidently do not know. Helena has been dead these ten years or more."

I confess that at that moment I was at a loss for words. I stared dumbly at Mrs. Meachum and she, sensing some kind of petty victory, turned and flounced triumphantly up the staircase. I would have remained rooted to the spot awhile but was obliged to hurry in pursuit of the bobbing pool of light that was the only source of illumination. By the time I caught up with her I had found my tongue.

"Do you realize what you are saying?" I gasped. "Why would any man leave his worldly possessions to a dead woman?"

"Because he is insane, poor devil. What better reason could there be?" She pushed open the door to a chamber at the top of the stairs and went inside. She put the candlestick down on the dusty surface of a dressing table.

"This is lunacy!" I cried. "How can I be expected to put Mr. Lawson's affairs in order if I cannot trust what he says to me? I had better have a long, frank talk with him in the morning."

"You must do as you think fit young man. And now, if you will excuse me – " She moved towards the door and then paused for a moment, a sarcastic smile playing on her lips. "The season's greetings," she said; and she went out of the room laughing unpleasantly.

With a sigh, I turned to survey the room in which I stood. My already low spirits sank to even greater depths. The bedchamber was a bare chilly garret that seemed to make the rest of the house presentable by comparison. The dressing table was the only item of furniture besides a large, verminous-looking bed. A pane of one window was broken and a terrible night breeze came rushing into the room. I could not help reminding myself that it was Christmas Eve and that by rights, I should be in some warm city tavern now, drinking good ale and enjoying the company of my friends. Instead, here I was with the bleak prospect of suffering the entire holiday in the company of two lunatics.

I was so depressed by my own bad fortune that I felt like weeping and I would gladly have walked out onto the moors in the direction of home, if I thought I had the slightest chance of reaching it. Deciding to make the best of a bad job, I removed my overcoat and placed it on the filthy bedclothes. Then, laying myself down on this I shrugged my jacket tightly around me and resolved to try and obtain some sleep. I left the candle burning because the thought of lying in darkness in that horrible room was too daunting a prospect to entertain.

I kept thinking of how Mr. Lawson had spoken of his wife, not in the past tense, but as though she was living with him in this very house. Perhaps with the morning, would come some kind of explanation.

Luckily the long journey across the moors had wearied me and after an hour or so of yawning and turning, I finally found refuge in the sanctuary of sleep. But even there lay mystery and intrigue. I began to dream, the most horrible, vivid dream I have ever experienced.

I was standing beside a lake, a vast, calm, moorland lake. It was a warm sunny day and the moors were alive with the rich sounds of birdsong. I felt calm and contented and I strolled along the banks for some time, my hands in my pockets. I did not know how I had come to be in this place and it was certainly not familiar to me, but nevertheless I was happy to be there.

Suddenly, I came upon a small rowing boat beached on the shore. I stood regarding it for a moment and then in one of those curious lapses of time that occur in the world of dreams, I was actually in the boat, rowing out to the center of the water. The sun was most uncomfortably hot now and I felt a thick acrid sweat break out on my body. Then I realized that for some reason, the boat was no longer moving forward. Glancing over the side, I saw that it had drifted into an area of thick, clinging water lilies and not feeling inclined to exert myself further, I lay down in the boat, so that I could gaze over the side of it and trail one hand in the water.

I stared down into the dark, shimmering depths. The coolness of the water on my hand was soothing. I examined a clump of weed closely. The stems were thick and green with sap, the leaves broad and veined as though with hundreds of tiny blood vessels. Then, I noticed that some other growth was tangled in the weeds, long strands of a silky substance that waved rhythmically in the water. Curious, I reached down and took hold of a bunch. I gave it a playful tug. I became aware of something shifting beneath the boat, something heavy. I pulled again, harder this time and the object rolled around beneath the blonde strands and bobbed abruptly to the surface.

A hideous face came lurching up out of the water at me, a corpulent bloated face that was framed in a tangle of water lilies. The eyes were empty sockets, the teeth were grimacing stumps of hideous decay upon which water-snails and leeches had fastened their slimy bodies.

But most horrible, most hideous of all was that the face was not dead. It was animated; it leered at me in feral jubilation as I snatched back my hand with a cry of revulsion. I screamed something, I cannot say what and I fell back sobbing into the boat, a terrible sickness rising in my throat. And then, to my dread, to my loathing, I saw a pair of skinny hands rise up on either side of the boat and abruptly, it was overturning, I was tumbling down into the water where the thing waited for me, its filthy arms outstretched in welcome.

I woke from terror, a thick sweat heavy on my brow. I could scarcely contain my breathing and for a moment, panicking in the unfamiliar room, I opened my mouth to scream. But the cry that reverberated through the house then was not of my making. It came from one of the downstairs rooms, a cry so desperate, so fearful, that I thought for an instant, that I had not woken at all, that this was just a vivid continuation of that same dream. But the scream came again and this time I recognized the voice of Victor Lawson.

With an oath, I clambered off the bed, snatched up the candlestick and hurried out of the room, flinging myself down the staircase with all the speed I could muster. I burst into the library and found Mr. Lawson kneeling on the floor in the middle of the room, his arms clasped over his head as if to ward off some kind of attack. He was sobbing frantically as though he was in pain and as I reached out my hand to help him to his feet, he cringed like a whipped dog, whining pitifully.

I took him by the shoulders and shook him until his weeping subsided. He stared at me in confusion for a moment and then he said quietly, "God help me. She is here in this house. Helena has come home."

I bid him be still and helped him to his chair. Then I stooped and taking some coals from the scuttle, I placed them on the fire.

"Where in God's name is Mrs. Meachum?" I complained. "Surely she must have heard you cry out?"

"Oh yes, she'll have heard all right, but she will pay no attention. Why should she? She's heard enough of my screams over the years. She thinks me mad and aye, perhaps I am. " He laughed bitterly. "I need a drink, a strong drink. In that cupboard over there you'll find a bottle of brandy... please, I need something to soothe my nerves."

I went to the cupboard and brought the bottle. He grabbed hold of it, uncorked it and took a long wolfish swig from its contents. He wiped his mouth on his coat sleeve, grimaced and set the bottle down on the hearth beside him. "She's here," he said again with quiet conviction. " She's in this house. She passed by the open doorway there, a moment before you came in - and she - she smiled at me." He shuddered violently.

"But Mrs. Meachum told me that your wife was dead," I told him.

He laughed a short, derisive laugh. "Oh yes, she's dead right enough! Whatever that means...."

"Then why the will?" I asked in exasperation.

"Had to. I had to give it all back to her. It's hers, you see, all hers. And I... I knew she'd get in here this time, I could see how close she was getting, year after year. Closer all the time." He reached out suddenly and grabbed my shoulder. "I can tell you," he said and there was a trace of exultation in his voice. " I have to tell somebody. All these years of silence there was only Mrs. Meachum and I could never bring myself to speak of it to her. But you'll listen to me, won't you, good Sir? You'll not brand a man a lunatic until you've heard what he has to say?"

"Well, speak then," I replied. He began to talk, slowly, haltingly at first but with growing confidence as the story progressed. He told me about Helena; beautiful, elegant Helena, the woman he had married for greed.

Victor's Father had been a worthless sort, a man who spent his days at the gaming tables. He had squandered his inheritance on frivolous pleasures and when the drink had finally carried him off in his middle years, he had nothing to leave his son but the large rambling house on the moors and a series of unpaid debts. Victor's Mother had promptly remarried and sailed off for a new life in Ireland, making it clear that her son was not welcome to join her there.

As is so often the case, Victor had inherited all his Father's faults. Though hopelessly in debt, he continued to live the life of a society blade, for he was gambling on securing a wealthy woman to support his vices. For once, the gamble was successful. He had met Helena at one of the endless series of society functions that he attended week by week. From the very outset it was plain that she was besotted with him. Her parents, recognizing Victor for what he was, did their utmost to dissuade her from marrying him, but it was to no avail.

Helena was a headstrong, willful girl, the only daughter of a wealthy family. She had been courted by many worthier suitors but this was the first time that she had lost her heart to one of them. For his own part, Victor pretended to return her affection and told himself that after the marriage, there was no reason why he should not grow to love her. She was a beautiful, intelligent and highly articulate woman and she would doubtless have been much sought after, even if she were not the heiress to a considerable fortune.

And so they were married and they retreated to that lonely house on the moors. Helena settled all of Victor's debts and began to learn a role that was entirely new to her, that of a dutiful, loving wife; and she did love Victor, so fiercely, so totally, that she was at his elbow every hour of the day. He quickly began to feel suffocated by her presence. The reciprocal love that he had hoped might flourish in time, became instead an irritation, open wound that he was unable to scratch. And as the years passed, that irritation became resentment, then dislike and finally a deep simmering hatred.

He was painfully aware that without her, he would quickly lapse back into his old ways. At that moment, he had wealth enough to pay off any debts that might occur, but when did he have an opportunity to visit the gaming tables with Helena hanging on his arm at every moment? He began to pine for the old times, the rowdy taverns and brothels that he had frequented in his bachelor days. What times he would have there now with the unlimited funds at his disposal. What he needed was Helena's fortune but not Helena. After that, the logical solution was an easy step to take.

"There was a lake we used to visit in the summer," he told me. "Scarcely a few miles from here." Lawson's voice was slow and painful and the faraway look in his eyes suggested that he was remembering, reliving the events of ten years ago. "We kept a boat down there, a simple skiff. Helena loved the place in the summer. She would just sit in the boat with her eyes closed and her hands trailing in the water, while I rowed her out across the deeps. And so, that last time we rowed out, I had taken into my mind the notion that for once, I would be the master of my own destiny.

She was sitting in the boat, leaning forward to gaze into the water. I took a firm hold of the paddle and I struck her once, very hard, across the head. She overbalanced and fell into the lake but she was not finished. She turned, floundering and she looked up at me. In her eyes I saw not anger, not fear, but dull surprise, a sense of betrayal. She reached out her arms to me as if begging my mercy and I took the paddle again and God forgive me, I pushed her.... I pushed her back down beneath the surface until she no longer came up again." His voice dissolved into a flurry of weeping and he covered his face with his hands, his whole body wracked with shame.

I stood there dumbfounded, for the memory of that hideous dream had come back to fill my mind with unspeakable images. After a while, when Lawson's sobbing had subsided, I asked him a question. I had to ask it, even though I felt sure that I already knew the answer. "Your wife, Sir, she had long blonde hair, did she not? "

He snatched his hands away from his face and glared at me.

"How did you know that? You have seen her also?"

I shook my head. "No. That is, not directly. But I had a dream - a dream of the lake. And rising out of the water - "

But I could not continue.

Lawson's face took on an expression of demonic triumph, the eyes blazing wildly at me as though he was on the very brink of insanity.

"They did not find her body you know, though they searched that lake for days. And I, the distraught husband played my role with such distinction. Tearfully, I explained how poor Helena had fallen, dashing her head against the side of the boat; and how I, unable to swim, could only watch helplessly as my beloved wife drowned right in front of my horrified gaze.

Perhaps if they had found the body, all would have been well. But the police told me they feared that the weeds and water-lilies had snared her somewhere deep below the surface; and I knew that she was waiting down there, passing the long cold hours away in her unhallowed grave. For my part, I returned home and shortly afterwards, I received the wealth for which I had craved. But I could not bring myself to spend one penny of it. Guilt is a terrible thing to bear Sir. It can change a man, alter the whole course of his life."

He got up from his chair and paced over to the window.

"The next time I saw Helena was the following Christmas," he said. "She was out there on the moors, just standing, watching the house. At first, I thought my own guilt had finally driven me insane - but then I remembered something that Helena had told me, at the time of our very first Christmas as man and wife. We'd been sitting in this same room, oh, but you would not have recognized it then, for it was grandly furnished and a great fire was blazing in the hearth. We were just exchanging our Christmas presents and dressing up a beautiful tree that Helena had insisted we should put in the window, even though there was nobody out there to see it.

She suddenly told me that this was the happiest moment of her entire life. Then she grew uncharacteristically serious and she asked me if I believed in life after death. When I told her that I did not, she seemed sad; and she said that she could not bear the idea of being parted from me in any way, even by the black veil of death. She said that if she were ever to die before me, she would strive with every ounce of whatever will remained to her, to visit me; and if she could choose to return and relive one day from her former life, it would be this one.

And so it has been for me every Christmas since her death. She comes across the moors and each year she gets a little closer, draws a little more strength from whatever hellish power motivates her." He turned to stare at me, his face contorted with horror. "Last year, she was at this very window, scratching at the glass with her putrid fingers, calling out to me in that loathsome childlike voice, begging me to let her enter. But this year, she needed no such help from me. Listen, she's singing now! She sounds like a little child lost in the darkness! For God's sake man, can you not hear her? Can you not sense her presence?"

I shook my head. "You are ill Sir, you are sick with guilt and little wonder after what you have done. These visions are but phantoms, conjured out of your own grief and suffering. I do not doubt that once you have been submitted to a fair trial for murder, you will be purged of them."

"Aye, purged by a hangman's noose, you mean! " He laughed mockingly. "You disbelieving fool! You say you've seen her yourself and yet-"

"I saw only a dream," I reminded him.

"A dream. And what is the distinction between dreams and reality?"

"I cannot say Sir, but for my part, I am bound by the laws of reason to reveal all that you have told me to the proper authorities. Tomorrow, you will accompany me back to town where you may confess your crime to the police."

He seemed to find this statement amusing. "What makes you think I shall be here tomorrow?" he retorted. "Tomorrow, I shall be with Helena. That is why she is here, don't you see? I had hoped that the will might appease her. I thought that returning all that I had taken might send her back to her rest. But I see now that I was wrong. It is not vengeance she craves. She wants what she has always wanted." He gave a grimace of revulsion. "My love," he whispered. "My body, my heart, my soul. After all I've done, how can I deny her that?"

I gazed boldly around in every direction. "If Helena is here, why does she not show herself to me?" I demanded.

"It is not yet midnight," replied Lawson calmly. "Not yet Christmas Day. That is the time when she is strongest." He returned to his armchair, threw himself down in it and snatching up the bottle of brandy, he gulped down some more of its contents. With a sigh, I sat myself down opposite him. I did not believe his fanciful tales but I feared that after his confession to me, he might attempt to steal away into the night, or worse still end my life as cruelly as he had ended that of his wife.

And so we sat, the two of us, staring silently into the flickering fire as the coals slowly burned away. As the hours wore on, no terrible vision came into the room. Lawson kept drinking the powerful liquor and rapidly, he sank into a drunken stupor. Seeing that there was no possibility of him attempting to flee. I relaxed a little and lulled by the warmth of the fire, I too fell into a slumber, which this time was not colored by bad dreams.

I know not how long I slept, but when I woke, the candle had burned out and apart from the faintest of glows from the fire, the room was as black as pitch. As my senses returned, I became aware that the atmosphere of the room had changed dramatically, It was icy cold and I could almost taste my breath clouding in the darkness. And there was a smell in the place; Lord, what a smell! A stench of corruption and slow decay. I tried to control my emotions but I could sense the fear rising up within me. I spoke my companion's name but there was no reply. And then, I heard a sound, a strange slithering noise as though some heavy damp object was moving across the rug beneath my feet.

Abruptly, there came a scream, a hideous drawn out howl of pure terror. I started up from my seat and immediately tripped over something in the darkness, which sent me sprawling across the hearth. My hand brushed against something cold and slimy and I recoiled with a gasp of disgust.

There were other noises now, the sounds of two voices. The first I recognized as Lawson's and it was sobbing fearfully, begging for mercy. Across the top of this cut a shrill piping cackle of glee. Then there was a crash as Lawson's chair overturned in the darkness.

I remembered the bottle of brandy on the hearth and began to grope about for it as the voices built to a frenzy of cries and grunts. My questing fingers touched glass and snatching up the bottle, I flung the remainder of its contents into the grate. The fire blazed up with a roar and in the sudden glow, I saw something that my eyes could scarcely credit.

Two figures were grappling a short distance away from me. The first was Lawson, his face horribly white and contorted with terror as he struggled to push away the creature that was against him. This was something from a man's darkest nightmare. It had once been a woman but now it was a monstrosity of exposed bone and withered flesh.

The cadaverous, slobbering face was pushed up against Lawson's chest and the creature was making strange, sighing calls as she enclosed Lawson in her skinny but powerful arms, hugging him against her in a gesture that was, most hideous of all, a declaration of eternal love.

I do not know what happened then. I think I screamed something though I cannot say what it might have been. The next instant there was an almighty crash as the big bay window of the room was smashed outwards as though by an incredible force. A gale rushed into the room, beating the flames back into submission, so that the light was extinguished. I heard one last despairing cry from Lawson and then silence fell, harsh and terrible.

I must have fallen into a state of exhaustion, for when the daylight came creeping into the room, I was still stretched out on the hearth and it was some hours before I could bring myself to speak. The room was completely wrecked and nobody could explain why the place was wreathed with fronds of slimy water lilies and stained with pools of stagnant water. Lawson was never found. The police, suspecting suicide after his confession to me, dragged the nearby lake with as much success as they had achieved when looking for Helena all those years ago. The weeds, they said. They held things down far below the surface.

The place is quite popular these days. In the summer months, young couples go boating there. On occasions I have been asked to accompany some of my older grandchildren. But I will not go. I am haunted by the thought of what might lie hidden in those dark, mysterious depths.

And so you see, Lawson's misery has passed on to my keeping; and I cannot greet Christmas with the same good-natured cheer that my friends enjoy. For late on Christmas Eve, when all the ghostly tales have been recounted and my young wards are tucked up in bed, dreaming eagerly of the festivities to come, I am left alone to stir the dying embers of the fire and to remember how it was, all those long years ago, the night that Helena came home.

Family Reunion

Catherine Nichols

Kory picked up the yellow jar and traced the letters on the red label with her finger. "Mom, what does M U S T A R D spell?"

"Mustard." Her mother continued dicing a bell pepper into confetti-size pieces. "Now put it back and hand me the mayonnaise like I asked."

"How do you spell mayonnaise?" Using both hands, Kory took out the blue and white jar.

"No more spelling. I have to hurry and finish this potato salad for the reunion."

Kory climbed onto a stool. "I want to help."

"If you really want to help, go tell your dad to fetch the cooler. Nevermind." Her mother held up her hand like the school crossing guard. "Here he is. Roy, get down the cooler. I can't reach."

Her dad rumpled Kory's hair as he passed the stool. "Your family's reunions," he grumbled to his wife. "Why are they always when the Mets are playing?"

Her mother tossed the empty mayonnaise jar into the trash can, and Kory covered both ears as glass clattered against metal.

"We see my folks one day a year," her mother said in her angry voice. "For once can't you go without bellyaching?"

"Your family treats me like an outsider. Always has."

"They do not. They like you just fine." Her mother patted her dad's arm with the back of a wooden spoon. "Except for Uncle Ted, of course."

Her dad grinned. "That old SOB still kicking?"

Kory reached over and tugged her dad's tee shirt. "What does SOB spell?"

"Sob," her mother said quickly. "Kory, go put on your blue jumper. Then I'll braid your hair. Cousin Charlie will be surprised to see how long it's grown."

Kory made a face. "He always pulls it."

"Well, Charlie's only teasing. It doesn't hurt to let him pull a braid or two."

Kory poked her head out of the car window and stuck out her tongue. When she popped it back into her mouth it would be ice cold, like a Popsicle.

Without turning around, her mother said, "Kory, stick that head in, now."

"Mom, what does R O U T E spell?"

"Route." Her mother sighed. "That child had better learn to read but soon."

"She has a healthy interest in learning, Nell," her dad said. "She gets it from my side."

Her mother snorted. "Right. *Like* Cousin Charlie *didn't win* the state spelling bee for spelling 'astronomical.'"

Kory leaned forward. "Mom, how do you spell 'astronomical'?"

"Pipe down."

Kory shut her eyes. She didn't remember much about last year's reunion. Still, a funny feeling came over her whenever she thought about her mom's folks. They were nothing like Grandma and Grandpa, her dad's parents. Grandpa had a scratchy face and threw her high in the air. Grandma smelled of cinnamon and would spell for Kory till she ran out of words.

Not her mom's people. Their faces were smooth, not scratchy, and they all had the same whispery voice. And they didn't smell of cinnamon. They smelt musty, like the dress-up clothes her mother kept in the cellar for her.

Except for Cousin Charlie. He didn't smell musty. He stunk. Motor oil and gasoline clung to his clothes, especially if he was working on some old car, like he usually was. Kory hoped he'd be there today, even if he did pull braids. Kory opened her eyes. Another sign was coming up "What does B R O O K L Y N spell?"

"Kory, not another word, I mean it," her mother snapped.

"Brooklyn," her dad said, braking. "That means we're almost there, honey."

"It will sure feel good to set eyes on Charlie again," her mother said. "Remember last year, Roy? He drove us to the reunion."

"Like I'll ever forget!" Her dad tightened his grip on the wheel. "Young fool came this close to getting us killed."

Her mother rooted in her purse for a rumpled tissue and dabbed her eyes. "I miss him."

Her dad slowed down for a turn. "Well, you'll see him today."

"It's never the same, though, once it happens." Her mother stuffed the tissue back in her purse and snapped it shut.

"Mr. Daredevil should have thought of that before he raced down a slicked road at ninety miles an hour."

"Dad, what does S T – "

"Kory, enough!" her mother said. "Anyway, here we are."

The car bumped down a narrow side street. Kory peered out the window at the grassy hills. As the car passed through the iron gates, Kory saw a sign. What did it say? She tried to resist their spell, but the letters beckoned.

"Mom, what does - "

"Kory!"

"Come on, Nell." Her dad reached across to pat her mother's thigh. "How else is the kid going to learn?"

"This is the last time today, Kory. I don't want you pestering the others."

Her dad pulled up next to the sign.

Before Kory could say the first letter, her mother jumped out of the car. "Look, Roy!" She waved frantically at shadowy figures on the hill. "There's Cousin Charlie." Her mother ran to the hill, arms outstretched.

After her mother had hugged Charlie it was Kory's turn. As he lifted her into his arms, she sniffed not the stink of gasoline, but the musty smell that clung to all her mother's relatives.

She had meant to ask Charlie what the letters on the sign spelt, but now she didn't. Instead she looked again at the sign, memorizing them. Next year she would know how to read. Next year she would unlock the mystery hidden in those black letters. She whispered them as she followed her parents up the hill, C E M E T E R Y.

Bring Out Your Dead

Laura Capewell

What better place to bury a body than in a cemetery. It had seemed so perfect last night during his drunken rage. He had been so drunk he couldn't remember driving here, so drunk he couldn't remember killing her. So maybe he hadn't. Now, hours after the backbreaking job of digging the grave, Peter was waiting for his wife to claw herself out. And that's just how he imagined it, those long red fingernails pulling and scraping at all that dirt. Feeling it fall in small avalanches around her as she frantically *dug...She should have been out by now.* He had buried her last night, nearly twelve hours had past and she should be out by now.

"Meg?" His voice was just a whisper but Peter knew that it carried down into that fresh grave where his wife was trying to dig herself out.

Peter shifted and his back dug into the rough headstone he'd been leaning against all day, the stone was surprisingly cool in the heat and humidity of a late August afternoon. Somewhere in the distance thunder trumpeted and he now saw the sky was an ominous shade of black. It would rain soon and Meg still hadn't dug herself from the grave.

"Come on Meg." He whispered. "I didn't hit you that hard. You're not dead."

She couldn't be dead even though last night she'd been so still and heavy in his arms. *Dead weight.* But he had buried her anyway. Frantically digging in this old graveyard in the middle of the night like some lunatic treasure hunter. Digging under a full moon while crickets chirped a background concerto. At one point their singing had threatened to drive him mad and he'd actually screamed at them to shut up and for a wonder, for a moment, they had.

"Come out, come out wherever you are Meg." He whispered and laughed. *Peter, you are mad.*

Peter heard the swish of tires as a lone car passed by on the two-lane blacktop behind him. The cemetery and old church attached to it were so remote that only a few cars had gone by the entire day. No one had stopped at the church, no one would and no one could see him sitting behind the headstone at the very back of the graveyard waiting for his wife to dig herself out of her crude grave.

"You're too heavy handed Peter, too quick to temper." That was his father's voice echoing from the past. *"So what?"* He had said at the time. Peter had been much younger then and over the years that heavy hand had just gotten heavier. He'd hit Meg before, several times, usually after a binge, the anger so bright it hurt his eyes. *Slap.* Enough for a bruise or two, enough for some tears, enough for an apology and then it would start again a month or a week later. And what had it been about last night? The argument, the beating? He had been drunk of course. *Now don't hold that against me.* He'd said that last night as he cut the seal on another bottle. Meg had given him a cold look then, so cold that he'd felt something click inside his head. *"I want you to stop Peter." "Stop what, the drinking or hitting you?"* And so it had come out, after five years with her. *I beat you Meg, now it's out in the open.* She'd given him that cold look again and her face had gone white. *"Both."* She'd whispered. Peter had started laughing. One of those stupid, drunken laughs, a high pitched giggle. A mad man's laugh. *You were already crazy then* Peter. And so he'd said, *"No can do Meg." "Then I'm leaving you."* And that's what that click in his head had been about and that's why he'd hit her, breaking her arm first with the full whiskey bottle that he'd just uncapped. He'd swung hard, just like he had as a kid

playing baseball, then he'd heard that horrible crack and Meg had screamed, whiskey spraying everywhere. *A waste of damn good liquor.* And he'd said that last night, actually said it and watched Meg's eyes widen in disbelief. And then she'd turned away, holding her broken arm and he could hear her crying and the rage had been blinding, a white, hot volcano. *She's leaving.* The thought had blotted out everything else, all common sense. He'd grabbed something, something hard and heavy and swung again. *Home run.* He'd hit her on the side of the head and she'd dropped like a rock.

But he didn't hit her that hard, not hard enough to kill her. *Then why did you bury her?* The thought made him jump and he went back to staring at the grave, watching for the freshly turned earth to move and Meg's long, slender fingers with the bright red nails to poke through.

"Meg, come out." If she didn't come out soon, then he'd have to go in and get her. *It's too late for that. She's dead.* "No she isn't, she can't be." She'd been unconscious when he'd buried her, that was all. He'd acted too quickly, thought she was dead because her eyes had been open, blank and staring. Peter pushed the thought away. No, she wasn't dead and she would dig herself out. It was possible. Hadn't it happened in the Middle Ages when Black Death victims had been buried alive? They'd dug themselves out. He'd read that somewhere.

Bring out your dead! Bring out your dead! Peter saw the horse drawn cart clomping through the plague-ridden villages, the driver dressed in black, his face not even visible, yelling for all to bring out their dead.

"Bring out your dead Peter." Peter jumped and around even though the voice had been in his head. *"You are mad, Peter, screaming at crickets and hearing voices.*

He went back to watching the grave, his eyes now stinging from the effort but still the ground didn't move, the mound of fresh dirt didn't tremble and Meg's blood red finger nails didn't pop up like a nightmare jack in the box. The thunder rumbled again, now closer and the sky had grown so dark it brought on a false twilight. If she didn't come out soon he would have to dig her up because it was going to rain and if it rained the ground would -

"Bring out your dead Peter."

"I have no dead." The sound of his own voice surprised him. *Now you're answering. You are mad.* But that time he had clearly heard each word, someone was speaking to him. *Maybe it was a ghost.* A ghost from one of the graves. But this cemetery was so old that the ghosts here had long since gone onto other lives, been born and died again and were buried in yet other cemeteries. *Where are you buried? Oh here, there and everywhere.* Peter laughed and he didn't like the sound of it.

"Meg, come out please." The desperation in his voice, now a notch above a whisper.

"Bring out your dead Peter."

"I have no dead!" This time his voice well above a whisper. A shout actually.

You are insane Peter, Peter pumpkin eater. Again that image of the horse drawn cart, the black man with no face. *He's the one who's calling for me to bring out my dead. But I have no dead I didn't hit her that hard, she'll come up out of there. Just wait.*

Then he felt the first drops of rain and Peter jumped up from the headstone, every muscle in his body shrieking in agony. "Damn it Meg, come up out of there now or this time I will kill you!"

"Bring out your dead Peter."

"I have no dead!" Another scream at a faceless voice, another step closer to madness. *We'll just see who's right, we'll just see.*

He picked up the shovel and muscles trembling in his arms, he dug at Meg's grave. The rain was nothing more than a heavy mist but already the ground was wet, already the damp earth heavy. "Damn it Meg, why didn't you come out! You're going to make me do this aren't you? You're going to make me dig you up you bitch!"

"Bring out your dead Peter."

"I HAVE NO DEAD!" The scream hurt his throat and even the old headstone seemed to tremble in response.

"You're awfully quick to temper Peter." The black man said, sitting atop his cart. Now Peter could see the bodies thrown carelessly inside and all those sightless, staring eyes.

"Don't talk to me, I can't even see your fucking face!"

"Bring out your dead Peter."

"I have no dead! You'll see, just wait!"

Peter shoveled earth again, another lunatic treasure hunt. The rain stopped and a mist crept up from the ground burying the cemetery in a shroud and still he dug, arms screaming in agony, sweat soaking through his clothes. The smells of last night's liquor mingling with the stench coming up from the hole.

"Bring out your dead Peter." The black man taunted from the death wagon.

"I TOLD YOU, I HAVE NO DEAD!" The scream echoed through the white mist and came back to him. "YOU'LL SEE, I HAVE NO DEAD!"

Dirt sprayed out around him, disappearing into the mist as Peter frantically dug. His shovel hit something soft and went right through. He stopped digging so suddenly he was thrown off balance and realized that he was now standing inside the grave. The thing his shovel had hit was Meg. He pulled the spade free ignoring the squelching sound it made and stared as the dirt still inside the grave shifted and Meg's long fingers appeared. One arm was raised, the fingers curled, clumps of dirt under those red nails. "My God Meg, you were trying to dig yourself out."

"Bring out your dead Peter."

"I have no dead, can't you see that you fucking bastard!" Another echo from the mist.

Peter reached down and brushed the dirt from her face and those sightless eyes that were still wide open. "I'm sorry I frightened you, Meg but, my God, you've got to learn."

"Bring out your dead Peter."

"I have no dead! See she's alive! Come on Meg, I'll help you up." Peter pulled that one raised arm and heard it snap a second time. *You broke that arm, remember? That's why it's raised, she couldn't bend it. You broke it when you hit her. Never mind that now.* He pulled her and howled with the pain in his back. *Dead weight.* "Come on Meg, you're not that heavy."

"Bring out your dead Peter."

"You fucking bastard, where are you! I have no dead! Look!" And those long fingers with the bright red nails closed around his hand and Peter screamed.

The black man laughed a sinister sound that echoed through the mist in the graveyard. *"Bring out your dead Peter."*

McCandless parked his patrol car behind the church and walked to the gate at the back of the cemetery. The ground mist made it difficult to see so he would have to walk the graveyard to find the source of the "screaming and yelling" a nearby resident had complained about. Screaming from the graveyard at the old church, someone yelling about the dead. It was too early for Halloween but he would have to check it out anyway. He stopped when he saw the fresh grave and an icy wedge of fear ran up his spine. *What the hell is this?*

"I brought out my dead." The voice came out of the mist in the graveyard and again

McCandless felt that chill. "I brought out my dead."

The mist broke apart and the apparition appeared. A man stumbling through the cemetery, carrying a large bundle in his arms. The bundle took shape in McCandless's eyes and he backed away. He saw her arm first, hanging down at an impossible angle and then the fingers and long red nails. Dirty fingers, as if she'd been digging in the ground. And then he saw her face, thrown back against the man's arm, the eyes wide, sightless and flecked with dirt. Dirt flew off in clumps from the long blond hair.

The apparition was in front of him now and McCandless was drawn to those mad eyes, helpless to look away. "I brought out my dead." The hoarse voice whispered. "I brought out my dead."

Isle of the Dancing Dead

Rick Kennett

"Is it true," said young George as he filled in his first grave, "that the best place to hide from a ghost is in a cemetery?"

"Aye," said the gravedigger, shoveling. "Most times you'd be right aholding to that notion. But not here. Not in this particular cemetery. Not with the Chenoweth Grand Tomb not five hundred yards behind ye."

"A haunted grave?" George turned about, studying the lawns and masonry. "Which one?" George wanted to be a gardener, and was still a little amazed that this work experience job came with the added responsibility of burying people.

"You've not seen it yet?"

"I've only been on the job six hours."

"Well, you'll know the Grand Tomb when you see it." He chuckled "Or, if you're a Chenoweth, when you hear it."

"How's that?" "Later, lad. One grave at a time."

When they'd finished and patted down the earth, Monty conducted George through a maze of headstones to the center of the cemetery where the young gardener suddenly found himself at the edge of a small lake. In the middle of this lake was an island, and in the middle of the island was a squat black marble building.

"The Chenoweth Grand Tomb," said Monty proudly. "One hundred and fifty year old and the grandest mausoleum in the Southern Hemisphere -- and its maintenance and the keeping of its doors are my responsibility alone."

"Haunted?" asked George.

"Aye. Haunted by the Wailing Woman. There's been times in the past eighty years that its coffins have been danced about, higgledy-piggledy, when it's opened to put another Chenoweth to rest. But as they say, there's no rest for the wicked, and the Chenoweth Grand Tomb is proving it.

"You see, lad, eighty year ago some Chenoweths massacred some blacks camped on their land. What with the Chenoweths being rich squatters and the blacks just being blacks, nothing ever came of it. Not as far as white man's law was concerned, anyway, because it's said the family was cursed by a Koradji man a sort of witch doctor -- and since then the murderers and their descendants have danced in death to the crying of the Wailing Woman."

"Have you ever heard the Wailing Woman?"

"Nay, lad. She canna be heard by any but Chenoweths about to die and those already dead."

"Why is there a lake?"

"It's a defense. It was dug seventy year ago in the belief that spirits canna cross water, and that a defense is more convenient and dignified than shifting all the dearly departed."

"Does it work?"

"Aye. Most times. I remember five year ago a summer that burnt the lake to little better than mud, and that's when I last saw the Grand Tomb open."

"And the coffins?"

Monty smiled. "What do you think, lad?"

George thought, and over the next few days asked other gardeners at the cemetery about the tomb, discovering little that Monty hadn't already told him, other than, when the occasion arose, the island could be reached by a pontoon bridge stored in a special shed. Unfortunately for George's curiosity, maintenance of the island's lawn and garden was a once yearly job, and unauthorized entry onto the lake and island was strictly forbidden. George had to make do with standing at the lake's edge during lunch hour, staring out at the black tomb on the island, thinking.

As it happened, George had only been at the cemetery a few weeks when the millionaire W.W. Chenoweth senior became critically ill. Like discreet vultures the cemetery management hovered in anticipation, assigning Monty the task of grooming the island. Permitted to choose his own assistant, he chose George.

George pressed his ear to the black marble wall and heard a voice say, "Take your partners for the Danse Macabre!"

He twisted about, coming face to grinning face with Monty. Embarrassed, George went back to his weeding.

"Five year they've had to jig," said Monty with a chuckle. "Do you think they'll pick today?"

George poked at the dirt with his weeding tool. "That's not what I was listening for."

"Sorry, lad, but I couldna help it. What was it you were listening for?"

"Water."

"Oh, aye."

"No, Monty. I'm serious. I've been thinking over this dancing coffin caper, and I reckon the Chenoweths are causing this so-calling curse to come true themselves."

"Themselves?"

"Aye." It was now George's turn to grin. "Just before school finished for summer we started a short course in hydrodynamics, you know, water pressure and that sort of thing. The tomb is airtight, right? It also has its foundations below the water level of the lake. Right?" He indicated the three stone steps leading down to the door of the tomb. "What if hot weather were to effect the air pressure inside, causing the lake water to seep in and flood the tomb? It would float the coffins about. Then when the weather changes, the water disappears, the coffins settle higgledy-piggledy, and there's your dancing dead."

"Well, firstly, lad, the floor of this tomb is tiles."

"Tiles crack, tiles break."

"Secondly, the Chenoweth coffins are lead-lined; too heavy to float."

"If the coffins are airtight they'd be buoyant. Steel ships float, you know."

"Aye, and pigs may fly. Let me tell you again that I've seen - that's seen - them coffins danced about: upside-down, against the wall, lying atop each other. There's nothing natural about this particular grave."

"Wouldn't you like to be sure?"

"How do you mean?"

"I mean have some method to see if I'm right - or wrong."

"I canna see how it can be done."

"With a glass jar."

"A what?"

"We leave an empty glass jar, weighted so it won't float, in the back corner of the tomb next time it's opened. Then, if I'm right, the next time the coffins are found danced about our jar will be full of water."

Monty nodded. "There's something in that, I'll admit. But what exactly do you mean by 'we'?"

"I'll supply the jar if you like, but you're the one responsible for opening and closing the tomb. A little sleight of hand before you lock the doors after the next funeral, and the following time the tomb is opened we may have our evidence, one way or the other. Haven't you ever wondered what really goes on inside this tomb, way down deep in the dark? In the unknown."

"All we'd be tampering with is the tomb's ghostly reputation."

"Laddie, there's nothing phony about the Chenoweth Grand Tomb."

"Then prove me wrong."

"With a glass jar, a lump of lead and a little sleight of hand?"

Next morning the news broke that W.W. Chenoweth had died during the night.

The day before the funeral Monty opened the tomb in the presence of the cemetery manager who, with an air of businesslike solemnity, stepped into its shadows. When he re-emerged, his expression was one that belied any belief in curses or rumors of curses.

"Very good, Mr. Montague. Carry on."

Duly checked, the mausoleum was closed for a further twenty-four hours.

On the morning of the funeral George handed Monty a glass jar coiled about with a thickness of lead. An hour later when he re-opened the tomb, Monty secreted the jar in a back corner, beneath the rear-most bier. That afternoon, as the last mourners left the island, he closed and locked the doors. All he and George could do now was wait for hot days and low water.

They got them two years later in a summer full of hot days.

The summer George worked there was one full of hot days, and standing by the lake edge he could almost swear to seeing its level drop day by day. But his time at the cemetery was nearly over, and school would soon be starting again. He grew restless and impatient to the extent of having vague fantasies of waylaying a Chenoweth just to get the tomb open.

The lake was little better than mud when the late autumn rains finally broke the dry. But by then George had long ago returned to school.

Many months passed before George laid eyes on the Chenoweth Grand Tomb again. It was a sunny afternoon, and he'd decided to skip school that day and look up Monty.

He found him gardening by the lake. Almost immediately their conversation turned to the tomb. George expressed disappointment that the tomb hadn't been opened since he'd left the job. Monty smiled with mock agreement, saying how irritated he was that none of the Chenoweths had had the common courtesy to drop dead yet.

"Why wait?" George asked suddenly.

"Why what?" Monty's smile evaporated.

"Why wait for a Chenoweth to die? Why not take a look ourselves?"

"Now?"

"Tonight. The water's what? Knee deep? Easy wading."

Monty shook his head. "It'd be my job, lad. It's nor worth the risk."

"Then lend me the keys. They can't sack me."

"The keys'll nor be leaving my keeping. Ah, it was a stupid thing I did, putting that jar in there."

"The only stupid thing you did was failing to see that the dancing dead are caused by a series of circumstances all very natural in origin."

"There's nothing natural about the Chenoweth Grand Tomb, lad. It's what I've always said, and it's what I believe."

George pointed to the tomb on the island. "Proof of what you say is there right now, Monty. The lake went dry last summer; plenty of time for low pressure within the tomb to suck up water, plenty of opportunity for your Wailing Woman to cross and call the next dance. Whether I'm right, whether you're right, the coffins must have been disturbed by now. The drying up of the lake is the common factor. But if you want to wait for a Chenoweth to die before you'll take a look inside that tomb, then you may be waiting a long time. In fact you may be dead yourself before – "

"All right." Monty looked across the lake. "All right. We'll go tonight. But if the coffins have nor been disturbed then I'm waiting for the proper time."

George nodded. "Agreed."

The mud oozed between their toes and the midnight water was cold about their knees. They climbed onto the island and padded across the lawn to the tomb.

Monty unlocked the door.

"The torch, lad."

George handed it over. Monty pushed against the door until it opened wide enough to admit half a face, then flicked the torch beam around inside. What he saw he saw in fragments: a bit of wall, a dried wreath, the glint from a glass jar. He pushed again. He stopped.

"Go on, Monty, open it'" George said a little nervously. "I canna! There's a coffin jammed against it!" Several minutes of steady pushing eventually opened the door wide enough to permit George to slither through. He took the torch and made his way over and around the scattered Chenoweth coffins, trying not to look behind him, his eyes fixed ahead on the beckoning glint of glass. At the rear-most bier he stooped and plucked the jar from its corner. He didn't dare look at its contents. Should it be dry he knew he could not long vouch for his reason there among the dancing dead.

Back at the door he handed Monty the jar, then squeezed through.

Monty held the jar up to the torchlight and they saw.

After a moment George said, "I'm sorry, Monty."

The gravedigger shrugged. He produced a lid from his coat pocket and screwed it down on the jar of water. "Well, maybe the Chenoweths will reward us if we can show the Wailing Woman is just a tomb full of cold water. Perhaps you could take the water to one of your school's science teachers and get it checked. You never know, it may come from a different source than the lake, an underground stream, perhaps. Or perhaps - perhaps it's only condensation." Monty's eyes glistened in the torchlight. "You never know," he repeated softly.

"I'll get it checked," George promised.

Monty met George a week later, standing in his usual spot at the edge of the lake, staring out at the black marble tomb on the island.

"Did you get the water checked, lad?"

"Yes," said George, still staring outwards. "In fact I got the answer back today."

"What's the matter? You're nor acting like the one who proved there's no such thing as the Wailing Woman."

"I wouldn't say that, Monty. It wasn't just water in the jar." George finally turned around. "It was tears."

Paradise Lost

Carol MacAllister

During the day he crouches low, like an animal, down in the swale among the overgrown cedars. At sunset, when occasional mourners leave the old cemetery, he wanders the grounds, mindlessly scavenging for food.

Months before, he had planned to take his life when the dementia and pain of his cancerous brain overwhelmed his failing body. Because of legalities, no one was allowed to assist. So, he lied to his doctor about sleeplessness and stashed away the prescribed bottle of sleeping pills. This would be his ticket out, so he thought.

The time arrived. Knowing the high water table of the delta ground mandated shallow graves, he ordered a simple wooden box. Immediate burial with no embalming or viewing confirmed, he dressed in his blue suit.

His two daughters sat at his side. Tearfully, they watched their father force down the pills. He rested back clutching their hands. Slowly, his eyes closed and his tight grasp lessened until his fingers fell limp.

Jacob Whittiker eased into a catatonic state. Barbiturates hadn't ushered him on to his passage, everyone mistook his lifeless appearance as death.

The local clerk pronounced him dead and signed the certificate. Within hours, he was placed in his waiting coffin and driven to his final rest through the gates of *Paradise*. A modest group awaited his arrival.

A brief eulogy, broken with cries of farewells, the humid air as the coffin lowered into the grave. Touched bottom, a sudden crack of thunder resounded the evening sky. Instantly, the unexpected deluge drove mourners from the muddy grounds.

The open grave filled like a vessel. Jacob's coffin floated up and drifted to the far side of the property. It stopped against the border of old, iron fence.

A sudden surge lifted the pine box and it angled upright against the pickets. Winds beat on the hinged lid. It swung open and cold rainwater drenched Jacob. The sudden chill shocked his body. Shivers sparked like an electrical current through his muscles and slowly he woke from his self-induced sleep.

Spreading tumors and deprivation of oxygen had deteriorated more brain tissue. Now, hours later, his impaired mind woke to a semi-lucid, dream world. With only fragments of conscience thoughts, he stepped from his coffin, shivering in the heavy down pour.

The muddy ground swelled with water and shifted. The coffin slipped down off the fence and the lid slammed shut. The sudden thud startled Jacob and he limped away. Confused and barely aware of his surrounds, he climbed on top of a burial vault canopied by overgrown cedars.

Throughout the stormy night, he cowered at the wallowing noise coming from graves as saturated ground split open and coffins floated upward. Winds moaned like the dead lamenting the desecration of their final resting places. The cemetery had turned into a shallow creek, edged by an iron fence, dotted with floating caskets, filled with howling, mournful sounds.

Two days of heavy rain passed. Chemical imbalances further diminished Jacob's awareness as hunger increased. Primal urges caused him to scavenge for food in the confines of the rain-battered property, but there was nothing to eat.

He turned to the drifting coffins. With a strange, primitive strength, he pried open the lids and routed through the boney remains for food. He found Marianne Heck, buried two weeks before. Jacob tore off chunks of spongy, embalmed muscle and like a ravenous carnivore devoured the infested flesh.

On the third day, the storm eased. A crew of workmen came from the parish to straighten out the disaster at *Paradise*. Disoriented and bewildered, Jacob hid fearfully in the craggy swale as workers reburied the coffins.

The men labored for days. Each night, when they left the property, Jacob crawled up the muddy incline to the plots and tore open the remaining coffins to pick through the decaying cadavers. After he had fed, he had returned, like a penned animal to sleep in the safety of his hiding place.

Caged by the surround of iron pickets, he has sustained himself for several months with no concerns, except to survive. His mental capacity continues to fade. Oddly, his body remains steady. He has learned the sound of arriving funerals and scurries to watch each new service from the undergrowth.

When evening comes, he limps through the cemetery to the new gravesite knowing only that flesh is buried in a box. In the moonlight, he feverishly uncovers the newly entombed. He pries open the coffin, then drags the corpse out, across the old burial ground and stashes the cadaver in the swale near his bed.

Cunningly, Jacob returns to the open grave, recloses the coffin, then refills the hole. As usual, workers return on the second day to retamp the loose dirt of the new gravesite and seed the rich, black soil. Jacob watches from the undergrowth, unaware the same had once been done for his peaceful rest in Paradise.

Till Death Do Us Join

James O. Dukes

"Carol, if you want the money, you have to do it," the young man said. Running a hand through his thick mane of brown hair, he stood up and walked over to the wet bar standing in a corner of the hotel room.

"Screw the money, Richard," the lithe blonde lying on the bed replied as she turned onto her back and pulled the sheet tightly around the lush angles of her nude body, crisp white cotton standing out in sharp contrast to the rich brown of her allover sun-bed tan.

Dropping a handful of ice into a glass with a sweet tinkling sound, Richard poured the contents of a small airline bottle of Absolut over the small cubes and tossed the empty bottle into the trash with an echoing thud. Raising his hands in an expansive gesture that took in the richly appointed suite they were sharing for the afternoon, Richard said, "What do you think pays for these rooms or the German cars or the ski trips to Aspen?" Agitation showing in his voice that was just a shade too loud, Richard said, "I can go back to waiting tables and living in a one room apartment smaller than your dead husband's crypt and be happy. Can you?"

Her hands gripping the sheet firmly beneath her chin, Carol pouted. "No," she said finally in a sullen whisper.

Picking up the glass of vodka, Richard, his body covered in a terry robe provided by the hotel, went over and sat down on the bed next to Carol, his graceful walk betraying the time he'd spent as a stage dancer.

"I didn't think people could put things like this in their wills?" Carol reached out and took the glass from her lover's hand and sipped from it gingerly.

"They can, and with a lawyer like Davitz as executor of the estate, he is going to make you carry this out to the letter. You could fight it, but with what? Until you officially inherit Joe's money, you haven't got anything to fight with," Richard replied, taking the glass back from Carol.

"I know." Turning onto her stomach, shoulder blades moving sensuously beneath taut skin, Carol asked, "You'll be with me?"

"If I can?" Richard set the glass on the nightstand and grasped Carol's shoulders firmly. He felt the tension in her neck and kneaded the taut muscles, eliciting a pleasant rumbling from the woman who had been his lover for three years.

Shrugging off Richard's hands, Carol pushed herself up from the bed and looked over her shoulder. "Why don't you come back to bed, there's still another hour before my appointment with the lawyer."

Standing up, Richard let the robe fall from his shoulders and got under the sheets with Carol, the subtle scent of her perfume growing stronger as he wrapped his body around hers.

The graying, rotund hulk of Frank Davitz, Esquire sat behind a mammoth teak desk and looked on sternly as his receptionist opened the door from the outer waiting room and ushered Carol in. With a nod that had clearly been rehearsed, he angled his head toward a leather sofa to indicate where Carol should be seated.

"Thank you, Miss Clarke, that will be all for now," the man said as Carol sat down, the leather giving off a muted rustle. As the receptionist slipped silently from the room and closed the door, Davitz rose up from his chair and, with a definite roll of one foot to the other resembling a duck's waddle, walked over to an armoire and opened its doors to reveal a television and VCR.

Carol hadn't expected her dead husband's attorney to give her a warm welcome, but Davitz had never been overtly rude. It was clear however the attorney's mask of civility had died with his client.

Turning back to face Carol, Davitz said, "I'm sure it's been clear from the beginning that I do not have a high opinion of you, or more specifically, your relationship with Joseph Grant, a man who was my friend for over thirty years."

"I never would have guessed, Frank," Carol quipped, assuming an angelic smile.

"Don't," he said, "I'm just trying to say that despite my dislike of you, I am not happy to be a part of this request. I told Joe when he made this codicil to the will that it is was unfair to you."

Caught off-guard by the sudden candor, Carol's false smile gave way to a look of concern.

Seeing the change in expression, Davitz hurried on, "Don't misunderstand me, Carol, I will execute this request exactly as Joe wished. I just wanted you to be very clear this was Joe's idea entirely and that I wanted no part of it."

"Is that supposed to make me feel better, Frank?"

"No. I just wanted it clear that I urged Joe not to make such an unusual request a condition of inheritance."

"That's wonderful. Now let's watch this tape and get on with what I have to do to inherit 'my' money?"

Like a malevolent moon, Davitz beamed rays of hatred at Carol before turning to face the television inside the armoire. Fumbling with a tape on top of the VCR for a moment, he finally inserted it and turned on the television set. Standing back, the lawyer watched as the image of Joseph Grant, III came up on the screen.

"Hello, Carol," the thick voice of the old man said. "I hope you're happy to see me." Joe laughed hard, causing an involuntary bout of coughing that left him gasping for breath.

His breathing back to a normal rhythm, Joe continued, "You've already heard my will and know about the night I've got planned for you." His left eyebrow twitched a nervous tic he'd had as long as anyone could remember. "The people at the cemetery weren't very happy when they heard what I wanted. It just goes to prove that being the majority stockholder in a company still counts for something."

"You will be taken from this office to my crypt before sunset and placed inside where you will remain until dawn tomorrow morning. Frank will have already taken care to provide a few things that will make your stay more comfortable." Joe smiled wanly, his left eyelid fluttering again ever so slightly. "Of course, should you decide not to fulfill this condition of inheritance, Frank will be happy to notify the various philanthropic organizations I have selected as alternate beneficiaries."

Joe pushed back on the chair he was sitting in and put his arm on the desk before him to stand up. Pausing, he looked into the camera again, "Oh, by the way, give Richard my best when he sneaks in tonight." Carol's dead husband chuckled malevolently. "Just be sure you're still locked in the crypt alone tomorrow morning when Frank comes to let you out, Carol, or be prepared to forfeit any rights to my estimated 1.3 billion dollars in assets."

On the television screen, Joe stood up, his gray suit hanging baggily around his stooped body, and dabbed at a corner of his mouth with a handkerchief he'd taken from a trouser pocket. He coughed and the microphone of the video recorder picked up the thick liquid rattle in his chest. Looking into the camera again, Joe said, "Until later, Carol," his eyelid fluttering as the television screen went black.

The sun hung low in the autumn sky as the limousine turned from Highway 30 onto the narrow gravel lane that passed through the rough hewn stone and wrought iron gates of Halcyon Bluff Cemetery.

Carol watched rich gold and black shadows slither ominously like some forgotten reptile through the branches of hearty live oaks draped in shrouds of gray Spanish Moss. Gravel crunching under tires, the car crept past modern bronze markers lying flush to the ground in the newest section of the cemetery. Following the winding lane it entered the older section where tall granite stones and crypts looked out from the bluff the cemetery took its name from over the dark waters of the Savannah River.

The car rolled to a stop in front of a crypt that, despite a place of prominence overlooking the river in the oldest section of the cemetery, looked utterly foreign. Stainless steel, glass and cool green marble had been wedded together by the designer, a close friend of Joe Grant, to create a gothic nightmare of soaring spires and sunken entryways that for some unexplained reason had always made Carol think the crypt belonged in some sick future where death wasn't just remembered--it was exalted.

Carol got out of the limousine and walked over to the river's edge. The final rays of the sun were golden on the gently swaying marsh grass across the river from the cemetery. A cool breeze blew across the water, filled with the scent of the marsh. To the uninitiated, the marsh smelled of death and decay, especially on hot summer days at low tide when the thick mud at its base lay bare.

Moving his bulk gingerly over the uneven ground to a spot close to Carol, Frank Davitz said exuberantly, "Wonderful!" He sniffed at the air as though it were a rare scent, knowing it for what it really was, an almost primordial staff of life, a thick organic soup whose scent promised life eternal.

Native of Atlanta's twisting lines of automobiles and concrete bleakness, Carol turned to Frank and said simply, "Stinks."

"Let's get on with this," he replied grimly, turning towards the crypt where Carol would spend the night.

Carol knew that somewhere beneath her feet rested the remains of her late husband, Joseph Grant, III. Until tonight, she had never been inside the crypt.

Joe hadn't wanted an elaborate funeral. His body had been taken from the hospital intensive care unit where he'd died and placed in the *crypt*. The whole thing had been overseen by a group of friends, the same men who had celebrated the crypt's completion five years before with an elaborate party.

Despite his wealth and social position, or, perhaps, because of them, Joe Grant was beyond being merely eccentric. Along with the five boyhood friends who would later bury him, Joe had done much as he pleased. Remarkably, Frank Davitz, despite his close friendship with Joe, had not been part of the exploits of the six men. Frank had always been the fixer, always there, always ready, but apart.

Thinking about it for the first time, Carol realized how strange it was that Frank, a man who clearly had considered Joe a close friend, had never really shared much of anything with his friend. It was almost like Carol's relationship with Joe Grant. They were together, but not. There was always something between them, some shadowy something that kept them from being truly close.

"Well," Carol said aloud, her voice sounding strange inside the tomb, "let's see about some light." From the table provided in accordance with Joe's directions, a heavy circular mound of dark cherry, Carol picked up a simple Bic lighter and lit the large candle centered upon it. The wick caught fire smoothly but not before the metal of the lighter became unpleasantly hot against her fingers.

There were other candles mounted on the walls. As Carol visited each of them, as though following perverted stations of an ungodly cross, the final light of day spilling in from thick glass apertures high in the dome of the chamber disappeared.

Amazingly, even as she rubbed her arms to warm them in the damp chill, Carol found herself more at ease than she would have thought possible. She had light. There was a chair, modestly padded, for her to sit on. There was even a bottle of vintage cognac and a snifter. Most importantly, however, Carol knew that somewhere along the highway Richard was parking his car. After making sure that Frank or someone working for the attorney wasn't around, Richard would make his way to her side. With luck he would be able to open the lock on the crypt's door. They would be able to sit outside, together, even if it was in a cold cemetery at night. At worst, Carol would have her lover outside to shout to occasionally, his muted reply proof that the world of the living had not forgotten her.

Thinking back to the videotape of Joe she had watched that afternoon, it came to Carol that her dead husband had not only anticipated Richard being at her side--no great surprise as Joe had been aware of her lover almost from the start, impotent old man that he was--but had seemed to be looking forward to Richard's presence, all in a tape made months before his death.

Carol poured half a snifter of cognac and sat down. Sipping from the glass, a warm flush spread through her body. A few moments later she was unconscious, mind unheeding as the glass slipped from her fading grasp and shattered on the stone floor.

Crouched behind a low bush near the entrance to Halcyon Bluff Cemetery, Richard looked warily about the landscape, searching for any sign of a watcher. There wasn't one. He was alone in the night save for the crickets, their song pulsing irregularly from all around him. Raising up to his full height, Richard made one last sweep of the desolate highway in the failing light of day. Empty. He angled his way across a shallow ditch and headed through the beckoning gates of the cemetery.

Carol had been robbed of all volition by the drug. She was a passive receptacle, a gatherer of sensations.

The clean rasp of stone moving against stone came first.

The lids of her eyes, transformed now into narrow, unmoving slits, allowed her eyes to make out dark shapes billowing like smoke from the floor of the crypt and gather around the chair where her body hung limply

A strange odor preceded the spectral shapes. It was a thick smell that spoke of water and earth and fire.

Something pushed at her lips and Carol tasted a rancid liquid that clung thickly to her tongue.

Then came the hands - pulling, pushing and prodding Carol's body as they lifted her from the chair and carried her back to the stone staircase leading down into the earth under the crypt.

Even with the beam of the penlight Richard had thought to bring, he moved awkwardly through the cemetery. Whether following the gravel road where tree roots caused unexpected upheavals of an otherwise even surface or working across the grass where marble and granite bases of flat bronze markers turned green with age tilted at imperceptible angles, Richard stumbled and lurched his way to the river.

Jogging along, the going only got worse as he entered the older part of the burial ground. Huge monuments of carved stone, often black and chipped with age loomed up at him out of the thickening darkness. Finally, dodging to avoid a low-hanging branch, Richard tripped on a ragged edge of marble jutting up into the air and fell to the ground, striking his head against another monument.

Warm air enveloped Carol as she was carried into the earth. But it was damp. Though the drug had made her begin to see faint halos about everything, the reason was very clear. The wall of the stairway, lit by the sultry glow of torches that gave off an oily smell, was a massive clot of roots and dirt. Where the roots were thickest, making an almost solid piece of wood, some mad artist had shaped grotesque masks, human faces contorted in pain.

Mixed with the rustle of heavy fabric hanging over the shapes carrying her, Carol heard the grind and moan of the stairs fashioned from thick wooden beams and shells from oysters.

Finally, after what seemed an eternity, she knew they had reached some sunken plateau.

Blood flowing freely from a scalp wound along his hairline, Richard pushed himself upright and leaned back against a cold headstone. Mildly dazed, he shook his head vigorously. It hurt but the dizziness cleared. He reached into the darkness where the thin beam of his dropped light still burned and picked it up. With his other hand, Richard prodded his wound gingerly and shone the light on the result, bright blood covering his fingers. Shakily, Richard stood up and went on.

Carol knew consciousness had slipped away briefly as she found herself lying flat on the hard surface of an altar. Ah instant later, the hands prodded and pulled at her again as they used sharp knives to slit her clothes, bra and panties into pieces. One set, quite cold, moved across the sensitive skin between her breasts and grasped the remnants of her bra, pulling it roughly from under her body. With the heat of a fiery ember, another hand clamped down erotically over her panties and snatched the red silk from between her thighs brutally.

"Should a widow be wearing red underwear," Carol heard a familiar voice ask.

"I don't think so," another man replied, barely concealing the mirth behind his words.

Still a third voice said, "Be quiet, both of you. This is a solemn occasion." A hand caressed the outline of Carol's ear. She tried hard to focus her bleary vision in its direction, discerning a face she knew only too well nestled in the folds of thick black fabric of long robes.

"I see you recognize me," the man said quietly. "We've been waiting for this moment a lot of years, Carol," he continued. "Ever since the six of us found this place as teenagers and pledged ourselves to the Keeper."

"Yes," another of Joe's old friends said from a new direction, "it's time to test what we learned from him."

There were sounds of fire; the crackle of bugs buried deep inside old logs bursting and the sputtering hiss of heated water from green wood grew louder. The chamber grew lighter as the flames of fire licked higher into the air.

Carol's vision continued to sharpen and she saw clearly the five men circled around her, holding her firmly against the rough slab of stone. They chanted strangely accented words in rhythms unheard by any outsider for at least a thousand years and the earthen walls echoed the call.

Richard saw Joe Grant's tomb outlined against the lighter color of open sky in the distance. Somewhere along the river, the thick bass horn of a returning tugboat sounded.

The heat of the growing fire felt unbearable against Carol's naked body. Her head echoed painfully with the chanting, growing louder and louder.

In the end there was an explosion of light followed by impenetrable darkness and despairing silence.

Richard heard a wild scream of hysteria from beyond the tomb somewhere near the river and knew without doubt that it was Carol. Running around the corner, he saw by the waning beam of his flashlight that he'd been right. There was Carol lying unconscious.

"God, are you alright, Carol?" Richard asked as he ran to his lover's side and knelt down.

"Yes, I. . guess I just let myself get scared," the woman replied, her eyebrows fluttering open.

"How ever did you get outside?" Richard asked as he helped Carol sit up.

"That's not important, Richard," Carol answered excitedly, obviously growing stronger with each passing second. "You have to come with me now. There's something I have to show you," she said, the shadow of a malevolent grimace shading her face.

Richard shone the dying beam of his light into Carol's face and studied her intently. "Are you sure you're alright, Carol?"

Her left eyebrow fluttered. "I haven't felt this good in years, Richard," she said with a laugh. "Let's go."

Harold

Gayla D. Bassham

My mother was nine years old when Grandma took her to see Harold. They stood in the living room of Grandma's childhood home and waited for the toddler ghost to materialize. "It took forever," my mother said. "We waited and waited, just stood there and stared at that bare patch of floor." Grandma finally saw him and pulled excitedly on Mother's arm. "Do you see him, Lily?" she asked.

"Did you see him?" I asked her when she told me the story.

"Rachel," she said, "I do *not* believe in ghosts."

On sunny summer days, when my mother was at work and I was out of school, Grandma took me to the "old house," as she called it-the house where she had grown up and where her parents had lived for sixty years. The porch was constructed of raw, grayed wood; the roof was tin. A tarnished mirror, whose purpose I never understood, hung next to the door. The mirror was so worn I could not see my reflection-it was like looking at the bottom of a metal bowl. Only a pinkish blur looked back at me.

The house was haunted by a three-year-old ghost. "His name was Harold," my grandmother told me, and I imagined him as he would be today - short and pudgy like my Uncle Jerry, or lean and gray-faced, like Uncle Curtis. "He'd be seventy-five now," said Grandma. She still took flowers to his grave on Memorial Day, honoring the big brother she'd never met. "He would have been fifteen, when I was born," Grandma told me. But he'd died of a fever twelve years before.

We went to the old house ostensibly to feed Grandma's chickens. She still kept them at the old house-she said there was no room at our home, and the houses were only across the road from each other. It was just as easy, she said. We always fed the chickens as soon as we arrived. Grandma tied a red and black calico apron under my arms and had me lift up the corners. "My mama and I used to do this," she told me, "when I was just your age." She poured gritty, greasy corn feed into the apron and grabbed handfuls at a time, scattering the corn to the chickens while I stood there holding the apron, frozen in awkward mid-curtsy.

When the feed was gone and its residue was brushed from the apron and my clothes, Grandma would take me on a tour of the old house. No one had lived there since my great-grandparents had died some years before my birth. Their clothes had been given to charity, the food had been emptied from the kitchen, and most of the family photographs had been distributed among their living children. But the house was still very like my great-grandparents had left it. A partially-sewn quilt piece rested in the antique black sewing machine. The radio, the huge old-fashioned kind larger than a modern TV, was tuned to Grandma and Grandpa Collin's favorite station (the station had since gone out of business; turn the old radio on, you'd only hear static.) A crocheted afghan-blue and white granny squares-was spread on the couch. "My daddy had this covering his knees when we found him," Grandma told me. "He'd had a heart attack and just drifted away."

Parts of the house had been a shrine to Harold since his death over seven decades before, and those parts my grandmother and her siblings also left untouched. A varnished wooden bucket, with a golden rope handle and stenciled letters reading "Harold" in fancy cowboy lettering stood on top of the ancient refrigerator. It was still full of toys: blocks with letters and numbers and shapes painted on them; a dried rubber ball that was once red but was now a dusky pink; a toy duck on wheels with a braided red pull. We never touched the toys. Of course, I examined them studiously from below. "My daddy carved them blocks when they were waiting for Harold to be born," Grandma told me. "He'd whittled that duck for his third birthday, the one he had just before he died. Poor little boy. He'd hardly got a chance to play with his toys before he took sick." The toys, Grandma said, had been put up on the icebox for when Harold got well; and in the decades after his death, his parents could never bear to take them down again

    Harold's photograph was the only family picture that the children had not removed from the house in the aftermath of their parents' deaths. It stood on the mahogany buffet next to the couch. A vase of plastic roses, once red but now nearly white with age, stood next to it, as if in tribute. I often stood on tiptoe at the buffet in an effort to get a better look at Harold as he had been; I was too superstitious to touch the photograph and too fascinated to leave it alone. I remember the frame particularly. It was oval, of a yellowed clear plastic, with indentations all around it, like a piecrust. The picture revealed a boy with straight light hair and a dimpled body, wearing a sleeveless sailor suit with shorts. He did not smile in the photograph; he looked glumly forward as if he could foretell his own death.

    Some days, Grandma and I saw Harold. We nearly always heard him; his childish babble carried to the chicken coop and, on windy days, even to our house across the road. But seeing Harold - that happened rarely enough to be a treat and often enough to be a possibility. We had to stand in the doorway, Grandma and I, squinting our eyes at the red and white rag rug in the center of the room. If we stood there long enough-if we didn't move a finger or an eyelash, if we didn't make a sound except the sounds of our own breaths-we could sometimes see him materialize on the rug, wearing his sailor suit and playing with the set of blocks. He would look up at us, laughing; he would appear solid enough to touch, and more than once I reached out for him before he slowly evaporated.

"When I was a girl," Grandma told me, "I'd get messages from Harold all the time. He used to come to me in dreams. But after I grew up and moved out of the house, I didn't see him so much. I hardly ever see him now." She shook her head, standing in the center of the living room. "There's something about this house," she said. "It's the only place I can ever see him regular."

I made my mother go with us to the old house once. Only once. Once was enough to learn my lesson. But I was young, excited by Harold, pleased that my mother had taken one day that summer off. "Mama, you have to come see!" I said. I refused to tell her what she would see. "It's a surprise," I told her.

"Only takes two to feed the chickens," Grandma said when I told her that Mother was coming with us.

"Rachel has a surprise for me," my mother said. She thought it was a picture I had drawn, maybe a little patch of garden Grandma and I had tended at the old house. I had never discussed Harold with my mother.

"Don't expect too much," Grandma said. I don't know who she was talking to.

We fed the chickens and then went into the house. I put my finger to my lips as we approached the entrance to the living room. "You have to be quiet," I told my mother. We stood silently for a moment, and the plump toddler appeared, placidly building a house with his blocks. My mother gasped and bit her lip; I watched the ghost reverently. As soon as Harold disappeared, I tugged at my mother's blouse. "You saw him, Mama! I know you saw him!"

Instead of responding to me, she looked over at my grandmother. "What have you done?"

she asked.

"I could have told you your mama wouldn't see him, sister," Grandma said to me. "She never has had the heart for it."

Mother knelt down and looked at me. "I did not see anything because there was nothing to see," she told me. "It's just imagination."

"But it's not," I said.

"But it is. You see him because you think Grandma sees him. You'll understand better later. Just remember that there's no such thing as ghosts."

"But there is," I insisted. No one answered me this time.

My mother is an even-tempered woman. Only one time do I remember her becoming unreasonably angry.

We had just moved to Harper Rock, and I was chattering on about what I would do when I grew up, where I wanted to live - on a grassy patch near the banks of Miller Creek, as I recall - how I wanted to sew my own clothes and grow my own vegetables just like Grandma.

"I don't want to hear that again!" my mother said.

I looked up, startled. Too startled to say a word. My mother had never shouted at me when I did not expect it.

She cupped my chin in her hand and leveled her face to mine. "You have to understand this," she said, calm again. "We are here to take care of your grandmother. We are not here for always. You, especially, are not here for always."

"But I like living here," I said.

She pulled me to the plate-glass window. "Look around you," she said. "Do you see nice houses like the ones where we used to live? Do you see people who can even feed and clothe their children properly? How many kids in your grade do you think will go to college? I know all about the nonsense your grandmother's taught you. People here cling to their superstitions because that is all they have. Do you understand? You are not here for always. I left this place for a reason."

"But you came back," I said.

"Yes, I did," she conceded. "Because your grandmother needed me. But I won't need you. Not here. I promise you that."

Every few weeks, after we moved into Grandma's house, my mother and grandmother would disappear behind the closed door of my grandmother's bedroom. Mother would never explain what went on that I could not be privy to. "Just talks," she would say when pressed. She would squeeze me and smile, making a joke out of it. "Would you want me to tell Grandma everything you and I talk about?" As close as I was growing to Grandma, I wouldn't have minded, and Mother could see that. "You'll understand someday," she said.

Once when Mother and Grandma had hidden themselves in the back room, I stood at the door and used a water glass to listen. A trick Grandma had taught me; maybe she wanted me to hear. "She can see Harold as well as I can. Better, even," I heard Grandma say. "And you hadn't taught her a thing about it."

My mother's voice was less distinct. I heard something about "backwoods nonsense"- my mother's customary way of dismissing country superstitions - something about "my daughter, not yours."

"How can you talk like that? It's what our family does, same as your daddy's family grew rice. Same as the Hillocks have a preacher ever generation," Grandma said.

"It's just superstition. I've never 'seen' anyone. She only sees what you tell her she sees."

"So you really haven't taught her a thing about it."

"No," Mother said. "No, I haven't." Unexpectedly, she opened the door, and I stumbled back. The water glass clattered to the floor. Mother looked at me, eyebrows raised, and shook her head at me. She cast a look at Grandma. From then, their talks were carried on more quietly, and *I* never knew what conclusions they reached.

We had lived with Grandma for two years when Mother decided to sell the old house. Grandma was getting too old to walk over there every day, she said. She might fall and break her hip at the house, Mother said. If I were at school, she would be all alone. Maybe for hours, Mother said. I'm thinking of you, she told Grandma. It only makes sense.

Grandma would have fought Mother's decision-it was, after all, not Mother's decision to make-but she was outnumbered. Her own siblings sided with Mother. "Come on, Ellie, we've held on too long," Uncle Jerry said. "We can't take care of it anymore," Uncle Curtis said, "it's time to let it go." Aunt Mona lay in a nursing home, dying; her daughter spoke for her. "We sure could use the money, if we did find a buyer," she said, "we've run through Mama's savings, and do you know how much those places cost?"

Mother, always efficient, found a buyer in six months-a man who made wooden frames for his wife's oil paintings, who bought the land for the house's wood; when the house was demolished, he'd hunt deer on the land, he said. How perfect, Mother told him, my grandfather used to hunt there, too. And the deer are just running rampant these days, she told him. We found three in the garden at one time last summer. Can you believe that, three, she said. And we'll all be glad to see the old house put to some use, she added.

Grandma raged and glared at Mother for a week, but Mother was reasonable, as she always is-"How else do you expect to sell so-so land with a falling-down house on it, Mama?"

she asked.

Grandma muttered something indistinct about restoring the house.

"It's too far gone, Mama," my mother said, and waited for Grandma to get over her anger.

"It's your birthright," Grandma said.

"You will get over this," Mother said. "You'll see I'm doing what's best. You'll see this is even best for you." But Grandma never saw that.

Over the Christmas holidays, I made the sorrowful trip to the old house with Grandma to collect the chickens and say goodbye. It was several trips, really: the chickens had multiplied and it took three trips for the two of us to transport all the cages to our fenced backyard. The chore took a long time, most of an afternoon. Grandma's chickens were "free range" chickens, none too eager to get into cages. "C'mon Lou," Grandma called to them. "In here, Becky; Polly Sue, get in the cage. It'll just be a few minutes," she pleaded with them, as if they would understand. "I'll let you out as soon as we get to the house."

When the last chicken had been freed in our backyard, Grandma and I headed back to the old house. "Reckon we should check and see that everything's gone," Grandma said.

"Reckon we'll see Harold today?" I asked as we crossed the dirt road. I savored the taste of "reckon." To my mother's chagrin, I was picking up country vernacular.

"I don't know, sister," she said. "Maybe so."

The house was empty; everything was gone, after all. The naked boards groaned and crackled underneath our feet. "I've never really seen it like this," Grandma said. "Never seen it without rugs. Mama always kept rugs on the floor. Said it softened the noise and made the rooms pretty." I nodded silently, too absorbed in my own grief at losing the house to reply.

"Listen," Grandma said, as we walked up the stairs to check the loft, "do you hear that sound, sister?"

At first I didn't, and I shook my head. But then the house began to move, to shiver, and to vibrate with life. For a second or two it was as it had been in the past: crowded with furniture and handmade quilts, rugs on the floor, and curtains in the windows, full of six people talking and laughing and running up the rickety staircase. For a moment I saw the house, and my great grandparents and their children as my grandmother remembered them; for a moment, I was the ghost and they were reality. But the vision, if that's what it was, vanished quickly, and I was left holding my grandmother's hand in a dusty, empty room that would soon be torn down.

That night I told my mother what had happened. "You have a wonderful, vivid imagination," she said. "But it's just imagination. And don't mention it to Grandma," she added. "She's upset enough as it is."

For Mother's Day that year, my mother had a surprise for Grandma-an oil painting of the old house, done by the wife of the man who'd bought the property, with a frame taken from the wood of the old house. "I took several photographs before the demolition," Mother told her, "and she painted it exactly as it was. So you'll always have it to look at."

It was, in fact, a lovely painting-"much better than I would have expected, from Harper Rock," Mother told us in private. "The woman seems to be talented," she said. "It's nearly as good as a Grandma Moses." But Grandma seemed unimpressed. Although she dutifully thanked Mother for the trouble she had gone to, she hung it in the darkest corner of the hallway where it was rarely seen by anyone.

"It's a real nice painting," she told me, "and I appreciate your mama's thought. But a piece of canvas and a few hunks of wood-it don't make up for it."

"Make up for what?"

"Make up for what I lost. That house was the only place I could still feel my mama and daddy. The only place where I ever saw Harold. But she had to tear it down."

"Mom didn't mean to upset you, Grandma," I said. But of course she had known it would.

"The cruelest thing about growing old is watching your world disappear. You can't stop it from happening; maybe you can slow it down. But your mama-she just speeds it up. She's as bad as them thieves," Grandma said. "Every bit as bad."

My grandmother died when I was fifteen years old. She died at home, in her bed - the easy way to die, we all believe. My mother went to check on her before we turned the lights out and she was gone, cold to the touch. "She must have drifted off just as she went to sleep," my mother said, calmly.

I ran outside, to where the old house had stood, ignoring the orange "No Trespassing" signs the new owner had tacked to the trees. I climbed over the barbed wire fence the owner had put up I sat there cross-legged, waiting for Harold. I could feel animals clustering around me-raccoons and squirrels, a deer at one point, two wild turkeys. After an hour or so, my mother came out of the house. I looked at her eyes, but it was too dark to tell if she'd been crying.

"Don't you want to come in?" she asked.

I sat there, looking down at my feet. I was playing with a rose that I'd plucked off a wild pink bramble. I pricked my finger with a thorn and it started to bleed. I began to pull the thorns off the rose one by one.

"Your grandmother used to say she could see the ghost of her brother that died here," my mother said.

"I know," I told her. "I saw him, too."

I don't know how long we sat there together, but it must have been an hour or two. My rose had begun to wilt and I'd abandoned it next to the tiny pile of thorns. It must have been midnight two or three o'clock when finally I saw Harold-or rather, I heard him, a high-pitched, full-throated baby's cry. Not a cry for food or a diaper change, I fancied, but a cry of mourning, the cry of a child who has lost his sister.

"Do you hear that?" I asked my mother.

"I don't hear anything," she said.

The cry came again, a little louder this time.

"You really don't hear that?" I asked.

"I think it's just the wind," she said.

The cry subsided. Harold did not appear, as I'd hoped he would. I gave up. "I think I'm going back," I said to Mother. I stood and brushed the dust off my jeans. She sat there. She was wearing one of those sack dresses that were so popular then; she'd pulled the skirt over her knees and sat hugging them.

"I think I'll stay here for a minute," she said. I crossed the road and turned to look at her. She sat hugging her knees on the site of my Grandma's old house, cocking her head, listening closely.

Bitter Pills

Deborah Markus

Laurel's mother had expressed a preference for being burned rather than buried and her ashes scattered quietly over the sea, but when the time came, Laurel, without explanation, gave her a funeral that might have done honor to a minor nobleman. There were flowers, there was singing, there was a viewing and an open casket (solid, somber, beautiful) and a good long eulogy. And afterward a lavish wake for the many friends and admirers, with more blossoms and enough food to satisfy without seeming festive. Laurel arranged it all herself, a little clumsily but with a good eye for detail.

She paid for it, too. As is common now, Laurel inherited nothing from her mother but expense. No insurance, unpaid bills. Even the house she'd grown up in was gone - sold years ago when her father died. Neither Laurel nor her mother had been able to live with the memories the place held. Besides, they needed the money.

Everyone gathered at Laurel's apartment afterward. The usual things were said, the usual quantities eaten. Laurel noticed as she had before that people always seemed starvingly hungry after funerals. She, herself, ate nothing, but held a drink to be polite.

She wondered if it had been a questionable touch to dress her mother in the wedding gown. (She'd left off the veil, after some thought.) Tiny and beautiful, dwarfed by the coffin and billows of lace, her mother had looked ready to be christened. She would have resented the infantilization. But what else could be done? She had to wear *something*. She did have some evening gowns, but most of them were brightly colored and all of them were low-cut. Surely décolletage at a funeral would be in bad taste, even for the guest of honor. Laurel supposed she could have just bought a new dress but there had been so much to do already without running such a strange errand, and there was the money to think of -- she couldn't dress her mother in something cheap, on this last big occasion. The only other option would have been lending something of her own, which was unthinkable even if she'd had anything remotely appropriate. Laurel's dresses would have been much too big for her mother. Unbecoming.

But everyone seemed to like the gown. It gave them something to talk about, especially the ones who had been present the first time it had been worn.

"To think it still fit her after all these years," one woman marveled over a cucumber sandwich. "She would have been so pleased." She lowered her voice slightly. "It *did* fit, didn't it? You didn't have to - -"

"Oh, no," Laurel said. "Not at all."

"Absolutely not," another woman, listening, said authoritatively. "She was terribly thin. Toward the end she could hardly eat a thing."

"Oh, good," the first woman said. "Such a lovely gown. I'd hate to think of it being cut. Such a lovely service, my dear."

"Thank you."

"Yes, a very good job," the other said. "Quite a lot of work under trying circumstances. You're to be congratulated. Really did her proud."

"Thank you," Laurel murmured. "She always said she wanted something simple, but -_"

"Modest." The first woman had spotted the cakes, was leaning toward them. Always so modest, such a sweet --"

"She'd have loved all the attention," the other woman pronounced firmly. "Anyway, not to speak ill of the dead, but I've always thought that funerals were more for the living anyway. After all, *we're* the ones trying to feel better. *Her* troubles are over."

Yes, yes.

"What troubles?" A woman whose hair was just starting to go blue joined them, seemed startled by her own querulous tone, and adjusted it slightly along with her hat, a construction of false fruit and flowers. "I'd like to know what troubles we're talking about here. Never had to work a day in her life. Married a man who adored her and had the sense to kick off before he lost his looks, not like some I could mention."

The second woman cleared her throat, glanced at Laurel. "Really, dear," she said. "You're talking about her father, after all."

"Her what? Oh, *her* father. He was a good man," she said judiciously, emphasizing the adjective as if it had been of her own invention. "No one ever thought she'd marry him -- good's all very nice, but you have to understand, she could have had *any*one. And he knew it, sweet man. He told her he'd give her anything, anything, everything she ever wanted. And he did, didn't he?" She sighed bitterly, then looked at Laurel listening politely and summoned one of the smiles everyone had been handing to the next-of-kin today. "And she had you, of course," she added. "Her own little girl. After she thought she couldn't even *have* children."

Yes, I know. Laurel cast her eyes down and smiled shyly.

"And then you took care of her all that time. You two were always together. You loved her. Everyone loved her." Her hat was askew again, her tone slipping into belligerence. "So, please, what troubles are we talking about here?"

"She went to such a lot of trouble," the lady of the cakes was explaining to a man who looked a little lost. He had, Laurel remembered, asked her mother to marry him twice. No, three times. "Such a dear girl." She licked one finger delicately, pretending not to. "So sweet."

Yes, Laurel thought later when she'd finally cleared everyone out, pressing food on willing takers and politely refusing offers of company or help. ("No, thank you really, but I just want to be alone. I can manage. No, no, really, I have my own system. I like to do things myself.") I am sweet. And now everyone knows it.

"I did it," she said to no one. "Did you see? Did you hear? I'm a good girl, I am."

She sat at the table with the last of the leftovers all around her, rich delicates that her mother never would have tolerated in the place even before she got sick. Who could object to them now? Who could object to a large, loving funeral, even if it went against the express wishes of the deceased? That was the kind of disobedience that looked like respect. An homage. Not the sendoff Laurel knew it was. Everyone had a chance -- was required -- to say goodbye, the way they wouldn't have with a cremation and a sea sprinkling. Laurel could just imagine the ones who spent most of their retired time sitting in

the sun in the park overlooking the ocean. "Every time I see it, I think of her."

No, you don't. Don't think of her, don't think of me. Leave me alone. I never want to hear about her again. It's over now.

"You two were inseparable," one gauzy, teary soul said on her way out. "You were never apart. I remember when you were just a little girl and you wouldn't let go of her hand. She took you everywhere, said she had to. Or you'd cry and cry and - "

"Yes, thank you."

210

We were always together. You knew who I was from the first time you saw me. As soon as they handed you to me, you never wanted to be put down. I couldn't even hand you to your father - you wanted Mummy, just Mummy.

I know.

You can't remember those days. But I do. We were together every minute. I'll never forget it.

Yes.

They told me I could never have children. They swore I'd never be a mother. And then --

"I know," Laurel said, and stopped and took a cake to quiet herself. There wasn't much she could do about the other voice. She'd lived with it for so long, she supposed it couldn't disappear right away just because its user was dead.

But, oh, to eat in privacy, in peace! To eat slowly, savoring, knowing that no one would call out to her for the time or a new magazine or help getting up just as she'd taken her first bite.

Laurel?

No. She wasn't needed anymore. Wasn't necessary.

Free.

Laurel finished her cake and had another one. Cloying, sticky things, now beginning to melt into one another after sitting out for so long. Funeral baked sweetmeats. And they were all she'd eaten today. Her stomach protested the belated attention.

You've got to take care of yourself. For both of our sakes.

She crammed another one into her mouth, teeth gritting through unadulterated sugar,

All you have is your health

then stood up, wiping her fingers on the front of her dress. She'd never wear it again; it ought to serve *some* use.

Time to get to work.

Packing was simple, since Laurel was getting rid of almost everything. She'd been paring down her own possessions since her mother first took ill, and was surprised at how much space they still took up, how many of the boxes she'd bought were filled with them. Clothing, dishes, books. She marked each one with what it contained and which charity it should be given to.

See what a good person I am?

Haven't I been a good mother to you?

She finished her own things, the house things. Sorted, wrapped, boxed. Then there was only her mother's left. By then it was nearly dark. She didn't turn on the lights, though. Not yet.

Instead, Laurel went and got the bottle of champagne she'd bought the day before. Would have stolen, really, if she'd thought she could get away with it. What if someone saw her making such a purchase on such a day? She who had never taken a drink in her life? And cham*pagne*? Wine at the wake, all right, but *this* --

It's for my health.

Oh, well, of course.

She had to use her toothbrush glass to drink it, which might have accounted for the less-than-uplifting taste. Carbonated mouthwash. She made a face but didn't pour it out. It didn't matter if she didn't like it. The point was that she was now a woman who drank champagne.

In the half-light, she went through her mother's clothes. Pretty, frivolous, strong. In decent shape, considering how old they were -- most of them from before Laurel was born. They still looked good.

But they smelled. Fake flowers and something powdery and unpleasant and indefinable, claustrophobic. Her mother's perfume battling it out with her mother's illness, neither quite winning, neither willing to surrender.

What a tiny waistline!

They said I could never be a mother. But then I had you.

Shut the box, tape the box, label the box. Have another drink, I'm buying.

These didn't go to the women's shelter Laurel's things did. She was giving them to a local Jewish thrift store. Why, she wasn't sure. Her father hadn't been observing -- his family didn't even care that he'd married a semi-Christian. But Laurel liked the idea of it. A good Jewish wife getting some innocent, pretty pleasure. Or a retro-fashion teenager who knew how to poke around in odd corners for a bargain.

Laurel touched the fine fabrics regretfully. She could have sold these herself. The money, always the money -- but she wasn't avaricious, she just didn't like waste. And it was a waste to give away something that could be sold, especially after she'd just spent so much. Everything for today had been more than she expected. But selling took time, and it would have been so easy for someone to find out.

A flare of bright, brief anger, and she poured champagne over it. She'd been taking care of her mother for how many years now, working at a job she didn't even like because it paid well, putting aside thoughts of school. No one blinked an eye at that, even when her mother had been strong as two horses. With her fine arts degree and her Cordelia voice and her friends in all the right places, she could have found some kind of work. Ornamental functionary for some big company. Laurel knew that kind of job: the less you do, the more you make. But no. Everyone had taken for granted that Laurel would take care of her mother, because she was used to being taken care of.

And Laurel certainly wasn't.

They said I could never be a mother.

"They were right," Laurel snapped.

But let Laurel try to get any kind of return on those years, and she'd immediately be damned as the most dutiless of daughters. Never mind how much she'd laid out for the funeral. No one had even offered to help. That was her job, her responsibility. Always. Who else's could it be? She was an only child.

They said --

"Stop it!"

Her voice echoed flatly in the dim room. No, this wasn't right. She shouldn't be spending her first night of freedom sitting in the dark sparring with old words.

Laurel moved through the apartment and switched on all of the lights, every one. She was surprised at how bright the place could be. Her mother hadn't liked light. Dimness was more flattering to a woman past a certain age.

In the pitiless glare, Laurel could see faint signs of age in the clothes she was handling. She felt the same surprise she had on seeing her mother laid out at the funeral. Still lovely, still timeless, but -- worn. Prettiness just this side of quaint.

Laurel shut the last box and taped it up.

Say old-fashioned, rather.

Her mother would have hated to hear that word applied to herself. But what else could you call a woman who lived off of her daughter rather than lifting a finger to do for herself?

Vindictive?

Her mother looking at her from across the room. No one else ever saw that stare. No one else saw her without a smile. Let the phone ring, the door echo behind a knock, Laurel's father walk into the room, and her face would shift magically, showing no trace of what had been there a moment ago. Laurel didn't think her mother even knew what she was doing. No one could be that good an actress. She showed whatever she felt, and what she felt when she was alone with Laurel was

They told me I'd never have children. Swore I couldn't. That's the only reason I got married. Your father knew and he said he didn't care. We wouldn't have children, we'd just have each other. Just have fun. And then --

"Then I came along," Laurel said, writing HADASSAH THRIFT SHOP with a thick black marker. The same story, over and over again. Like a child's bedtime ritual. Only this one was never grown out of.

Your father cried when he saw you. Kept going on about the new life. He didn't understand I only wanted the old one.

I want my life back, damn it.

You took my life. I want it back.

Laurel stood up abruptly and went into the living room, taking the bottle with her. She sat on the worn couch under all the bright light and had another drink.

That last bit was a little much, wasn't it? Her mother hadn't actually said that, had she?

Well, it didn't matter. Her mother wasn't saying anything anymore. And if she were, the words would fade away with time, with nothing to support them. Had to.

"I supported you," Laurel said. "Maybe I took your life, but you lived off me and that's the same thing."

After you were born, nothing was ever the same.

Yes, that was more like it. That sounded familiar. One of those lines her mother could use no matter who was in the room. And only Laurel would know what it really meant.

"It's a good thing I came along after all, though, isn't it?" she asked. "Somebody had to take care of you. The man with all the fun in his pocket didn't stay around long enough to do the job right, did he?"

Oh, but that hurt. She'd loved her father; he'd loved her. Really thought it was wonderful when she was born. Didn't even care that she wasn't a boy, even when people teased him. He'd been proud of her, just for being his daughter. A good girl.

"Take care of your mother. Be good."

"I will."

And then he was gone and she'd mourned him, properly, almost happy to have something so normal to do. She could be just plain sad because her just plain sweet father was gone. Nothing to it.

Laurel swallowed more champagne. It went down a little easier now.

She looked at the ring on her finger. She was glad that it only fit on her right pinky. Wearing her mother's wedding ring on her own wedding finger would have been a bit much.

Not that she was going to wear it long. As soon as she was in another city, somewhere no one would possibly recognize it, she was going to sell it. At a good place, too. Somewhere she'd get some real money. It was a good ring. Valuable, she was sure of it. Anything that heavy had to be worth something. Her father wouldn't have bought something cheap. Certainly her mother wouldn't have worn it.

Ironic, that everyone talked about the dress and no one noticed that the ring was missing. Of course, her mother had lost so much weight, she'd taken the thing off a lot herself rather than have it rattling around on her hand. When she took a bath, when she was sleeping or playing those endless games of solitaire.

She'd been wearing it when Laurel took it, true. But it had slipped off easily enough.

Laurel had been a little nervous when everyone started shuffling past her mother's body to say their last farewells. Surely that empty circle around her finger would be glaringly obvious. But no one saw it. Why would they be looking there, anyway?

Laurel took the ring off for a moment. It felt like her mother's finger around her own, a cold tiny grip. But there was nowhere else safe to put it; nowhere she could be sure she wouldn't lose it. And she had to hang on to it long enough to turn it into money. It was her freedom.

I want it back.

"You can't have it. I need it."

Laurel was going to move to somewhere no one knew her. Her lease was month-to-month; she'd already given notice. The brief leave of absence from her work would be extended into a regretful resignation. No one would be surprised that she had to get away. No one would blame her. How could she live alone in this place?

How, indeed.

She could find somewhere small and cozy to live, just for herself. She could find work she'd really want to get up in the morning and do. Maybe she'd go back to school.

But most of all, she'd be going somewhere that she could stop keeping the big secret.

My mother? Oh, she passed away some time ago. No, it's all right. I hated her.

(No, too extreme. That would make people uncomfortable even if they hadn't known her mother.)

My mother and I aren't close. Never have been.

My mother and I had our differences.

My mother died in childbirth.

No one would ever know any different.

She remembered once, just once, she'd made the mistake of telling someone the truth. She was very young and it was so hard, carrying the secret all by herself. Keeping it from her father, because it would hurt him to know that his family wasn't what he thought it was. And so she'd told. Just once.

"I don't like my mother."

"I don't like mine either."

"And my mother doesn't like me."

Awed silence. They'd been whispering together, out on the playground away from all the other children and only five minutes left of recess, and it had seemed so safe. Susan. Her best friend and she lived far away. Far enough that she had to take the bus to school, anyway. And so they only played together at school, talked on the phone, and both of them said they wished they could go to each other's houses but Laurel didn't mean it. She liked things just the way they were.

Susan believed her. She was shocked, but she believed her.

Then Laurel's mother told her that she had to have a birthday party.

Didn't ask her if she wanted one. Told her she was having one. Laurel's mother was sketchy on the details of parenting, not having made a study of them. She didn't always get them right. And one day for some reason she figured out that kids had birthday parties and had all their friends over and played games. Maybe Laurel's father had said something. And how could Laurel say no?

She'd had to invite Susan. Word would have gotten around too easily. *You had a party? Why didn't I get to come?*

If Laurel was going to lose her anyway, she might as well at least get a present out of it.

The day came, and everything Laurel dreaded came to pass. She wore her new dress and had plenty of presents, already, even before anyone got there, and everyone could see them, lined up on the kitchen table. The house was perfect, immaculate, decorated. There were games and balloons and everyone got a special little treat to take home just for being so nice and coming to the party.

And Laurel's mother was enchanting. Wiping spills, telling jokes, patting heads, making sure everyone took turns. *Oh, Susan, what a pretty paint set! Laurel, think of all the pictures you can paint with that!*

Beautiful. Obviously enjoying herself. Flushed with triumph.

Haven't I been a good mother to you?

Laurel and her best friend still played together after that - at school, as always. But it was awkward. Susan was obviously baffled. And Laurel hated her for not getting it without Laurel's having to explain. Which she didn't, of course. Even if she'd had the words, she wouldn't have tried. She'd learned.

Mothers didn't hate their children.

Laurel sipped more champagne and realized she was beginning to feel just a bit fuzzy. It wasn't unpleasant.

She could say whatever she wanted now. Soon. Tonight was the last night of silence, the last night of lying.

She'd sell this ring and maybe someday she'd be given another like it. By someone she could tell the truth to and know he could believe her. No one would be there to tell him otherwise.

My mother and I don't get along. Didn't.

My mother died, and, well, it was a relief more than anything else.

Words still couched in conventionality, still more than she'd ever been able to say before.

My mother --

They told me I could never be a mother.

My mother and I --

Why did I have to be a mother?

She --

You wouldn't leave me alone for a minute. I'll never forget that. I never had a life again after you were born.

It was a relief when --

It was a relief when they told me I couldn't be a mother.

I --

And then --

Enough. Enough enough enough.

Laurel stood up, surprised to find herself a little wobbly on her feet. It was full dark behind the curtains, outside the lights. She hadn't eaten anything like a real meal today, but she wasn't hungry. She was tired. She'd been working hard and she wanted to sleep. Deep, uninterrupted sleep. The balm of hurt minds, and all that.

She took the phone off the hook -- what a miracle that it hadn't rung already today -- and went into the bathroom, where there were still a few personal things left unpacked. The things she'd known she'd need, even if everything else got swept away in her grand fit of giving.

Hairbrush, toothbrush, comb.

And the pills.

Her mother's, of course. Heavy-duty painkillers. For toward the end, when there was nothing anyone could do for her.

I didn't take your life, Mother. I could have, but I didn't. Not even when you begged me to.

Of course she'd kept these locked away from her mother during the day, when she was at work. And there was always a friend or would-be beau there to help, to make sure Laurel's mother was all right and had everything she needed. And didn't have anything she didn't need.

The bottle was three-quarters full. Plenty there to help Laurel along to the first decent night's sleep she'd have in --how long? Too long to count. No calls, no voices. Sweet, dreamless sleep. And then tomorrow. The first day in her life that she'd ever looked forward to. Well, the second.

She started toward the bedroom and then hesitated. So tired, but she was filthy, too -- ink all over her hands from folding newspaper around cups and dishes, dust and grime from all the rest. Perspiration. She wouldn't want to wake up with herself like this. Not on the first day.

A bath, then. A quick one now, and a more leisurely one in the morning.

She started the water and stripped her dirty clothes off into the hamper, then slipped into the tub. Hot, hot water. Heavenly.

Just to make sure she didn't stay in too long, she took a pill, swallowed it with a little more champagne, which was beginning to taste good now. An acquired taste.

Yes, very good. She leaned her head back, letting her hair get wet. Champagne tasted very good after all, and it made you feel -- just lovely.

Her mother never drank. Maybe she had at all those parties she didn't get to go to any more after Laurel was born, but not after, not during Laurel's lifetime. Not that Laurel knew of.

Laurel looked at the familiar name on the bottle of pills. Her mother had liked these. Pretended not to, feigned indifference, but Laurel could see the light in her eyes, the faint greedy gleam, at medicine time.

She tried another one. Two? They were small.

They *were* good. Made your troubles seem so distant. And shut up all the voices, and replaced them with a lovely hum.

Hummy hum hum.

Laurel giggled. She was starting to sound like Winnie the Pooh.

But really, why *didn't* her mother drink? Not now, of course, but when she'd had the chance? Life would have been easier for everyone that way. She would have felt better, and Laurel would have had something definite and acceptable to pin on her.

My mother drinks and I hate her.

Now, now. The voice was gone, all gone, at last. No replacing it with another one just as unpleasant.

But if drinking makes you feel better, that means you felt bad in the first place. And for her mother to admit that even to herself would be a little too close to admitting why. Which she couldn't do. Not nice. Mothers didn't hate their children.

She should have put some music on. Before she got in the tub. Then she'd have something real to listen to, something happy. She wouldn't feel so lonely.

One more pill might crank the humming up a tune, actually, if you listened closely for it. Sweet, like the pills. She'd thought they were a little bitter at first they were sweet now. Like swallowing vitamin C she was a kid.

Oh, it felt so good, so good, so good to be alone.

And yet she was lonely. How did that work?

It didn't matter. Nothing mattered. She'd get a night's sleep, and then tomorrow she'd get up and make batch of new friends and never feel lonely again.

Really, she ought to go to bed now. Early to bed, early to rise. And she was so sleepy.

Too sleepy to scrub. She should have put some bubble bath in. Even some dish soap. (You're soaking in it.) Then she'd be getting clean just by sitting here Lying. Whatever.

Well. Time to get out. Time enough to get clean tomorrow.

Laurel started to sit up and her head spun like a globe inside a globe.

Oh. So this was why people didn't drink. Hard to do much else if it made you feel like this.

But this couldn't be just the champagne. She hadn't had *that* much.

She fumbled by the side of the tub for the glass to check (but how many glasses?) and found the pill bottle instead. Almost empty.

Really? She didn't remember taking so many.

It's just as easy to be careful.

Maybe not, Mother.

But now it was really time to get out. Baths and drinking and pills didn't mix. She'd heard that somewhere. She was pretty sure.

But she couldn't get up. She really couldn't.

A crashing sound. Echoes. No, nothing bad. Just the pill bottle (almost empty, how could it be so loud?) hitting the tile floor.

Now she was really alone.

Well, she'd just rest here for a while. Just until she felt better. Just until bedtime.

A twist of panic and weak sanity. She couldn't stay here, not like this. It wasn't safe.

She didn't drink, and she'd been drinking. She'd never taken anything stronger than aspirin, and now she'd taken who knew how many -- what were they called? Didn't matter. Prescription only. Handed out to those who had nothing left to worry about. Side effects not an issue.

She had to get up.

She couldn't move.

She needed help.

All right. She couldn't get out to call anyone, but surely someone would call her.

But the phone was off the hook, because she hadn't wanted people wondering why she wasn't answering. Worrying. And she'd told everyone she'd need a little time alone. A polite hint to back off that most seemed to have taken.

And no one at work would worry, because she wasn't due back in for at least another week. And she was friendly with everyone there, but not *friends*-friendly. Not enough that anyone would think to check up on her.

Oh, no. Please no.

One last try and this time nothing moved. The water was cooling around her and she could barely feel it. Even her thoughts were sluggish, fueled only by panic.

But I'm supposed to get out! This was my chance to get out!

You two were inseparable.

Another voice, an old one. One that had been to a lot of funerals.

You were never apart.

Never, never.

She thought of being found, here, here, like this. The pills, the drink. Her apartment clean. No food but the leftovers from the funeral, not even breakfast for the next day. And everything she -- they -- owned packed in boxes, marked. Please give me to charity. Remember me when this you see.

And the old gossips at it again.

She was her whole life. Poor dears, they just couldn't live without each other.

Well, at least they weren't apart long.

No! Not like that! Death, all right, but not to be remembered like that!

The devoted daughter. Never kept her mother waiting, even now.

It's not true! she struggled to say to someone, anyone. I didn't do this to be with her. I only ever wanted to escape.

And knew she never would, as the drowning began in earnest.

Little Voices

Matt Doeden

Sometimes Susan heard voices in the attic. It was a place she dared not go, a dark and fearful place of ominous regret. It was a place that beckoned her, one too much a part of her to be shoved to the periphery of her perpetual depression.

She thought there might be ghosts up there, in that attic. Angry ghosts. Ghosts that could never forgive her. Ghosts of her children, those lovely babies she'd let die.

They'd said those beautiful twins were evil -- red eyes, twisted, deformed limbs, banshee cries -- unnatural, born of some cruel genetic flaw; whispers of demons amid masked shudders.

She had let them die. Hadn't been strong enough to stop it. And now they waited in her attic. Those beautiful children she'd never seen. Now they waited for their mother.

She stood atop the old staircase with fingers gripping the dusty knob that crowned the oak railing. She stared at the ceiling where the attic latch dangled just within her reach. This was her barrier. This latch, this final bit of separation from the ghosts that stalked her. She'd stood here before, caught between fear and resolve, a dozen times at least. Today the voices were too insistent. Today, she had to pull it.

She lunged for the latch, let the sting wrap about her extended middle finger and rested it there, quivering, tremors of wafting regret and encroaching madness overwhelming her muscles.

She had to do it, had to pull lest she fall completely mad. Had to silence those tiny voices that tormented her, haunting her during the night, laughing and mocking during her lonely daylight hours.

Her hand found cool purpose gave the slightest of tugs. The latched popped a ghastly creak of rusted hinges as gravity finished the task. Three distinct thumps as a frail ladder offered passage upward.

A stale gust of decay, cold fingers of winter invading from above. Tiny voices, sharp and piercing, no longer muffled by layers of wood and insulation. Angry demon voices bent on torment and revenge against such a wicked mother.

Would they believe her? Could they believe that she loved them still, that she'd been drugged and without will, that she thought of them constantly, wrenching her soul with sorrow and tears?

Could they forgive her? Such a wretched mother, unable to save her beautiful babies from the uncaring hands of doctors, nurses...

Their father.

The whispers, maddeningly just beyond the range of her comprehension, seemed to thrive on her regret, her ebbing terror. She felt did not see two lancing pairs of red eyes from the darkness, bloody shapes without form waiting, waiting.

Laughter.

Her knee cracked as she placed a foot onto the ladder's bottom rung. Two more trembling steps up. Her head rose out of the comforting reach of glowing lamplight below, ascending into the attic's preternatural gloom. Taped up cardboard boxes, the smell of decay and a packaged, forgotten past. Her breathing grew loud and intrusive against the hollowness of the place. She was aware of her body's every sound. But most of all, she was aware of the voices.

They grew nearer, their chattering more fervent. She felt eyes from all around, a rageful lust that beckoned from just beyond the column of light that feebly reached up from below.

"Hello, little ones." Her voice was weak, uncertain.

A shuffling, like tiny feet against the floorboards, echoed from all directions, beyond the shadowy dank her eyes could not penetrate. Whispers and footsteps, peering eyes.

She took two final steps upward, hoisted herself up by the edge of a splintered floorboard. A long, excruciating silence -- judgement, perhaps. Then, the familiar creaking of the house's front door, the cold plop of a briefcase against the kitchen table.

"Daddy's home, little ones, " she whispered.

Footsteps below, a faint whistling -- <u>Oh Suzanna</u>.

"Are you upstairs, honey?" a voice called. So false, so full of transparent pretense. This man who'd surrendered the lives of these precious children, this man who pretended to love her, pretended to care, forever pretended things would be better.

The time for pretense was over.

Whispers rose from the confusion: *Mother. Mother. Mother.* Her heart swelled -- her babies loved her, forgave her, understood her role, too, had been the victim. Those beautiful little ghosts hated him. Not her.

A vein pulsed behind her eyes as rage crept in over her senses, triggering in her some repressed, visceral mother's instinct. Unconsciously, she scooped up a forgotten bundle at her feet, slid quietly out of the attic and down the staircase. The old stairs did not creak as she descended -- they knew her too well.

The bedroom door stood closed, but unlatched, at the foot of the stairs. She pushed it open gently with her free hand, stepped inside, carefully sheltering her bundle in the other. The murderer stood in the adjoined bathroom, faucet running. She stepped softly to the bed, laid down her bundle, and sat beside it.

A moment later, he emerged, smiling. "You're up, " he said, smelling of minty aftershave. "Are you feeling better?"

He leaned over to kiss her, froze.

He stared at them for the longest of moments, some awkward disbelief, as if his stare might wipe the murder from his eyes. He staggered fell back, grasping the wall as if he lacked the simple strength to stand. His mouth opened, but he said nothing. His face grew pale.

"Is this the way a father greets his family?" she asked sarcasm sweet upon her lips. The loving, ghastly whispers encouraged her from behind.

Mother, Mother, Mother.

"My God, Susan, what have you done?"

"What have *you* done!" she snapped, scooping the corpses from the bed and thrusting them into his face. They hung there, joined at the shoulder, shriveled, hairless heads, tiny hands and feet jutting out from all the wrong places, sunken eye sockets and open, hollow mouths. Dry and cracked and reeking of death. "You killed them! You killed my babies!"

He was shaking, tears welling up in the soft brown of his eyes "Put it down, Susan." His voice quivered.

"You said my beautiful babies did not deserve to live."

He swatted her arm. The decaying corpses flew from her grasp, landing with a sickening *thwop* against the half-open bathroom door.

"Stop!" he shouted, his voice regaining its masculine bass. "They weren't going to live -- don't you remember? They couldn't live, Susan. They were already dead."

"No, " she protested, throwing out a fist in rage. In it she grasped cool metal, something large and heavy and blunt. She recalled neither holding it nor exactly what it was. The object struck his nose, fell squarely and with more power than she'd expected. Something popped. A distant pang of worry.

But this was how her beautiful babies had felt as he beat and murdered them. And the voices, slightly muffled, echoed, *Mother, Mother, Mother.*

She lashed out again, again, feeling the give of his flesh beneath her anger. He did not resist, did not defend himself against her onslaught. Those tiny, tortured voices in her mind seethed, boiling up like a cauldron as she leveled blow after enraged blow.

Soon, and again without her immediate knowledge, it was the joined corpse of her babies she clutched as she punished him, scraps of their flesh caught beneath her ragged fingernails, broken, severed bits of their bodies scattered horribly about the room.

And her husband lay still, blood dripping from his mouth and nose. He did not move, only bled. She fell still, unconsciously dropping the brittle, broken corpses.

She watched him for hours, waiting for him to look back at her, waiting for his soft eyes to comfort her, to tell her everything was all right. She loved him so.

But he did not move, and Susan found herself growing tired. She staggered from the room, closing the door behind her. She sat alone in the dark, those ghastly voices again seducing her from within.

Only days later when a man came knocking at the front door did she wonder where her husband might have gone. She watched the well-dressed man from the window as he knocked. Such a strange time for a visit.

She opened the door cautiously.

"Hello," the man said, holding a hat against his slick raincoat. From outside wafted in the wet smell of rain, of earthworms.

Mr. Devitt, what brings you here?"

"We've missed Steve at work, Mrs. Brenkford. Is he here?"

"Let me check," she answered, gesturing him inside the darkness. "Have you seen the babies yet? They're just gorgeous."

The Buried Past

Phil Locascio

The haggard, thin-faced lawyer, Darrell Demety, cleared his throat and continued with the reading of the last will and testament of John Simon Hathers, Jr.

"To my youngest son, Lon," Demety looked up at Lon with an embarrassing scowl. Lon held his breath. He knew there was an ocean of hatred and disgust between him and his father. Nothing could change that now. But his good for nothing, drunken older brother, Junior, and his callous, spiteful sister Sarah had already been awarded two million dollars each. Damned if he wasn't going to get his.

Demety started again, "To my youngest son, Lon, who has, through the years, been a source of great pain to his mother and immense disappointment to me, I leave a single, sealed envelope, the contents of which are to be read by Lon, and Lon alone, in private, immediately following the reading of the will."

The room fell silent. Lon frowned at Demety. "What is this, Demety, some kind of sick joke?"

"I swear to you Lon, I knew this to be your father's intention but as God is my judge, I do not know the contents of the letter." From the upper pocket of his aged suit coat, Demety produced the white envelope and handed it across the table to Lon.

"Looks as if father's made a fool of you Lon, eh? The final coup de grace, if you will."

Junior blushed, the juicy words slithering off his tongue.

"Go to hell, Junior!" Lon retorted.

Sarah feigned sympathy with all the warmth of a viper. "Oh come now Lon. Did you really think father would be so forgiving after all that's happened between you two?"

"I don't know what I expected but I came here with a forgive and forget attitude:"

"How appropriate a time for you to want to forgive and forget," she chuckled sarcastically.

Lon softly spoke, his anger rising. "So, this is it, eh? The final humiliation! Well, fine. If father wants to take one last shot at me, fine! Who gives a damn! It'll be the last thing I ever have to do with this whacked-out family! Are we done, Demety?"

"Well actually no," sighed the old man. "There is one more caveat to the will which, for reasons unknown to me, John insisted I include." Demety paused as if, once again, embarrassed. "Under no circumstances is the body of my wife Eva, nor mine, ever to be exhumed *for* any reason whatsoever."

Sarah blurted out a guttural laugh. "Why the hell would anyone want to exhume their bodies?"

"Demety, father did die of natural causes, didn't he?" asked Junior.

The attorney looked rebuffed. "Of course. Why, Bailey and I were with him right to the end. The cancer was everywhere. Look, this stipulation was put in when Eva died eight years ago and John would never tell me what it was about."

Lon turned to Bailey, butler for the estate since ... well since Moses parted the Red Sea. The frail, hunched man peered through the two tiny slits that perforated the wrinkled lines of his face. Lon detected a look of amusement.

"Look here Bailey," Lon said, "what the hell do you know about this nonsense?"

"Oh Master Lon, I wouldn't be privy to such matters." After Lon turned away, the look of amusement twisted into a sneer.

Lon grabbed his letter from the table and stood defiantly. He had a good mind to open it up right there and read it out loud but why cause himself further embarrassment. Mumbling in disgust, he left the room.

Bailey had his coat waiting for him at the door. Lon snatched it out of the old man's hand and opened the door to leave. Then he remembered something. "By the way, you old fool, why the hell did you book my room for a whole week? Surely you knew this would take no longer than a day."

"Well I thought maybe you would want to visit for a while longer – "

"Oh sure, with my wonderful family, huh! I'm out of here first thing tomorrow morning." He stepped through the doorway and headed for his car.

The stiff white collar chaffed the butler's neck as he turned to watch Lon walk off. His piercing eyes squinted through the bright sun. His look turned devious. "I don't think so, Master Lon," he chuckled. "I don't think so."

Lon screeched out of the parking lot. His little plan hadn't worked. Now Lon Hathers, son of one of the richest men in New York State, could live out the rest of his stinking life scratching and clawing. He took out his anger on the gas pedal cursing under his breath the man he hated now more than ever.

When he got back to his room he angrily grabbed a beer and ripped open the letter. "OK you son-of-a-bitch, go ahead, take your last shot."

Dear Lon,

Well, how did the reading go? A tad upset are you? I'm glad you decided to read this because your greedy little hopes have not been dashed.

Cheer up, I have good news for you. I'm leaving you two million dollars too, just like Sarah and Junior. Oh, make no mistake if it was up to me I wouldn't leave you a dime. But your dear mother, you remember her don't you Lon? You know, the woman who bore you, whose heart you broke. The woman who after you left was never the same. The woman who waited for years for you to return while you went on your merry, selfish way, too proud to call or write or visit or nothing: Well she made me promise, on her deathbed no less, that I would treat you no differently than the others and I'm keeping my word. I have left you two million dollars. It's sitting in a safe deposit box in your name right now. All you have to do is go get it.

Do you know what your mother's last dying words were? She uttered your name and wished she could have seen *you* Just one *more time before she* went. She was crying, Lon. Crying for a son too proud to even attend her damn funeral!

Well, Lon I'm going to grant her last wish. You want your two million? The answer to where you can find it is in an envelope, a tiny envelope, cradled in your sweet mother's hands. Those precious, ivory hands buried so long ago.

By the way the safe deposit box is in a very obscure bank in a very obscure place. Trust me, you will never find it on your own.

Ah ... you understand now the purpose of that caveat to the will about our bodies not being exhumed. If I were you, I wouldn't tell Sarah or Junior about this. They might just make sure that caveat is held to. Besides, you couldn't really trust them, could you? They might decide to go digging themselves some night, you never know? No, I'm afraid you're on your own on this one Lon.

So you go see your dear mother and please, give her a kiss for me.

All my love,
John Simon Hathers Jr.

Lon slumped into the chair, the letter falling from his hands. He was mad, Lon thought, mad. Would he have the remains of the only thing ever truly loved desecrated to appease his vile, demented revenge? Lon gazed down at the letter as if it carried the plague.

Father was right about one thing. It was his pride that had kept him away all those years, even when mother was sick. He remembered back to the last time he had seen his parents. He had taken $2,000 from his father's stash. The wads of cash he kept around the house just in case he needed it to wave in the face of some prospective rival. Humiliation, father had always been good at humiliation.

Lon remembered his final parting words, "I hope I never see either of you again." His father viciously retorting, "You'll be back. You may not give a damn about us but you can't leave the money. We'll see you again, you son-of-a-bitch."

Those parting words, that's what had kept him away. He harbored no real ill will towards his mother. She had just been caught in the middle. But father - that was a different story.

However, Lon was getting too old to care about pride anymore. He wanted his rightful share. But not this way, this ghoulish, twisted way.

Outside, the western sky glowed red as the last rays of the sun fell below the horizon.

The dying twilight shone down on a gently sloping hill on the outskirts of town, on a gray, weathered headstone that leaned slightly from years of settling. The headstone of Eva Hathers.

Lon did not sleep well that night. Bizarre questions raced through his head. How long would it take to dig up a grave? After eight years, what, if anything, would remain of the corpse? Would one even be able to open the casket? What if the whole thing was just a sick joke?

In the morning he loaded the car and headed for the hotel counter to check out. On the way he detoured into the restaurant. The caffeine from the rich, dark coffee inflamed his already boiling blood.

When he finally reached the desk, the clerk asked, "Checking out, Sir?"

Lon paused, a quizzical look on his face. "Ho ... no ...but tell me, where might I be able to purchase a shovel?"

At 11:45 p.m. Lon guzzled down the last swallow from a warm can of beer. He sat parked behind a dilapidated shed across the road from Lakeview Cemetery. He was drunk, damn drunk and he was thankful he had not been pulled over by the squad car he had passed.

He got out, stumbled to the trunk and popped the lid. He took out the shovel, gloves and flashlight he had purchased. He grabbed one more beer. He would need it out there, he thought.

He ran across the empty road and dropped his things through the six foot iron grating that ran the length of the graveyard. He boosted himself up and began climbing the cold grating. Suddenly he heard a car speeding towards him down the dusty back road.

He climbed faster.

As he got to the top he saw the headlights cast his shadow onto a nearby headstone. He jumped to the ground and laid still. The car sped past, the radio blaring, kids, young punks, laughing, yelling, out for a joy ride. The car disappeared down the road; the dust billowed up behind it and then slowly settled to the ground.

Lon spotted the tall mausoleum where the family plots were and soon found his father's grave. Recently dug, it was void of grass. Directly to the left was the grave of his mother.

The cemetery was peaceful, the light from the 3/4 moon turned the marble stones chalky white. Lon set up his flashlight pointing it directly on the grave. A mild breeze bent the trees back and forth providing a layer of white noise for Lon to work through.

The fear began to well up inside him. "Forgive me mother," he mumbled as he rammed the shovel's head into the moist earth.

The top layer of ground was easy to remove due to the heavy rains of previous days. After the first foot or so however, he met with a thick, pasty clay. Every scoopful required heavy exertion. By the time he had dug down two feet he had to stop and catch his breath. He leaned against a nearby headstone and popped open his remaining beer.

The idleness, Lon soon discovered, allowed macabre thoughts to enter his head. To avert the panic he was feeling, he returned to his disgusting task. His intense nervousness and the alcohol running through his veins fueled him on. Scoopful after scoopful of earth was removed, deeper and deeper he thrust the shovel into the pit. Just when he felt he needed another rest, the shovel was stopped short by a solid object. Through the hole left, Lon saw glistening metal.

He began digging like a frightened dog trying to escape under a fence. The top of the casket was quickly exposed. He clawed with his hands trying to find the latch. He located it and pulled on it as hard as he could. It would not give way. He shook the casket and beat on the top of it and still the latch would not give. Filthy dirty and sweating profusely, he stood on top of the casket and jumped up and down. The thunderous booms reverberated in the dark pit like a tolling bell. He returned to the latch and finally it gave way. The lid popped up slightly. A small gushing sound, like a lover's whisper, emanated from inside the dark enclosure.

The hinges creaked and groaned but the wall of the hole was not dug out far enough to allow the lid to raise to a sufficient height. Lying over the coffin, Lon clawed desperately, digging away the earth that blocked the way. After digging the wall away, he returned to the casket. He tucked the flashlight under his arm and began raising the heavy, metal hood. As the lid reached chest level, he shifted the position of his hands and began pushing up with his palms. With a powerful last thrust, the last mound of dirt which blocked the opening fell away. The lid swung open and rocked back and forth on the rusty, squealing hinges.

Lon shined the flashlight into the box.

In a small room on the second floor of the mansion, Bailey poured himself another cup of tea. It was not unusual for him to awaken in the middle of the night. He wrapped his velvet robe tightly around his skinny frame to keep out the chill.

He gazed out the kitchen window to the east. The morning sun had not yet pierced the horizon. Slowly, he sat down and thought about the unfortunate occurrences of the last few days, the death of his gentleman, the funeral and that nasty business about the will.

Slowly, the lines of his face formed a lurid smile. He peered off across the sky in the general direction of Lakeview cemetery. He chuckled under his breath, "I wonder how Master Lon is coming along?"

The withered corpse that was his mother, rotting inside a lovely sky blue dress, leered up at Lon. A huge diamond broach sagged from above her breast. The dank stench of decay rose from the coffin encircling Lon as he gazed down. His mother's head was shrunken, the remains melded into the silky pillow. The face was almost entirely skeleton except for a few black patches that clung, here and there, to her skull. Her left eye, set in a blackened recess, glared out. The shriveled orb seemed locked on Lon. The vile stench and the vision of the mummy before him petrified Lon.

All that remained of his mother's hands was skeleton. Her wedding ring, now oversized on the bony finger, glistened in the glow of the flashlight sending prisms of yellow sparks all about the soft white padding. Through the rosary that draped across her hands, Lon could see a small yellowed envelope. He cautiously tried to pull it out but it was stuck in the death lock grip of the corpse. As he tried again, he exerted too much pressure on her left hand and two of her fingers fell away, crumbling into ash.

Lon jumped back and let out a stunned cry. Now in a panicked frenzy he grabbed at the envelope pulling it free. Black, decayed flesh stuck to the side of the brittle paper.

Lon's hands accidentally slipped from their hold on the coffin. The lid slammed down with a thunderous boom that shook the walls of his self-made crypt. He quickly pulled himself out of the hole and began clawing dirt back into the pit. To the east the first gleam of morning rose. Sweating and hysterical, Lon worked at a fevered pitch.

An owl hooted in the distance, a dog barked from afar, a low plane was approaching from the north. Lon had expended his last ounce of courage. He quickly grabbed up his things and ran for the car.

Twenty minutes later, his hands shaking, Lon sat at the table of his motel room. He ripped open the envelope. Inside was the key to a safe deposit box along with a typewritten note. It said, "Medville Savings and Loan, Medville, Pennsylvania. Box 377."

Lon felt relief for the first time since his ordeal had begun. After a shower and a change of clothes, he collapsed on the bed. The silent shroud of sleep engulfed him.

Lon awoke to someone knocking at the door. It took him a moment to gather his wits. "Yes," he mumbled.

"Mr. Hathers, it's the police. May I have a word with you?"

A stream of panic flooded his brain. He looked at the clock that read 4:35 p.m. "Eh, hold - hang on a moment."

Lon quickly looked around. Everything was in order, no telltale signs of what had occurred the night before. He quickly combed his hair in the mirror and went to the door. He took a deep breath, looked around once more to reassure himself and slowly opened the door halfway.

"Yes, I'm Lon Hathers. What can I do for you?"

"Mr. Hathers, I'm Sheriff Reins. May I come in for a moment?"

Through a gush of fright Lon replied, "Sure, come on in."

Reins took off his hat as he entered the room. Lon noticed him turn the long way as he came in as if to give the room a quick once over.

"Please," Lon said as he motioned towards the table.

Reins remained standing. "Mr. Hathers, I'm afraid there's been some trouble."

"Trouble, what kind of trouble?" Lon felt he gave a good impression of stupidity.

"Well I don't know what exactly to make of it your father's butler, he suggested that perhaps I should have a word with you about it." The officer looked over at the unmade bed. "You usually sleep this late in the day?" A suspicious tone hung on his words.

"No, no, I - I was just napping."

"I see. Well I called Luther over at the front desk and he said you hadn't checked out yet so I thought I'd come over. Come to think of it maybe I will sit down." Lon was aware of the quick scan the sheriff made of the room as he sat himself down.

The slightly paunchy officer laid down his cap and ran his hand through his thinning hair. "Would you mind telling me where you were last night, Mr. Hathers?"

The question stung Lon like a bee. He started to pace and then realized he didn't want to appear uneasy. He eased himself into the chair next to Reins. He moved the empty beer can that sat in front of the sheriff. Off to the right, he noticed the stained envelope and crinkled note.

"Last night? Last night I did nothing. I sat around here most of the night. I did go out for a bite to eat about seven, came back here, watched TV and went to bed."

"What time'd you go to bed?"

"I don't know, eleven or so. Look here, are you going to tell me what this is about?" Lon felt he might have been too overanxious.

"Well your father's gardener Mr. Shafer, he got up early this morning and took a bouquet of flowers out to your father's grave. When he got there, he noticed someone had been digging at your mother's grave."

"Digging at my mother's grave? What the hell do you mean?" Lon thought he sounded convincing.

"The grave's been dug up. Possibly all the way down to the casket. It had to happen last night cause Shafer was out there yesterday morning and nobody would try a damn fool thing like that in the daytime." Reins leaned back in his chair and peered across the table at Lon. Lon could tell the interrogation was about to begin. A tiny drop of sweat trickled down his neck.

"Bailey tells me you were pretty upset at the will reading. Care to tell me about it?"

Lon was glad he had the chance to tell the truth about something. "Yes, I was upset. I don't know if you know it or not but my father and I weren't exactly close. Yes I was mad at how I was treated in the will. But what has that got to do with this?"

Reins noticed the note on the table. Slowly he reached over, picked it up and began reading it. Lon's mind spun in a thousand directions. He breathed a sigh of relief as the sheriff pushed it aside with a look of unconcern.

"Is that your blue Taurus out there, Mr. Hathers?"

"Yes, why?" Lon replied.

Reins studied Lon once again. His eye's squinted slightly. "I been sheriff going on ten years now. I knew you and your father didn't get along. He told me all about it. Him and me, we was pretty close you know." Reins paused a moment and leaned back in his chair. "So, ... tell me ... what'd you need a shovel for?"

A jolt of fire ran up Lon's spine. Fireworks exploded in his head as he reached over and brushed off some crumbs from the edge of the table, stalling, his mind racing, desperately searching for an excuse. En shovel, what do you mean?"

"Luther told me you wanted to buy a shovel."

Lon cleared his throat. His pulse was on fire. He tried to think, focus, as a stampede of horses trampled across his mind. "Yah ... well I had some time to kill. I'm a gardener. I - I figured I could get one a little cheaper here than at home." Lon realized the ludicrous statement he had just made. He was tempted to try to repair it but decided not to say anymore about it. Instead, he attempted to change the subject. "Look here Reins, you don't mean to suggest I would dig up my own mother's grave do you? Why the hell would anyone want to do that?"

"The jewelry's my only guess. Everybody knows she was buried with a ton of it." An eerie silence fell over the room. Finally, Reins broke the spell. "This shovel you bought, is it out in your car?"

That damn shovel again: Lon's hands were tied. "Yes," he said as defiantly as possible.

The sheriff leaned in a little closer to Lon. "I don't suppose you'd want to show it to me, being as miffed as you are, now would you?"

Lon hesitated not knowing what to say. Slowly, a snicker trickling from his mouth, Reins stood up. He looked at the beer can on the edge of the table. "You always drink Miller, Mr. Hathers?"

"Sometimes, why?" A cold shudder turned in the pit of Lon's stomach as he realized the implication of the question.

"Seems our body snatcher or grave digger or whatever the hell he is likes Miller too. Left an empty can out there." Reins smiled with a wide, fake grin. Their eyes met and for a split second they read each other's thoughts. Then unexpectedly, Reins snickered, went for the door and stepped outside. Lon followed him out. The sheriff turned, nervously fidgeting with his cap.

"There is one other thing though, Mr. Hathers. You say you went to bed about eleven. Well," Reins chuckled as he spoke. "I was on duty last night and I passed a car ... oh about midnight I guess it was, only car on the road mind you, and I think that car could have been a blue Taurus and that car was headed out towards the cemetery. But you know I just wasn't paying all that much attention and to tell you the truth," Reins paused and gazed up at the sky. "I just can't for the life of me remember if it was or not. No sir, I surely can't."

The sheriff stopped fidgeting with his cap. He lifted his gaze to Lon, his eyes glaring like white hot pokers. This time he wasn't chuckling. "Your business is done in this town. You leave here today and you don't never come back, you hear me. I don't know all of what this is about and a part of me don't want to know but in this county our dead rest in peace. So you pack your bags and you take your shovel and you get in your blue Taurus and you get the hell out of town. And if I ever see you around here again or there's ever anymore trouble at the estate or the cemetery, then I'm gonna come looking for you. You hear me."

With a spiteful smile he tipped his cap to Lon. "Now you have a good day Mr. Hathers."

Lon was packed and gone within an hour. He made Medville by 9:00 p.m. and found a motel room. He was at the bank waiting when the guard opened the door.

Lon reached the counter where a young blonde was counting receipts. "I have a safe deposit box here, number 377, I'd like to enter it please."

The girl asked his name and Lon produced his driver's license. "Let's see," she remarked searching through the card file. "Yes, here it is, 377, one of our larger boxes. Please follow me."

Lon's heart began to race as he was led down the aisle into a private room. "Please wait here. I'll be right back with your box."

An eternity went by and finally the girl returned. She carried the box like a waitress would a tray. She had to stoop down to lay it down on the table.

"Will there be anything else, Mr. Hathers?"

No ... no thank you," he replied.

"Very well. You may want to lock the door after I leave, it's up to you but we always recommend it to our customers."

She turned and walked out. Lon quickly locked the door and fumbled in his pocket for the key. Panting with excitement, he unlocked the box and lifted the lid. The box contained a single hand-written note. Lon immediately recognized the handwriting.

Dear Lon,

Congratulations. I never thought you would have had the guts to make it this far. How was your visit with mother? Pleasant I hope? Now, as I promised, you can collect your two million dollars.

No Lon, the money's not here but all you have to do is go get it. It's waiting for you in a safe deposit box just as I promised. It's just not this safe deposit box.

You see, Lon, I want to see you one last time too. You'll find the key and the location of your little treasure chest nestled in the palm of my hands. Come see me anytime you like, you're always welcome. I'll be waiting for you. I'm just dying to see you, Lon.

With deepest regards,
John Simon Hathers Jr.

Down the hall the cashier heard a loud shriek, a demented half-laugh, half-scream followed by a low, somber moan. She turned to a second cashier who had heard it also. Shrugging her shoulders, she laughed and went back to counting the previous day's receipts.

The Lovers

Edo van Belkom

The woman fell to her knees and broke the hard crust of the earth with the sharp jagged tips of her fingers.

Somewhere beneath the ground was her mate, trapped inside the tight pine box, crying out in the darkness.

"I'm here, lover," she said in a gravel-throated voice. "I'm here."

She dug into the earth with both hands now tossing aside great mounds of dirt at a fantastic pace.

The hole rapidly deepened.

He was in there, she knew, clawing at the walls on all sides, calling out her name and wondering why she'd left him alone.

"You'll never be alone again," she whispered. "I'll never leave you. Not now. Not ever."

Her hardened fingers struck something solid. The casket. She increased her efforts twofold, wildly brushing the dirt from the top of the box and throwing it aside.

The piles of earth surrounding the hole grew larger.

"Soon, my love. We will be together." Her voice had become even more hoarse and ragged.

Suddenly, there was a rap from inside the box, the dull thudding knock of a knuckle against the lid.

She felt like crying, she felt like laughing. He was in there and he was all right.

She wedged the fingers of her right hand into the tight space between the casket and the surrounding earthen wall and pulled upwards. The lid did not budge. For a moment it seemed as if she'd come so far only to fail. She raised her head and let out a raspy wail of exasperation.

There was another knock from within.

With a second try, she pulled with almost inhuman strength and the lid moved. Dust and earth broke away from the walls as the lid slowly rose up, pulled from above... and pushed from within.

She looked into the casket, saw his deep, dark eyes and fell in love all over again.

He looked up at her and smiled.

She moved back from the edge of the grave, stood up and tried to wipe the crusted dirt from her knees.

He rose from the casket slowly, looking like a cat awakening from a long, deep sleep. He stretched his arms skyward, raising up to the full light of the moon. His time-stiffened joints them snapped and popped like dead twigs.

"My love?" he said.

"Yes," she said, giving her hand to him and helping him from the grave.

"How long has it been?"

"Too long."

She spread her arms wide and brought them together around the body of her long lost love.

She opened her mouth in preparation for a kiss, and her mottled gray cheeks fell away from her face like October leaves.

His lips felt good against hers as they kissed, parchment-tongues scraping together in clouds of dust as they probed deeply into the mouth of the other.

His hard bony fingers caressed her cold rotting flesh. Her dead dried breast felt wanton as it crinkled against his touch. She could almost feel heat rising up from down there, between her legs.

He broke off the kiss.

"I knew you'd come back to me," he said.

"I couldn't bare being without you any longer."

"You have me now, forever."

She let out a sigh. Her dusty breath fell to the ground like snow.

"After you," he said, making a wide sweeping gesture with his bony arm.

She hesitated.

"Of course." A pause. "How stupid of me."

He lifted her up into his arms, holding her there effortlessly as he stepped down into grave. He laid her down in the casket, then joined her.

The casket lid slowly squeaked shut.

A rat peered over the edge of the grave, wrinkled its nose and waddled away.

In the darkness, a single muffled giggle broke the continuous whispering of the wind between the trees.

Summer House

Calvin K. Bricker

The old house was disconsolate, like a mother bereft of her children. It used to be their summerhouse, but his family didn't vacation there any more. Not since his sister had died thirteen years ago.

Greg had driven upstate alone just to see the place, but there wasn't much left worth looking at. He parked his car by the roadside, got out, and strode through the withered timothy grass. The warm breeze smelled of rain. Unseen crows cawed raucously in the nearby oaks as he stepped onto the dilapidated porch.

Planks nailed across the door frame barred entrance to the house. He tore away the rotted wood and cast it on the sagging porch floor. Termites skittered from the porous chunks.

When he pulled the screen door's rusted handle, the door divorced its hinges and clattered from the casing. The tarnished knob of the inside door rolled off the threshold and came to rest between his feet.

He kicked the door, and it swung open on the living room. Swirls of dust waltzed in the afternoon sunlight that filtered through gaps in a boarded window. It smelled old and dead inside. The only furniture they had left downstairs was an aged, puffy sofa draped with a moth-eaten sheet, half of which lay rumpled on the floor. He slapped the faded, olive upholstery, sending up a cloud of dust. He used to think the sofa was huge but, like everything else he had seen so far, it seemed smaller than he remembered it.

Memory is a strange thing. Sometimes it serves you well, offering happy recollections of birthday parties, camping trips, baseball championships. Sometimes it causes you heartache, dredging up remembrances of sweet departed grandparents or a favorite dog that ran away. And sometimes it brings on agony, confusing you or withholding what you'd give anything to remember clearly. That's why Greg had returned: to remember everything that had happened-- and to stop the torture.

The broken hearthstones were piled with dark gray ashes that spilled from the fireplace mouth like petrified vomit. A mountain pie iron lay discarded on the floor.

He stepped into the kitchen. Above the sink, shreds of lace curtain fluttered in the breeze that whispered between boards nailed to the window casing. Across the room, the stairwell to the second floor waited silently in the darkness.

He tried to determine if the steps were safe, but it was too dim. He climbed slowly and, although he was trying to be careful, he stumbled on a piece of broken railing halfway up. At the top, the air was hot and musty.

The hallway was dark, and the wood flooring creaked beneath his feet. Cobwebs drooping from the ceiling shrouded his face unexpectedly. Shuddering, he wiped them away.

At the end of the hall, he stepped into the bedroom where he and his little sister, Lisa, used to sleep. Two sets of bedsprings without mattresses crouched on frames against the far wall, looking lonely and skeletal. The heat was stifling, and the room smelled like baked peat. He sat down on the bed nearest the door, staring at the grimy dresser. The silver had peeled off the back of the mirror, and it offered no reflection now. The faded wallpaper behind it was stained from water that had leaked through the roof. Although he wasn't sure, he seemed to recall there had been little wildflowers on it.

That last summer they had vacationed at the house, he was twelve, and Lisa was seven. He remembered their midnight pillow fights when they weren't sleepy. How they fished in the lake or just lounged on the bank watching the newts play tag and the bass glide gently through the water. They hiked in the fields and picked daisies for the supper table.

When it rained, they played in the basement. In one of the three cellar rooms was a huge iron coal furnace that was never used; the house needed no heat in the summer. He and Lisa fancied they'd discovered a mountain cabin and, claiming it for their own, they scrubbed off and swept out the worst of the cinders then lined the inside with flattened cardboard cartons. It was a dirty job, but he always thought the best adventures started with a little hard work. He could still remember the taste of rust and coal dust.

Lisa said, once they got the place fixed up, she'd go inside to cook and clean house, and Greg could go out to the other corner of the coal cellar to kill grizzlies or catch salmon to eat.

House. She always wanted to play house.

Pleased with their accomplishment, they marched upstairs to scrounge more furnishings. However, when their father discovered how they had gotten so filthy, he marched downstairs and nailed shut the door to the furnace room. And their mother marched them upstairs to the bathroom. "Why do they have to spoil all our fun?" Lisa glumly asked fussing with her dollbaby's frazzled nylon hair. Her own was wet and tangled from her bath. She smelled of Ivory soap.

As fresh water thundered into the tub for his bath, he simply shrugged. He figured that Mom and Dad, being high school teachers, had burned out and grown tired of caring for kids, including their own.

He convinced himself they vacationed at the house so his parents could ignore him and Lisa. He resented their assumption that, just because they were in the country, he and Lisa would be safe without their attention. Yet what was the country for? Why take a vacation if you couldn't enjoy an escapade now and then?

At the time, his parents had been having marital problems. That's why they had bickered so much the previous year. He hadn't understood until later that, embarking on that last vacation, their relationship was crumbling and they were entering the stage that would culminate in divorce. Only recently had he admitted they hadn't been as selfish as he thought; they'd merely been self-absorbed. But twelve-year-olds weren't always so rational and understanding. His parents' inattentiveness had made him bitter, and he'd taken it out on Lisa.

Being younger, she had needed more care than he did. However, with their parents so preoccupied, she turned to him, and he didn't know how to parent her. He resented what he saw as a forced responsibility and treated her spitefully.

He had been on the verge of puberty. His attitudes and interests were changing. He felt strange inside and wanted to be alone more. He'd grown sick of being stuck with Lisa, having to watch her and play with her all the time. Except there was no one else to bum around with at the summerhouse.

One July afternoon, Lisa had fallen from the willow tree out front. Landing flat on her back, she knocked the wind out of herself and lay there shocked, choking. All she needed to do was relax, and the breath would come, but she panicked and started convulsing.

He hollered for Mom, for Dad, but they didn't come. Had their ignorance made them deaf?

When Lisa turned blue, he burst into the house, screaming that she was dying. His mother came out of the kitchen, drying her hands on a dishtowel, looking cross. His father followed her, and they found Lisa lying pale and unconscious in the grass. She revived a few minutes later, and his father carried her into the house.

Greg was so frustrated he broke into tears and ran to the basement to hide. That's when he discovered under the workbench the chute between the second room and the coal cellar where the furnace was. He crawled through the chute into the furnace room and hid in the furnace where he recovered from crying by making angry vows about his parents about Lisa He decided he would do what he pleased and would no longer be responsible for his little sister. When he set his mind to something, good or bad, there was no one more stubborn than he was in following through. From then on, when she looked to him for answers, he'd insult her. When she came to him for reassurance, he'd antagonize her. When she clung to him for comfort, he'd push her away.

He wiped his face and hardened his heart. Yes, that's just what he'd do.

On a rainy morning, Lisa had wanted him to play house, be the husband, the dad, but he wanted to go fishing. Alone.

"You can't go fishing," she said, "it's raining." She cradled her doll in her skinny arms. Its eyelids dipped dreamily.

He looked out the living room window. "Sure I can - it's clearing up." It *had* stopped raining, but the sky gave no indication it was clearing up for good.

"Where are you going?" She followed him to the front door.

"To dig bait." He yanked the door shut, leaving her behind.

The rain held off and later that afternoon the air grew sweltering. As their parents prepared to make the eighteen-mile trip to town, their mother called him into the kitchen.

"Watch Lisa while we're gone."

He felt his lip curl into a sneer.

"Would you rather come with us?"

"What, so we can listen to you argue?"

She glared at him and snapped her purse shut. "Just stay away from the lake. If it starts raining again, get inside. And no fighting."

"No fighting," he sang and smiled sanctimoniously.

She slammed the back door behind her.

As the station wagon trundled down the long dirt driveway to the road, Greg gathered his fishing tackle.

"What are you doing?" Lisa asked.

"None of your business."

"Greg – "

"What's it look like I'm doing?"

"We're not supposed to leave the yard when Mom and Dad are gone."

"And how they gonna know?" He looked up at her in disgust. "They'll be gone at least an hour, and that's plenty of time to catch some fish."

"You heard what Mom said. We're not supposed - "

"What do you mean, 'we'? I wanna go fishing, and I'm going *alone*."

"But I'll be - scared." Lisa clutched her doll to her chest. It was a wetsy doll she called "Missy."

"I don't care - that's your problem."

"Greg – "

"You got Pissy to keep you company."

Her blue eyes narrowed. "Her name is *Mi*ssy."

"Missy, Pissy, what's the difference?" He latched the tackle box and headed for the back door.

Fluttering about, she slipped between him and the door. "Why don't we play house instead?"

He glowered at her as she stood there, wide-eyed, her hand on the doorknob.

"How many times do I have to tell you? I don't want to play stupid *house* any more."

"Okay, okay. Then lemme come with you."

He threw down the tackle box, and it crashed to the linoleum.

Lisa cowered against the door.

"I said, I want to go alone. I'm *sick* of you always tagging along."

"But look at the sky. It's gonna rain again."

He glanced out the window. "All the more reason to hurry."

He pushed her out of the way and barged out the door swinging the tackle box. He grabbed his fishing pole leaning against the back of the house, his creel, and the coffee can of earthworms he'd hidden in the shade of the porch.

He turned and saw the top of her head, her tear-filled eyes, between the lace curtains in the kitchen window. He set out through the field for the lake, accompanied only by the angry buzz of insects.

Dark clouds billowed across the sky, and the buckwheat tossed fitfully in the wind, its tiny white flowers like snowflakes against the whispering leaves.

The lake was deserted. Having poor drainage, it was muddy and full of what Lisa called "seaweed."

He settled on the bank, baited the hook, and cast his line into the dark water. Soon, two nice-sized fish lay in the creel beside him. Sensing another tug, he yanked on the pole.

A frantic bass struggled on the end of the line, the hook stretching open its mouth. He reeled it in, relishing the lively vibration of the rod. As he lifted it out of the lake, the fish arched and wriggled, splattering water warm as urine in his face.

"Greg – "

He whirled around. "What are you doing here?"

Her eyes pleaded as she said, "I, we were scared." She held out the cherubic doll with its drooping eyelids and pursed, pink lips. Behind it, Lisa grinned sheepishly, showing new front teeth that looked too big for her mouth.

Lightning burst brilliantly over the lake, and a clap of thunder followed.

Lisa shrieked.

The fish shivered in his hand, driving its spiny dorsal fin into the soft flesh of his palm.

"Dammit!" He dropped the fish, and it flopped into the water, darting away in a streak of silt.

He threw down the pole. "*Now* look what you done. I lost my fish--the biggest one--and I - I'm *bleedin'!*" Gritting his teeth, he held his hand up to her.

She looked alarmed. "I'm sorry, Greg, I didn't mean it!"

"I told you I wanted to go fishing alone, and you come and ruin it."

"But, Greg, I was scared. Missy was scared, too."

"Oh, you and that stupid doll. Give it here."

"No!"

He wrenched it from her grasp and twisted its head off.

"Greggie!"

He flung the body in the lake. The neck hole filled with water and, spitting bubbles, it quickly sank.

She covered her head with her arms and started to wail.

"Oh, shut up, you big baby. It's about time you grew up. Mom and Dad don't care about us no more - they can't even stand each other- and *I'm* not gonna be your dad. You're on your own." He hurled the head at her, and it bounced off her chest.

"I hate you!" she screamed. She grabbed the open creel and dumped his catch in the lake. "There! How's it feel?" She started running.

"You idiot! When I catch you, I'm gonna dump *you* in the lake. Enraged, he chased her along the edge of the water, dead grass crunching under his boots.

She screeched and ran faster, but he was right behind her and soon caught up to her. She turned and kicked at him, but he shoved her hard. Screaming, she flew into the water and immediately submerged.

"Serves you right." He watched her long, golden hair sink into the greenish scum while he stood there, wiping blood and fish slime off his hands.

Barely reaching the surface of the water, her hands groped frantically. A mass of bubbles rose and burst.

"Aw, come off it," he said. "Pretendin' you're drowning don't fool me--I know you can swim."

But she didn't come up.

"Lisa - "

He realized she wasn't pretending.

Frightened, he kicked off his boots and leaped into the water. He tried to run to her, but the mud pulled at his feet. The seaweed was slimy, and it wrapped its olive strands around his ankles. He kicked free and swam to where the bubbles had erupted. Because of a sudden drop-off, the water was much deeper than he thought. Ducking under the surface, he opened his eyes and saw a dim shape moving a few feet away. He reached for her and missed.

He splashed to the top, gulped a breath, and dove again. Thrashing about, he found her, grabbed her wrist, and pulled upward. Although she clutched his arm, she was apparently stuck in the mud. He pulled harder. She inched toward the surface

He tried to get her to the air but couldn't lift her. Pulling her by the elbow, he kicked toward the bank. He reached a place where he could stand, but then his feet slipped in the mud. He went under and she sank down with him.

He pushed her toward the surface. She no longer grappled for him. She felt heavy now.

He broke the surface of the water, gasping. He picked her up and slogged through the mud to the bank, pulled her limp body onto the grass, and parted her tangled hair from her face. Mud clogged her nostrils; he tried to squeeze it out. He had read a book on water safety once, but he couldn't remember what to do first. He knelt over her, waiting for something--anything-- to happen.

Her throat gurgled, and foul-smelling water dribbled from her mouth. Little bubbles like frog eggs formed in the green slime that coated her ashen lips. Her body stiffened and her eyes flew open. She looked like she was about to cry and then, suddenly, she relaxed.

He moaned. He shook her and pushed on her chest to force the water out, but she didn't respond.

Lightning flashed and thunder cracked. He began to sob.

Violent now, the wind tossed his wet hair across his face. The water churned in the gale, slapping the shore, as an icy torrent burst from the blackened heavens.

His parents had found him in the corner of the bedroom, his legs drawn up, eyes staring at the wall. He had bitten his knee until it bled. His hair was plastered to his head, and his face was streaked with tears. When they discovered Lisa was missing, they asked him what had happened. He shook so violently he could hardly form the words, but managed to blurt out where they had gone. He didn't tell them he'd pulled Lisa out of the water.

They ran to the lake. His father jumped in the water and dove for her body. His mother stood in the mud like a crazed woman, her hands clawing her head, a wild look in her eyes. Greg huddled on the bank, clutching Missy's head, while the rain poured down.

They had been unable to drain the lake. He recalled policemen in diving suits going under the water to search for the body. Over and over they dove, coming up with nothing.

His parents knew he'd been in the water. They questioned him anxiously, desperately. The police grilled him about what had happened, but he swore he remembered nothing except her sinking hair, her frenzied claw-like hands, the bursting bubbles. He said he'd tried to rescue her but couldn't find her in the mud. He never revealed to anyone what he'd done with Lisa's body. All these years, they thought she lay at the bottom of the lake somewhere, hidden in the muck.

He and his parents abandoned the summerhouse that night for a local motel. The last one out, he remembered pausing at the living room door. It was so quiet, he thought he could hear his heart thudding in his chest.

He tossed the doll's head on the sofa. Its eyes dipped once then snapped open to watch him shut the door.

The following spring, when his parents divorced, his father hired a moving company to clear the house of anything valuable. His dad went back later to board up the outside, but Greg hadn't returned until now.

Doubts had harried his broken family the following year, yet he'd kept secret that he'd pulled Lisa out of the water. He wasn't sure any more why he'd lied; perhaps he was just being obstinate about his decision to deny responsibility for her. In any case, whenever he was asked how she drowned, he recited his litany, concluding with, "Beyond that, I just don't remember."

As he grew older, he reconsidered his decision to lie. Many times he'd wanted to make things right and tell the truth, but it was much too late. What good would it have done?

For thirteen years, he'd assured himself that it didn't matter what had happened to her body. There was an accident and she had drowned. In a moment of irrational terror, he'd hidden the body, believing it would somehow conceal his guilt.

For thirteen years, he'd told everyone - tried to convince himself - that Lisa's death was an unfortunate accident, one which, yes, he had caused, but which had scarred his adolescence, perhaps his entire life. Considering how his parents' marital problems had affected him at the time, he'd told himself it wasn't really his fault.

For thirteen years, he'd suffered from the guilt, and thirteen years was long enough. Despite the anguish he'd endured, it was high time he acknowledged *he* wasn't the victim--Lisa was.

He'd done his best to block out the tragic events of that summer, but they'd recently come back to haunt him. The antidepressants hadn't worked. They'd only made his muscles twitch, aggravated his sleeplessness.

When he did sleep, nightmares plagued him. During the day, confusion badgered him to distraction; he couldn't concentrate at work. He was a computer software trainer for CompUSA. Last week, during the data queries segment of a Microsoft Access class, he'd gone blank, blacked out for God only knows how long. When he came to, he found himself standing in front of the whiteboard, staring into space, while his students eyed him suspiciously from behind their PCs.

If for no other reason, he had to end the torment lest he lose his job. So he'd driven north to visit the summerhouse.

Sitting there on the bedsprings in the oppressive heat, he watched a large fly beat itself against the dirty bedroom window. Then, as if the memory was being fed from outside him, he saw his recurring nightmare again.

"I hate you!" Her blue eyes and freckles, her hair like new corn silk, her aggrieved innocence accused him, exposing his guilt. Beside the lake she screamed against a menacing sky.

When would she stop? He could not shake it from his mind. As it happened in the nightmare, he drowned her again and again, but she would not stop the screaming. Words bubbled from her lips as he once more shoved her under.

"Stop!" he cried.

Grinning malevolently at him, she sank into the black water, her golden hair sliding into the murk.

"Stop," he whispered, finding himself crying again.

The years of torture he'd endured, not willing to confess all that had happened that day, the wounded looks from his mother and father, the frustrating sessions with the psychiatrist. "You've got to stop blaming yourself," the doctor had said, peering over the rims of her blue glasses. "It was an accident, Greg - a tragic accident, and you must come to terms with the fact that her body will never be found."

He knew better.

Because he'd never admitted what he'd done with the body, his haunting had deepened. No longer merely a psychological suffering, it had swollen to a torment that rivaled reality. Acknowledging his entire crime now, the agony intensified.

Unlike in his nightmare, he hadn't purposely drowned her, but he knew what he'd done with her body, knew it all along. He'd hauled her from the water and parted her slime-sodden hair. He tried to resuscitate her but couldn't. He picked her up, staggered with her through the storm-swept field. Struggling through the back door, he'd borne her into the kitchen and carried her limp body down some steps, almost dropping her. .

For all his denial of what he *could* remember, an insidious paranoia gripped him. Try as he might, there was something simple yet crucial that he could *not* remember.

He knew he'd find peace only when he stopped denying his responsibility for all he'd done that summer.

His heart hammered wildly in his chest.

"I'm coming, Lisa."

He sprang from the bed and sprinted down the hall. A startled rat sitting on the top step scrambled into the darkness. He took the steps two at a time until one crashed through, ripping a gash in his calf. He shook his leg free, ignoring the searing pain, and kept going.

He bounded into the kitchen and stopped to find his way.

He turned and saw the basement door.

He went slowly now, fear welling inside him. He twisted the knob, but the door was stuck. He yanked on it and it shuddered open, showering paint chips on his head. He peered down the basement steps into blackness.

Somewhere in the kitchen, they had kept candles for emergencies and summer storm blackouts; he pulled open drawers until he found a candlestick. It was hard and felt more like wood than wax. He fished in his pocket for his lighter then lit the candle with some difficulty. It held only a small flame that flickered constantly, threatening to go out. He inched toward the basement door.

The stone steps had never been very good. They were worse now, cracked and displaced from the house shifting over the years. His cut leg throbbed. His shoe squished with blood as he descended.

At the bottom, the pungency of mold was overpowering. He noticed the greasy trail and the droppings that rats had left along the wall. A half-eaten rodent skeleton lay in the corner of the first room. He approached a doorway laced with spiders' webs, which he burned away with the candle.

It was cool and even darker in the second room. Against the far wall, the workbench still concealed the chute into the third room, the coal cellar. He knelt and pulled away the rotting pegboard he'd used to hide the entrance. It was entirely black on the other side. Being careful with the candle, he climbed through then straightened up.

His hand trembled, making the candlelight waver and the shadows dance. In the far corner of the room, the rusty iron furnace hulked. He shuffled over to it and crouched before the door. When he turned the handle, it screeched hatefully, like a tortured witch. His heart pounded as if it were a prisoner trying to escape his chest.

In his mind, he saw the lightning flash and heard the thunder crack. He heard the lake water splash - Lisa's helpless squeal, her hideous gurgling.

He pulled the handle and the furnace door groaned. The candle flickered in a cold puff of fetid air. Hunkering down, he held the candle inside. In the wavering circle of light lay a mound of gray bones.

His heart skipped a beat. Averting his eyes, he glimpsed the back wall. On the cardboard they had lined the furnace with, something was scrawled in what looked like hieroglyphics. He didn't remember drawing anything on the cardboard. Perhaps this was his missing memory. He had to discover what the symbols were.

Hesitantly, he forced his shoulders through the tight opening and climbed into the furnace. He slipped and scattered the bones. He squeezed his eyes shut, muttering in shame at his sacrilege. When he opened his eyes, between his knees, he saw Lisa's dusky skull wobbling in the flickering flame. Tatters of hair veiled hollow, black eye sockets.

He forced himself to breathe deeply until his heart slowed. The gritty taste of coal dust, rust, and powdered bones made him gag and spit.

Remaining hunched, he crab-walked to the back of the furnace where he held out the candle to light the marks on the cardboard. They were jumbled, broken letters scratched with coal, a twisted chirography, as if the message had been written in the dark.

GREG IE IHATE YOU
FO REVER

Behind him, the door creaked. He lurched around, toppling into the bones. They snapped beneath his knees. His sister's skull grinned back at him. That's when he noticed the cardboard by the door. It had been torn away. No - gnawed.

Then, beyond the door, he saw her bending over, peering in. Her pallid face grinned like she grinned in his nightmare, like she grinned between his knees. In one translucent hand, she clutched a nubby doll's head with pinched black lips and its eyes poked out. With the other hand, she shut and latched the furnace door.

On the inside of the door were more scratchings. But these were claw marks.

Hot wax dripped onto his hand. He jerked and dropped the candle; the dying flame blinked out. Moaning, he crept about desperately, crunching bones in the blackness.

Outside, laughter like the tinkling of broken glass faded into silence. He scrabbled at the door, but there was no handle inside. He pounded on the door, the walls, but it made only a hollow, thudding noise.

Clutching his head in the darkness, his heart thumped frantically in his chest. Now, he remembered what he'd forgotten, realized what he'd heard the night he and his parents abandoned the summerhouse, and why he'd always felt so guilty.

Then he screamed.

The Mako Shark Society

Ray Roberts

Roger paused a moment by the battered black mailbox and glanced inside. Empty again. He whistled softly and then grinned wryly. The magazines must be dead this week, he thought, as he walked back toward his house on the wooded acreage. Roger made a mental note to replace the mailbox. He hadn't remembered it looking so old and weather worn.

As he came to the front door the gathering twilight created a brief illusion. For just a second, the door seemed to be half rotted away and hanging precariously from one lone and rusted hinge.

But the illusion was gone as quickly as it had come and Roger shrugged his shoulders. Things often looked strange in the twilight. But even so, he was glad the writer's group was meeting at his house tonight. He'd welcome their company because the midsummer air that hung heavy and warm like an oppressive woolen blanket also held just a trace of something in it, something odd, indistinct.

Trying to ignore the feeling, he stepped inside the house, crossed into the living room and glanced around. A large bowl of chips and two kinds of dip sat on the rustic two inch-thick wooden coffee table that sat in front of the couch. The living room lights were on and the beige carpet was recently vacuumed. He actually had the place pretty well picked up for a change, but it did seem a bit dusty. The bookshelves around the fireplace especially so. Darn, how long had it been since he'd dusted? Not that it was something he liked to do, but it was starting to look as if he'd let it get a little out of hand.

He glanced at his watch. Almost nine. Well, it was too late to deal with dust now. The group would be here in a few minutes. Roger crossed the room and sat down in his favorite chair, leaned back and kicked off his boots. He fished a letter out of his shirt pocket, unfolded it, and glanced at words he knew by heart.

The letter was from DAW. A reject on his novel, but pretty encouraging for a reject. An assistant editor had written to say that the novel showed promise, but it didn't quite meet their current needs. But they definitely wanted to see his next novel and please mention this letter when submitting again.

Roger re-folded the letter and stuck it back into his pocket. Lately that was the story of his life. And the rest of the group for that matter. Oh sure, they could string words together well enough to fight their way out of the slush pile, and plot and structure weren't usually a major problem. But more often than not, what they wrote just seemed to fall a little shy of the mark. Good, but not quite good enough. There always seemed to be just a little something missing. Not much, because they all made that occasional sale that kept them going, but if the stories or novels could be just a hair more imaginative, or had a tiny bit more . . . what?

He glanced at the manuscripts beside him on the end table. They were a good example. All of them were written well enough, but where was the spark? That little bit of magic that made the characters jump out at you, to make the story or chapter literally *grab* you? But the manuscripts all seemed to lack that tiny something that forced you to read to the end and then go "Wow." To know you'd just read something that was going to stick with you for awhile, make you think about it, be disturbed or moved, and maybe even want to read it again. And where the hell did you find that missing bit of magic? It damn sure wasn't in books or seminars or classes.

And, if it was something you simply had to be born with, well, if that was the case, they were all in trouble. He and the group would be doomed to be mediocre writers, only occasional sellers, for the rest of their lives.

The doorbell rang, jarring him from his thoughts.

"It's open, come on in," he shouted.

Karen and Tim entered the living room, packets of manuscripts under their arms, and Tim with a six pack of beer.

Roger grinned. He liked Karen the best. She could really turn out a story, but unfortunately, wasn't very prolific in her writing. Tim on the other hand had a wit so sharp that Roger often didn't get it, and then found himself laughing some two or three minutes later. Both had degrees in English and were technically professional writers with a handful of sales to major magazines. Tim, a tall blond man in his late thirties worked at a used book store while Karen, in her early thirties, with jet-black hair and striking green eyes, worked at the state mental hospital. Temporary jobs of course, only until they could support themselves with their writing.

They exchanged familiar pleasantries, and asked the age-old question: "Sold anything recently?" But none of them had. Oh well, there was always tomorrow or maybe next week.

In a few minutes Alex and Angelina showed up. Alex, a reporter, was the youngest of the group and the only true full-time writer. But non-fiction was just work to him and didn't count. Fiction was his true love and he'd actually sold a story to *Omni* once, but oddly enough, it was the only professional fiction sale he'd ever pulled off. Angelina on the other hand had fiction published in some twenty-five different magazines. But for all that, she'd yet to make her first professional sale to a major market. All her stories ended up in the smaller magazines, the ones that paid anywhere from a tenth of a cent a word to a penny a word. Encouraging, but not quite as encouraging as a truly "professional" sale to a larger more prestigious magazine.

They soon settled down for the meeting, Tim, Karen and Angelina on the couch and Alex to the side in another easy chair. Tim broke a potato chip in the French onion dip, fished it out with his fingers and dripped a globule of dip onto the clean carpet. Roger winced, but Tim seemed oblivious.

"Well, lets get started," said Karen, the unofficial leader of the group.

"Who's should we do first?" asked Alex.

Karen wrinkled her forehead in thought. "Oh, let's start with Roger's time travel story."

He started the critique first, and it went slowly from left to right. Roger jotted down notes and soon realized why they called it The Mako Shark Society. There'd be a compliment or two to get you off guard and then the person giving the critique would usually turn, shark-like and suddenly rip your story or chapter to shreds.

The worst part was they were usually right, and you knew it. Roger looked up as Alex started.

"Well, I always hate to be the last, because everyone else has usually covered what I was going to say. But, I've got to agree. There's just something missing. I feel there needs to be something - and I don't know what - but something that the story needs to turn on, that just isn't there. You've got a twist on the end and all, but it's not *enough* of a twist. I guess it's that old problem; there's been hundreds of time travel stories published and it's nearly impossible to do anything really new with that subject. I mean, you came close, but you just didn't quite pull it off."

Roger glanced toward Karen who was nodding her head in agreement, and for just a second the lights seemed to dim. The brightly-lit room suddenly became darker, and shadows danced, played in the corners where field mice had made their nests. The clear plastic bowl of chips sat empty, except for a dried leaf at the bottom, and the ceiling had fallen in places. A heavy coating of dust lay everywhere and the windows, instead of simply being open, were now *broken out. It was as* if the *room* was part of a house that had been abandoned for years.

Karen, sitting on the rotted remnants of the couch seemed suddenly indistinct, merely a wispy apparition of something that had once been a person.

Roger blinked his eyes and the momentary impression was abruptly gone. It had only been a flash, a mere fraction of a second, but he felt a shudder run up his spine and was glad to be in the well-lit living room. Karen and the others had substance and form again, but Roger felt inspiration strike. He knew he had an idea.

The group moved on to Angelina's chapter, but Roger paid scant attention. His mind was wheeling, a story forming. What if there was a writers group? One just like this, but in some fashion only ghosts? Yeah, that was ticket. Ghosts only hang around because they've got unfinished business. And what if everyone in that writer's group had almost made it? Had come *that* close, but never got there? Never quite became successful writers, but were so close they could *taste* it?

And if they died one by one, wouldn't their business on earth be unfinished? Wouldn't they hang on as ghosts, and come together forever, in an effort to perfect their craft, endlessly writing and rewriting, and critiquing their stories and novels? A group of *true* ghostwriters?

Roger grinned. Now *that* was a story idea. But had someone done it already? Was it trite, hackneyed, done to death? He wasn't sure, but he didn't think so. And maybe for once, he'd finally come up with a truly gripping idea? Something that might grab and hold a reader, an editor?

But no, he saw a problem. If this group met as ghosts, how could they ever succeed? They couldn't. There was no way. Damn, a ghost couldn't even mail out a story.

But that might make it even better, more frustrating or at least more tragic. And what a tug at the heartstrings of editors. They were mostly writers too. And picture this poor ghostly group of writers with no possible way to succeed, and therefore doomed forever to meet, to write, to rewrite and suffer endless critiques, and the longed for sales would *never* come. A true horror story and a dilemma with no escape. Ever.

Roger jotted down some notes on his idea, but was soon forced to abandon them. It was his turn to critique Angelina's chapter. He kept his comments brief and went back to his notes as quickly as possible. Yes, he was convinced. This was a story with some possibilities. But, add one more thing to make it even better, scarier. Have it such that the ghosts didn't know they were ghosts. Yeah, the idea was getting better all the time. Have them endlessly writing the same dull stories and meeting to endlessly discuss stories that had been critiqued a thousand times before. Doomed like some sort of latter day flying Dutchmen on an endless sea of frustration. And never knowing. But maybe once, once in a great while, suspecting.

The stories and chapters finally critiqued, Roger visited with his friends for a time, discussing the idiosyncrasies of editors and the frustrations involved in writing. Tim and Karen left and then, some twenty minutes later Alex and Angelina drove away into the night.

Roger grinned, satisfied with his new idea. And hopeful, perhaps this one would have that special something that would make it work.

Despite the hour, he felt compelled to get a start on the story. He had a feeling that this was one of those stories that would practically write itself.

He stepped into the recreation room, sat down at his desk and turned the computer on. He had the start of the story in his mind already. Just make it like any other writers group meeting. He began to type and the words simply flowed, came pouring forth.

But as Roger's fingers danced across the keyboard, the cobwebs and dust that covered it remained undisturbed. The computer screen with the bullet hole through it remained blank.

The Grave

K.D. Wentworth

Ruth Ann followed her husband through the chill star-lit night as his green Taurus turned off into the tree-lined driveway of Memorial Park Cemetery. It stopped before the tall wrought-iron gates. The loss she still couldn't face surfaced again, raw and angry, big enough to drown a universe. Her throat constricted until she couldn't breathe. In the name of God, was this where Robert had gone night after night these past three agonizing weeks when he'd thought her asleep - to their child's grave?

She watched his long lean frame get out of the car, then hop over the solid stucco fence, holding above his head, of all things, a tiny Christmas tree shimmering with tinsel. Shaken, she drove another block and parked in the deserted lot of a strip shopping center.

The December air blasted her unprotected face and hands when she emerged from the sheltered warmth of her car. Dressed only in a robe and slippers, she had followed Robert on impulse and was unprepared for an open-air trek. On the other side of the fence, red and green ornaments swayed on the small pine as Robert wove in and out around the grave markers. She clicked the car door shut, then darted across the empty street, shivering. Poor little Bobby's grave was close to the nearest corner where the cemetery bordered an adjacent field and she could follow Robert along the outside fence.

Streetlights illuminated the winter-bare bushes that lined the wall. They trailed nervous black shadows back and forth over the bleached grass in the bitter-edged wind. Even before she reached the corner, she could hear the steady murmur of Robert's voice. Lowering her head, she crept along the shoulder-high fence. What Robert was doing was so personal that he hadn't felt he could tell her about it. No doubt, he would be embarrassed if he saw her.

"And of course I saved the star for you." Robert's voice was jolly, as though he and four-year-old Bobby were decorating the family tree at home "Don't you want to hang it yourself?"

Tears welled in her eyes as she remembered the downy curve of her only child's eager face last Christmas when their lives had been so rich, so full of hope and expectation for the future.

"All right," Robert said, "if you don't want to I guess I'll have to do it myself."

"No. Me, Daddy."

Her heart shivered into a thousand million pieces.

"Give Daddy your hand then."

The child spoke again, so faraway and wispy that she might have been dreaming it. "But I'll have to start over"

"Son, give Daddy your hand. Now."

A thin-edged whimper began, rising and falling like the wind. Ruth Ann gulped the icy air and clung to the stucco wall with desperate fingers. That was Bobby's cry. She'd never been able to sleep through it. Bobby's cry, Bobby's tears. Shaking so hard she could barely stand, she made herself peek over the fence. Before her husband's dimly outstretched hand, a faint blueness quivered then solidified into the blue-diamond outline of a small child. The sobbing grew louder.

"There's nothing to cry about." Robert knelt on the frozen ground and clasped the translucent blue hand to his cheek.

"But - but it's so dark here," the blue child whimpered, "and I'm scared." Its eyes gazed pensively around the bleak night-shrouded cemetery and the islands of polished granite. "All the others have already gone - "

"Don't start in about that light again." Robert's voice was firm. "Only sissies go there, and you're not a sissy, are you?"

The blue figure shook its head and the crying ebbed.

Robert pulled something shiny out of his coat pocket. "Now put the star on your tree."

The tiny blue figure reached for the silver star in Robert's hand. As it turned toward the fence and the wan yellow light of the street lamp, she caught a full glimpse of her dead son's face. Her fingers gave way and she fell backwards into a well of darkness.

The paramedic squeezed her hand "I'm so sorry " he said in a low voice "but it was too late. His neck - there was nothing we could do."

"Too late?" Her voice had an odd squeal to it. Like a record needle skidding across the grooves. "Robert?" Dropping her groceries on the driveway, she pushed her way through a shocked murmuring crowd whose faces were as white as the ornamental rock in her flowerbeds.

Her next-door neighbor, Mrs. Higgins stepped into her path. "Ruth Ann, it's Bobby." She put an arm around her shoulder. "He fell going down into the basement. It was - ," She stopped and closed her eyes, fighting the tears that leaked down her wrinkled cheeks.

Refusing to understand, Ruth Ann shrugged her arm off and stumbled up to her front door where a policeman stood, writing in a little book. "Mrs. Jackson?" he asked, his tired eyes wary as though she were going to explode "I'm very sorry. It seems to have been an accident."

"He - fell down the steps?" Her throat ached with the effort of not screaming. "But that's not possible. He's not allowed to go down there by himself, and he's afraid of the dark."

Robert came to the door then, his lean face streaked with tears. his eyes red and swollen. "I - " he said. then stared helplessly at her. "Just for a second. I only turned my back for a second!"

"There must be some mistake." She looked at the policeman. "I already have his Christmas presents."

Robert caught her wrist as she tried to slip past, then pressed her against his chest in a bear hug "I'm so sorry!" his lips whispered brokenly into her hair "It's my fault, all my fault!"

She opened her eyes and blinked up at the frosty stars. They looked like broken bits of rhinestone someone had forgotten to sweep away. The stiff grass rustled as she moved her head, then she remembered her dead child's face as he reached for the silver star, the child she had buried here only three weeks ago.

No, she told herself, it couldn't have been real! Robert must have been talking to himself and she'd had a hallucination, a side effect of grief. The minister had told her to expect such things, whispers, footsteps where there were none.

Groggily, she struggled to her feet, then looked over the fence again. Robert was gone. On the small grave, the tiny Christmas tree stood at a crazy angle, thrust into the still-raw mound of dirt. A glimmering silver star dangled from the top, Bobby's favorite ornament.

Her head hurt where it had struck the ground and her chest ached as she tried to breathe the savagely cold air. She had to get home. It was too cold to stay out here like this, and Robert would be wondering where she was. Shivering, she pulled her robe around her shoulders and crossed the deserted street to retrieve her car.

When she unlocked the front door, Robert was standing there, worry written in his tensed jaw, his clenched fists. "Where have you been?"

She stared back at him, trying to speak of the scene at the cemetery, but it was too strange, too awful. The words buried themselves deep inside her head, refusing to come. She edged around him and sank down on the sofa, clutching her car keys to her chest. "I--had to get out," she said haltingly. "I couldn't sleep - and you were gone."

"I know." His face crumpled. "I couldn't sleep either. Every time I close my eyes, I see - " He bit his lip. "I went for a drive to clear my mind." He sat beside her and pulled her head onto his shoulder. "I was frantic when you weren't here. I couldn't bear it if anything happened to you too."

Numbly, she let him stroke her hair with the same hand that had given Bobby the silver star.

The next night, she lay under the covers of their king-sized bed and feigned sleep with long, slow breaths until Robert eased out of the bedroom. After she heard the front door click, she dressed in a sweater and jeans, knowing there was no hurry. If he was going to the cemetery, she'd have no trouble following.

All the way across town, she kept telling herself she was mistaken, last night had been an illusion. In his grief, Robert had taken a Christmas tree to his dead son's grave as though it could give poor little

Bobby any pleasure. But it couldn't, she thought, turning into the same parking lot. Nothing in this world could affect her child now. That was her only comfort. Bobby was at peace, just as the minister had said at the funeral when he had spoken over that pathetically small bronze casket.

Crossing the street, she hugged the cemetery wall as before, then heard her husband's voice as she neared Bobby's grave.

"See what Daddy's brought you tonight? A pinwheel! Remember when Mommy bought you a big striped one last year and you ran with it in the park?"

Pressing her shoulder to the stubbly wall, she listened for an answer, but there was only the restless crunch of Robert's feet in the dead grass.

"Bobby, answer me."

The wind shifted, moaning against the tombstones.

"Do you want me to take it back?"

"No, Daddy," the faraway voice said.

Stuffing a knuckle into her mouth, she straightened up to stare over the wall. Robert held out a shiny red foil pinwheel spinning furiously in the night breeze.

"Then come and get it." Robert glanced over his shoulder into the night. "I can't stay very long."

"They say I should go into the light," the heartbreakingly familiar voice said. *"They say I don't belong here. It's almost too late."* A tinge of irregular blueness formed over the small grave and hung there, a faintly shining cloud in the unrelieved darkness of the cemetery.

"What *they* say doesn't matter, young man. I'm your father and you'll do as I say!"

The whimpering began again, distant, reedy, fading in and out.

"You come here right now!"

The blueness coalesced into the shape of a small child, its head hung just as Bobby's always had when his young world had been laid desolate by some tragedy.

"That's better," Robert said cheerily. "Pinwheel."

A sense of wrongness swept over Ruth Ann as she watched the hesitant blue hand reaching out.

"No!" she cried, climbing onto the wall, her legs scrabbling furiously against the rough stucco. "No, don't touch it, Bobby, leave it alone!"

"Mommy?" the small voice cried. *"Mommy"*

"Ruth Ann?" Robert whirled around as she wrenched herself over onto the frozen ground.

A cold scintillating blue body ran into her arms. icy hand touched her cheek. *"Mommy, I missed you!"*

"I - I - ," Shivering, she held him, even though a cold beyond anything she had ever known pierced her all the way through and she could feel it was wrong, terribly wrong, for him to be there like that. "I missed you too, Bobby-socks." Holding him back a little, she looked into his sad blue face. "What are you doing here?"

"I have to stay here or Daddy won't be able to find me"

The small head turned to stare into the impenetrable night. *"But it's cold and dark. I don't like it."*

"Of course you don't." With trembling fingers, she smoothed an icy tendril of shining blue hair out of his eyes.

"Can I come home with you?" Bobby threw his chill arms around her neck again. *"I want to sleep in my bed."*

"No, sport." Robert took the child's hand and pulled him away. "I told you why you can't come home with us anymore.

"Please, Daddy."

"No, you misbehaved and now you can't ever live there again."

"That's not true!" Ruth Ann jerked to her feet, her heart racing. None of this could be happening. In another moment, she would wake up. Her son would be asleep in his room and life would be bearable again.

She reached for Bobby, then forced her hands down at her sides. "He fell, but it wasn't his fault."

"I made a mess with Daddy's stuff so he sent me downstairs," Bobby sniffed. A glimmering blue tear rolled down his cheek. *"I had to sit in the dark so I could remember to be good."*

Startled, she turned to Robert. "But we never let him go down there. The steps were too steep."

Robert's lips tightened. "Bobby, take your pinwheel. Mommy and Daddy have to go now, but we'll be back tomorrow night so you stay right here where we can find you." He thrust the pinwheel stick into the grave's hard-frozen mound, then gripped Ruth Ann's arm above the elbow. "Say good night to Mommy."

"Don't - don't leave me," the blue child whispered brokenly, then began to cry again. "Mommy. Don't go."

"Let go of me!" She twisted in his grip, but his fingers bit into her flesh as he hustled her back to the fence.

"I'm sorry, but we're out of time." He boosted her to the top, then hopped over himself. "The security patrol sweeps by here about once an hour."

"I don't understand." She stared down at him, seeing angles and shadows in his face that she'd never noticed before. "Why are you doing this?"

He met her eyes, then looked away. "Ruth, I can't give him up!" His voice was strained.

She slid down the other side of the fence. "But he's not supposed to be here." Scalding tears streamed freely down her cheeks. "He's supposed to be at peace!"

"You don't know that for sure. No one does." Robert started back toward his car. "This way we can still be together."

She ran after him. "We can't be together," she said. "Our son is dead. You have to let him go on or - "

"Or what?" He knuckled away the tears in the corners of his eyes without slowing. "You'll tell someone? Go ahead. No one will believe you." He darted across the grass to the driveway where he had parked his car.

Her heart pounded as she watched him. He seemed so different, almost a stranger. As his car screeched out into the street, she glanced back into the cemetery and saw a spinning glint of red catching the light.

She waited out the rest of the night at a truck stop just outside of town, sipping cup after cup of bitter coffee that tasted of unrinsed soap. She couldn't face going home, at least not yet. What could she and Robert possibly say to one another? He had sent Bobby to the basement, of all places. He had caused her son's death, and now his guilt was driving him to this terrible extreme.

He was right about one thing, though; although her mind had run the full gamut of possibilities from priest to psychic, she couldn't tell anyone. No one would ever believe her.

Still, there had to be some way to make him leave Bobby alone to do whatever it was he needed to pass on into the next life. Her fingers tightened on the cracked mug. Perhaps if she could keep Robert away from the cemetery for just one night, that would be enough. What was it Bobby had said? *"They say that I don't belong here, that it's almost too late."* Evidently, time was running out, but if she could keep Robert home tomorrow night, then maybe Bobby could find peace, and the two of them could pull the shattered fragments of their lives together and try somehow to forgive each other and start over.

After grinding the engine several more times, Robert flung the car door open again, then wrenched up the hood and peered inside with a flashlight. Behind the garage, Ruth Ann pressed her back against the wall, heard the hood crash down, then a few seconds later, the front door slam. She exhaled slowly, limp with relief; she must have pulled the right handful of wires, but everything depended on what he did next. Opening her purse, she peered down inside at the gleaming black automatic, a forty-five and, as the clerk had warned her earlier that afternoon, "not a lady's gun."

If Robert persisted in this madness, she would follow him to the cemetery and threaten him with it, even shoot into the air if she had to; that would at least bring the security guard, and perhaps the police. Even if he got away, they would watch the cemetery more carefully after that, and he wouldn't be able to get back in at night, at least for a while.

Half an hour later, her ears were numb even under the woolen scarf wrapped around her head and her feet felt like blocks of ice. She was almost sure he had given up, when the front door opened and

Robert strode out, carrying something under his arm in a paper bag.

She held her breath as he turned up the street and then turned again at the first corner. Waiting until he was out of sight, she hurried to her car around the corner, then drove cautiously after him. Three blocks down, she saw him waiting at a bus stop, and her heart sank. He was still going to the cemetery. The best she could manage now was to get there before him.

Hiding her car two blocks down from where she had parked before, she jogged back, her fingers sweating inside her gloves, her gun-heavy purse bouncing against her side at every step. Why was Robert persisting with this when she had begged him not to? The memory of his fingers caressing her skin came back to her, the funny squint he had when he was thinking over something important, his exultant grin when Bobby was born. In spite of his temper, there had been good times.

She climbed the fence in silence, then stared at the small grassless grave under the starlight. The tiny Christmas tree planted crookedly in the dirt, the pinwheel spinning crazily in the night wind, what on earth must the grounds-keeper think of people who brought such things brought to a dead child?

Nervously, she watched for some sign of the blueness with which Bobby had manifested himself before, but there was only the bitter December wind howling around the squat tombstones and the somber pines whispering overhead. Icy dread spread through her body and she huddled inside her coat. What an incredibly cold and lonely place this was at night, full of broken dreams and lost promises. How could anyone condemn a child, much less *her* child, to exist here when something else obviously waited for him?

Hearing a rustle on the other side of the wall, she pulled off her glove and reached into her purse for the forty-five.

Robert's blond hair caught the light from the street lamp as he pulled himself to the top of the wall and hopped over with the paper sack still jammed under his arm. "So there you are." He sounded almost cheerful. "I wondered if you were going to desert us on Christmas Eve."

"Robert, go home!" Her searching fingers closed around the cold metal of the gun. "You can't do this anymore! You have to let him find whatever peace he can."

"Nonsense." The paper sack crackled as he opened it. "Do you want our son to think we don't love him?"

"I love him enough to let him go!"

"That's not love, that cowardice." His breath puffed white as he pulled a black velvet Mickey Mouse doll out of the sack, as tall as Bobby had been, dressed in a bright red fireman's hat and uniform. "Bobby? Come and see what Santa's brought you for Christmas."

"No!" She clicked the safety off, then, raising the gun in both trembling hands, took aim at his chest. "Leave him alone!"

"Ruth Ann, you aren't fooling anyone with that thing. Put it away before you shoot yourself in the foot and scare Bobby." He balanced the Mickey on the frozen dirt beside the Christmas tree, then sat back on his heels. "Come on, old sport, Daddy hasn't got all night."

Then, out of the corner of her eye, she saw a scattering of blue sparkles. "No, Bobby!" She shuddered with the effort of keeping the gun's muzzle trained on Robert. "Don't come back here! Go into the light!"

"Daddy?"

"Right here, son." Robert smiled at the gathering cloud of blue light. "You wouldn't let your old dad down, would you? Not again."

Features formed in the blueness, a small upturned nose, legacy of her maternal grandmother, a determined chin and widely spaced eyes from Robert's side of the family.

"Bobby, no! Go into the light--please!" Tears ran down her cheeks until she could hardly see, but she didn't dare loosen her hold on the gun to wipe them away.

The sparkling blue face turned to her. *"What's wrong. Mommy?"*

"See the Mickey Mouse?" Robert picked up the stuffed animal and held it out. "Just like you asked Santa for at the mall. Remember?"

As Bobby's pudgy blue fingers reached for the Mickey's plush black arm, she pointed the gun into the air, squeezed the trigger as the clerk had showed her, and fired. The resulting report staggered her backwards onto the icy frozen ground and echoed through the emptiness of the cemetery, ricocheting from tombstone to tombstone.

Bobby wailed as Robert snatched the gun from her fingers. "Goddammit all to hell!" he snarled, then flung her against the nearest grave marker. The granite caught her hard across the ribs. "Get over there and shut up!"

As she struggled for air, he stomped back to the grave and snatched up the stuffed Mickey. "Come here and take your present, Bobby."

In answer, the child's wails only grew louder and more distressed.

"You're letting Daddy down again. It's your fault. This whole stinking mess is your fault, and you know it!" Robert's voice rose in an effort to override the crying. "If you'd been a good boy, like Daddy told you, we would be home, sitting around our Christmas tree right now! Come here and take your Mickey before Daddy gets *really angry!*"

"No!" she whispered hoarsely, but the word couldn't get past the hard knot of pain in her ribs.

"All Daddy wants for Christmas is for you to come here right now, Robert Alan Jackson!"

Far off across the gentle rolling hills of the cemetery, she saw a tiny pair of headlights approaching. Perhaps the guard had heard her shot. Bracing an arm across her throbbing ribs, she struggled to her feet and lurched at Robert. "Leave--" She wrenched at the gun in his hand. "--him--" Her fingers found the trigger and pulled at it. "--alone!"

The gun roared again, striking a marker a few yards away, sending granite chips flying. One of them cut her cheek. The blueness that was Bobby became fuzzy, more indistinct.

"Stop it!" Robert's face blazed with anger as she grappled for the pistol "This is stupid! Even if you killed me, you still wouldn't win, because then I'd be with him, and I'm definitely not going into the light!"

She could hear the security patrol's car now, its engine racing, tires squealing, and still there was Bobby's crying, thin and heartbreaking.

"Bobby-socks, go into the light like Mommy told you!" she cried. "Go right now!"

"I'm scared." he wailed. "I'm scared to go by myself. Hold my hand."

"See?" Robert glared down at her as she slipped to her knees, still wrestling for the gun. "See what you've made out of my son? A goddamned sissy! But I'll fix it. If I have to, I'll come back here every night for the rest of my life. I'll make a man of him yet."

"Like you did when you sent him down the cellar steps?" Her fingers found purchase on the gun's chill metal again, curled around the grip.

"That was an accident! I never touched him!"

The blood stopped in her veins. With a rush, she finally understood the full measure of this man she had called her husband. Almost from the beginning of their marriage, she'd known better than to argue with him, but she'd thought they were slowly working things out, coming to respect each other's differences. Now she realized that she had never known him at all.

Whether Robert lived or died, he would win. Even if the guards came and the police were called, they couldn't watch Bobby's grave twenty-four hours a day. He would still be free to come back here, playing his sick games with her baby, and no one would ever believe her. And even if she could summon the courage to kill him, he would hold Bobby here with him in this grim twilight, suspended between life and death, and her child would never know peace.

Loosening her fingers, she let Robert get a grip on the gun, then leaned against his chest and looped her arm around his warm neck to hold him close like a lover while her right hand suddenly tightened around his finger and squeezed the trigger. The blast thundered through the night, so loud, she thought she had gone deaf. The universe shuddered and fell away, taking her with it.

From a great distance, she heard Robert cry out. But it was all right, she wanted to tell him. Unwittingly, he had shown her the only way to go.

"Mommy will you hold my hand?" Bobby sounded closer this time.

"In a minute, Baby," she whispered.

The security guard flashed his light down into her face, then knelt on the icy ground and fumbled at her coat, eyes wide with shock.

"Mommy's coming."

Red Whiskey

Tina L. Jens

"Sheriff's here," May said, peering out the front window at the Brown Mountain Grill parking lot.

She didn't bother opening the sliding window to take the lawman's order. She knew he and the deputy would come on in the back room where a long table served as a meeting place for the regulars.

"I'd better put their burgers on, they'll be hungry," Louida said, turning toward the grill. Louida prided herself on being the older, more practical sister.

"They mightn't be in the mood," May said to her sister. "Will looked pretty green. That body musta been something."

"No body's a pleasure, 'specially one that's been sittin' awhile," Alice Chester said.

Louida nodded at the old woman' wisdom.

Miss Alice sat perched on a barstool next to the meat freezer where she could keep an eye on things.

"Y'all want your usual?" May asked doubtfully as the two men tramped through the back door. Calvin Haskel was followed by his deputy, Will Seagal.

"Just coffee for me, " Cal said, easing himself wearily into a chair at the long table.

"Make mine a Sundrop," the younger man said.

Miss Alice waved at the men. "Got another dead one up there at Pine Hollow." It wasn't a question.

The sheriff raised an eyebrow at her. "We got a body in strange shape, but I didn't know it was common knowledge already."

"Word doesn't have far to travel in a small town," she told him.

"That's a fact, Miss Alice," the sheriff said.

"What'd it look like?" May said, setting a cup of coffee in front of Will and dropping into the seat across from him.

"It looked like one of them squirrels out of Cal's stew pot!" Will exclaimed.

"Lord, Almighty!" May said.

Louida raised an eyebrow at the sheriff. Cal was always slower to talk than Will, but he made more sense.

"I went to Viet Nam," Calvin said finally. "I've seen a lotta sights. But that man was boiled alive. I've never seen nothing like that in my life, the flesh was so tender it was falling off the bones!"

"Calvin Haskel, you got a poor memory for a young man."

The sheriff looked at the old woman. "Well, shore it up, Miss Alice. If it ain't knowed by you, it ain't fit to be knowed."

"Hell, I got a customer at the counter," Louida grumbled. "Don't you tell anymore till I get back, you hear?"

"You were saying, Miss Alice?" Cal asked, when Louida returned to the high-backed wooden chair beside him.

The old woman shook a bony finger at him. "I hadn't said nothing yet. Just you don't rush me. There ain't no mystery about that dead man up there. Your Granddaddy and your Pa seen this a'fore. Your Granddaddy even took you up to Pine Hollow to see the body. Your Ma squalled the whole time that it'd put yer mind over. Hell, you don't even remember it."

"Pine Hollow, that's the same place this one –"

"It's 'xactly the same place, cause he was using the same still, making the same shine. That red stuff. Looks like fine aged whiskey. But it *ain't* aged, it runs red right outa the worm-pipe."

"There's been some whiskey like that floating around the market lately," the deputy said.

"You got any left?" Cal asked with a straight face.

Will nodded, then blushed.

"Well, don't drink no more of it. We may need it for evidence." Cal sighed. "Boy, don't you know better than to buy from short-term operations? Ask me out of uniform and I'll give you the names of the reliable bootleggers."

"Oh, I know the reliable ones, sheriff. I just figure it being illegal and all, it's up to us to do quality control. I buy whatever's on the market. About a year ago I spread the word that you and I'd shut down anyone making popskull, but we'd leave 'em alone as long as they kept it healthy and kept the prices reasonable. Quality's up, sheriff," Will added helpfully.

Cal sighed again. He had to give the deputy credit, the boy wasn't lacking in motivation.

"The moonshiners I know use a shotgun or a torch to put their rivals out of business. I never knew one to cook a man to death. What's the red whiskey got to do with the dead body?"

"That red whisky comes 'bout every twenty years," Miss Alice told him. First appeared round 1931, during the Depression. You may a been too young to remember it in '52, but you shoulda had a lick of sense in '71."

"I was away at the war. Don't remember my folks writing about it though."

"Probably figured you had enough news of the dead. But mark my words, Calvin Haskel, when the red whiskey comes, the dead body always follows."

"Cotton Whisnant, I ain't a climbing in that pot for you to stand out here and hammer on it. I'll go deaf or get hit one," Sarrie told her new husband.

They'd been down to the courthouse that morning to be married. Repairing her daddy's abandoned whiskey still wasn't exactly what she'd had in mind for the afternoon.

"You'll get hit out here if you don't do as I say. Now get in there."

Sarrie gave her husband one last pleading look before she swung herself over the edge and ducked down into the copper pot.

"You gotta hold it firm while I patch it. The mash'll stick on any of the dents. You're gonna want this right honey, cause you're gonna be stirring. Dents just mean more work for you."

Sarrie hated moonshining. She'd had her fill helping her daddy -- digging up the jars out of the woods when the customers came by the house, keeping watch out for the law, driving whole wagon loads into town right under the sheriff's nose. She hunkered her head down into her shoulders trying to block out the noise.

"Sarrie, push harder! You're letting it dent."

"Pushin' as hard as I can, Cotton! Hold a minute."

She slid further down into the boiler pot and planted her tailbone against the back corner so she could brace the side wall with both her feet and hands.

"Now try it."

Cotton commenced hammering.

She couldn't fault Cotton for wanting to start up the old still. There weren't enough land to farm nor any jobs to be had in town. Everybody in the county was laid off. Cotton said that as long as Herbert Hoover was President, things were bound to get worse.

When he paused, she sighed and put a finger in each ear to shake it out. "Lawd, Cotton, you almost done?"

The neighbors would be bad off come winter. But moonshining paid. The whiskey would keep food on the table and leave them money to spare. Pure corn whiskey, doubled and twisted was what her daddy had made. But Cotton said that was old fashioned. Took too much time and too much corn. He was going to add a thumper barrel to the rig. A thumper would cut the stilling time in half and sugar would more'n doubled the output. Maybe moonshining Cotton's way wouldn't be so bad.

She adjusted her position and braced the copper wall as Cotton began to hammer in the second set of rivets.

She felt the metal give.

"Wait a minute Cotton, it's coming through!"

Sarrie's warning came too late. The old copper flaked loose around the rivet Cotton had been pounding. The metal patch bored through the hole and the soft web of skin between the thumb and first finger of Nora Jean's hand, nearly cutting her thumb off.

"Cotton! I'm hurt! I'm hurt!"

Sarrie's head reeled back against the copper wall. She slid down the side, unconscious. Blood started to puddle in the bottom of the pot.

She was still lightheaded when she came to. But she couldn't be sure if that was from pain, loss of blood, or her position. She was hanging upside down half out of the still. Cotton was squatting on the ground below her, his neck twisted around so he could see her face, which he continued to slap, despite the fact that her eyes were now open.

"Come on Sarrie, wake up honey."

Sarrie grabbed at his wrist before he could slap her again and moaned as pain throbbed through her hand. At least Cotton had tied the wound up with his bandanna. Blood still oozed out from under the fabric. The shack was spinning. She closed her eyes but it didn't help.

"Get me out of here, Cotton."

"If I get you out now, I don't think I could lift you back in.

She flopped her head toward his voice and tried to focus her eyes.

"We're going to finish the patch first, honey. Now come on, it won't take long..."

"Sarrie showed up on my porch the next day," Miss Alice told the group. "I faith-healed her hand, till it was right good as new."

Will snorted. May slugged his shoulder for mouthing off to his elder. But Miss Alice could fight her own fights.

She snapped at him, "You young'uns go off to college and come back with less sense than you started with. Faith heading's in the Bible, boy. Anybody can do it, if they know the right passages."

Surveying the group, she could tell the rest didn't believe either. They'd just had better manners than the boy.

She sputtered at them. "Calvin, you were seven years old when yore mother brought you to my house. Had the measles so bad you liked to died, and you were scratching at them. Your poor mother was afraid you'd be one big scab and scar. I blowed on them and the itching went away, and the marks too."

Calvin said, "I don't remember it. But I reckon it's so. Ma always told it that way."

Sarrie dropped a cake of lye soap into the huge kettle of water, then added more wood to the fire underneath. The sheets would go in when the water boiled. Meanwhile, Sarrie had to string up the clothes wire, or she'd have no place to hang the clean laundry. It was just one more chore Cotton hadn't gotten around to.

He'd been in a black mood for a week. His first batch of whiskey had failed. He'd rushed the mashing process, hadn't let the corn sprout properly before taking it to the mill. Of course the liquor had come out sour. Sarrie had tried to tell him.

Day before last, he'd gone down to the mill, bought somebody else's sprouts and hired a couple of colored boys. They'd spent the last two days and nights up at the still, drinking, cursing and getting set to cook a new batch.

She shoved the bed sheets down into the water with her paddle. Cotton had marched down the hill yesterday and declared the still off limits to her. Claimed she'd jinxed the first batch, and that a still were no place for a woman.

There was a time when Cotton had said nice things to her. When they were courting, he had told her she had skin the color of moonlight and hair the color of snow.

Sarrie snorted. She ought to thank the Lord for small blessings. Getting the cabin in order and putting in a late garden was work enough for one woman. Course, a man oughta come home at night. Last night, layin' alone in bed, she'd heard him sitting up there, howling at the moon and singing as them boys plucked guitar and blowed harmonica.

Sarrie gave the kettle of sheets another stir then headed into the cabin to make Cotton some lunch.

Sarrie had to fight the briars off as she climbed the hill. She knew better than to use the same route to the still twice. Cutting a path would be like setting out a welcome mat for the law.

After a half-hour of climbing, she saw the cluster of laurel bushes that hid the still. She poked her nose into the shack, but no one was there. They were probably out cutting wood for the fire. Or shoring up the fresh water trough that cooled the copper worm and condensed the liquor. Cotton had said the water flow had been weakly the first batch.

She sat down on a stump in the shade to wait. She lifted her skirt and fanned her legs with the hem.

Sarrie spotted her husband coming out of the woods, his arms full of kindling. She waved at him. "Cotton, I brought you some lunch."

He gave a growl that reminded Sarrie of her daddy's hunting dogs. He dropped the wood and charged at her.

She screamed and ran behind a nearby tree.

"It's lunch, honey, I just brought you some lunch!" She dangled the bag out in front of him.

He knocked it out of her hand. He grabbed her arm and dragged her out into the open. Then he slapped her.

"I thought I told you to stay away from the still! Spoiled it, ain't you?"

"I didn't go anywhere near the still. I just sat out here - honest."

Cotton Mather was a big man, and there was meanness in his eyes. He dragged her to a spot just beyond the doorway of the shack.

"You stand right there -- and we'll see."

She stood frozen as he thrust a Mason jar under the worm and collected several ounces of liquor. He lifted it to his nose, sniffed it and frowned. He took a drink. He cursed and spat it out.

Sarrie took off running before the liquor hit the ground.

"Woman, you git back here!"

Cotton drug Sarrie's limp body into the shack. He staggered in the doorway and swallowed hard. He hadn't meant to kill her. Just knock some sense into her.

The woman had no business coming up here, getting in his way. Didn't appreciate how hard he was working to get something set aside before winter. Now he'd pay for her foolishness.

As he stared at the limp form laying face down in the dirt, he heard a shout. Someone was at the foot of the hill. Probably Sheriff Owens. He'd been sniffing around last week. T'wasn't fair - the law hounding him before he sold a drop.

The harassment hadn't worried him, then. A first time moonshining offense couldn't mean more than a thousand-dollar bond or a month in jail, if he couldn't put up the money. But for murder -- they'd send him straight to the chain gang, for sure. Frantically, he looked for a place to hide the body.

The only thing big enough was the boiler. He grabbed a hammer and knocked away the clay molding that sealed the funnel-shaped cap on top of the pot. He shoved Sarrie's body down into the boiling beer, slammed the cap back down, and did a quick sealing job with some fresh clay. Then he reached for his rifle. It was never far from a moonshiner's hand.

He'd sent the colored boys to town to buy sugar and Mason jars and quietly drum up some business. Cotton would have to face the sheriff alone.

As he left the shack, he thought he heard a moan. He looked back, uncertain. Surely, she couldn't still be alive. But there wasn't time to check. The sheriff was just breaking through the laurel thicket.

Cotton stepped out of the shack and cocked his gun. The sound of the action crackled through the woods.

"Easy there! Don't get jumpy boy!" the man said.

It wasn't the sheriff. Cotton lowered the muzzle of his gun, but kept it pointed at the stranger.

The man raised his hands in the air. He wore a white ribbed undershirt tucked into brown work pants. As he came closer to the shack he pulled a red bandanna out of his back pocket and ran it over his bald head then down around the back of his neck.

"That walk can do you in, in the noon-day heat. I'm Ode Benefield. One of your neighbors. I got me a thirst for a little white lightning." He winked at Cotton.

"Pleased to meet you, Ode," Cotton said, cautiously, switching the rifle to his left hand so he could shake hands with the stranger.

"I was a steady customer of Sarrie's daddy," Ode told him, as they walked toward the still. "You using his same recipe?"

"Yeah, sure."

"Well then, let me have a gallon now, and add me to your delivery route. I'm just down the hill a piece on old Saulmon Road."

The stranger followed him into the shack. It made Cotton uneasy, but he didn't see any way to keep the man out without insulting him. He couldn't afford to drive off his first customer.

Cotton looked on nervously as the stranger examined the boiler and four-barrel operation, inspecting the shiny copper pipes that connected it all. He looked down into the running water flowing through the flake stand that condensed the spirits. "What are you using as a worm, son?"

"A 1921 Ford radiator -- I cleaned it out real good though," Cotton said quickly, as the man looked up suspiciously.

The thumper barrel started pounding. Both men jumped.

"That gave me a turn," the stranger laughed. "My pa always said it was the spirit of the alcohol knocking, trying to get out. A thumper can shore speeds things up, warming the next round of mash up," Ode said.

Cotton tried not to stare at the boiler as he pulled two jars of whiskey out of a half-packed box.

"I see you're brewing up some brandy, too," Ode Benefield said. "Mind if I take a sip?"

He helped himself to the aluminum dipper that hung nearby, and plunged it deep into the bucket that collected the distilled spirits.

The alcohol was running a dark red coming out of the worm. Cotton felt the blood rush from his face. He reeled back, barely catching himself on a chair.

The stranger sipped thoughtfully. "You got an interesting blend of fruit there, son. But you might not want to skimp so much on the sugar. It's a bit sharp for my tongue."

Cotton took the man's money and followed him on shaky legs to the break in the laurel thicket.

"Say 'Hey' to Sarrie for me," Ode told him. "And son, you better get yerself a lookout man. I coulda been the law. Them revenuers, they ain't so neighborly."

Louida hooked the coffeepot off the warming tray and poured another round. Calvin pushed the sugar bowl toward Miss Alice. They waited as the old lady measured out two level teaspoons and stirred them into her cup.

"Well, what happened?" May asked, impatiently.

"I'll tell ye, directly," Miss Alice said, testing the flavor of her coffee and nodding as it passed inspection.

"Soon as his customer was gone, that old snake hightailed it out of there, never went back into the shack. He drove in to Shelby to find those colored boys. He sent them up to the still. Told them to clean everything out. Get rid of everything they found there. Paid them handsome, and made them swear on the Bible they'd never say a word of it to no one. Not even him. See, that way they'd be a feared to talk -- afraid the devil would take 'em.

"So they does it. But the next run red and the next." Miss Alice cackled with pleasure. "No matter how much that old snake made the boys scrub out the still and barrels, the liquor always run red."

She grew quiet and pulled her sweater closer around her shoulders.

"They say there's three kinds of moonshine. You ever heard that, Cal?"

The sheriff nodded his head. "The fighting kind, the crying kind and the fun kind. As the law, we mostly gotta worry about the fighting kind."

Miss Alice told him, "The red whiskey's always the fighting kind, you remember that."

With a shaky hand, Cotton poured himself a shot of the blood-red moonshine. He couldn't account for the color. But it wasn't hurting sales. There were twenty stops on the delivery route, now.

He stared at the glass. He poured the same shot night after night, but he could never bring himself to taste it. He'd been buying his white lightning from a moonshiner outside Shelby. A mason jars half full of that liquor sat in the middle of the table. Clear and pretty as could be. He pulled it closer, unscrewed the lid and took a swig, then banged the jar down beside the shot glass. The red whiskey sloshed at the sides of the glass, a single drop splashed over the rim and crawled down the outside.

Cotton lurched forward as he heard a knock at the door. He tried to stand, but the moonshine stole his balance. His chair fell over and thumped on the wooden floor. Cotton staggered across the floor. He didn't welcome visitors who came calling after midnight. Rifle in hand, he threw open the door.

A woman stood there, beautiful in a long white gauzy dress rustled softly in the wind. The moonlight glistened on her hair as a smile played around her full red lips.

"Sarrie?"

He couldn't believe his eyes. He was sure Sarrie had died up at the still. But he had never asked the boys what they had found in the boiler.

She seemed to float past him as she entered the cabin.

"Where you been, honey?" He followed her nervously as she rounded the kitchen table.

Silently, she stoked up the cast-iron stove and moved the coffeepot onto a burner. While her back was turned, Cotton grabbed the two jars of moonshine off the table and searched for a place to hide them. But the shelves were bare. The dishes were all dirty in the sink, and the pantry was depleted. Desperately, he shoved the jars down into the flour bin.

Sarrie turned around just as his hand closed around the shot glass. He crossed his arms behind his back and edged toward the sink.

"You know, I been worried about you," Cotton stuttered.

Sarrie smiled demurely and moved toward the door.

"There ain't no milk in the well, I ain't had time to get none," Cotton said apologetically.

She frowned slightly, then moved toward the sink to get cups.

As the last incriminating evidence trickled down over the dirty dishes, Cotton's confidence returned to him.

"You been gone a long spell. A man can't make a living and do woman's work, too. Ain't had a decent meal in a month. Haven't got a clean shirt to wear."

He strutted across the kitchen. It was upper hand, and the whiskey made him brave.

"I've been busting my back while you're lazing about somewhere. It's about time you account for yourself, woman."

"It won't happen again, Cotton." Sarrie'5 voice was soft but it had an edge of strength that Cotton hadn't heard before.

"Damn straight," Cotton said loudly. But as he looked into Sarrie's unwavering blue eyes, he wasn't so sure they were talking about the same thing.

Cotton gave her wide berth after that. They never spoke about what happened at the still and she never told him where she'd gone. She spoke very little. But she worked tirelessly and did all he asked. It scared the living daylights out of him.

Cotton stomped through the door. The house smelled of lye soap and wet newsprint. He found Sarrie in the kitchen, studying the Sears catalog pages that papered the walls.

"Cotton, your muddy boots are tracking up my clean floor," she complained mildly.

"It's delivery night. I'm running late," he growled at her. He kicked his boots into a corner, and concentrated on the supper Sarrie set before him. "Get my clean boots."

A second pair of shoes was a luxury few in the county could afford. But moonshining paid well and Cotton rewarded himself accordingly.

Sarrie poured him a cup of coffee and sat down across from him.

"I want a bath."

"You know where the creek is," he said, without looking up from his plate.

"I mean a tub, Cotton. A ceramic one. They got one in the catalog. It's not expensive. Less than the suit of clothes you bought."

He slammed his coffee cup down and glared at her.

Sarrie flinched.

"What do you need another suit for, Cotton? We don't even go to church."

"Who's making the moonshine, woman?"

"You are, Cotton," she said quietly.

"Then I'll spend the money."

He shoved his plate away and pushed back from the table.

"And put that lamp out. You're wasting kerosene."

She fingered her warn dress as she watched him leave. When she was sure he was gone, she fetched her sweater from its peg and slipped out the door.

Miss Alice cackled again. "The revenuers caught him with thirty cases stacked in the back of his car. And I don't mean the local sheriff, the federal agents got him."

Will whistled. "A hundred and eighty gallons of moonshine? They catch you with that, you're in a heap of trouble."

Calvin shook his head. "If he had that big an operation, he could pay the fines and be back in business the next night."

"Bond was set, but it weren't paid," Miss Alice said, mysteriously. "Cotton Whisnant spent six months on the chain gang."

"What happened to Sarrie?" Louida asked.

"Some people say she knew where he kept his money hid, but didn't care to bail him out," Miss Alice said. "Others say he was so full of blamed meanness that he'd rather spend six months on the chain gang than share a penny with his wife. And," the old woman dropped her voice to a scandalous whisper, "that she found a personal way to raise some pocket money while he was in jail."

"Miss Alice!" May said, shocked.

Louida rolled her eyes.

"Anyways, when he got home after his spell on the chain gang, he found her just a laying in a big old ceramic tub, heels propped up on the edge, hot water and bubbles up to her ears."

"You couldn't raise the money to post my bail, but you could buy this damned tub?" Cotton roared.

Cotton stood, fists jammed against his hips, glaring at his wife. The tub sat in the kitchen corner next to the cast iron stove.

Water kettles sat nearby and the stove's fire door stood warming that corner of the room.

"You've walked a hard road, Cotton. Why don't you climb in here with me and relax a bit?" Sarrie splashed the bubbles with her toe, invitingly.

Cotton's anger surged through him like poison. He struck quick as a copperhead, grabbing her ankle and jerking it toward him. Sarrie's head cracked against the back of the tub and she slipped beneath the water. Cotton dove his hands into the tub, holding her down. Plumes of water splashed through the air as she kicked her legs and fought to get free.

Suddenly, her hands shot up through the water and raked across his face, leaving bloody furrows behind. Then cold fingers circled his neck. With a strength Cotton had not known she possessed, Sarrie pulled him down.

Their bodies twisted and their positions reversed. The water closed over Cotton's face. He realized the muscles he had built on the chain gang could not match those of his wife.

Dripping wet, Sarrie stepped from the tub and lifted Cotton in her arms.

The pale moon glistened on her naked skin as she carried his body up the dirt path to the still.

"That's a good spook story, Miss Alice," Calvin said, when she had finished. "But what's it got to do with the body up at Pine Hollow?"

"I knowed a man was gonna die, just like Cotton Whisnant did back in '31. And I knowed there weren't anyone who'd believe me."

"How'd you know?" the sheriff asked her.

"Cause Garland Hennessee died in '52, and Buck Carver in '71," Miss Alice said, solemnly. "And cause Sarrie came to me a couple weeks ago -- to have them same wounds healed.

"I used to think she was a demon or a haint. But the word wouldn't heal her if that were so. I don't know what she is. All I know is, she shows up on my doorstep 'bout every twenty years, with a gashed hand and burns all over her body. I heal her and send her on her way...and pray that the nest man'll be good to her."

<u>For my uncle, Fred Chester, a retired bootlegger, and gentleman.</u>

<u>Thanks for the stories</u>

Grounded

Robert Devereaux

"The Lord be praised, honey, Momma just got lucky!" Millie Rae Hattersley whapped the folded newspaper with a backhanded swat and swore in delight.

"What you got, Momma?" said Betty Lou, her voice a swatch of weariness flopped open on the day bed where she forearmed the heat of August off her forehead.

"A way out, honey. A way to be rid of our difficulties."

"Jesus, Momma!"

"Yes! You listen up, Betty Lou, and listen good! No more creditors hounding you, no more godforsaken probation officer poking his nose where it don't belong, and no more worry about cooking up alibis when you and your momma play fast and loose with other people's money."

Betty Lou, a dark-haired rail of a woman with tired eyes and a straight, pinched nose, propped herself on an elbow and shaded her face with her other hand, squinting out from under it like a tortoise. "Lay off the whiskey, Momma. They got us licked and you know it."

"All we need to do," said Millie Rae, crossing from her chipped plastic dish of burnt toast and sitting beside her daughter, "is find us the right stiff." Impelled by a scheme sprung full-blown, Millie Rae clamped an excited hand upon the bony shoulder of her offspring. "A corpse your size, honey, unclaimed? A little playacting at the morgue? A quick burial? A death certificate in the name of Betty Lou Hattersley?"

"Now calm down, Momma," said Betty Lou, suddenly interested. She knew when her mother was on to something, and this particular something had the makings of freedom about it. "Stop waving that paper about and give it to me slow, dribbing and drabbing one tiny bit at a time."

- rest of em call me jane doe 'cause I'm not claimed by any breathers - they lie there and shun me - they mumble and snigger into themselves like the breathers did when I was one of them - cant recall much - just being pushed around- do this do that button your lip young lady here suck on this it makes me feel so fine - bossy breathers everywhere and me always erasing myself on their behalf - the others they come and go - don't stay long - not buried though - lots of anger about that - put in warehouses instead- me , I been stuck here five solid weeks.

"My momma and me," said Betty Lou into the phone, "we just come back from Europe? Been gone awhile. We thought to check the morgue? For my beloved sister Betty Lou."

"What makes you think she might be here, Miss--"

"Jeanine Anne Hattersley. That's with two T's and an L-E-Y at the end. It's not like my sister, sir, to just disappear. We've called all the kinfolk we could to call and spoken to every friend she had."

"Now calm yourself, Miss Hattersley." The man at the other end sounded like a snippy officious busybody. Betty Lou pictured him dressed in dull brown, his dull gray lips flapping into the receiver. Mr. Boscom indeed! "When was the last time you spoke with your sister?"

"Oh it's hard to say. You so lose track of time when you travel. A couple of weeks, maybe three.

"We've had no Jane Does in that period of time."

"Jane Does?"

"One came in, four five weeks ago, still unclaimed. We call them Jane Does, you see if nobody - "

"Come to think of it, Mr. Boscom, it *was* the end of June we last roused Betty Lou on the phone. Lordy, you don't suppose it could be her!" She pulled wide eyes at her mother, who sat sipping black coffee on the couch and grinning behind her fist.

"Now stay calm. It's probably someone How old was your sister?"

"About my age. Early thirties - "

"Oh well then- "

"Course she didn't look her age."

"Older or younger?"

Betty Lou cursed him inside, then flipped a mental coin. "Younger. She looked somewheres in her twenties."

"Height?"

"Well, under six feet, that's for certain. I'm so muddle-headed at this sort of figuring. Let me picture her standing beside me. Oh this is so upsetting!"

"Ours is five foot six."

"Oh God, let me check with Momma." Hand over phone. "Caught ourselves a fish this time, Momma, a minnow and a half!" Back to Boscom. "Oh my dear sweet Jesus, that was my sister's height exactly. What color's her hair?"

"Let's see. Says blond here - "

"Oh my God - "

"No wait - can't read my own scrawl - it's brunette."

"Oh my God, brunette! That was her precise color! Mr. Boscom, do you suppose we could come down and take a peek at this . . . this Jane Doe? Oh Lord in heaven, our Betty Lou is dead!"

"Please, Miss Hattersley. Yes, do come down, if only to put your mind at rest. I'm sure our Jane Doe is not your sister."

- something new in the boscom breather - something about me - good god who dont exist and I always knew you didnt i hope he's not going to go disgusting again all over me - no this feels different - new mumblers picking up on the difference - raising the specter of respect for me among the others - not that i need them - insufferable prigs on their hoity-toity slabs - why dont they go get shipped to their precious warehouses - leave me be-

Betty Lou fluttered about Boscom's desk, showing just enough bosom to make the poor soul as pliable as a chicken bone set out overnight in vinegar. Made Millie Rae proud. He sat there dumbstruck in plaid, his thin, elbowed arms sticking out of a short-sleeved shirt and coming into enfoldment over the blotter in a puffed flurry of hands. Boscom's face reminded her of the beaky creatures in *The Dark Crystal*, but his eyes were bland as warm milk.

Together they plied him.

At last he led them to the wall of drawers. He tugged on one, waist high. Out it slid, easy as butter. Loathsome. Millie Rae suddenly wanted things to differ, wanted a normal Ozzie-and-Harriet kind of life for her and her daughter. Not this rootless gallimaufry of oddments that had come upon them when Willy pulled out of her life, taking everything not bolted down but his debts, leaving the two of them to fend off the wolves that came loping in.

"Oh Momma, hold me, I'm going to die."

Betty Lou collapsed in her arms, but Millie Rae kept her eyes fixed on the waxen face of the corpse and made her throat all tight and breathy with grief. "It's my Betty Lou, as sure as we're standing here." She squeezed out a tear and gave her best sob. "The life's drained from her pretty face, but there's no mistaking my first born baby girl."

"She was such a sweet sister."

Mr. Boscom was contrite. "Please accept my deepest condolences, ladies."

"Tell us, Mr. Boscom," said Millie Rae, "how did my little girl come to this dreadful conclusion?"

He closed the drawer first and helped them back to his desk. His aftershave affronted Millie Rae's nose; he smelled like a barber's accident. Then he told them as delicately as possible about the drugs, the needle, the cheap motel room they'd found her in. Millie Rae put on her sterling best performance. And Betty Lou matched her, sob for sob.

Boscom drew up the necessary papers for city hall and told them which office to go to for the death certificate. Everything was proceeding according to plan.

But then the conversation turned to funeral homes and burial, and Mr. Boscom got out his scrapbook of clippings, and that's when things went all to hell.

- thought rest was upon me - heard my momma and sister claim me - name me - betty lou they said but i cant recall it - others say thats common - family claims you - festoons you with flowers and music and weepy words - puts you under the earth and marks the spot in stone - helps you keep your identity about - but why i ask betty lou not being buried - why no one being buried - the angry dead rumble all around me - breathers refusal to make their shovels delve dirt in graveyard - want more money bulging out their pockets – only then shove in the spades - make coffin holes - dead stacked up in warehouses waiting - bursting the seams of mortuaries waiting -

waiting for one breather group to break or bow down to other breather group - dead fury raging all about me - fury raging inside me - growing stronger now that i know who I am and feel the tug of the ground -

Betty Lou burst through their apartment door, still cursing a blue streak. Millie Rae came after, defensive to a fault.

"Christ, daughter, you saw the clippings," she said. "The strike hasn't been front page news for months." She followed her daughter to the stack of newspapers piled by the day bed and watched her riffle through them.

"Look at this," Betty Lou threw back at her. "Page two, yesterday. Grave Diggers Turn Down Latest Proposal. Momma it was staring you smack in the face. Here it is in the first paragraph: 'Members of Cemetery Workers and Greens Attendants Local 622 voted by a two-to-one margin to reject the latest offer by Associated Cemeteries in a bitter two-month dispute that shows no sign of ending.'"

"So I missed it. So sue me!"

"You know how much I hate this town?"

"You think I like it any - "

"You just had to weep and wail and tell Harry Boscom and those bozos down at city hall that you've *got* to see your precious Betty Lou buried." She hurled the newspaper at her mother and flounced down on the day bed.

Millie Rae gripped her purse. "At least we got the death certificate, honey. We're halfway home."

"We're nowhere's where *we* are, Momma. Stuck in this stinking cow town for the Lord knows how long. Christ in heaven, I feel like that junkie stiff waiting for someone to shove her in the ground. I envy the bitch. Leastways she's got a cool slab to lie on."

"They're moving her to a refrigerated warehouse."

"Even better. Get me a community of cadavers going, a little music, a little loving. Get us organized. Go out and put a scare into Local Six Hundred Whatever. Jesus, Momma, can't we even pop for a fan?"

"You know how low we are on funds. Go take a bath, why don't you? Then we'll see about getting some work."

"Let's scam the hell out of this place. Do some sob-and-rob among the old folks. Christ, anybody who'd choose to retire to this hellhole's got to be dumb as dirt."

"No way, honey. We need to keep our faces clean till the strike's settled and our number comes up." Millie Rae dug into her handbag and pulled out the papers from the funeral home. "We're eighty-three at Holy Cross."

"Eighty-three, ain't that grand. Feels like we're at the meat counter, and with my luck that's just the kind of work I'll get. Wrapping bleeding hunks of liver for wimpy housewives."

"Don't fret honey," said Millie Rae, brushing back strands of her daughter's hair. "Soon's you're buried, we'll pull up stakes and head over to Las Vegas, maybe roll us some high rollers."

Betty Lou sighed. "Sounds like heaven, Momma."

- feels like a powerhouse being here - surrounded and enclosed by new others - anger's everywhere and growing - we crave earth – finality - want to strike out and torque the minds of spademen - drag some in here - smother them with rotting flesh - twist their heads about - get them digging again - i want to feel my momma hovering over me sobbing - feel my sister sobbing - get the music - get blessed - get a headstone and an armload of blooms to remember betty lou – me - proud in my identity - proud to be betty lou - proud of my momma's love - the others clench

like fists about their anger - i can feel our power growing with the delay - my own power growing like outrage -

"Hang on just a little longer, honey." She laid a black-gloved hand on Betty Lou's long black thigh and watched the blur of colors slide past outside.

Betty Lou brought her head close to her mother's ear and whispered impatiently: "Christ, Momma, it's October. I'm tired of slinging hash. And I'm tired of Harry Boscom coming round to see me."

"Hush, girl, or he'll hear you," said Millie Rae, but Boscom in the driver's seat of their spit-and-baling-wire Chevy Impala appeared to have his mind on tailgating the shiny black hearse. Besides, she noted, their old clunker was not of the quietest. "Daughter, don't crack on me now. Unless I'm much mistaken, that's Holy Cross just ahead. We get that little gal in the ground, we can pack up and be out of here before noon."

"Promise, Momma?"

"No later than one o'clock, I swear." It was hard for Millie Rae to judge her daughter's expression, what with both their faces veiled in black netting and the day dark and threatening rain; but from the way she slumped back in her seat, she seemed mollified.

Around the gravesite, the air felt oppressive under the lowering sky. They'd gotten some hoary old minister assigned to them. Good Lord, she thought, he looked like a wounded cow chewing the cud of holy biblicity. Unctuous drippings bibbled from his lips. Meaningless crap about heaven and God's mercy and the prematurity of poor Betty Lou's death.

"Preacher-man's giving me the creeps, Momma," came the veiled voice beside her.

"Me too, Betty Lou," she whispered. Miles away, a swift drum roll of thunder sounded. "Hang on, girl. What with the backlog of bodies, they've only allotted us half an hour.

Somebody's bound to cut him off and usher us out of here."

Across the way, Harry Boscom had the nerve to put a sanctimonious finger to his lips and silently shush her.

- betty lou - my momma called her betty lou - but thats who theyre burying - wrong daughter is being sunk into the ground - nothing but injustice - a world full of bad deeds and spite - first I felt the fury of the unburied - then the relief of getting ready to go down like im sposed to - now new fury rages inside me and im glad they postponed the shoveling and the shoving me under the turf - my mommas brain must be addled - calling her betty lou but burying me her eldest - must be in thrall to my sister – yes - reaching out I can feel her wickedness - thoughts thick with sludge and meanness - some scheme to divest me of whats properly mine-- feel like I can burst the bonds that bind me - gotta reach out and touch that evil sister of mine - feel shoots of fury push out through the pine lid - probe into her -

A wash of lightning lit the sky.

"Momma, I'm not feeling too good," said Betty Lou. There was queasiness inside. It hit her stomach first but spread rapidly into her chest and throat. She felt the urge to pitch forward onto the coffin, felt insanely as if that would help.

"Steady, girl," came her mother's voice, ringing in her ears like anesthesia taking hold.

The old minister crossed himself and closed his worn bound book of prayer against his chest. "Go in peace," he said, and a roll of thunder rumbled out of the distance as if in answer.

It sounded to Betty Lou like the growl of a stomach beneath which she felt oddly enwombed. The tight pocket of air enveloping her head buckled and warped like the cervix of the universe effacing. "Momma?"

Through gritted teeth: "Keep it together, honey. We're on our way to the car." Her momma's words crushed her skull like long forceps. She wanted to scream but couldn't. Her entire body was wracked now with the awful feeling, bound tight as spider's prey. She felt as if she were sliding headfirst into the ground, although she could see, as through a telescopic lens, her legs carrying her unsteadily across the grass. Momma's gloved hands gripped her upper arms with high tension.

Then a swift dilation twisted like an iris at the top of her scalp and she saw the scene slip away, felt herself slip away. Not into unconsciousness. Not into an absence of feeling. She was blind. Or there was nothing to see. Her body floated. No, her fingers, drifting over smooth cloth, were brought up short by unyielding planes of the stuff to either side. Drawing breath was getting harder. She raised her head, bonked it upward. "What the devil?" she said, and registered the dead dull confinement of her words. Without warning a rain of fists pounded above her, fists that laid down a sudden, battering volley along the length of her body, then vanished into stillness.

Her belly wrenched tight with fear.

Betty Lou knew where she was.

"Can I help?" Boscom's eager face poked its beaky nose around her daughter's far side as they walked.

"No," said Millie Rae, ready at last to haul off and give the smarmy, mealy-mouthed son of a bitch what for. But then: "Why, yes, Mr. Boscom. Would you kindly open the car door for my daughter? There's a dear."

Boscom galloped ahead like an ungainly colt and right then Millie Rae felt a change ripple through her daughter. One moment, she was as weak and woozy as a rag doll. The next, her strength and solidity returned, even though she staggered in Millie Rae's arms like an invalid getting out of bed for the first time in months. She eased Betty Lou into the passenger seat, then, "Good heavens, girl, what's wrong with you!" She lifted her legs in and slammed shut the door. A chill drop of rain smacked against the side of Millie Rae's nose. Another slanted down the rolled-up window behind which her black-veiled daughter sat.

"Where can I drive you two?" He had one hand on the back door handle, ready to help Millie Rae in. The other he'd stuck palm out, feeling for rain. His round-lidded eyes blinked against the first plash in a sudden rush of water. "Oh, my heavens!" said Mr. Boscom, and opened the door for her.

But Millie Rae put her hands out and slammed it shut, nearly catching Boscom's thumb. Then she hurried around the Impala to the other side. Holding her skirts up, she caught her shiny black image in the grille as she passed. "Nowhere atall, Mister Harry Boscom. We're on our way out of this town and" - (a quick roar like someone had turned on a shower full blast) - "we have no further use for your services, thank you kindly."

She tucked herself and her dress into the driver's seat and closed out the downpour. Whipping of f her veil and hat, she sailed them into the back seat and gunned the engine. "Hold tight, Betty Lou. We're shaking the dust of this town right now!" In the side mirror, she caught a glimpse of Boscom standing there bewildered, his dark hair plastered in wet strands down his forehead, arms raised in supplication after them, glasses steaming up. At a bend in the road, she spun the wheel and he was gone. "Drip," she muttered.

Her daughter sat silent and unmoving, still veiled, staring straight ahead. The wipers slapped at the base of the windshield. Rainwater crawled and trembled like blobs of quicksilver along the side windows.

"Betty Lou, you all right? Answer me, honey."

Her daughter's neck, turning under the black collar, cracked like a knuckle. It made the back of Millie Rae's scalp tingle to hear it. Her jaw was making an effort to open. She could see it strain under the veil. She heard Betty Lou's lips plip open like one long asleep fighting drymouth. Then they eased closed.

A whiff of grave-stench assaulted her.

"Betty Lou, you're giving me the willies. Now you answer me this minute. Mind your momma, hear?" Outside, dark tombstones whipped by. Up ahead, Millie Rae could see the tall wrought-iron gate of the cemetery; beyond it, a stream of trucks and cars, surprised into headlights.

The voice was abruptly there beside her in the car. It sounded like someone moaning from the bottom of a well but up close, close as a grown-up looming over a child's misdeed. "Muh-muh," it struggled out. "Muh-muh."

Before she could stop it, Millie Rae's hand shot out and tore away the veil. And her brainpan filled with the blurry eyes of the thing blinking at her, the moving mouth and the taut vellum cheeks. "Muh-muh," the thing said, its tongue moving thick and dull behind the white worm-wriggle of its lips.

But Millie Rae couldn't hear what it said because her own screaming took up all her earspace. To push away the horror, she stiff-armed the steering wheel and jammed down on the accelerator. The car veered wildly then slammed into a stone pillar to the right of the gate. It canted sharply upward. Millie Rae's body pitched forward, then back.

Then the corpse fell like deadweight on top of her.

More dirtfists thundered and thudded like judgment above her. They thrilled her, made her feel like peeing.

"Let me out," she yelled, hurting her ears with the sound of it but that didn't matter. Fresh air and light and life were all that mattered. "I'll be good, Poppa, I'll be good." Poppa? Woolen winter coats behind her in the hall closet crowding her like grownups, stern as the face of judges; galoshes groping for her heels.

By God, she'd suppressed it.

But there weren't no poppa out there now to plead with, or if there was he was one deaf implacable son of a bitch. Hard fists pummeled Betty Lou's immovable coffin lid. She wept and cursed and kicked at it.

Pain flared in Millie Rae's jaw cracked against the steering wheel. dentists bearing down all at once in Novocain, gleefully drilling for roots.

Above her the corpse's mouth opened like the slitted seam of an overripe tomato, spilling juice and seed on her cheeks. "Muh-muh," it said, and then its head fell like a dead slab of meat onto her face and its lips smooshed into hers.

Millie Rae, her head flaring, drew breath to scream and choked on the unspeakable drool of the thing.

Then the engine deafened her and flames whipped up like a windstorm about them.

This was decidedly not her day, thought Millie Rae absurdly, not her day at all.

But it was.

Betty Lou's too.

Better Forget

Liz Holliday

"Remember me, remember me, remember me when I am gone – "

The insistent rhythm of the train echoed Sally's thoughts. She shifted around on her seat, aware that she was dozing off. One hand clutched the book of Christina Rossetti poems she had been reading. With the other, she cushioned her head against the window. Mustn't sleep, she thought, or I won't be able to sleep tonight. Don't go to sleep, don't go to sleep clattered the train.

But she did.

She woke feeling gritty eyed and disoriented. She rubbed her eyes with the heel of her hand. How long had she been asleep? She glanced at her watch. It had been a good hour.

Pete wasn't there. Sally felt oddly bereft for a moment, as if he had deliberately betrayed her. Silly, she thought. You think he'll stop loving you just because his mum doesn't like you. He's probably just gone to the loo. She took another look at her book. The scrap of newspaper she was using as a bookmark fluttered to the floor. She picked it up, then tried to settle down again. *For if the darkness and corruption leave...* She shivered. When Pete had given her the book she hadn't realized how overblown and depressing it would be.

She looked out of the window again. The countryside rolled repetitively past: trees, telegraph poles, field with cows; trees, poles, cows; trees, poles, cows. In the distance, a line of storm clouds cut the perfect blue of the sky. It would be raining in London, she decided. Just then, she caught a movement out of the corner of her eye.

"Hi, sweetheart," she said without looking up, "You've been a while, haven't you?"

When there was no response, she turned to look at Pete, only to find the steward with the refreshment trolley there.

"Sorry 'bout that," Sally said. "I'll have a coffee, please, and ummm.... a diet Pepsi for my husband, wherever he's got to."

The steward looked at her oddly, but served her without comment. Sally sipped her coffee. It was tepid and bitter, and there wasn't enough milk. She sighed. Bad coffee was definitely one of the drawbacks of the long trip from Lancaster. She looked at her watch again, and realized with a start that Pete had been gone at least half an hour. In fact, they would be getting into London very shortly. She decided she had better try to find him. The buffet car seemed her best bet. She put her cup in the ring on the wall, and stood up.

She lurched down the carriage, jerking first to one side, then the other, against the pale plush of the seats. The next carriage was a smoker. The stink of stale tobacco hit her immediately. She pulled a face, then hoped no one would notice. She looked hopefully in each row of seats as she passed. Maybe Pete was having a cigarette, though he was supposed to have given up.

He wasn't, though.

Sally began to hurry, stumbling more and more against the rhythm of the wheels. You must find him soon, you must find him soon, they muttered and each time they got to soon she found herself clinging to a seat back. She felt as tired as if she had never slept at all, and utterly desperate to find Pete.

Another carriage. Then another.

Finally, she came to the buffet car. The narrow space beside the serving counter was empty. She could have wept. She leaned against the wall and closed her eyes, refusing to be soothed by the train's lullaby. She would cry. She knew it. The tears welled up even as she stood there.

She took a deep breath and refused to give in to the panic. It's just stress, she told herself, that's all. She looked around again. Beyond the far door she could see a half-empty carriage. She started to walk towards it when a steward came out of the kitchen galley, into the serving area, bringing with him a faint smell of stale grease and old meat. Slowly, he began to wipe the Formica countertop.

Sally crossed over to the counter. "Excuse me," she said, "I'm looking for a man."

The steward said, "Aren't we all, love." He moved a tray of tired looking sandwiches, and wiped underneath them.

Sally bit her upper lip. "My husband," she said, "I'm looking for my husband. He's tall, dark with a short beard and glasses. He's wearing a green sweatshirt and jeans and..."

"Could be anyone. If I were you I'd go back and wait in your seat. He can't have gone far." The steward walked around to the front of the counter, and started to pull down the metal grille. "Unless you think he ran off with another woman somewhere between Kettering and Luton."

"Thanks," Sally said. "I'll do that." She walked towards the far door.

"That's first class, that is," came the steward's voice behind her. Sally ignored him, and kept on walking. "Suit yourself, love. See if I care."

He wasn't there, wasn't in any of the other carriages either. Fighting panic, refusing to listen to the song of the wheels, keeping her head high, Sally returned to her seat.

The lights came on as she walked. She glanced at the windows, and was surprised to realize that they were in the outskirts of London. Rain slicked the windows, smearing the slashes of neon light that came and went and came again. He'll be there when I get back, Sally thought, and immediately the train echoed it: he will be there, he will be there, he's got to be, he's got to be.

But he wasn't.

He'll come, she thought, he's got to. For something to do while she waited, she got out the poetry book. The newspaper bookmark drew her eye, but she resolutely ignored it. She wanted to read as many of the poems as she could before Pete came back. He had tried hard to conceal his disappointment when she hadn't liked them. At least now she could say she had given them a decent chance. She glanced at the index, hoping to find something more to her taste. *The Heart Knoweth Its Own Bitterness. A Dirge. What Good Shall My Life Do Me?* She gave up and stared out of the window.

It was still raining, as it had when - when - , she couldn't remember. She thought she saw figures move, clothes black, and faces pale against the darkness of the storm. When had it rained? When had the rain fallen like tears? She knew. She knew these people who were crying in the rain; but she also knew that if she let herself remember them the world would come apart around her-

She jerked awake. Her mouth was dry and her heart was pounding. It had been a dream, just a stupid dream. She would tell Pete about it when he came back.

She picked up the book from where it had fallen on the floor. The bookmark was still in it, a yellowing scrap of newsprint. It looked more interesting than the poetry, but she knew that if she wanted to surprise Pete she would have to concentrate on the book. *Remember me when I am gone away* - It struck her that that was exactly what Pete had done. She would have to point it out to him later. She imagined how they would giggle over it together, and suddenly she found that she was laughing out loud.

When she had calmed down she found that she was clutching the scrap of newspaper. She unclenched her fingers, suddenly realizing that she didn't want to see what was written on it.

Despite that, the headline jumped out at her: MOTORWAY PILE-UP. That sounded sad. She didn't want to be sad. She looked at the book again.

Better by far that you should forget.

She decided that she'd had enough of Rossetti. The woman was an idiot. How could anyone want to forget someone she had loved?

She didn't want to think about that, but now she only had the scrap of newspaper to take her mind off it. MOTORWAY PILE-UP KILLS FOUR. There. It was as sad as she had expected it to be. She turned back to the book: Better *by far that you should forget and smile, than that you should remember and be sad.* She had been right. Rossetti was an idiot. Sally threw the book on the seat beside her. She would just have to tell Pete she didn't like the book.

She glanced again at the newspaper. Pete's name leaped out of the page at her. *Local man Peter Lewiston was killed in a five-car pile up on the M25 near London-"*

No," Sally whispered. But it was no use. She remembered it all: remembered the drive up and how excited they had both been to be going home for the first time in a year, remembered the policeman's face when he told her, remembered the sweet, scalding tea the nurse gave her, the terrible argument with his mother about where the burial should be. Remembered most of all, the driving rain that had drenched them as they lowered the coffin into the mud.

She closed her eyes. It seemed to her that the darkness would overwhelm her. Tears burned down her cheeks. He was gone, dead beneath a pile of twisted metal. She opened her eyes to brush the tears away.

Pete was sitting opposite her. She looked at him, knowing beyond doubt that he was dead. The air around him shimmered with light. He put down the scrap of newspaper he was holding. His hands and face were pale, and his eyes were raw from crying. She wanted to go to him, to comfort him. He stared at her through the bright air, and she knew that he could see her.

"Peter?" she said, and at the same instant she saw his lips silently form the word, Sally.

She stood up and balanced herself against the rocking of the train. His eyes never left her as she took a tiny step across to him. She brushed her lips across his. Just no gentle kiss but coldness sliced through her.

If she had dared she would have tried to take his hand. She did not. But her gaze fell on Peter's paper, on the article that said, *Local woman Sally Lewiston was killed in a five car pile up on the M25 near London-*

Dear God, Sally thought. Am I dead, then? But the railway carriage was reassuringly solid, and she could feel her nails bite the palms of her hands.

She reached out to touch Peter, but the light surrounding him was fading. He grew slowly dimmer, more out of focus.

"Don't go." He mouthed the word silently. She understood then. He would live on without her, in his other world, as she would have to live without him. Then he spoke again: "Better forget."

What had the poem said? *Better by far that you should forget and smile/ Than that you should remember and be sad?*

Then she understood. He wanted her to do the hardest thing of all. He wanted her to be happy, even without him.

I can't do this, she thought. But she knew she wanted the same thing for him.

And so, before he was quite gone from her, she whispered in her turn, *"Better forget."*

And then the light faded and she was alone in the darkness.

I Know What Scares You

Greg Burnham

The bright red slit on the horizon stretched across the sky like a knife wound to the belly. The two men worked diligently stacking the freshly exhumed coffins in the storage shed at the back of the cemetery. The task was morbid and a bit foreboding, but the pay was good. One hundred dollars per coffin cash money, and for a couple of out of work, down on their luck handy men, it was perfect.

"Hey Bubba, it's gettin dark and this place gives me the heebie-jeebies. Let's get outta here and come back in the mornin."

"Damn, T-bone, quit whinin'! All we got is a couple more and we'll be done!"

T-bone, a gangly youth flashed a shaky smile and wiped his filthy hands nervously on his ragged flannel shirt. "Don't it feel weird to you? I mean these coffins, they full of dead people."

"Come on an get in the truck, jus two more by the front gate and we'll be done," Bubba hawked a wade of tobacco out onto the ground and wiped the dribble from his square chin with a soiled denim jacket sleeve. He was doing a better job at concealing his uneasiness, but as the bloody hue of sky faded into the fast approaching blackness of night, he too felt a sudden urgency to complete the task.

They were just able to navigate the old Chevy pick-up through the labyrinth of tombstones without adding to the assortment of dents that already littered the truck. More importantly they had been able to do this without the aid of headlights. This represented security for the two men, because as long as they didn't need headlights to see, it was obviously not yet night time, and no malevolent entity could roam outside of the realm of darkness.

They moved together quickly with the synchronization that comes only with repetition as they wedged the last coffin in the shed among the other hulking boxes. The freshly unearthed soil caked on the burnished wooden surfaces of the coffins acted as a lubricant allowing them to slide the cargo into place with minimal effort. They both smiled in silence as Bubba closed the heavy doors and snapped the master lock into place.

"Seventy-two of them sum bitches. That's $7,200 to me and you," Bubba sighed and started on the six pack of beer he had stashed in a small cooler.

"How'd you go about findin' a crazy job like this anyway, Bubba?" T-bone grabbed one of the cans and cracked the top.

"Ms. Sally Baker." Bubba gulped his beer.

"That rich lady that owns the real-estate company?"

"That's the one. She bought the cemetery and gonna build one of them outlet shoppin' malls startin' at the gate," he pointed his meaty finger toward the road.

"She said Springtown was the perfect spot for a mail being right smack between Chattanooga and Knoxville, lot of traffic she says. Then she said that the cemetery here is sittin in the best place since the interstate exit is just half a mile up the highway," Bubba took another swig.

"Anyway, she gave me a call and said she had a bulldozer ready to go and all she needed was a couple of guys to dig em and haul em into the Quonset hut back here. Said she couldn't think of nobody who did better work than us. Plus she'd pay us $100 a head if we got it done by today," he smiled and crushed the empty beer can.

"What she gonna do with all them coffins?"

"Relocate em I guess," Bubba slid off the hood of the battered truck. "Let's go, it's gettin dark."

"You ain't lyin'. I don't like bein' in no grave specially at night," T-bone said pulling himself up bench seat of the truck, that was little more than a tarp stretched over springs.

"Jesus Christ T-bone!" Bubba barked as he opened the driver side door, his hand cupped over his nose. "What the hell did you do, shit yer britches?!"

T-bone replied with a grimace. "Geez! It does stink in here! You musta stepped in dog shit or someth…" A terrified gasp choked off the words.

"Wh-wh-who the h-h-hell is that?" he mumbled, barely getting the words past his trembling lips. Bubba looked up to see what T-bone was babbling about.

By this time the moon had made its debut for the evening and the pale blue illumination of icy moonbeams allowed them to see the bizarre stranger. A tall dark figure wearing a dark suit with a top hat stood at the edge of the storage shed. It was a man, but even in the fluorescent light of the moon they could see that he was not human.

His arms and legs were elongated and slender to the point of being out of proportion with his torso. The skin was pasty white and luminous in the moon, it looked splotchy and lifeless as if it belonged to a zombie. His dull red eyes leered at them from sunken hollow sockets like an animal of prey evaluating it's victim. Both Bubba and T-bone were frozen by the hypnotic stare of the grotesque man, which easily penetrated their superficial thoughts deep into their minds' eye.

It suddenly became eminently cold, not because the sun had dropped below the December mountains of Tennessee, but from the presence of evil. This was a stone cold, a frigidity that crystallized every fiber of their beings into irretrievable blackness.

They felt the loathsome probe into their psyches as if it were a libidinous young boy tearing through the pages of a pornographic magazine in search of the centerfold. It was forceful. It was lustful. Then, like the climaxing orgasm of that refractory boy, it was gratified. It had found what it had come looking for.

A blinding flash cracked and T-bone blinked his eyes purposefully then leaned forward.

"Hey, where did he go?" He squinted to intensify his field of vision. "Bubba, where did he... Bubba?"

Bubba was no longer beside him. T-bone flounced awkwardly like a fish out of water, searching frantically out of every window of the vehicle before he caught the moonlit figure of Bubba in the rear view mirror. He was moving away from the truck at a high rate of speed.

"Bubba!! Wait!!"

T-bone grabbed aimlessly at the door latch. It would not open. Even when he pulled the door lock up yanking on the latch it still wouldn't budge. Stretching across to the driver's side door he was denied again. Thrashing violently, he punched and kicked at the windows, no use. He may as well have been a rotting corpse in the stagnant tomb this truck represented. He tucked his knees under his arms in the fetal position and closed his eyes tight, hoping this would protect him from the decaying zombie that lurked in the darkness.

T-bone jerked in response to the shrieking wind outside the truck. He rubbed his eyes and glanced at his watch, he had been asleep for over an hour.

"I know what scares you."

"Huh?" T-bone froze instantly in response to the hollow whisper. After a few minutes of intent listening he finally relaxed, it had only been the wind.

"I know what scares you." The faint voice echoed again, more emphatic this time.

"Who said that?!" T-bone screamed, looking desperately for the source. Nothing. He was alone.

A moment passed before something caught his attention, a shadow inching across the dashboard. He just stared as his mind tried to determine what the motion was that slowly darkened the cracked vinyl of the dash.

"A cloud must be crossing the moon," he offered under his breath and gazed carefully out of the window. Not so. The pure unadulterated brilliance of lunar rays glowed powerfully throughout the cemetery casting elongated shadows from the tombstones, but none over the truck.

"What the hell is that?" He nervously reached out toward the oozing flood of blackness. He squinted cautiously as he made contact. It was definitely moving, or crawling, which he found to be the more accurate description.

"Shit!!"

T-bone wailed uncontrollably as he bounced around the interior of the truck, pounding furiously at the windows.

"Bubba! Anyone! Let me outta hear goddamn it! Let me out!!"

The pain was unbearable, enveloping his body in small bursts like so many piercing needles invading his skin. Each bite was more excruciating than the previous, which eventually immobilized his limbs. Without the use of his hands to swat the attackers away he could only lie motionless as the swarms of spiders covered him like thick molasses.

The poison injected into his flesh from the relentless fangs of thousands of Black Widows left him blind with pain; he was totally helpless to the slaughter. Then, as if they were being directed, the uncountable arachnids bit down simultaneously filling his trembling body with a mass of deadly venom, and inevitable death.

"I'm tellin you it was like some kind of creature, or somethin. I mean whatever it was, it weren't human."

"If you keep up with this I'm going to have to sedate you again."

"No!" Bubba implored the nurse still groggy from the previous administering of sedatives. "Don't do that, I need to be alert. It's gonna come for me."

"Listen to me Bubba, you've had a rough night, try and get some sleep."

A knock sounded on the door and both Bubba and the nurse looked up across the room. It was a man in an overcoat with two uniformed policemen behind him.

"Please extinguish that thing, you are in a hospital," the nurse got up and started out the room. The man just smiled.

"Give me a minute, will ya boys?" He waved off the two men in blue and closed the door behind him.

"I'm Detective Branson. I read your chart out there. You really believe what you're saying to be true?" He pulled heavy on his cigarette.

"You gotta believe me, that thing read my mind. It fuckin knows my deepest fear. It's gonna kill me!"

"Hold on cowboy, who's gonna kill you?"

"T-bone's dead, I know he is, and I didn't do nothin'. I was jus' to damn scared, so I ran." Bubba stared blankly at the wall.

"Wait a minute. Whose T-bone?" He thumped his cigarette onto the floor and ground it with his foot.

"Go to the cemetery, you'll see, he's dead."

Branson jerked the door open and hurried out into the hall. He barked at the two officers and then motioned for a doctor. After a few minutes of debating he rushed back into the room throwing a crumpled piece of paper on the bed next to Bubba.

"Those are your rights, read em, you're under arrest. If you have any questions you can ask em at the station."

"What's goin on here?" Bubba looked confused.

"I talked to your doctor and he says there's nothing wrong with you physically. He said you just busted in the emergency room ranting and raving about the boogey man. He feels you need a psychological evaluation and since we've got a shrink at the station, and you just told me someone was dead at the cemetery, I figured I'd kill two birds with one stone," he huffed intensely while cuffing Bubba.

"But I didn't do nothin! T-bone's my friend!"

"Well, if you didn't do anything, just think of it as police protection. After all, you did say someone was going to kill you and I'm just doing my job to protect the citizens of Springtown, Tennessee."

The rusty hinges of the cemetery gate creaked in the howling winter wind as Sally Baker eased her Mercedes through the narrow opening. The headlights did little good to pervade the gloomy shadows that filled the graveyard like cobwebs in an abandoned attic.

She fiddled with the lock before swinging the shed doors wide with delight.

"All there! I knew those half-witted yard boys would do it without a question." The corners of her mouth curled into a devious smile.

"Bunch of worthless worm food if you ask me. By next week I'll be using you guys to fertilize my lawn and your headstones will be properly relocated across town at my new cemetery. Oh the beauty of being brilliant!" She spoke to the tower of coffins as if they could understand her vicious intentions.

She slammed the doors with malice and hurried back into the warmth of her car. After cranking the heater to full blast and blowing into her hands she placed the gear in drive and started out slowly.

"I know what scares you."

The almost inaudible whisper chilled the air and then vanished. Sally pricked her ear up and turned from side to side. Nothing. She turned the knob on the radio off and shrugged slightly.

She was already out on the highway when something darted into the road. After slamming on the brakes and losing control of the car she found herself in a shallow ditch on the side of the road. The wheels spun mindlessly as she tried to gun her way out of the slushy ditch, only digging a deeper rut with every turn.

"Shit!" she shouted and looked both ways down the road without any reassurance. No cars in sight. The temperature was well below freezing and other than the elegant evening dress and fur coat she'd worn to the theater, she was alone.

Upon situating herself for the hike into town, she noticed something down the road. As it approached she realized it was a man and he was heading straight for her. At first her reaction was of relief, but soon changed to terror as he came into focus.

"Shit," she repeated under her breath and reached into the glove box withdrawing a .25 caliber revolver.

The closer he came, the more ghoulish he appeared. He was very tall and lanky and was wearing a long overcoat and hat. With every step Sally became more nervous and as soon as he was within fifteen feet she cut on the headlights, rolled down the window and stuck her hand out waving the gun.

"I've got a gun, and I'll blow your ass away if you take one more step toward me!" she threatened in an anxious voice. The man never broke his stride and continued forward. "I'm serious you bastard, I'll kill you!!"

The man pulled his hands out of his pockets and cracked his knuckles, never slowing his pace. He was now within a few feet of her car and Sally let off six rounds, emptying the chamber. The fire and smoke from the bullets sank deep into his chest and head holding him up in his steps a few seconds before dropping him to the muddy ground.

Steam rose from his body as he laid face down in the icy slush water. Sally leaned back in the car and quickly pressed the button to raise the window and lock the doors. Her heart was pounding as she closed her eyes and threw the gun on the floorboard. After catching her breath she slowly peeked over the steering wheel. Suddenly her eyes widened and she frantically scanned outside in search of the man. His body was not there.

Once she was satisfied that he was not around the car she grabbed for the gun and started to dig through the glove box. After a few minutes of fumbling, she found two more bullets and quickly loaded them into the revolver.

An hour had passed and although she was still trembling she had convinced herself that he probably rolled in front the car, just out of her view.

"I blew him the fuck away! Dead as a doornail!" She laughed to herself before smelling a sudden pungent odor that filled the car.

"God, there must be a skunk around here! That's the most disgusting thing I've ever smelled." she gagged and pulled her coat up over her nose.

While squirming about searching for the cause of the repulsive stench, she glanced up at the rear view mirror and saw him. There he was, sitting in the back seat with a loathsome grin. Three bullet holes were visible, two in his forehead and one directly under his left eye, and other than a brownish oily substance draining from the wounds against his decomposing face, he was fine. Actually he was giggling in a high pitched demonic cackle.

Sally spun around screaming, squeezing off two more shots. The man laughed and pushed open his overcoat revealing a monstrous erect organ that was throbbing from his groin. Before Sally could move he ripped the sequined dress open and pushed her knees up to her shoulders. The car rocked violently as Sally screamed and begged for mercy with every jolt. Finally, after what seemed an eternity of the brutal impalement, her insides gave way as the molestation tore into her flesh. Then silence.

The car sat motionless as the moon peacefully illuminated the bright white frost that had calmly settled over it.

"What's all the commotion out there?" Bubba called and within seconds Branson was at his cell.

"We just found Sally Baker out on Cemetery Road," he opened the lock. "She was murdered in her car. The good news for you is that it happened while you in here, so you're off the hook."

"And T-bone?"

"Yeah, dead, at the cemetery."

"It knows what scares you. That's how it kills you." Bubba put his head in his hands and closed his eyes.

"Bubba, you said that something scared you out there earlier tonight. What was it?"

Bubba spent the next half-hour describing in detail what he had encountered at the cemetery. After the interview Branson told Bubba he could stay at the station, as it would be the safest place for him.

"Hey Detective, it was spiders wasn't it?"

Branson stopped at the door.

"That sum bitch was like a little girl when it came to spiders, specially Black Widows. He got bit by one a few years ago, nearly killed him, ever since when we gotta plumbin' job, or somethin', he wouldn't never go under a house, or up in the attic. He was scared of gettin bit."

"Shit," Branson breathed hard. "I-bone was killed by no less than two thousand spider bites, Black Widow."

"What about Ms. Baker, what happened to her?"

"Sally Baker was assaulted and grotesquely molested. Her vagina and stomach were shredded; internal organs burst like water balloons. I've never seen anything like it, she was nearly split in two." He shrugged. "And guess what? When she was a teenager she was attacked, raped and nearly bled to death. I'd say that qualifies as something that scared her, don't you?"

Bubba wrung his hands. "Doctors, that's what scares me. All them shots and scalpels, cuttin' and stitchin! Burrr! Makes my skin crawl jus' thinkin' about it. Hell, I had a hernia for damn near twenty years now, never had it fixed cause I'm scared of bein' cut."

Branson smiled politely and walked to the door. "Get some sleep, Bubba, I'll see you in the morning."

"I know what scares you."

"Wuh?" Bubba sat up straight on the cot in a cold sweat.

After looking around for a few minutes he remembered that he was in the small drafty cell and that he must have been having a nightmare. He rubbed his eyes and laid his head back down on the hard pillow letting out a disgusted sigh, when something caught his eye in the corner. He couldn't see very well as all the lights were off other than the security light, which actually threw shadows, making it darker in his cell. He didn't think much of it and was about to shut his eyes when something moved again, very slowly.

"Who's there?" he whispered, still not quite sure if his eyes were playing tricks on him. Although there was no answer he sensed something was there and decided to investigate. He rolled over and stood up from his bed finding the icy cold floor with his bare feet.

"Burrrr," he trembled in discomfort and quickly sat back down on the edge of the cot.

He stuck out his hand to feel around then suddenly jerked it back. Something was there in the dark. Before he even had the opportunity to speak, a vile yet familiar stench filled the air. He immediately retreated back into the farthest corner of the cell as his eyes adjusted to the dark

"Who is it?!" Bubba exclaimed terrified, trying not to inhale to deeply. The figure just leaned against the cell door, methodically rubbing his hands together.

"Who are you, goddamn it?!" he insisted again, becoming increasingly sickened by the foul odor.

"How you doin' Bubba?" A deep scratchy voice projected from the shadows.

Bubba felt every hair on the back of his neck stand up, accompanied by a bone-chilling breeze that enveloped his body. He stood silent in the corner shaking uncontrollably and slowly succumbing to the putrid fumes.

"What's wrong Bubba? Cat got your tongue?" he hissed and suddenly jolted forward forcing Bubba's mouth open, grabbing his tongue, and then slicing it off with the stroke of a blade.

Bubba immediately fell to the floor in agony as the blood poured out of his mouth in a continual rush. Somehow remaining conscious, while desperately squirming around on the floor, he managed to pull himself up onto the commode and stuff handfuls of toilet paper into his mouth. Although the pain was blinding, the wads of paper had drastically slowed the bleeding, allowing him to focus on his assailant. He held the rolls of crumpled tissue firm in his mouth and slowly raised his head.

What he saw filled him with fear so intensely that he could actually feel his heart swelling larger and larger with every rapid beat. There, outlined in the weak light, was the creature from the cemetery, more hideous than the nefarious stench it emitted. He was slightly hunched over devouring the freshly severed tongue that he held up to his mouth. After lapping up the bloody residue from his hands he leaned toward Bubba and belched.

"You don't look well," he whispered in a desolate voice and pushed Bubba flat onto the cot. "Maybe this will help!"

Bubba moaned and jerked convulsively as the polished stainless steel of sharpened cutlery hacked away in a spray of his own blood. Inch by inch, starting with his fingers, then hands, then elbows, then shoulders, his arms were mutilated. Next were his legs, starting with his toes and so on, in the same manner, until he was no more than a bloody stump.

As if it were some black miracle his brain continued to receive messages of excruciating pain, his heart continued to pump the blood out of the freshly amputated sockets, and his eyes watched in horror as the putrescent ghoul looped a stiff, black suture through the end of a long thick needle.

"Don't worry Bubba, I can fix it!" He laughed diabolically as the massive loss of blood slowly snuffed Bubba's torment.

"This is not tolerable!" Branson slammed the phone down and headed out the door.

It was 3 a.m. calls like these that made him regularly question why he had chosen to become a homicide detective, but never in all his years on the force had he ever heard of anything like this. As usual he'd fallen asleep in his cheap non-press suit, so getting ready was irrelevant other than downing half a bottle of Listerine to combat the whiskey fumes that he was filtering through his mustache.

"How in the hell could this happen in the middle of the jail?!"

"I don't know, but some sick bastard had fun," the coroner pulled the plastic away from the body. "It looks like they cut all of his appendages off in sections and then sewed them back on. Fucking Frankenstein wannabe."

Branson massaged his temples. "It's just like he said."

"What's that," the coroner zipped the plastic back.

"Uh, nothing. Does the chief know about this yet?"

"He's in there chewing some ass right now. You need to talk to him?"

"Just tell him to check out Sally Baker Real Estate. I think she shuffled some paperwork on that cemetery deal. See if she had all the environmental documents to exhume those graves and also if she had the proper regulatory agency approval to relocate the bodies. If I'm right she didn't have shit, but a bunch of corpses stacked up in a storage shed."

"What's this got to do with anything, Branson?"

"Everything, I think. Just do it, okay?" He pushed through the crowd of police and headed for the cemetery.

He parked outside the gates and slowly walked into the dark graveyard.

"Where the hell are you?" he whispered and eased up to the large rusty cast iron gate.

A sudden cold breeze blew from within the cemetery and a chill swept across his body. He continued to look into the blackness of the trees and tombstones. Somewhere in the dark lurched a monster and another chill shot through his body, only this time it was not from the brisk wind.

Although he was feeling uneasy being there by himself, he continued his search and began to cautiously walk down the dark little road leading through the cemetery. He made it about midway through before he caught the odor. It was decadent and he knew in an instant that this was it.

He hefted his flashlight and aimed it straightforward to cut through the towering shadows all around him. Then, as if it had stagnated, the icy breeze, the putrid bouquet fumed again and something moved. The terror swelled in his stomach.

"This is it," he mouthed quietly after placing the flashlight beam directly on the figure. It was the ghoul that Bubba had described to him.

It stood absolutely motionless on top of a tall headstone, feet planted firmly and arms hanging down below the knees. The tattered black suit, with a long bow tie and lace up dress shoes dated him to sometime around the turn of the century. His pale face was discolored with rot and the eyes had a hellish red tint. At about eight feet tall with spiderlike appendages he looked supernatural, but had enough human qualities to offset the elongated skeletal limbs.

Just as Branson felt the anxiety slightly subside to bewilderment, the creature started to bob up and down bending only at the knees, slowly and methodically. This gesture froze Branson back into his icy fear and all he could do was stare. It continued to make this rhythmic motion for about a minute when suddenly it jumped from the top of the headstone toward Branson. In unison, an invisible force jumped forward with the ghoul, stabbing deep into his mind.

Branson forgot about reasoning with this monster and turned to run, breaking off the probe. He bolted across the graveyard dodging and maneuvering through the merciless maze of tombstones and trees. He had not gotten far before the creature started appearing in front of him blocking his escape. Every time Branson would hysterically change directions to flee from his pursuer, there it was, right in front of him. Finally after becoming fatigued and at his wits end

Branson just stopped.

"What do you want!" he shouted in terror.

"I know what scares you."

"Ohhh, God!" Branson moaned and stumbled back a few steps sickened by the intrusive penetration into his mind and was instantly lifted off the ground by the monsters strong hand.

"Oh no, not God," it replied, dispelling its noxious breath with every word. The stench was like no other Branson had ever known and, had he not been strangled by the creature, he would have surely vomited.

Branson was dangling high above the ground, suspended in the air by the monster's hand wrapped tightly around his neck. His face turned purple as the lack of oxygen and the pressure from the grasp made his eyes bulge in their sockets. He strained to keep conscious when suddenly he was lowered to the ground, but not released from the death lock on his throat.

The ghoul placed his elongated forefinger on the corner of Branson's eye and began to slice downward across his cheek with a jagged fingernail. Branson could not feel the actual pain from the incision as his bloated face was already stinging with pressure, but he did feel the warm thick liquid running down his skin. He was dizzy and losing consciousness.

"This must be death," he thought and a silent calm fell over him.

"No, not so fast Detective Branson. It's better when these things take time, you know, a little longer for us to enjoy them," the monster hissed.

Branson suddenly found himself collapsed on his back gasping heavily for air. The wheezing deep breaths of cold December air stung his throat and lungs. As he slowly regulated his breathing he noticed that the hideous ghoul was standing directly over him emitting a low angry growl.

He stared at Branson for a few seconds then bared his long yellow teeth with a loathsome grin that widened the hellish red eyes. His gums were decayed and infected and had receded leaving only the rotted teeth.

"Suffocation? Now I would think a big tough cop like you would have something more scary than suffocation packed away in his slimy gray matter, but if that's what scares you. " The ghoul quickly pinned Branson to the ground, dropped down directly over him and licked his face.

"Eat this you little bitch!"

He pushed his mouth over Branson's and started to convulse in spurts, sending periodic chunks of regurgitated matter into Branson's mouth. The substance was decrepit and tasted like spoiled meat. Before long he was vomiting a steady flow into Branson, forming a tight seal around his lips to assure it was all being ingested.

Branson was nearly suffocated when he managed to get his gun from under his coat and start firing into the monster's head, hurling him back into the darkness.

Branson rolled over and started vomiting profusely until the entire contents of his stomach were emptied into a quivering loaf of rancid matter. He shook the lightness from his head and stumbled for the gate only to be intercepted by his gothically stoic nemesis.

Weak and beaten, Branson fell to his knees and groaned. "Who are you?"

"I am the keeper of this cemetery. Every boneyard has one and as the first body to be laid to rest here, it is my curse to guard the sanctity of these graves for all eternity."

"What do you want?"

"I want our resting place back and I will continue to kill until I get it. It is a domino effect, first T-bone because he pulled my grave out of the ground. Then Sally because she bought the consummated ground, and if she hadn't bought it then poor T-bone couldn't have exhumed me. Next would be Bubba, he got T-bone the job, then you for helping Bubba in the jail cell. It's

going to be the Chief of Police next because he employs you, and so on, and so on, and so on, until our bodies are back in hallowed ground."

Branson had raised to his feet by now and somehow managed to orchestrate a proposal for the ghoul. "What if I tell you I can get you the cemetery back?"

"Sally Baker's company never had the intention of relocating. She has instead signed the contents of the cemetery over to waste management, for a considerable fee, but nevertheless much more economical than total relocation of seventy-two coffins."

"No! Listen to me! I'm having my people check into that as we speak. By tomorrow afternoon, Baker real-estate will be under criminal investigation, and I will personally get a court order to have all the coffins put back in this cemetery." Branson's eyes shifted furiously in his head for signs of acceptance.

It was a long anxious minute before a reply came. *"You can do that?"*

"Absolutely! It's basically a done deal. I figured out Baker's relocation scam earlier today and had the department start collecting evidence immediately," he surged with a sudden relief.

"By tomorrow evening I want all seventy-two coffins in the earth," the keeper waves a crooked finger from to side.

"Done, but I need a promise from you as well." Branson gestured.

"You are in no position to negotiate." It drew close to Branson and the malodorous breath lurched through rotted teeth. Branson turned, still weakened by the violent convulsions earlier, and stepped away wearily.

"I need you to promise me that no one else will be killed. It's the only way I will agree. Please. ." His words broke off, no longer able to fend off the dry heave spasm from the pit of his stomach.

"You have a deal. But remember, you guarantee the serenity of my graveyard. Do not disappoint me. Ever."

"I guess this is kind of like a deal with the devil, huh?" Branson attempted humor to ease his own mind. The hideous ghoul bared it's teeth in a sinister grin.

A bright flash cracked, as if from a huge lightening bolt and Branson was alone. He scanned desperately, but only the rows of tombstones stared back. They resembled gnarled teeth of the monster, jutting out of the ground tainted and uneven. It was all he could do not to break down and sob, so he ran blindly through the pitch of blackness.

Ten years had past since the pact was birthed on that blustery December night in the damp and dark graveyard. Detective Branson was now Chief Branson and the case file labeled, *The Cemetery Stalker* had been long since forgotten. Although the case had remained unsolved for several years, after being promoted to Chief of Police, Branson had officially closed the file and successfully lost it in the infinite city archives.

It was twelve o'clock and Branson was out for his usual Friday lunch at the Chinese restaurant when the waiter brought him the daily paper and a fortune cookie. It was his routine to have stir fried rice with spicy chicken, a fortune cookie and then read the paper every Friday at lunch. It had not changed in seven years.

"Your fortune cookie and newspaper, Chief," the waiter offered with a heavy Asian accent.

"Thanks, Ping and tell Lei Pow that the stir fry was delicious."

The man bowed his head graciously and disappeared into the kitchen.

Branson stretched out the folded newspaper longways on the table and wiped the fresh ink from his fingertips before tearing the plastic wrapper from his cookie. He broke it half and pulled the white slip of paper out while crunching heartily on the brown shell. Mindfully sipping on his coffee he straightened the tiny scroll and adjusted his glasses to read the oriental prophecy.

Involuntarily, his eyes widened and his coffee to the floor. He gasped deeply to try and swallow erupting anxiety only to exasperate the situation. A piece of the brittle cookie lodged forcefully in the tender folds of his throat and immediately arrested his air flow.

The suffocation was just as he remembered it so many years ago in that cemetery, helplessness. Total unmerciful helplessness. The unreleased pressure within his lungs stung like so many wasps and it felt as if a sledgehammer was repeatedly slamming into his chest. Everything exploded into a crimson red hue as the delicate vessels behind his eyes burst in the swollen sockets.

"No! We had a deal!" The thought echoed through his mind as if he were yelling it directly to the hideous ghoul himself.

"This can't happen! I had the graves put back a decade ago!" he continued the silent plea, but the only answer was relentless pain and deafening silence until finally the icy hand of death pulled him away into blackness.

When the police arrived at the scene they examined body which was now hunched over and lifeless on the table. The waiter was babbling frantically in broken English.

"I think he choke! I try to help, but he just fall over dead! I call 911!"

When they lifted Branson's head, the doughy remains of a fortune cookie oozed out the corner of his mouth onto his newspaper, the front page of which read in bold black letters:

Ten-year-old project to construct Shopping Mall over old cemetery starts today at noon.

The officer collected the newspaper from the table allowing a small slither of paper to drift to floor as he did. The tiny black letters of the fortune cookie prophecy read simply:

I know what scares you.

Caretaker of the Ring

Michael C. McPherson

Percy Tretsmire placed his lantern-styled flashlight down alongside his tool bag on an angle so that its light would shine directly onto the coffin lid. Rubbing his hands together, he cracked his knuckles for good luck. Not that he felt he really needed it. Everything was going great so far. He had climbed over the spiked fence with no problem at all, had picked the lock on the iron door leading into the mausoleum like he was professional. It took him less than two minutes to enter the cold dank room, a world record in his books.

Placing the smooth flat end of his pinch bar between the lid and the box, Percy put his weight against it until he heard both catches snap free. Losing his balance as it gave way, he did a little Russian dance with his two feet before falling down on his rump on the hard floor. The pinch bar clattered noisily as it hit the concrete beside him, and Percy winced at the sharp echo of it bouncing about the small chamber.

Jumping back up on his two feet, he hurried over to the iron door and opened it slightly, peering cautiously out into the darkness of the cemetery. After a few moments of leaning an attentive ear to the crack he created, he breathed a sigh of relief and returned to his work.

Crouching down Percy studied the coffin lid to make sure he hadn't caused any noticeable damage. "Good," he announced in a low whisper as he ran a bony rough hand along the seam. "Ain't nobody gonna suspect a thing." Lifting the lid, he looked fearlessly in at the supine and unsmiling face of Ivan E. Roffgelt, the former millionaire industrialist.

"Look at you," Percy scoffed. "You're all decked out in a thousand dollar suit. Tch-tch, what a waste of good money. Good thing I don't let my greed bowl me over. If I did, I'd strip you of those duds in no time." His eyes widened as they fell upon the object he had come to steal. It was a large ruby ring surrounded by a cluster of small diamonds, set in a golden flower petal.

Resting both arms down on the sides of the box, the thief in the night stared down at the grim-faced Roffgelt with a mischievous twinkle in his eye. "Why, you old sonofabitch," he laughed dryly. "You even tried to take that big beautiful rock out of this world, didn't you?" Reaching down and lifting the cold and rigid index finger, Percy wormed his thumb and forefinger around until he had hold of the thick and shiny ring. He tugged at it greedily, his eyes mocking the dead. Unable to free it from Roffgelt's finger, Percy grabbed hold of the lifeless wrist and began to twist the ring back and forth with all his might, but it still wouldn't budge. "I'm afraid old chum," he panted. "I'm going to have to get nasty with this finger of yours." Percy reached over and pulled the monogrammed handkerchief from Roffgelt's suit pocket. Opening it, he allowed it to flutter down, covering the old man's face. It helped to ease his guilt a little. In the act of dismembering a corpse, any corpse, Percy always covered the face.

Stooping back down, he wrenched open his tool bag and yanked out a set of bull cutters.

Reaching into the box again, he spread Roffgelt's fingers apart. He then placed the scissor edges over the finger in question and grunted as he closed down on the cutters. He closed his eyes until he heard the bone snap. A sickening stench made him turn away momentarily. He began to gag as a pus-colored fluid seeped out of the stub. Percy knew it was a mixture of body fluids and formaldehyde. It turned his stomach, nonetheless.

Something caught Percy's eye, made him blink. He held his breath and studied the form of Roffgelt with a renewed interest. He could almost swear he had seen the old fart's chest move. He shook the thought out of his mind. Percy knew what fear could do to a man under these circumstances, especially in a mausoleum in the middle of the night. Reaching back into the casket, he picked up the sticky and wet severed finger and dropped it into one of the bags he kept tucked away in his pocket.

Without looking at Roffgelt directly, he closed up the coffin and hurried his tools back into the bag. After shutting the iron door behind him and padlocking the gate, he raced across the graveyard until he reached his former entry point by the fence. Tossing his bag over the top, Percy clambered up one of the slim metal spiked shafts and pulled himself up. Once there, he slid his feet carefully in between the wrought-iron spear points and stood up, balancing himself on the slender rail. It was the only way he could jump over without getting caught up in the fence.

Something made him turn and look back, a sixth sense -- a hunch, a subconscious safeguard on his part to make sure nobody was following him. His eyes strained in the darkness and came to rest on the familiar gray stone of the mausoleum he had just vandalized. He only saw it for a second before losing his balance completely and toppling headlong over the fence to end up dangling by one leg. His jeans got caught on one of the spear points of the fence. The rugged material was holding fast, keeping him suspended. His cry of terror came out in a weak thunderous moan. With hands clawing at the air, inches away from the earth, Percy began to wail at the sight of the figure standing and staring out at him through the mausoleum window. Squealing like a half-starved pig being made ready for slaughter, Roffgelt added fifty years onto the age of the terror-stricken Percy as he shook his four-fingered fist at the ensnared form of the thief dangling on the fence.

The more the dead man waved a threatening fist, the more Percy clawed frantically away at the air. Finally, his jean material gave way and good old gravity sucked him earthward. With his pant leg torn and his ankle all blue and bleeding, Percy hopped across the grass to his waiting pickup truck.

Later, and after a couple of belts of good cheap rye whisky, Percy calmed himself down enough to tend to the wound on his ankle. It had swollen to almost double in size. Ripping a strip of cloth from one of the bed sheets in the linen closet, the young caretaker took a container of ice from the fridge and wrapped a number of cubes around the pulsating foot. It helped bring the swelling down a little.

A shard of fear began creeping into his bones again. Percy swallowed noisily and took to downing more rye to help boost his courage. Although the sight of Roffgelt's face in the window of the mausoleum seemed so real, Percy began to reason it all out. The big maple tree alongside the tomb had no doubt played a shadows game with his imagination. A flicker of moonlight dancing across the branches of the tree would warp anyone's mind into believing anything, he decided. Yeah, that's what it was. Total freaked-out imagination. Of course, working as a caretaker in a funeral home had a lot to do with it too. Seeing all those stiffs coming and going year after year was bound to bother him sooner or later. Make him see things that just weren't there.

His face soured as he thought of Roffgelt. Alive, the man had been the most miserly, inconsiderate bastard that ever walked the face of the earth. The only bonus he was ever known to have given anyone of his employees was a Christmas card to all reminding them that they still had a job to return to once the festive season was over and behind them all. Even in death, the man still grimaced with the haunting look of a money-grubber. Percy believed that even in death Roffgelt was upset at the world of business making money without him being around to share in the spoils.

Pulling the baggie out of his pocket and hopping over to the kitchen sink, Percy withdrew a large carving knife from out of the drawer. Slicing the bag open, he hacked mercilessly away at the finger until the ring fell off. Throwing the hacked-up piece of bone back into the bag, he opened the garbage container below the sink and tossed it in. After washing his hands with a common household cleanser, he hobbled back over to the couch and sat down to study and gloat over his prize. "I betcha this baby's worth almost a hundred grand!" he cried excitedly. "Tomorrow, first thing I'm gonna do is take the bus into L.A. and see Charlie. He'll love me for this item. It's not even hot. I should be able to scoff at least thirty grand for it." Percy looked around the room for a decent hiding place. For the rest of the night, he finally decided that the best place for the gem of gems would be on his own finger.

Percy tried to pinch himself to see if his dream was real but he couldn't find his arm. Sitting up in bed, he gawked at the woman sitting in a chair by the bedroom door. She was crying and moaning, tears streaming down her reddened cheeks. Percy heard himself ask, "What the -- what's wrong with you, miss?" But his lips never moved.

She was wearing a fancy blue velvet cloak with matching hood and had the sweetest face Percy had ever lain eyes on. "Please, give me back the ring," she pleaded with him, dabbing her eyes with an ocean-blue colored handkerchief. "If you don't, we'll be ruined." She began to cry again. Just then, the door burst open and in walked a mountain of a man dressed in what looked like a chauffeur's uniform. Unafraid, the woman glanced up at the mean-faced brute and said, "He won't give me back the ring." The man smiled at her reassuringly. Walking stiffly over to the bed, he lashed out and punched Percy hard in the face. "Give the lady the ring," he said huskily. Percy wanted to answer, but the force of the blow had knocked him back against his pillow. His eyes flickered. He was seeing three chauffeurs, maybe, four. He was also feeling so tired all of a sudden. So - very - tired.

The alarm clock went off at six-thirty sharp. As he sat up in bed, Percy came close to playing a clawing game with the ceiling. Sliding out from the sack and jumping to his feet, he moved over to the closet and began hauling out clothes he planned to take with him on his bus trip to L. A. It was then that he remembered the dream. "Boy," he laughed aloud. "That old penny-pincher Roffgelt is playing games with my head."

Turning round to lay out his clothes on the bed, Percy screamed as he caught sight of a patch of dried blood on his pillowcase. Something else, he noticed was odd, too. He looked down at his ankle. It was not cut or swollen. It looked perfect in every way; as if his bout with the wrought-iron fence had all been part of an unforgotten nightmare. He specifically remembered the dream and the chauffeur punching him. Running into the bathroom, Percy studied his own face. There were no cuts. No bruises, either. But still, one question remained to be answered. Where had the blood come from, the stuff that was all over his pillow? Percy looked at the shiny ring on his finger, wondering if the object was somehow responsible.

It was during the bus trip that Percy gave his pulsating ego a round of applause. It wouldn't be long now and he would be on easy street. He would have enough money to tell his boss to stick his job once and for all. Maybe, he'd go south a ways, find a different line of work. But, first things, first. He'd party until the cows came home, drink himself into oblivion for at least a week. Yeah. He earned it!

At one of the rest stops along the way, Percy casually picked up a newspaper from one of the stands. There was a story on page three that literally had him hyper-ventilating.

SHARES AT ROFFGELT INDUSTRIES DOWN $4

Firm wastes millions on purchase of worthless Pottery.

The story went on to say how furious stockholders were over such waste. It also spelled out their demands to the surviving heiress to submit an immediate press release to explain the reasons in behind the loss.

Percy folded the paper and put it down. *I sure hope they don't run out of money too soon, he worried silently. I wouldn't want them opening Roffgelt's coffin and looking for that ring to help save their bacon. That would lead to an internal investigation at the funeral home. Sooner or later, someone would point a finger at me.*

By the time Percy's bus rolled into L.A., it was almost midnight. Climbing off the bus with his battered suitcase in hand, he started walking until he found an old motel that still rented rooms for less than twenty-five bucks for each crack of dawn. As tired as he was, he fell asleep in no time.

In the middle of the night, Percy woke to find himself bound hands and feet to the bed. Seated in front of him was the woman from his dream along with the wrestler that masqueraded himself off as a chauffeur. Neither one of them were smiling. "I will only ask you once," she said stiffly. "If you don't answer me correctly, Francois will pound your miserable carcass into a substance similar to gruel."

Percy swallowed noisily. "What is it you want?"

"You know what we want," she scowled at him. "We came for the ring you stole off my father's body. Now, where is it?"

"I have it hidden," Percy said shakily. "I'll get it for you, no problem. But I want something in return."

The chauffeur began to laugh. An icy look from the woman cut him short. "You're not in a position to bargain for anything," she said.

"My needs are small," Percy said weakly.

"What is it you want?"

"A soft job. Something in one of your Wall Street offices. A job that would mean very little work, and a nice little apartment to boot, and a salary to whisk the pains of poverty away." He bit down on his lip.

A small smile cornered the woman's mouth. "Would cleaning a single ashtray and emptying out one wastepaper basket be what you're looking for?"

Percy smiled. "That sounds like something right up my alley."

"Consider it done," she said, smiling it back. "Now, what about the ring?"

"How do I know that I can trust you?" Percy asked nervously.

Lady Roffgelt frowned at him. "The Roffgelt Family never draw back on their word," she said icily.

Miss Roffgelt held the ring up so that it sparked in the light. "Father will be glad to have it back," she whispered to Francois. The beefy-faced individual haunting her every movement nodded in agreement.

"What about my job, the apartment?" Percy said, his heart pounding, as he thought out the worst. They weren't going to keep their promise. He had been a fool to hand over the ring. They were going to kill him right here and now, toss his body into a sewer.

"Don't worry," she told him, smiling. "We haven't forgotten our promise to you at all." She nodded to the chauffeur. Francois pulled a Beretta - complete with silencer - from out of his jacket. Turning toward the caretaker, he shot him right through the heart without a second thought. Percy was dead before his head slammed back into the pillow.

At exactly twelve midnight, Ivan E. Roffgelt pushed back the lid of his coffin and climbed out. "Come, Percy," he muttered in a raspy voice. "We have work to do." The new casket situated against the opposite wall opened and Percy climbed out and stood beside his new employer. Stiffly, he followed the old man to the door. Silently, both wanderers of the night waited until Miss Roffgelt undid the lock and let them out.

"Good evening, father," she said cheerfully. "All your papers are on your desk waiting for your approval. Also, the Board members are interested to hear your recommendations on disposing of the Pottery." The rotting corpse of the elderly Roffgelt nodded understandingly. He marched right on past his daughter toward the waiting limousine.

Percy stood nearby, motionless, his dead eyes staring straight out ahead of him. "Percy," she commanded fiercely. "You will look after father's office. Make sure the waste paper is disposed of nightly and all his cigar butts cleaned out of the ashtray before dawn. No one is to know that Roffgelt Industries continue to survive on the ingenuity of one man, a member of the undead. Is that understood?"

Nodding, Percy pushed his way past her and followed the senior Roffgelt's trail in the direction of the awaiting car. He failed to notice or even thank Miss Roffgelt for the identical family ring adorning his own index finger.

Mr. Aberystwyth and the Three Weird Sisters
Robin Lochlann Spriggs

Three sisters, each one draped with a heavy gray veil of cobweb and dust, sat in a moldering parlor among the peeling walls and antique furnishings. The middle sister, blue-eyed and golden-haired, perched motionless before a rickety piano, her fingers lingering on the perfect chord of silence. The eldest, her plump chinaberry face blank beneath her bonnet, roosted on a rattletrap davenport, still as stone, halted in the act of knitting, pinching a frayed noodle of baby-blue yarn with chopsticks of stainless steel.

The youngest, flaxen-curled and chicken-bone thin, nested on the floor, frozen at the feet of the eldest, dotting a secret *I* on a jasmine-scented page of her diary.

The soft, delicate light of the fading April day worked its magic through the shattered window of the parlor, anointing the room and all within with salt-and-pepper sprinkles of shimmer and shadow, while the green smells of grass, dandelion, daisy and wild onion arose spirit-like from freshly mowed graveyards and wafted through the shivered panes, haunting the parlor with the fragrance of life.

The grandfather clock stood armless in the shadows, his pendulum arrested, tired of counting the hours and minutes and seconds that fill the gaps between beginnings and endings.

Thirteen fire-shrunk candles slouched on rusty candlesticks like ancient kings on tarnished thrones, waiting wearily to be supplanted. Under the davenport the skeleton of a mouse lay snapped in two upon a trap.

Minutes passed like years. The parlor held its breath. Nothing, not even the dust, dared stir. While, outside, the world raced on and the tiny town of Widdershin, Georgia, did its pitiful best to keep up. Some cars still heading home from work, some just now heading out to play. Wednesday night Bible study finishing up at Crimson Creek Baptist Church and choir practice about to begin, ten-year-old Jimbo Kemp rounding third base, just three seconds away from an inside-the-park home run; Sidney Elrod and Maxine Smallwood up in the barn loft rolling in the hay, and Butch Cassidy, the addled bird dog, chasing his bloody tail round and round, his eyes filled with hatred for his half-eaten enemy; and the sun, blushing deeply, teetering for a moment on the brink of one world's evening and another world's morning, then sliding on its way, going, going, gone.

The parlor went dark--but only for a moment. Then the thirteen fire-shrunk candles whispered up thirteen dancing flames. The grandfather clock groaned hoarsely, wagged his rusty pendulum and tolled the last syllable of a proclamation begun but left unfinished long, long ago.

The three sisters exhaled in unison and blackish clouds of dust billowed from their mouths and noses like sooty smoke from chimney tops. Mildred dropped her noodle of yarn and laid down her stainless steel chopsticks; Virginia lifted her fingers from the silent tomb of black and white musical bones; and Bobbie Ann closed the leather-bound story of her life, marking her place with dried baby's breath.

And, again in unison, they peeled themselves from their silken cobweb shrouds, emerging like forlorn moths from cocoons immemorial, tearing away the dust-laden layers of their protracted hibernation and pulling forth the colors and textures of their long-buried lives.

"It's almost time, girls," said Mildred, her round cheeks trading their yellow for red.

Virginia spun round on the piano stool to face her sisters and crossed her shapely legs.

"Indeed it is. How do I look?"

"As lovely as ever," said Mildred.

"What about me?" demanded Bobbie Ann, rising to her feet and pursing her lips.

"Pretty as a daisy," said Mildred.

Bobbie Ann smiled, her silvery braces glimmering in the candlelight.

"We'd better straighten up a bit," said Mildred. "This place is a sty, and he'll be here soon, you know." She rocked back and forth, trying to heave her great weight from the sagging depths of the threadbare davenport. Bobbie Ann giggled.

"Laugh while you can," said Mildred. "You'll be fat someday yourself."

"Nuh-uh," said Bobbie Ann, wrinkling her brow.

"You most certainly will be."

"How do you know?"

"It runs in the family."

"Virginia's not fat," argued Bobbie Ann.

"I would be if I didn't starve myself," said Virginia. "As it is, I'm none too thin."

Bobbie Ann looked deeply concerned.

"Well, don't just stand there," said Mildred, stretching out her hands. "Help me up, will you, girls?"

Virginia took one hand, and Bobbie Ann took the other. They pulled with all their might and slowly hauled Mildred to her feet.

"It's not so dreadful being fat," said Mildred. "A pretty figure's a lot like a diamond ring. Once a girl's got one, she lives in fear of losing it. But when you start out stout like me, you needn't ever worry; the damage is already done, and you can get on with the business of living." The three sisters laughed and set about putting the parlor in order. Virginia dusted the keys of her piano; Mildred set a crooked doily straight; and Bobbie Ann wrote I love you with her finger in the viscid layer of dust on the window.

"By the Horns but it does a body good to be expecting *company,*" said Mildred. "It wakes you right up, starts the blood to flowing, gets you up and moving, makes you feel alive. Old Nick knows it's good for this house. It's about the only time we ever clean it."

"Why, Mildred," said Virginia "you know good and well we clean this house every evening."

"And why is that?" asked Mildred. "C-O-M-P-A-N-Y."

"Mr. Aberystwyth isn't company," said Virginia. "He comes a-calling every night. Practically lives here. In my book, that's not company."

"What is it, then?" asked Mildred.

"A pain in the neck," said Virginia. "The man's obsessed."

"Well, obsessed or not," said Mildred, "don't pretend you don't enjoy it. I've seen the way your face lights up when he looks in your direction."

"Me too," said Bobbie Ann, drawing a heart on the window.

"You shut up, Bobbie Ann," said Virginia. "You're a fine one to talk, purring and posing like a cat in heat every time he comes to visit!"

"That's enough, girls," said Mildred. "If truth be told, we're all a little sweet on Mr. Aberystwyth. Who wouldn't be? A charmer like him."

Virginia frowned at the back of Mildred's head.

"I like his mustache," said Bobbie Ann. "It tickles."

Virginia gasped. "How would you know?"

"Same reason you do," said Bobbie Ann, giggling, then stuck out her tongue.

"You little liar!" yelled Virginia, starting towards her.

Mildred stepped between them, clapping her pudgy hands.

"Girls! Girls! Quit squabbling. What's done is done. What's past is past. Water under the bridge. We're beyond all that now. The storm's over and we're still afloat. A little shaken, maybe. A little down on our luck, perhaps. But still afloat. I know we've seen better days, girls. I know how you miss the way things used to be. So do I. But the important thing is we're still together. Inseparable. Indivisible. Just like we promised. Just like sisters ought to be. Let's not spoil it now, after so many years. Let's not fall apart just when things are looking up, just when the tide is shifting, just when the stars are lining up favorably again." She paused and looked at Virginia, then at Bobbie Ann, then at Virginia again. "Please," she added tenderly. "If not for my sake or your own sakes, then for the sake of Mr. Aberystwyth. He has certain needs, you know, certain expectations. And we must not disappoint him, not when we've come so far, not when we've come so close." Virginia's tight jaw slackened. Bobbie Ann's scowl disappeared. They came to Mildred in the center of the room, and the three sisters joined hands, smiling.

A knock at the door.

"Oh my," whispered Mildred. "There he is now. Places, girls. Places."

Virginia returned to the piano stool. Mildred sank back into the yielding depths of the davenport, adjusted her faded blue dress, then took up her knitting and nodded to Bobbie Ann, who undid the latch and slowly opened the door.

It groaned in protest.

"Who is it, Bobbie Ann?" called Mildred, her voice a crystal bell.

"Mr. Aberystwyth," Bobbie Ann answered.

"Well, don't just stand there. Show him in."

Bobbie Ann stepped aside, giggling, and Mr. Aberystwyth stepped inside.

He was tall and as spare and brittle looking as a winter twig. His once-proud Sears-and-

Roebuck suit hung loose and bedraggled upon the sharp, cruel angles of his bones like a soaked black sack. His complexion was hoary, his cheeks concave, his chin weak, retrograde and in need of a beard. His crooked, knife-edged nose divided his face into unequal halves and crowded a mustache that drooped on both sides of his mouth like broken silver wings. His eyes, deeply sunken in his wilted face, were disturbingly huge and blue, bright water in dark wells. An intricate design of crisscrossing scars wrapped around his forehead, disappearing beyond his temples into the umbrage of his long gray hair. He stood there, barefooted, hunched over, staring at the floor, gnawing his nether lip, twitching his bushy mustache, clutching a tattered billycock in his dark-veined hands and worming a bony finger through the moth-eaten felt.

"Why, good evening, Mr. Aberystwyth," said Mildred. "What a pleasant surprise!"

Mr. Aberystwyth continued to stare at the floor and did not say a word.

"You're looking awfully handsome today," said Mildred. "Won't you have a seat?"

Mr. Aberystwyth shambled toward the rickety bent wood chair near the davenport.

"Wait!" exclaimed Virginia, rising and rushing toward the chair. She wiped a thick coat of dust off the seat with the hem of her yellow skirt. "Now then. Now it's fit for a gentleman."

Mr. Aberystwyth sat down, never looking up.

Virginia returned to the piano. "Would you like to hear some music?"

No answer.

"How about the 'Maple Leaf Rag'?" she asked.

"That's his favorite," chimed Bobbie Ann, skipping about the room.

"It certainly is," said Mildred. "He was whistling it the first time he ever came a-calling."

"Remember?" asked Virginia. "'So bright and happy and full of life, traipsing down the walkway, flowers in your hand."

"A box of chocolates under your arm," added Mildred.

"Whistlin' like a bird," said Bobbie Ann. "Remember?"

No answer.

"Remember?" asked Virginia.

No answer.

Mildred cleared her throat. "Remember?"

Mr. Aberystwyth nodded.

Virginia played a few notes. "Is that how it goes?"

"Sure it is," said Mildred. "We never forget a melody, do we, 'girls?"

"Or a face," said Virginia.

"Or a name," added Mildred.

"Especially if it's a funny name," said Bobbie Ann, taking a porcelain unicorn from a cobwebbed knickknack shelf.

Mr. Aberystwyth shifted in his seat.

Virginia stopped playing. "It's just not the same on the piano, though. It's better when you whistle it. Whistle it, Mr. Aberystwyth." No response. "Go ahead," said Mildred. No response.

"Please," begged Bobbie Ann, caressing her unicorn.

Mr. Aberystwyth began to whistle, his cracked lips trembling. The notes came out raspy and broken.

"That doesn't sound so good, Mr. Aberystwyth," said Mildred. "You sound parched. Would you like something to drink?"

Mr. Aberystwyth said nothing.

"Get Mr. Aberystwyth a drink, Bobbie Ann," said Mildred. "You know what he likes."

"Already did," said Bobbie Ann, giggling. "It's right there on the coffee table."

"Why, so it is," said Mildred. "Have some, Mr. Aberystwyth. It'll wet you whistle, quicken your instrument."

Mr. Aberystwyth did not move.

"Have some," said Bobbie Ann.

Still he did not move.

Virginia brought her fingers down hard upon the keys, pounding out a chord that shook the parlor walls. "Have some."

Mr. Aberystwyth reached, hand shaking, for the tall, dark, web-draped bottle. He lifted it from the table, pulled the cobwebs away, brought it to his lips and took a token sip.

"More," said all three sisters.

Mr. Aberystwyth raised the bottle again and guzzled deeply, grimacing at the taste. Then he wiped his reddened mouth with the back of his hand and returned the bottle to the table, placing it directly on the dust-free spot he had taken it from.

"That's more like it," said Mildred. "That's the Mr. Aberystwyth we all remember. Isn't it, girls?"

"Boy howdy!" exclaimed Bobbie Ann.

"No doubt about it," said Virginia.

"Ah, memories," crooned Mildred. "This house is full of them. It remembers everything, Mr. Aberystwyth. And so do we."

"Do you remember everything, *Mr.* Aberystwyth?" asked Bobbie Ann, hopping on one foot.

No reply.

"Do you?" asked Virginia.

No reply.

Mildred stomped her foot. "Do you?" she demanded.

Mr. Aberystwyth nodded but kept his eyes glued to the floor.

Bobbie Ann crept up behind him and tickled his ear with the dried petal of a red rose.

"Memories are all we've got, Mr. Aberystwyth," said Mildred. "Isn't that right, girls?" Bobbie Ann giggled.

"That's right," said Virginia. "Our memories keep us together."

"Without them," said Mildred, "the girls and I might have drifted apart a long, long time ago. But here we are, still together."

"Thanks to Mr. Aberystwyth," said Bobbie Ann.

"Yes, indeedy," said Mildred. "Yes, indeedy. You're the reason we're still together, Mr. Aberystwyth."

"We're boring him to death," said Virginia.

"He's tired of that story," said Bobbie Ann.

"Is that right?" asked Mildred. "Are you tired of our little story, Mr. Aberystwyth?"

No answer.

"Are you?" asked Virginia.

No answer.

Bobbie Ann dropped the unicorn, and it shattered on the floor at Mr. Aberystwyth's feet. "Are you?"

Mr. Aberystwyth seemed to wither in his seat. He tore at his hat with long, jagged fingernails and shook his head.

"Good," said Mildred, "because we do so love to tell it." She paused and smiled a fine-china smile. "Shall we tell it again, Mr. Aberystwyth?"

Mr. Aberystwyth licked his bone-dry lips with a leathery tongue that failed to moisten them.

"Shall we?" asked Bobbie Ann, pirouetting barefoot over the sharp-toothed shards of unicorn, leaving footprints of blood in the dust.

Virginia slammed the mahogany cover over the piano keys, striking a demonic chord. "Shall we?"

Mr. Aberystwyth closed his eyes and nodded.

"Well, all right then," said Mildred. "If you insist." She cleared her throat. "You see, Mr. Aberystwyth, after Mama and Daddy passed away, it was up to me to raise Virginia and Bobbie Ann. It was hard at first, but soon I grew to love it. After a while it just seemed like the way things should be. I know I made a lot of mistakes, but I did the best I could, and for the most part I think we were very happy.

"I'd given up a long time ago on finding a man. The Great Lord knows, I wouldn't want to wake up next to something that looks like me every morning for the rest of my life--not if I had a choice. So I immersed myself in the girls. Invested everything in them. All the time and care and love I could muster. Then one day I woke up, and Virginia had turned into a beautiful young woman, and Bobbie Ann was surely soon to follow.

"I'd asked them to promise me, way back when they were little-bitty things, that they would never grow up and leave me, that we would always stay together and care for one another and that things would never change. And of course they promised. Little children are sweet that way, Old Horns bless 'em.

"I knew they'd outgrow their childhood promises someday, though. Everybody does. I knew that someday somebody special would come along and take them both away, Virginia first and then Bobbie Ann, and that I'd be left here all alone to rot among the dust and cobwebs, unloved and unremembered. That's just the way things are. That's life.

"Still, though, I prayed the day would never come. I knew it was a selfish prayer, but most prayers are, so I prayed it just the same. I prayed it every day and every night. And if you pray for something long enough, sooner or later whomever or whatever you're praying to is bound to give you what you're asking for, if for no other reason than to shut you up and finally get some peace. It's the first rule of Magic. That's how it works. That's how it's always worked. So I persisted, and at last my prayer was answered.

"That's where you come in, Mr. Aberystwyth. But to be honest, when I first saw you whistling up the walkway with a box of chocolates under one arm and a dozen roses in the other, you didn't strike me as the answer to my prayers. Quite the contrary. As a matter of fact, I thought you were the very thing I'd always feared the most. I thought surely you were here to see Virginia, that you'd been courting her secretly for a long time and had finally come to show yourself and take her away for good. Then I thought it might even be little Bobbie Ann you were after; some men are like that, you know. And that really *did* give me a scare.

"But then you handed *me* the roses and chocolates. Me. Fat, homely, resigned-to-spinsterhood me. Then you sat down beside me and commenced to sweet-talk. Lordy Green Vines, the things you said! Nobody had ever said such kind and wonderful things to me before. My head was swimming. I didn't know what to say. So I asked if you wanted to come in and sit with me in the parlor for a while. You said yes, so in we went. We sat right here in the early evening glow, and you picked right up where you left off, talking up a storm, words all full of honey and brown sugar, filling my ears with enough sweet nothings to make a woman drunk in love forever. Then--"

"Then I came in," said Virginia. "I couldn't believe my eyes. There you were, Mr. Aberystwyth, all cozy and intimate on the davenport with Mildred." She pointed to where Mildred sat. "On that very spot. You, the man I caught snooping just one week before, in the Sacred Grove down by the lake. The man I took an instant liking to. The man I met secretly every night afterwards. The man with whom I shared the Mystic Lore. The man I let kiss me and swore to worship forever. There you were, holding hands with my sister. And as if that wasn't bad enough--"

"As if that wasn't bad enough," said Bobbie Ann, crouching down behind him and whispering in his ear, "I came in with some daisies I had picked for Mildred, and there you were, right in my very own parlor. Remember how I screamed, Mr. Aberystwyth? You promised you would stay a secret. You said you wanted to stay a secret. Remember? You bought me that ice-cream cone to make me stop crying and told me I had to help you stay a secret. And I never told, Mr. Aberystwyth. Honest I didn't. I promise. But you came to my house, anyway. You came to my house and showed yourself to Mildred and Virginia. That's not a secret, Mr. Aberystwyth. That's a lie. Why did you lie, Mr. Aberystwyth? Why did you come to my house?"

Mr. Aberystwyth began to tremble and sob. "Do you remember what you did then, Mr. Aberystwyth?" asked Mildred, laying down the tiny blue sweater she had almost finished knitting. Mr. Aberystwyth moaned. "Do you?" asked Virginia. Mr. Aberystwyth groaned. "Do you?!" Bobbie Ann shrieked.

Mr. Aberystwyth wailed and nodded his head wildly.

"So do we, Mr. Aberystwyth," said Mildred. "We remember it very well. But there's one thing we *don't* know, Mr. Aberystwyth. One thing that's always puzzled us. One thing we've never been able to figure out, not in all these years." She paused as a single plump tear rolled down her cheek and into her mouth. "Why did you do it?"

"What did we ever do to you?" Virginia asked sincerely, her blue eyes needing to know.

"Was it because you thought I'd tell?" asked Bobbie Ann, weeping silent rivers.

"Did you hate us?" Mildred asked. "Did you fear us? Or was it just a silly whim? Just one of those things? Or did you plan it, Mr. Aberystwyth? Did you watch us, scheming unseen? If so, for how long? Days? Weeks? Years? Centuries? Millennia? Why did you do it, Mr. Aberystwyth? Why?"

"Why?" asked Bobbie Ann.

"Why?" asked Virginia.

"Why?" asked Mildred again.

"Why?!" they all screamed.

Mr. Aberystwyth did not answer. His wails and groans and moans and sobs all ceased. He fell completely silent. His long, shriveled frame hung limply in the chair, a blade-thin sack of bones. The scars on his head began to bleed, and so did his hands, and so did his feet, and so did the old deep wound below his ribs, slowly and secretly at first, then profusely, drenching his Sunday suit.

Not far away Jimbo Kemp was fast asleep, dreaming of inside-the-park home runs; Sidney Elrod and Maxine Smallwood were sneaking in their respective back doors with salty grins on their faces; Butch Cassidy, the addled bird dog, was snoozing peacefully by what was left of his bloody tail; and choir practice at the Crimson Creek Baptist Church was drawing to a close with a final chorus of "Almost Persuaded."

"Well, then." said Mildred.

"Well, then." said Virginia.

"Well, then," said Bobbie Ann, producing a dried black carnation and pinning it to the old man's lapel. Mr. Aberystwyth rose shakily to his feet and staggered toward the door, leaving behind him a spreading wake of blood.

"Mr. Aberystwyth?" Mildred called.

He stopped in the threshold but did not turn around.

"We'll see you tomorrow evening," said Mildred.

Mr. Aberystwyth shambled into the night, dragging his blood-soaked feet.

The three sisters lifted their hands to their lips and blew the gentleman a kiss, and the thirteen fire-shrunk candles flickered out again, leaving the women forever in the dark.

When Sparrows Fall

Lisa S. Silverthorne

It begins with a chill wind and screams. Burnt scent of jet fuel and whistle of air across torn wings. I toss in my bed, desperately wanting it to be a dream, and flail against the terrified voices, the hush of descent. There is a horrible, rushing sound in my ears. At the whisper of death and the gouging of metal against ground, I bolt up from the bed, my skin clammy with sweat. My stomach aches and tears gather in my eyes. Please -- not another one.

Turning on the light, I sit up and hug my pillow. Icy fear trembles through my body and my teeth chatter. I rock against the headboard, trying to dislodge the images. My hands hurt. I glance down at them. They're burnt and smell of jet fuel. My hands haven't burned in a long time. It's a bad crash -- a jet. Lots of people.

Sunrise is a couple of hours off and he'll be calling. Maybe by then I can pull myself together?

In a short while, my shaking stops, the blankets at last warming me. I rise slowly and go into the kitchen to make some coffee. After two cups, I slip into the shower and dress. The horizon is fiery now. I pour myself another cup of coffee and wait.

Finally, I lay my hand against the phone and a heartbeat later it rings. My trembling returns.

"Hello, Mark," I say, my voice raspy.

"Uh -- Stacia?" NTSB Investigator Mark shakes more than usual this time.

"It's a jet, isn't it?" I ask, my hands still throbbing.

A long sigh hisses through the receiver. "Yes, Stace. Two hundred people dead. Only one survivor. We're still looking for the black box."

My heart twists at the ghostly feel of a stuffed bear and the image of a little girl clutching it like a life preserver, her head down. The whistle of air across the plane's fuselage echoes in the phone's static. The impact is sharp then numbing. I lurch forward. The silence is heavy. They always call me when the black box is lost.

I glance out the window at the darkness beginning to lighten on the horizon and I hear the fragile chirp of birds. Morning will come soon.

They say that God hears even a sparrow when it falls to the ground. What must He hear when two hundred of his own fall?

"I'll be there in four hours," I say finally, my voice still hoarse.

"But I didn't tell you where the crash site is."

I sigh. I've been working with NTSB investigators for almost a year now, yet Mark hasn't gotten used to what I see.

"I know where it is," I say calmly. "An old growth forest northwest of me." I can smell the tang of pine nettles and the raw stench of fire. And I see the blackened furrows and broken trees, the long, white plane a greenstick fracture poking through the earth's brown skin.

"We can't find the box and the little girl's critical. The tower thinks it was pilot error. What went wrong?"

I clutch the receiver. "We'll know soon enough," I say and hang up the phone.

The morning coolness mists the fir trees and frames the highway. It swirls ominously across the twisty road that winds through the ancient forest toward the crash site. The heater huffs low, softening the drone of the radio that fills the silence with distraction.

Finally, I reach a roadblock where police cars huddle in the road. The grim-faced officers move almost mechanically in their rain ponchos. A policeman steps toward my car and I roll down the window. He is bleary-eyed from a sleepless night.

"I'm Stacia Evans," I tell him and offer my driver's license. "Investigator Vincent sent for me."

"Yeah, he's expecting you," says the policeman and hands back my license. His gaze falls to the gloves on my hands. "Pull your car off the road over there." He motions toward a small clearing. "You'll have to walk up to the site."

After parking my car, I start up the hillside, bracing myself as I crest the hill and stop.

Torn suitcases and mangled seat cushions, foam and springs erupting, litter the forest floor. Airplane panels lie shattered like eggshells, stark against the nettles and moss blanketing the autumn ground. Bits of fabric and seat belts cling to fir tree branches. Empty plane seats twist around tree trunks and crumple against blackened ground. I suck in a breath, but it hangs in my throat at the rows of yellow body bags lining the horizon. Slowly, I move deeper into the crash debris. At my feet is a torn, sooty tennis shoe. Just one.

Stale smoke scent is cold in the gray drizzle that has started early today. A crane squeaks nearby, loading hunks of gutted plane onto a flatbed truck. One chugs past me and lurches down the hill. I fight the urge to reach down and pick up the lone shoe. Not yet. Not until I've seen everything.

Yellow hazard suits weave through the old forest, investigators combing wreckage for clues -- and the black box. A sandy-haired man, looking all of his thirty-five years, moves through the damp forest toward me.

"Stacia," he calls. "Glad you're here."

Mark Vincent's angular chin is stubbled and smudged with dirt, his blue eyes dull. His rain-dappled hazard suit creaks as he extends his hand. I hesitate then shake his hand quickly, trying to avoid images that will haunt me for weeks. They always do.

I nod toward the investigators and cleanup crews. "Have they recovered the bodies?"

"What's left of all two hundred." He glances at the crane raising one of the engines onto another flatbed. "When will you want to start?"

The hazy image of an old woman slips up from a section of crushed seats. Her steely hair is swept back in harsh curls that reveal deep wrinkles furrowing her brow and cheeks. Her blue pantsuit is spattered with blood and dirt as she flits between workers. She reaches out to them, her misty face a mask of confusion, but they just walk past. Behind her, a young man in a torn Rugby shirt and jeans crouches. He stares blankly at ruptured plane panels and luggage strewn everywhere.

A child rushes toward her mother and falls into a ghostly embrace.

The pilot walks grimly behind the investigators and surveys damage. He grips the arm of his younger copilot, shaking his head and rubbing his eyes.

One by one, the passengers find each other and many go on, disappearing into the woods until I stand alone in the debris.

I watch them all as they search. They cling together while the last broken remnants of their lives are swept away, leaving them only this drizzly hillside -- and each other.

Even ghosts collect their dead.

"Stacia?"

A hand waves in front of my eyes and I glance up. Mark steps closer, concern on his face.

"You look like you're about to pass out." He steers me toward a pickup truck where I climb onto the open tailgate and let my muddy boots dangle. Mark slides a warm cup of coffee into my gloved hands.

He stares out at the debris. "You never get used to seeing things like this."

I shake my head and watch two hundred ghosts slipping in and out of the wreckage and I nod.

Now a woman in a denim dress stands at the center of the wreckage, her gaze encompassing the forest and debris. In her eyes, I see panic. She calls out, but the sounds are lost in the whir of the crane, the buzz of trucks. Finally, her gaze falls to me. The graying, stuffed bear dangling from her hand makes me realize why she waits. I sigh.

"They're all so lost," I mumble, mostly to myself.

"Yeah," says Mark, "two hundred of them lost."

"I meant after the crash. It's not quite over for them yet. Not until they're finished here. It's important to them."

He stares uncertainly at me. I know he tries to see what I see. He never knows what to make of it, but he believes me. He stares at the broken plane and I know he sees nothing beyond the hazard suits and the drizzle.

"What do you mean -- important?" he asks.

Sometimes, it really doesn't make any sense. Why some people survive and others die. I remember a cold autumn morning so painfully close to this one. The spray of hot jet fuel burning my flesh, the choking billows of black smoke smothering the dark compartment. I gasp, shoving that bit of broken memory away from me. It's a place I haven't gone in a long while, but the specter remains, cold and dark inside me. Like this gift of mine.

"How's the little girl?" I ask, changing the subject.

"Weaker. Still hasn't regained consciousness."

I rise from the truck and set down my cup. Then I move into the heart of the crash.

I wander with the ghosts through the rubble until the investigators and crew thin out. There is closeness about these souls. They gather together, helping each other. At times, I feel like an intruder, but they accept my presence because I accept theirs.

I move toward the body bags and piles of luggage that have been moved back. Bending down, I pick up a black purse and that lone shoe. I run my hands across the purse and my eyes well with tears. Twenty-two C and D. An elderly couple. Toward the wing, they'd insisted the travel agent seat them there. It's safest over the wing. Inside the purse are the boarding passes. I run my finger over them, catching wisps of excitement and exhaustion -- twinges of apprehension at so much money spent to fly. The shoe belongs to a 50-year-old account executive in 2A who just had a surprise birthday party and was returning home.

When I glance up, the elderly couple stands before me, bewildered and shaking their heads. The account executive stands beside them, his other tennis shoe clean and white. I reach out to them. I can't touch them, but they understand my gesture.

"Tell me, please," I say. "What happened?"

"It was so fast," says the elderly man, his voice thin and tight. His ruddy, hooked nose flattens as he talks. "One of the engines on the right side caught fire. The other one just stopped."

"The flight attendants told us to put our heads down and we just prayed," says the woman. "Now, we're here. Why?"

I shake my head. I have no answers for her.

The account executive shoulders past the older man. "The lights went out. Then a flight attendant whispered that one of the engines had stopped working." His gaze falls to the shoe I hold.

The woman's husband takes her hand. She turns toward him. Gently, the elderly man lays a hand against the account executive's sleeve and the younger man nods. Together, they walk out of the wreckage and disappear into the forest.

I see the pilot and move toward him. The investigators watch me as if I'm insane. Ignoring them, I drop down beside the pilot.

"Captain? Can you tell me what happened?"

"Engine failure." His voice is gravely and low, the pain thick in his words. "One of them ignited. The extinguishing systems didn't kick in either. Then we suffered a massive power loss and everything went off-line." He points somewhere in the distance. "I tried to land her in the clearing over that ridge, but we dropped too fast." He shakes his head, his ghost fingers gripping his brown hair. "Some of us might have made it. What have I done?"

I lay my hand against the air where his shoulder would have been. "Your best. Captain, you had no engines. You were over mountains and forest. You did your best. But the tower suspects pilot error. That's why I'm here. You've got to help me find the black box, Captain."

His lined face lifts toward me. "They can't find it?"

I shake my head.

"And they think it's my fault?"

"Not if we can find the black box. Can you help?"

"I'll call my crew together," he says urgently, rising from the ground. Having a purpose stirs him to action. "We'll find it." He flits toward his crewmembers, but stops and turns to me again. "How long do we have?"

I smile. "As long as it takes."

Soon, I'm alone in the debris again. I pace the rows of body bags that are being loaded into trucks. Shortly, the bodies will be carried away to next-of-kin. I reach down and touch a few of the bags, 14B, 6A, 26A - Seattle, Buffalo, Phoenix. So many stories, so many places. So many ripples. They play behind my eyes, a granddaughter going to her grandparents' fiftieth anniversary, a couple on vacation, a woman going to a wedding. I see their stories as if they are my own and it chokes me up. I inhale sharply and continue to pace.

I glance toward the trees and realize I'm not alone. The woman in denim still waits. Ten years fold back like the ragged plane panels at my feet and the image of another plane crash makes me shiver. I was ten. As someone shoved me out of the burning wreckage, I looked back, expecting it to be my mother stumbling out behind me. But it wasn't. I never saw my mother again. Even now, I can't help but wonder if she stood in that wreckage like this woman, searching for me, calling to me.

It's nightfall when the captain and his crew emerge from the woods. He surges toward me, his frame pearly white against the darkening forest.

"We found it! It's here!"

"Take me there."

He nods.

"Mark, I know where to find the box."

I'm surprised by the calmness of my voice. In moments, Mark Vincent, flanked by a handful of investigators, rushes toward me. I nod at the captain and he hurries into the woods. I follow, the others not far behind.

The captain leads me across the nettle-laden ground, deeper and deeper. His ghostly gleam is my only guidance. There, battered and hidden by brush, lies the small orange casing of the black box. I tear at the brush, pulling away branches and leaves until I have uncovered the box.

I step back as the investigators descend on it, gently lifting it from the foliage and carrying it back to the site. Mark hovers beside me. I walk behind the investigators as they carry the box out toward the trucks.

When I reach the site, I see the woman in denim still waiting. I close my eyes for a moment, feeling a closeness that makes my chest ache, and approach her. The woman holds the stuffed bear against her chest.

"Have you seen my daughter?" asks the woman. "I've been looking for her for hours!" Her ghostly face is tear-streaked and she looks utterly lost. "Please, where is my daughter?"

"She's in a hospital," I answer, my voice thin. "She survived the crash."

"Oh, thank God," the woman cries and slumps to the ground, clutching the bear. Her relief is overwhelming. "Thank God she's safe."

Shards of memories stab back into focus. A voice long dead calls my name through the roar of fire, through shrill screams. But never have I been so far from that voice as I was that chilly October morning. Ten years have passed, but I clench my eyes closed, my mother's voice haunting my memory. How she shouted at me from the plane's burning wreckage, but they couldn't get to her in time. I inherited my curse that morning. Now, I relive every jet crash as if it were that awful October morning outside Spokane.

I drop to my knees, a sob tearing at my throat. I never saw my mother again. Never got to tell her goodbye. Why didn't she hear me? I called and called, but she never answered. If only she could have followed my voice to the exit. If only ice hadn't formed on the wings. My sobs wrench free, the rain pounding the ground now. If only.

While Mark and the others carry the black box toward a truck, Brittany walks out of the woods. Her form is translucent, milky and soft like fairy dust. I am afraid to move. I crouch there in the pouring rain.

"Mommy?"

The woman turns, her face contorting. "Brittany. I thought you were safe."

Her mother runs toward her and clasps the child to her chest. Sobbing, the little girl holds onto her mother. "I couldn't find you, Mommy. I couldn't find you!"

"Sssh, honey. It's all right." She lays the bear in Brittany's arms.

Shortly, Mark's cell phone rings. I watch the heaviness in face. He shakes his head. A battle lost. He rushes into debris and drops down beside me.

"The little girl passed away a few minutes ago," he shouts above the rain.

I nod and watch the last of the ghosts of flight 1155 melt into the woods and fade into the air. For a moment, Brittany's mother remains. She gazes at me as if she knows about my mother. There are no answers to these whys -- to my whys --just acceptance, I realize.

"Could you -- " I stop in mid-sentence.

She moves toward me and nods, urging me to continue.

"Could you tell my mother -- that I miss her?"

"I'm sure she's already heard you."

The woman takes hold of her daughter's hand and slips after the others.

Peace settles warm and calm against my shoulders, as if someone has put an arm around me. My hands stop hurting. I pull off my gloves. The burns are receding . . . my gift is fading. I feel it. And for the first time, I understand this gift. I've been hearing my mother's voice for ten years through these images. They were the good-byes she never got to tell me.

I step out of the wreckage, knowing that tonight, I leave my gift behind. I trudge toward the investigators as they load the black box bound for D.C.

"They'll find that all engines failed," I tell them. "One engine caught fire and the other stopped working. The fire extinguishing system failed to come on-line, too. There was no evidence of pilot error. Goodnight."

I don't even turn to see their expressions. It doesn't matter if they believe me or not. They have the plane's flight record and I have mine. As I climb into my car, I look back at the forest and wonder, if a sparrow falls, does it rise again and sing?

Water This Cold

Terry Campbell

The porcelain was smooth and unblemished. The flowing lines of the facial structure - the soft curve of the cheeks, the subtle valley of the eye sockets the gentle kiss of the pursed lips - were exquisite. The color was shocking white, even after years and years of wear. Who had played with it? How often had it been played with? Who could tell? How could anyone tell? These were questions Collin Hayworth asked himself every time he viewed a new doll. And this was the most immaculate doll he had ever had the fortune of laying his eyes upon. And he had laid his eyes upon many. His collection numbered into the thousands, and it was insured for one million dollars. It was truly the envy of doll collectors all over the world. And here was one more, nothing overtly spectacular, just one simple little turn-of-the-century depiction, and Collin made up his mind that he must have it, he *would* have it. But this doll was in no elegant antique shop, no clearly marked price tag hanging from one dainty toe; it was not sitting atop a velvet table in a booth in some collector show waiting for her price to be haggled over. This doll was two and a half miles below the surface of the Atlantic Ocean, partially buried amid the sunken ruins of the White Star liner <u>Titanic</u>, and Collin would not believe that peering at the beauty through binoculars and a nine-inch thick glass window was the closest he was going to get to it.

He knew that several groups had been retrieving relics from the doomed ship for some time now. Hats, watches, eyeglasses, that sort of thing. Dr. Robert Ballard had placed a plaque on the stern of *Titanic* in 1986 when he had first discovered the tragic remains imploring future explorers to look, but not touch. It now seemed that his wish was going unheeded. The overwhelming success of the James Cameron movie had seared dollar signs into the eyes of many, and anything Titanic-related was sure to fetch an equally titanic price, especially if it was the genuine article.

The small submarine slowly moved away from the doll, casting a veil of ocean floor silt over it, and Collin stepped back from the small crowd of folks pushing its way to the small windows. He shivered; it was so frightfully cold in the tiny craft.

Collin Hayworth was a man who knew how to get what he wanted, and he had the means to accomplish it. He smiled the face of the doll etched into his memory. It wouldn't take much - the right individual, the right price - and he would hold her; the first to claim ownership in eighty-six years.

His vacation with friends of equally sound financial status on the French Riviera had been extremely monotonous up until the morning Sophia mentioned that a Swiss submarine company was offering underwater tours of the *Titanic* for five-thousand dollars a head. And even then, there was really nothing of interest as far as Collin was concerned. He knew of the marine disaster, how the ship had struck an iceberg on the night of April 14, 1912, had gone down in two hours, how she had been deemed "unsinkable." But he had only a passing interest in the history at best.

But Sophia Renfield and her fifteen-year old daughter, Amy had become addicted to the movie, and the entire group had decided to take a break from their summer on the Riviera and head for cooler climes. Collin had reluctantly agreed more so for the fact of not wanting to be left out of the group's adventures than anything else.

Collin smiled the smile of a man who had achieved his goal. The trip had been worth it. Well worth it. It had cost him one million dollars, but now, looking at his bounty, he knew he would've paid twice that amount.

The doll was complete, and in surprisingly good condition. The clothing had long since succumbed to the harsh salt water of the Atlantic, but the porcelain was immaculate. It seemed that years of lying in the ocean floor had polished the surface of the porcelain, rather than deteriorated it, if that was possible. The paint on the eyes and lips was gone, if there ever had been paint there. The overall effect of the stark white face was no less eerie to Collin than the moment he saw the ghostly pale face peering at him from the murky depths of the Atlantic. Here was the crowning glory to his already spectacular collection. Who else anywhere at all, in the entire world, could claim to have a doll salvaged from the wreckage of the greatest ship disaster in all of history?

"No one," Collin chuckled, caressing his prize. "No one at all."

"We should have a seance," Stella Lloyd said.

"'A seance?' her husband Leonard asked. "Are you mad, woman?"

Collin's group of friends had all been impressed with his acquisition, even if they thought the price tag was a little steep. Collin now kept the doll locked up in his safe, nestled cozily inside an ornate wooden box, its interior lined with red velvet, he had built specifically to house the doll. Sophia and her daughter were not as impressed by the doll as Collin imagined; perhaps seeing it separate from its grave lessened the emotional impact for them, or perhaps they were more infatuated with Hollywood's *Titanic* than the real one. The others were probably just not all that interested in the history of the ship. It was something to keep them occupied at the moment, something to coax them away from the every day monotonous existence of the wealthy, and when it was over, forgotten. The fact that the doll came from where it did meant little to Collin himself. It was a beautiful piece, and it was *unique*. And that meant it was valuable, extremely valuable. Therein lay the lure for Collin Hayworth.

"Yes," Stella said. "A seance. We could try to contact the spirits of the Titanic. After all, tonight is the anniversary of the sinking, is it not?"

"Yes," someone agreed. "Eleven-forty tonight. Eighty-six years ago."

"Wouldn't that be fun?"

"What do you know, what do any of us know, about conducting a seance?" Collin asked.

"I've read books," she replied. "I know a little."

Curious glances were exchanged, as if each individual mulled the thought over and sought to seek the approval of the others. Sophia's husband shrugged and puffed on his pipe. Sophia and her daughter seemed extremely intrigued by the idea. Thomas Wilford refilled his drink, a sign that he was content. Without words being spoken, it seemed the clique was in agreement.

"I don't know," Stephanie Ashley said. "I don't like the sound of this."

"What's wrong with it?"

Stephanie shook her head. "It just doesn't seem like a good idea." The crowd began to mill around the dissenting voice. Stephanie was the only one who had not tagged along on the two-week sail to the *Titanic's* resting spot, and she seemed no more ready to partake in this invasion of the spirit world than she did the probing of the burial ground of over fifteen hundred souls. "You people seem to have lost touch with reality. That movie has destroyed your way of thinking. You've let Hollywood glamorize this whole event. You've fallen victim to the romanticism. You're forgetting what a terrible tragedy the *Titanic* was. People died, fifteen hundred people died. It may seem wonderful and glorious to have gone down with it when you watch a movie or read a book, but I'm sure if you asked any of the people who were actually there, you'd get a different story. A much different story indeed."

There was a heavy silence in the room for an uncomfortable period of time. Eyes met each other and then locked onto Stephanie. A moderate rain had begun to fall just outside the veranda of Collin's villa suite.

"Well," Mr. Lloyd said, finally breaking the silence. "We'll find that out tonight when we ask them, I suppose".

Stephanie sighed, making it clear she would have no part of this particular evening's festivities. The group broke off into sections, some heading for the liquor cabinet, some to the lobby of the magnificent hotel.

Collin glanced over at the safe that housed his newest acquisition and walked out into the steady rain. It was the middle of summer in France, a pleasant eighty-two degrees.

But the rain falling from the monotone sky seemed ice cold.

The scent of the candle--some kind of apple/cinnamon mix--was assaulting Collin's senses. He found himself wishing this nonsense would be over soon. He looked about the dark room, studying the curious highlights and shadow's the flickering candle created across the faces of his friends. He started to reach for his brandy when Stella shot him a warning stare. She was obviously striving for the proper theatrics in this childish game, and any disruption would spoil the effect.

"The night is April 14, 1912," she whispered, sounding for all the world like some gypsy fortune-teller in a black-and-white monster movie. "We feel your sadness, we can feel your fear."

Nervous eyes glanced about the room. Collin knew that no one believed, but there was that faint degree of uncertainty, that gnawing possibility that this could actually work, that Stephanie could be right about her anxieties at contacting the spirit world.

"Come to us," Stella continued. "Come through the murky depths, come up through the cold waters."

--Water this cold--

"Join us here tonight." She paused for effect. "Speak to us. Share what you're feeling with us."

Collin closed his eyes, not to partake in the ritual, but merely to rest them. He was beginning to think that this summer escapade was more draining than it was relaxing, but then major acquisitions usually left him feeling this way. And his latest acquisition was the grandest of all. Collin smiled, his eyes still closed, and pictured the lovely doll, resting snugly in her velvet bed, safe from all prying eyes and hands inside the sturdy metal safe. Collin let himself relax, Stella's voice becoming merely a hum of background noise to his ears. The candle scent drifted into his nostrils. A tinge of brandy followed. Soothing. Collin breathed deeply, and let the white noise of utter relaxation fill his mind. He thought he could hear the rain returning to splash along the cobblestone drive that led to the hotel. It has a pleasant effect. But underneath the aromas of candles and liquor was another odor, a faint underlying scent that Collin could not quite place, a cold, chilling smell he couldn't begin to describe. Somewhere in the distance. .

...water...

...waves crashed gently..

...this...

...upon the shore.

--cold...

Running water. He could hear running water.

"Give us a sign," Stella's voice broke through the lull. Not running water.

Collin opened his eyes.

<u>Cascading</u> water.

"Give us a sign."

Collin heard terrifying screams in his head, and the sound of crashing waves, of roaring water, was deafening. He could see the others staring at the candle or at Stella in her faux trance, but he could not hear them. He could see Stella's lips moving, but all he heard was the sound of many people, crying and screaming in a fit of mass hysteria, and an ear-splitting wrenching sound he could not place.

"Come to us.

--could stop a man's heart in a matter of minutes-

"Speak to us. Come up from your watery grave."

--would feel like thousands of knives digging into your skin—

"Share with us."

--as cold as porcelain--

Collin opened his eyes and looked at Stella. He wanted to scream, but he could force no sound to escape from his throat. Stella's face had changed. It was not longer the subtle face of a wealthy middle-aged woman fighting the effects of aging with plastic surgery. There was nothing plastic about her face. It was porcelain.

Stella bore the same smooth untainted face of the doll that had stared at Collin through the submarine window. Startled and frightened, Collin fell back in his chair and landed hard on the floor.

There was laughter. "Are you all right, Collin?"

Collin looked up from his prone position. Thomas was standing over him, offering his hand. The smell of the candle was fading from the room, replaced by several flavors of pipe tobacco and various liquors. But that other unexplained odor from his dream still lingered.

"I think I may have fallen asleep," Collin said embarrassed. It was the only explanation he could come up with for the strange sequence of events he had just experienced. "I'm sorry, Stella."

"And just when we were about to make contact," she said, and gave Collin a pert pout.

Collin took her hand and kissed it, as a proper gentleman should. He had fallen asleep and had a short, terrifying nightmare; that was all it was. He took in a deep breath and crossed into his bedroom, anxious to check on his prize.

Collin knelt to work the combination on the safe's lock when he felt a cold dampness on his knee. He looked down at the dark spot on his slacks and then to the top of the safe.

"Who sat their drink on my safe?" Collin called out to the others. But the party was rapidly returning to full swing, and no one answered him.

Grumbling to himself, swearing to put a lock on his private bedroom door, Collin pulled out his handkerchief and wiped away the icy water that had formed on the surface of the safe.

That night, Collin had strange dreams.

He felt as if he was floating in gelatin, and that he was trying to fight his way out of the cold, thick substance. It was dark all around him, but there was a light above him, a light that seemed to get farther away the more he struggled. He tried to call out to the light. Why wouldn't it answer him? There were dark objects surrounding him, and Collin was reminded of banana slices suspended in lime green gelatin, a concoction he'd often had in grade school. But each time he reached for one of these dark objects, they would disappear.

Collin sat up in his bed, the bizarre nocturnal adventure rapidly fading from his mind. He swung his legs over, slipped into his night slippers and robe, and shuffled down the hall toward the bathroom.

Collin flicked the switch and turned the faucet on. The water was ice cold. He turned the hot water all the way, but it seemed to only get colder. The water heater must be malfunctioning, he thought, and made a mental note to call the desk in the morning.

--water this cold--

--and stopped.

What was that noise he just heard? It sounded like running water in the distance. Was it raining again'? So much for the sunny Riviera. He heard the sound again. No, not rain. It was a wet sound, as of someone walking around in drenched slippers.

Collin wiped his hands--they were numb from the cold--on a towel and flicked the switch when he heard a different noise.

It was impossible.

Outside maybe, but unlikely at this hour.

But impossible inside his suite.

--water this cold-

It was the carefree laughter of a child. Collin opened the bathroom door just in time to see the silhouette of a small girl running around the corner toward the front of his suite. He started to give chase when he slipped on the tiled floor. Collin caught himself and turned on the lights.

--water this cold--

Puddles of water lined the hallway, extending around the corner where the child had disappeared. He'd heard no door open or close. There was no means of escape.

But there was no child anywhere inside Collin's suite.

Collin rubbed his eyes. He could feel a migraine coming on.

The strange weather must be getting to him. The rain was making him feel as if freezing to death. It was summer on the French Riviera, and he was always cold. Maybe Stella's performance had unnerved him more than he cared to admit.

Collin made his way back into the bedroom and stopped suddenly at the foot of his bed. Small dark footprints wound their way from the door to the foot of the safe. When Collin removed a slipper and touched the spots on the carpet with his bare toe, he could feel their cold chill.

This is preposterous, Collin thought. *I refuse to even consider this possibility. I own many antique dolls and I have not once had their pasts come back to haunt me.*

The damp footsteps didn't bother him nearly as badly as the thin sheet of ice that had completely enveloped the safe.

Collin found himself trapped in the gelatinous sea again, wildly flaying his arms to either side in a mad attempt to reach one of the dark objects trapped beside him. At last, as he watched the last of the objects disappear, his hand bumped something else. It was a life belt.

--water this cold--

Collin quickly slipped into the flotation device. He seemed to be able to breathe, but he felt the need to don the equipment. Somewhere in his hazy state, he thought he could hear the gentle, bittersweet strings of "Nearer My God to Thee" floating somewhere above *him*.

At that precise moment, a tremendous roar of screeching steel and shattering glass drowned out the beautiful melody, and he felt as if he was now floating in freezing water. He looked up to find a gigantic ship looming above him, its bow sticking straight into the air. As the unnerving roar increased in decibels, the great steamer broke in half with a heart-wrenching grind of twisting metal, and screams filled the air as dozens of people fell from the decks into the frigid water.

--could stop a man's heart in a matter of moments--

Collin looked around himself to find that he was floating in water, the buoyancy of the life jacket holding him above the ocean's surface. A bright light exploded from overhead, and Collin looked up to see the rocket's sparks dissipate in the night air. Screams and chaos continued to fill the air. Collin panicked as a man attempted to use him to hold himself up. Collin pushed the man away, and watched with indifference as the man went under. Collin returned his attention to the doomed ship. It's bow bobbed up and down a few moments before it began to sink into the black, frigid water.

--would feel like thousand knives--

Collin turned to look about. Hundreds of others floated in the water around him, ice clinging to their faces and hair. In the distance, he could make out the shapes of the lifeboats, but they were out of reach, and none made an effort to come his way.

Collin looked back up at the stricken <u>Titanic</u> and saw a little girl.

Her mother was holding onto her even as the ship slanted to an almost illogical degree. The little girl held onto the ship's railing with one hand, and in her other tiny hand, Collin could see that she held a small porcelain doll.

Collin's eyes met the girl's, and it seemed as if she were right in front of him, instead of hundreds of feet above him in the cold, starlit night.

He watched in horror and the ship continued to slide farther into the water.

--water this cold--

... until it was gone.

A great suction created by the sinking ship swirled in a wide arc for many long moments. When it finally subsided, Collin was left floating in the freezing water, the cries and pleas of hundreds floating on the night air. The sky was moonless, but there were many stars out, millions of stars. Slowly, surely, the cries and screams began to subside as many succumbed to the frigid water. Collin let his head fall back. He could almost still hear the strains of the orchestra, and he stared up at the sky. He saw a falling star. Then another. He suddenly remembered something he'd heard as a child. Every time you see a falling star, it means someone has died. The cries diminished still. There would be many falling stars tonight, he thought.

Collin heard the gentle lapping of water to his right, and he turned to see the little girl he had spotted earlier on the deck of the sinking ship. She was no more than two feet away from him. Close enough to touch if he could move his arms. She did not shiver; she did not appear to be cold at all. The little girl brought her arms out of the water and Collin could see that she still held the doll in her hands. She extended the doll toward Collin as if to offer it to him, but he could not raise his arms. The little girl's cold blue eyes—

--water this cold--

--stared into his, but she never made a sound. Finally, the little girl released the doll, and it began to sink into the black depths. Collin followed its path as it sank further in the water, and pictured in his mind the slow, wafting journey in would take, two and a half miles into the Atlantic, where it would nestle amongst the remains of a once mighty ode to man's progress, among the mingled remains of hundreds and hundreds of souls (no separation by class down here, everyone equal,) joining them in a somber graveyard, where it would remain for eighty six years, until one man who thought only of himself, a man who believed that the all mighty dollar could save the world's problems--or at least his anyway--would choose to wrench it from its final resting spot.

Collin looked back up to find the girl, but she was gone, and he didn't have the strength left to look around for her.

He could not feel his legs, nor could he any longer feel his heart.

The water was just too cold.

Jonathan Denny could scarcely contain his excitement. This was a dream come true. A lifelong dream fulfilled at last. He was nineteen years old, a high school graduate about to partake of his first college semester. This was something he had envisioned since he was twelve, ever since the day he had picked up a book from the school library for a book report, a book by a man named Walter Lord entitled A Night to Remember

Ever since then he had absorbed every book, every movie (including Cameron's, which he had seen eleven times, so many times that even his girlfriend had gotten tired of seeing it), every article, every documentary on the subject he could find.

And when his father gave him the exciting news that he had booked his son on an underwater tour of the sunken liner as a graduation present (who needs a car?), it was the best news Jonathan had ever received.

And now, here he was, two and a half miles beneath the surface of the Atlantic. It had taken over two hours to reach this depth, and that waiting had been the hardest part of the entire trip. But now, the tour guide had instructed them to watch closely, that they were nearing the stern of the great ship. Jonathan watched intently as the submarine neared the sad remains. It gave him chills he would never be able to explain to anyone to see the dark outline of the stern slowly appear out of the murky gloom.

Jonathan listened as the guide explained all the visible pieces of the ship, pointed out the great gash along the side that had doomed the ship. But Jonathan had seen every picture ever taken of the wreck. Or so he thought.

The submarine had just passed over the last part of the stern, and was hovering just above the ocean floor where a great deal of the wreckage was strewn about. Jonathan had seen these pictures before in all the books he'd studied Toilets, pieces of wooden stairs, benches and all types of debris littered the some six hundred yards of ocean floor that separated the Titanic's stern from her bow.

And Jonathan remembered seeing the picture of the doll's face protruding from the silt on the ocean floor.

But he'd never seen any of the other pictures. Surely they had been photographed. How had he missed them? Why had he never read anything of them?

He'd seen the one photograph of the doll face, but only one. Nothing of the rest of them. And there were so many.

Scattered across the ocean floor, mixed in with the debris from the great Titanic, amid wreckage that had called the bottom of the Atlantic home for eighty-six years, were hundreds and hundreds of broken dolls.

Eight Words

James Van Pelt

The lock resisted at first, then clicked with a rusty thud. The door hung freely on its hinges and drifted open a black inch. Deep in the orchard the cicadas droned.

"Are you afraid of ghosts?" he said.

"Who believes in ghosts?" She pushed the door back.

He had insisted on the "traditional" tools, so, when they shut the door behind them, they fumbled for candles and matches, and, after a dark moment, unsure light illuminated a bare room. He held his candle close to the wall, and a faded gilt pattern shone back at him in intricate, complicated whorls, like the heart of a rose. He looked towards her and saw a candle and her hand floating in the middle of the room, and a reminder of her face drifting above them, eyes black and deep.

"The ghost won't be here," he said. "Not in the <u>living</u> room."

Her hand and candle swooped to a banister, and her flame showed the first steps of a flight up, warped paneling of the wainscot, an empty place where a wall switch had been, her arm, her shoulder, her hair a sudden corona around the eclipse of her head.

"It's not like you to be ironic," she said.

"I practice in the mirror."

"So where should we be?" She looked at him; the candle shadowed her face. A drip of wax flowed onto his hand; it seared for a second, then solidified.

"If not the *living* room, where?"

She thought for a second. "The dead room?" He touched his ear. She said, "Oh! Sounds like. The bedroom."

"Where it began - " He lowered his voice. " - and ended."

She laughed and some metal cabinet in an unseen kitchen reverberated. "So melodramatic." She climbed the steep, narrow stairs in front of him. He looked at her back, the pockets on her jeans, the seam, then his own hand scraping along the wall.

"A ghost doesn't like to be ignored," he said. "It's personal. Ignoring it doesn't make it go away."

"Ghosts are in your mind. If you dwell on them they hang around, otherwise they're vacuum." She laughed again. "People see ghosts who can't let go of the dead."

They held their candles in front of them and stepped into the bedroom doorway. A water soaked section of Sheetrock bowed from the ceiling, and from it some wires, red and black, dangled from a porcelain light fixture. Along the walls, the yellow lights flickered on a stained dresser, a pile of newspaper, ripped cloth hanging from a bent curtain rod, a boarded window, and a china cabinet on its back, its glass fronted doors shattered so jagged remains lined the empty spaces in the middle.

She cleared a spot off the floor with her foot, sat down, leaned against the wall and put her candle on the floor between her knees, which cast huge, twitching shadows. He sat on the edge of the dresser facing her and scrunched back so that his calves rested against the edges of the drawers. He watched the shadows on her face. The candlelight gave her skin a wheat-gold glow and he had a sudden memory of her in a similar light looking across a dinner table at Carbone's when he had said "I love you."   He shut his eyes and pressed the back of his head to the wallpaper, which crackled. He listened to a branch scratching the side of the house.

"Tell me a joke," she said.

"Why a joke?"

"Who needs a reason for a joke? This is a dreary place. You used to joke a lot. Tell me one now."

"A ghost joke?"

"I don't care. You choose."

"How many ghosts does it take to change a light bulb?"

"I hate that kind. That's not a real joke." She shrugged her shoulders together and shivered. "Does it seem cold to you?"

"Cold spots are a sure sign of hauntings." He brought his feet up to the dresser top and rested his chin on his knees.

She sighed. "Cut it out. I don't believe in them."

"You don't have to. No Tinkerbells here. A strong ghost will get a disbeliever too."

"Have you ever seen one?" She rubbed her arms briskly. He said nothing, but cocked his head to listen to wood beams and old nails creaking. Something skittered in the wall behind him, and he jumped.

"They're around me all the time. Not just in this old house, but it's a good place. Some people need this setting. Some people need to see a ghost."

"You mean me? You don't know what I need." She straightened her legs out, which raised a pall of dust when they flopped onto the floor. She coughed into her hand. "O.K. I give up. How many ghosts does it take to change a light bulb?"

He leaned to the side and blew out his candle. Now her candle provided the sole light. He could see her better. "None. Ghosts aren't afraid of the dark."

"That's stupid. That's as stupid as this one. Knock, knock."

"Who's there?"

"Boo who."

"Boo who who?"

"Don't be sad, I'll tell you in a minute."

Below them, in the kitchen or the living room, something moaned softly. He tried to inhale, but his lungs seemed paralyzed. She looked towards the door.

"I love the wind in a old house," she said.

He listened and the moan began again. Maybe a window in back was broken a whistle gap for moving air. He rolled a pebble beneath his finger, around and around, tiny motions so that one revolution was the circumference of his fingertip. "Are you ready?" he said.

"Yeah." She put the candle on the edge of the china cabinet. "Go ahead and tell me the story."

"You have to be in a believing mood." He picked up the pebble and held it up to the light across the room. It was a mouse dropping. He tossed it. "You've got to forget who's telling the story."

"Tell it good, and I will."

"No. It's important. Shut your eyes." She did. She leaned her head back, like his. The light distorted the proportions of the room. The ceiling seemed twice as broad as the floor, like they were at the bottom of a square funnel. They seemed so small, tiny legs, baby-doll arms, fingers too short to touch each other. "You feel the wall behind you?"

"Yes."

"It's dry wood, no varnish, rough kind of?"

"Yes."

"Rub your hand on the floor."

"Why?"

"Mood."

"O.K."

"The floor's gritty, isn't it?" he said.

"Yes."

"Do you feel your clothes on your skin?"

"Yes."

"Do you feel the air on your face?"

She turned her head side to side, eyes closed. "Yes."

"Take a deep breath with your mouth open."

She opened her mouth, a black hole, and inhaled. Her chest filled, he could see it rise. "Do it again." She did.

He said, "Say, 'I am here.'"

"I am here."

"Say, 'The time is now.'"

"The time is now."

"There is no other," he said.

"There is no other."

The wind noise stopped. The branch that rattled back and forth across the side of the house stopped. Slowly he breathed out all his air, pushed his diaphragm tight against the bottom of his lungs.

A stair creaked, distinctly. She twitched her chin to one side, canted her head, kept her eyes closed.

He said, "It could be something on the stairs. It could be nothing."

She nodded.

He said, "Say, 'All times are now, all times are here, we are in the here and now.'"

She did.

"This is the place it started. This is the place it happened. It is happening now, again, as I speak. It is always happening. All parts of it."

Another stair creaked.

He said, "Are you ready?"

"Yes."

The air between us, he thought, all that separates us is the air. Almost nothing.

"If you truly are, then maybe the ghost will come." He spoke the lines the way he'd rehearsed. "This is the story I've been told about the ghost that haunts this house. Others have seen it. I'm not the only one. This is what they say, in the time of the story, when this house was lived in, there was a beautiful man, a Greek god of a man. His name was Theodore and he threw discus in college. But it wouldn't matter if he were plain and unathletic. He could've been any man. He wasn't, though. He was Theodore the beautiful, and everyone loved him except himself. He strode to class, blind to the eyes that followed. His voice was clear and strong. When he spoke, the air quieted around him. Professors paused, not because of his brilliance, but only to bathe in that voice. People who barely knew him stopped to ask him how he was, just to hear him speak. And the music in his voice only hinted at the wonders of his laugh. But when boys and girls hung on him, he shrugged them away, and they loved him even more for his disdain. Like any man, he only knew himself from the inside. He saw nothing special.

"There was one woman, though. Her name was Katherine and she sat beside him in a mythology seminar. She, too, was moved by his beauty. Everyday others tried to sit in her seat, to sit next to Theodore, but she got there earlier than all of them. When the janitors opened the building, she was on the step, her books tight against her chest, her hair combed a thousand strokes, her face scrubbed and powdered, her clothes agonized over, and she sat in her seat, next to the one he always took and waited."

Two more stairs groaned under a weight ascending, some soft, slow movement upwards.

"The class met in a lecture hall, hundreds of seats bolted side by side, with swing-up desks for writing. Katherine rested her arm on the edge of his desk hoping he might accidentally brush her; so she could say, 'Excuse me,' and they would talk. He never did. She could not even look at him. Day after day he came to class, and she sat next to him in miserable ecstasy. Then, one time, she glanced over at his notes and saw that he was doodling. Around his notes of Daedalus and Icarus and the intrigue in the court of King Minos, Theodore had drawn tiny rocket ships balancing on long lines of exhaust. He was busy sketching in an armada of missiles behind the word *Perdix*, which Katherine had written in her notes too, but couldn't remember what it had to do with Daedalus. His paper was covered with ships and asteroids and cratered moons."

He listened to her breathing. The house was so silent, he thought he heard her heart. But more important, he heard, or sensed, or just knew, that a thing stood on the stairs, not breathing. He heard it not breathing.

"She thought, then, that she had seen the Theodore that no one else knew: the little boy inside, not a cold, stiff, unfeeling marble man. She relaxed. For the first time in weeks sitting beside him, she slouched in her chair. Katherine reached over with her pencil and drew on his page a flying saucer. He froze for a moment, then drew behind it, as a backdrop, a ringed planet. She placed a sun high on the sheet, and he added a single spacecraft orbiting.

"Because she saw his spaceships and played his game, he thought she was perceptive, intuitive, that they had touched on some higher level. She was not like the others. She knew the real him. They left class together, and he took her to his favorite spot, through a door shut with a broken lock and onto the roof of the tallest building on campus. There they met, day after day, and talked of inconsequential things, as men will to women and women will to men, though they never spoke of the spaceships or the ringed planet or the orbited sun."

In the hallway at the top of the stairs, he heard the quiet press of a foot onto the floor, the hiss of cloth scraping cloth.

"And, after a time, they became lovers, in this house, which his parents owned, in this very room. And as they were lying in bed, after their first time, he said, 'I don't trust myself to say I will be here for you forever.' And she said, 'We are modern. Nothing is forever.' They met many times in this room, and when he became frightened that she wanted things from him that weren't his to give, she reminded him that nothing is forever, and he was comforted.

"But as they walked together on campus, he saw that no one followed him anymore. The attention he never noticed when it was there, he missed when it was gone. And it seemed the professors were less interested in what he had to say. He laughed and no one looked his way. So it came to him, in a devious kind of logic, that Katherine had changed him, that she had wanted him to be different all along and was subtly working a woman's magic on him. She wanted him to be hers forever. Katherine had told Theodore that he was special, and he believed her, and he believed that she was preventing others from seeing it."

He felt a movement to his left, in the hallway beyond the door. A ghastly half-speed dropping of a sheet. A stir of air.

"So he told her here, after they had made love, 'I am leaving. You have diminished me,' and he left. Katherine didn't beg him, she didn't cry out after him, she didn't weep when she was alone, but she was empty. She thought about his little-boy rocket ships, and their private place on top of the building. She thought about that nothing is forever. After a while, she slid her feet out of the bed, wrapped the sheet around herself, wrote a note, just eight words, and left it on the dresser. She knelt, opened the bottom drawer, took out a safety razor and sliced her wrist. She died on her knees, her forehead pressed against the floor."

The candle caught a gust of air and almost went out as a shape glided through the door and into the room.

She said, "I'm freezing."

He said, "It's here."

She opened her eyes. "What?"

"The ghost. Katherine's ghost."

The misty shape drifted in between them. The girl smiled. "There are no ghosts."

He had been afraid she would say that, that she wouldn't see the ghost, but he had to try.

"You are not in the here and now, or you would."

"It's cold. Let's go."

The shape coalesced on the floor beneath him. Its back bowed the form of its head against the hard wood.

"No, I can't. You go ahead and I'll be along."

She stood, carried her candle over to him, walking through the ghost.

"I'm frozen! There'll be snow tomorrow." She lit his candle. He looked at her impenetrable eyes. He remembered her again in a similar light. She said, "Come with me."

"I can't. I'll meet you in the car. Give me a minute."

He thought for a second that she was going to touch him, but instead she said, "Being just friends isn't going to work out for you, is it?" She left.

He and the ghost stayed motionless. Only the shadows moved. He thought about Katherine alone in this room. He thought about her writing the note, the eight words. Then the ghost raised its head from the floor. It looked up. Hair fell down in front of its face, but there was no face behind, just emptiness. He wasn't frightened. He leaned over the dresser. He thought about the girl who was sitting out in the car now; he thought about the eight words.

Then the ghost spoke.

"It's not my fault I fell in love."

The voice was only an echo. He heard it more in his head than in his ears. But he knew the ghost was real.

He said, "I know."

The Man in Black

Carl Hughes

Martin damned his luck. A fifty-two-seat coach with fewer than twenty passengers, yet one of them had decided to sit next to him. Wonderful. Really set the seal on his day.

The coach backed out of its bay into miserable November rain and began the journey to London just over thirty miles away. Martin gazed through streaky glass at bobbing umbrellas, shop windows spilling orange light on to sodden-litter pavements and the ferment of a town five weeks before Christmas. A dreary time of year, he thought. All hustle and crush compounded by short days, incessant rain and anemic coldness. Given godlike power he would have created perpetual summer: Christmas and winter were for idiots.

He had intended to dump his case on the seat beside him but the fellow passenger had slipped in first. Martin thought briefly about slotting it into the rack above his head instead but as that would mean asking the other passenger to shunt aside, he kept it on his knee. They would be in London in less than an hour anyway.

He jumped as the other passenger laid one hand on his arm and said, "Excuse me, Sir, but you really ought to heed your wife's misgivings, you know."

Martin found the man staring with an intensity that startled him even more than the statement. For a second he felt he recognized the face but only vaguely, as though it had perhaps once looked at him from a crowd. Certainly, one would never forget such a face. It was white. That is to say, not merely untanned, as most faces were at that time of year, but bloodless, and crinkled like damp vellum dried in front of a fire; and it had wide, protruding lips reminiscent of something on a fishmonger's slab. It was an elderly face with almost colorless eyes, and framed by ringlets of silver hair. Contrasting with the white and silver was black: Quaker-style hat, overcoat buttoned to the neck, creaseless trousers.

"I know she meant well, Sir," the man went on when Martin didn't answer. His voice had a cultured edge but curiously lacked expression. After a moment he removed his hand, white and crumpled like the face, from Martin's arm.

Martin blinked, coughed, forced himself not to stare. "You must be mistaking me for someone else," he said.

"Oh no, Sir. You are Martin Dulson." A statement, not a question.

Martin hardly knew what to say. Eventually he asked, 'Have we met before?'

"No, Sir, but other members of your family knew me well. Uncle Thomas, Cousin Emily, to name just two."

Well, that was a fat lot of help, Martin thought. They were both dead and he'd never felt particularly close to either of them. He could only assume that this strange individual had once surfaced among other eccentrics at Aunt Jane's home. Jane always did have an odd crowd around her.

"I therefore strongly urge you to heed your wife and not travel by airplane today," the man said, suddenly smiling like some refugee from a nightmare.

Martin frowned. "What I should or should not do is a matter for me alone. And as for what Beryl and I discussed . . ."

"Discussed, sir? Hardly. You refused to listen — told her she was talking nonsense. Said you would not encourage stupid notions of air travel being dangerous."

Martin clenched his teeth. How dared Beryl go running off to some peculiar stranger, whining because she couldn't get her own way? Angry, he said to the staring old man, "You can inform my dear wife that I profoundly resent her involving people whose opinion in the matter is irrelevant."

The white face accepted this rebuff without visible embarrassment. In fact, it looked surprised rather than mortified.

"Your wife was concerned only for your welfare, Sir. She could as easily have remained silent and allowed you to walk into what she regarded as mortal danger."

"Yes, well . . ." Martin felt uncomfortable. There was no arguing with that, of course, but Beryl even so should not have dispatched some oddball character after him.

"And her fear is utterly justified," the old man insisted, inching his face closer.

Martin pulled back. The odious creature smelled of mildew, as though he had been wheeled up from a cellar.

"You see, the airplane to Edinburgh is going to crash. You can be assured of that, Sir."

Martin's irritation intensified. No doubt the old fool had said the same thing to Beryl and so added to her fear. Worse than that, though, he was obviously unstable and Martin found that vaguely threatening.

As though tuning into his thoughts the stranger produced that ghastly smile again, lips pulled back over his teeth, and said, "I assure you I am no madman. I know things others do not. Perhaps you doubt that such people exist?"

"Fortune-tellers, you mean?" Martin didn't attempt to disguise his scorn.

"Seers. Visionaries. Fortune-tellers merely hazard guesses. Seers and visionaries tell of facts. What I say to you is not a guess, my good Sir. The airplane you intend to catch will crash — I know it as certainly as if it had happened yesterday and I was looking backward in time rather than forward."

Martin sneered but it was a weak affair and he sensed it. He would not allow himself to be intimidated, however, and would certainly not allow this strange fellow to think his preposterous utterances were being taken seriously.

"Very well, Sir," the man said, withdrawing his face at last. "I can see you feel uncomfortable in my presence. Most people do — I'm accustomed to it. I will leave you, therefore, but do be assured that we shall meet again."

So saying he slid out of the seat and swept off towards the back, presumably to secure one of the many other vacant places. Martin sighed his relief, and was annoyed to find his hands trembling. From across the gangway a scrawny woman in glasses stared at him quizzically, and he guessed she must be as puzzled by the strange old character as he was. He shrugged his bewilderment, shaking his head. The woman merely frowned and resumed reading a paperback book.

Martin pulled a copy of The Times from his overcoat pocket but found he could not concentrate on the words. That white, dried-parchment face kept meandering into his mind, the strange warning repeating itself, chafing at his nerves. Irritating and ridiculous.

But what if he was right? What if the plane does crash?

Those doubts surfaced as though programmed to do so when least wanted. Nonsense, Martin thought. The man was an eccentric old fool. One had only to look at him in order to see that.

Yes, but what if -

He stared at passing countryside, sodden and dreary. Rain streaked the coach window, created geometric patterns, curled up and flicked into space. A miserable, wretched day: not one on which to travel by choice. Martin certainly hadn't wanted to make the trip but sixty business executives would be gathering for a conference in Edinburgh next morning, all expecting him as main speaker to produce wit and wisdom and vision. That was why he had opted for a shuttle flight rather than an interminable train. The plane would get him to the Scottish capital by mid-afternoon: plenty of time to relax, prepare his speech, perhaps even take in a film or show later.

But what if -

On the other hand, of course, he didn't want to appear selfish. Beryl had a phobia about flying and would suffer agonies all the time he was airborne. Then she would worry about his return flight. Perhaps, he thought, it would be more charitable to go by train after all and so eliminate her anxieties. Ludicrous, of course, to suggest the plane might crash, but foregoing his own comfort in order to relieve a nervous wife wasn't really too much to ask. Yes, giving in on this occasion would be the noble thing to do. It was the sort of self-sacrifice he could respect.

That still left the matter of his hideous old man in black. Even allowing for her phobia, Beryl ought not to have dispatched him on this idiotic errand. Martin considered her action intolerable and would have to tell her so. Not yet, though. She was neurotic enough. Plenty of time to raise the subject, tactfully, on his return from Edinburgh. He could then also point out that his plane had not crashed: that he would have been perfectly safe.

Unless, of course –

He frowned away thoughts of the old man. Appalling, crazy creature. Charity alone, not some idiotic prophecy, had influenced the decision to go by train: he would leave Beryl in no doubt about that, either. The rain continued thick like mist, congealing around London's traffic and slowing it to no more than walking pace. As a result the coach reached Victoria nearly twenty minutes late. When it finally labored into a litter-strewn bay Martin stood up and looked around, seeking his unwanted merchant of doom. Might as well tell him of the decision to travel by train, he supposed, if only to ensure that the wretch never bothered him again.

A mere handful of passengers occupied the rear section of coach, and none of them looked remotely like the old man. Puzzled, Martin turned towards the front, assuming that the stranger must have moved that way while his attention was distracted. Again, only a range of business people, a few elderly men and women, and a denimed teenager. No parchment face, silver locks, black Quaker hat, black overcoat. Frowning, Martin filed off with the other passengers, waited until the disembarkation ended, then he boarded again, convinced that the old man must still be occupying one of the seats. He told the driver as much and they investigated together, but there was no one.

"The gentleman must have got off just before you," the driver said without interest.

"No he didn't," Martin insisted. "I saw everybody and he wasn't one of them.'

"Well, where is he, then?" the driver asked practically. "If he isn't on board, and he didn't get off, it means he either got beamed up or he wasn't there in the first place."

Martin eyed him with scorn but said nothing because there didn't seem a lot actually to be said. The only reasonable answer, of course, was that he had somehow missed the old man, even if he couldn't understand how that was possible. Irritated, he turned up his coat collar and joined a hustle beneath leaky verandahs. Most people were either making for the buffet or they were in various stages of transit: arriving or leaving. A few, vacant-faced, lounged on benches staring into nowhere. Cardboard-city people, existing, not living, Martin told himself without sympathy. He forced his way to a line of phone kiosks, fretted several minutes before one became free, and finally pushed inside, stepping on a disgusting paste of rain, cigarette ends and urine.

As soon as Beryl answered the phone he said, "I've decided not to fly. I'm going by train after all."

"Really? Oh, I'm so glad." Her relief sounded gratifyingly fervent. "But why? I mean, what made you change your mind?"

"Knew you were anxious, decided to put myself out." He felt slightly shamefaced while uttering the words and couldn't understand why. They were true, after all.

"You really are a darling — I've been worried sick."

"I know, I know." It was impossible to keep the curtness from his voice. He still felt angry about her sending that dreadful old man after him. No doubt she assumed this change of heart had come about because of the hideous creature's warning, and that thought rankled. It had no bearing on the matter at all. He drew breath to tell her so, but remembering that he had decided to say nothing yet, he bit back the words. Instead he said, "I don't know what time the train leaves so I'd better hurry. Don't want to spend half my day sitting in a downpour waiting for the next one. I'll give you a call later."

Outside the kiosk again, looking for white parchment, he scanned a thousand milling faces; but he saw only humdrum human beings going about their business. Strange, he thought, that the face had seemed vaguely familiar. Really must have been one of Aunt Jane's oddball crowd. He grabbed a taxi and fumed in stop-go traffic all the way to King's Cross, staring balefully through misted windows. Eventually he reached the station, hurried to the ticket office and smoldered for another ten minutes in a disordered queue. It seemed everyone ahead of him had at least three queries and wanted to pay by credit card; and the ticket clerks were operating in slow motion.

Due to the delays he missed an express train by two minutes. A gleeful porter told him the next train to Edinburgh would not leave for an hour, and it would stop at virtually every station. Martin damned the porter, he damned Beryl and he damned the parchment-faced man in black. Sitting on a bench, bumped by a fat woman alongside, he reflected that he could by then have been on a plane. And in another hour he would have been in Edinburgh. Stupid man that he was, allowing his heart to overcome superior judgment.

The train was indeed as bad as he had expected: slow, dirty and crowded. It trundled through the murky November afternoon with all the urgency of a statue, sucking in people who smelled of wet cloth, and disgorging others who left behind a clutter of crisp packets, sweet wrappers and Coca-Cola cans. Crushed into a window seat by an elephantine woman (another one - they seemed to be taking over the world,) he occasionally ran his hand over the misted glass and stared at a ceiling of tumbling, remorseless cloud. Above the cloud there would be sunshine, and jets whisking sensible people to Edinburgh and other places in comfort and style. The train clanked to a stop and for nearly half an hour stood doing nothing. The short afternoon had begun to fade; distant farm lights glowed through smoky dusk. One of the passengers asked a uniformed man why the train wasn't moving and the man said he had no idea. Couldn't care less, either, Martin thought. The oaf was probably on overtime and consequently welcomed every static minute.
Many people disembarked in the Northeast and at last Martin had the luxury of a double seat to himself. By then full darkness had come down, and the train ought to have been in Edinburgh. Beryl would be worrying again, he knew. Serve her right. If she hadn't panicked he would already be settled into his hotel room, relaxed and content.

A tinny voice over the interior sound system told passengers there would be a twenty-minute delay at the next station because of trouble along the line. A universal groan went up, and Martin felt like weeping. Instead, when the train pulled alongside the platform, he got out and hurried to a line of phone kiosks to let Beryl know what was happening. He hadn't much sympathy for her worry but knew she would soon be getting on to his hotel asking why he hadn't called her, then like as not she would plead with the receptionist to contact the police and hospitals and goodness knows what, and he would feel idiotic for the rest of his stay. It didn't bear thinking about.

"Martin!" he almost shouted his name. "You're there at last."

"No, I damned well am not. I'm here." He wasn't sure where here was, and craned his neck for sight of a station sign. Her next words, however, drove all uncertainty, all frustration, totally out of his mind.

"I've just heard on the news that the plane you should have been on has crashed."

"What?"

"Yes, at Heathrow. One of its tires burst when it was taxiing for take-off, apparently, and it swerved into another plane."

"Good God."

"Nobody was hurt, thank goodness."

"Oh." He felt almost cheated. "Oh, that's good."

"Yes, but it made a mess and everybody had to get off down those long chute things. You wouldn't have liked that, would you? Not dignified."

He snorted.

"So you see, I was right all along about taking the train, wasn't I?"

He bridled at the note of triumph in her voice. "Maybe you were," he acknowledged acidly, "but even so it was intolerable sending that grotesque gargoyle after me. Who the hell is he, anyway?"

"Gargoyle? What are you talking about?"

"You know who I'm . . . oh hell, I've got to go." Other passengers who, like him, had left the train, were now being herded back by uniformed officials. The train must be about to move on again, sooner than the tinny voice had led them to believe. Typical abominable organization,

Martin thought. To Beryl he said, 'The train's ready to leave. I should be in Edinburgh in an hour or so. I'll call you then." In fact the last words were superfluous as he had already replaced the receiver and was thrusting open the kiosk door with his backside.

The train began moving before he had even resumed his seat, and within minutes it was hurtling through the joyless night. Martin pursed his lips. If only the wretched driver had developed this sense of urgency a little earlier it would have saved much inconvenience. Then again, if Beryl hadn't sent the gargoyle after him he would have been on the plane that crashed. Although, of course, he wouldn't have been injured. But as Beryl said, he wouldn't have enjoyed sliding down the chute with a lot of idiots watching, and then there -

His thoughts froze as the gargoyle appeared, stalking through the carriage as though looking for an empty seat, of which there were many. Martin instinctively shriveled up within himself and hoped the horrible creature wouldn't notice him and decide to occupy the vacant place alongside. Dread metamorphosed instantly to curiosity, however: he wondered why the old fool had chosen to board this of all trains; and how he had known the plane would crash. Was it a lucky guess or something else? And who was he, anyway? That bloodless face, silver ringlets of hair, the black hat and coat. All familiar yet not easily placed. It was on a reflex that Martin scrambled upright and called out, "Excuse me. You, Sir - just a minute."

The handful of other passengers glanced at him accusingly, frowned, got on with reading their papers. The man in black, on the other hand, took no notice but continued on his way, out through a sliding door.

Martin hurried after him, angry at such rudeness and determined not to be humiliated in front of the other passengers. He would get answers if he had to wring the creature's scraggy neck.

He followed into the next carriage only five or six paces behind, but when he entered he found merely a long, empty gangway between the seats, and about a dozen passengers in all. He lurched down, rocked by the speeding train, staring at every occupant and receiving bemused glances in return. None of the people had a parchment face, silver locks or colorless eyes. He went through to the next carriage, and the one after that, all the way to the front of the train, but he could not find the man in black. On his way back he checked the lavatories, wondering if the creature had locked himself in one of those, but they were all vacant.

The train roared on, pitching, rattling, swaying. Martin struggled back to his seat, bewildered and annoyed. Something, however, was beginning to shift in his memory. That face. Yes, he had seen it before, as he thought, but not at Aunt Jane's. His mind was finally bridging a chasm of years, recalling the Christmas he received his first bicycle. There had been jigsaws, too, and various games — and several books. One book above all the others had enthralled him, held him spellbound. He could see it now. A large, glossy book called Tales from the Crypt, with a cover picture of graveyard ghouls in the moonlight. A peculiar book to give to a boy of eight or nine, but typical of Aunt Jane to think of something like that. His parents hadn't altogether approved, he remembered, but he certainly had. He had taken that book to bed and read it over and over, scaring himself witless in the dark winter nights.

Yes, that book. It was within its pages that he had seen the parchment face, silver locks, colorless eyes, Quaker hat, and coat that seemed to exude shadows. The character had appeared several times in picture-strip stories. The Angel of Death.

No, Martin told himself. No, impossible.

He told himself impossible only once, however. For in that instant of denial something happened, something so sudden, so cataclysmic, that it banished all skepticism forever.

The train braked fiercely, bucked. A sickening impact, a screech of metal, and a slithering, sliding, grinding jolt as the locomotive and carriage jumped their rails. Another smash as the train demolished a wall and seemed to implode. And then suddenly the carriage was airborne, hurtling into space from a viaduct, and all the passengers were screaming, and people were being flung from floor to ceiling, smashing like glass marbles in a tin as the carriage turned and turned.

And as Martin somersaulted he saw the man in black sitting in the seat from which he had just been precipitated, and the man smiled. A knowing smile, cold and deep and empty.

Portrait in Graphite

John Urbancik IIII

Matt Lane moved in quietly on a Thursday afternoon. He carried his few boxes, alone, up three flights of stairs to the top apartment.

Darkness crowded the narrow, crooked steps, but the early evening sun illuminated the apartment. He had rented it because of the two walls of windows in the corner room. One overlooked the street and apartments and storefronts, which faced him. The other, before the neighboring building had been erected forty years ago, had given a grand view of the river and all the bridges.

An elderly woman on the second floor watched his repeated ascensions, box and bag laden, from behind a door she opened only as far as the inch a brass security chain allowed. When he smiled at her, she snorted and slammed the door.

Matt set his easel in the corner of the room, between the windows, after his last trip.

The provided furnishings were sparse, drab, and barely functional. He made up the bed with brightly colored sheets. He wished it was larger, but he had only one pillow. He stuffed underwear and socks in the top dresser drawer, then sat on the couch with his arms spread across the top and closed his eyes.

He woke, curled in the corner of the couch, after dark. Little light filtered in through the windows; the next building blocked most of it. He saw well enough to stumble through the dark, banging his knee only once on the heavy wooden coffee table.

The lamp was dim, as if the bulb and not just the lampshade was dirty. Something to fix, but there was a lot more of that than there was money. Light, however, was a priority.

A toilet and claw-legged tub crowded the bathroom, the porcelain discolored and cracked. He rinsed his face in the sink and stared a moment at his reflection. Blue eyes stared back.

Matt blinked. No, the eyes were brown, as they were supposed to be.

The image stuck with him, though. He sat with his drawing pad and a few colored pencils and drew a woman's eyes. Blue, of course, neither wide or thin but almond shaped.

He sketched a second set, then a third, oblivious to the time. They were pretty eyes, pale with darker flecks bursting from--without quite touching--the pupils.

Three of his five boxes had been art supplies.

In the morning, city-filtered sunlight through the window woke him on the couch. He had drawn seven pairs of eyes, even the hint of a nose with one. He closed his pad, placed it on the coffee table, and took a hot shower.

On the way to a job interview, Matt bought a bagel for breakfast. At the same shop, on his way back, he bought a fifty-cent package of cookies for lunch.

He drew, with his colored pencils, the view from his window before the obstruction next door had been created: the wide river, which bent slightly north half a mile from his apartment, two bridges, and a setting sun.

The sun had, indeed, settled for the night by the time he finished. He left it on his easel and went out.

The old lady on the second floor was in the hallway as he left. She paused as he rounded the staircase.

"Good evening," he said, nodding.

"You're not the first artist we've had up there," she said, disapprovingly. "At least you're quiet."

Matt smiled, ignoring the confrontational tone, and continued down the stairs.

At the nearest grocery store, he bought milk, cereal, bread and jelly, a couple of apples and a piece of chocolate. Returning to his apartment, he stared a moment at the old lady's door. It looked just as thin, but more badly worn, as his.

He ate cereal for dinner, cracked the window to let in the city sounds and chilly air, and opened his drawing pad.

He sketched the partly opened apartment door, in black and the old woman as he had first seen her. He might have added one wrinkle too many on her gnarled fingers, but figured she'd earn it in time.

He didn't have another job interview the next morning, so he never left the apartment. He watched the street for a long while, through his open window, picking a particular person and following them until they disappeared. He wanted to draw a person, but no one sparked his interest.

Near dusk, after dining on chocolate and an apple, he started painting the eyes. It required more time than the pencils, and he worked until well after midnight. Maybe twice, he looked up from the canvas as he wiped his paint-smeared brow with colored fingers. When rain began falling, he closed the windows and took a shower.

Matt crawled into bed and slept. He woke before dawn, poured out of bed, and trudged into the corner room. For a moment, he saw the river through the window as though the building didn't exist. It was the image from his sketch, or the moment after it. *Dreamy eyes,* he told himself. He sketched the outline of the river, without the bridges this time. They were too new.

They weren't as old as his apartment. He wished he truly had that view, but then he never could have afforded this apartment.

The painted eyes stared at him as he drew. After a while, he became very aware of then. He gazed back, wondering from whose face he had caught them before rendering them as his own creations.

"You look sad," he told the eyes. That's how they'd appeared originally. He'd tried to change that with more sketches, failing for the moment. When the right time presented itself, he'd make them wearing a different emotion.

A shiver spread from his spine to his fingers. Matt put down the pad and went to the window. Outside, a lady leaned against one of the lampposts. What struck him most was her hat. Tilted off-center like a beret, it exposed most of her short, curly black hair. From this distance, it appeared to be velvet or something equally as soft and textured. A black veil hung from it, close to her head and face, covering most of her hair and falling just above her lip. It didn't look dark, but glamorous. Her dress, too, was black, with tiny straps over her shoulders, but its details melted into the shadows. She was thin. The distance masked the details of her face, even when she cocked her head and looked directly at him.

Matt stared back, captivated. She glowed in the streetlight, unlike everything else around her which merely reflected it, and even wearing black in the night, she stood out as if she were a perfect onyx atop a mound of sugar. She waited for something. She kept her eyes on him. She made him nervous. She was too beautiful to be out alone at night, dressed for a gallant ball in the middle of a silent film

He wanted to get closer, to see her face, the curve of her lips and the shape of her eyes, the texture of her skin. Her arms were bare, and seemed a single perfectly curved line to her shoulders, throat, and cheek. He wanted to see them from closer and then draw what he could remember.

He ran down the stairs, taking them three and four at a time and rounding the corners blindly. At the front door, her lamppost remained out of sight. With a deep inhalation, he stepped into the night.

The street was empty, with neither moving cars nor living souls. It was nearly three, too early for the morning people to be out, too early even for the night people to come home.

Dreamy eyes, he told himself, slowly returning to his building and climbing the stairs.

On the second floor, the old lady's door stood ajar nearly two inches. She stared through it, relentlessly, and narrowed her eyes when Matt looked at her. She said nothing, and gave no response to his half-hearted smile. He heard her finally close her door as he opened his.

"Sleep," he said, a command to himself. After rinsing his face, and finally shutting the window--and confirming that the woman was, indeed, gone--he went back to bed.

In bed, images of the first artist flashed through Evelyn's mind. She didn't just remember the year, she remembered the exact day they first met.

Outside this very apartment building, when the neighbors were pretty and extravagant, he had moved into the top of the building. Through her partially opened door, she watched the young man ascend. He carried one bag over his shoulder and a drawing pad under his arm. Her father disapproved.

"He pays for that apartment by drawing women without their clothes," he told her. "Keep away from him. Seventeen at the time, the suggestion only heightened Evelyn's intrigue. Maybe he'd draw her picture.

"He captures their souls," father continued. "Puts them on paper with wretchedly black pencils and collects ten dollars a piece for the theft." His rants rarely lasted so long; perhaps he'd never seen Evelyn so enraptured before.

The artist's face belonged in a painting. His eyes were perfect, wide and soft, and very unlike those of a gentleman. They revealed wildness, something pure, which touched Evelyn at a spiritual level. His were the most kissable of lips, thick and tender, and when he curved them into a smile he might charm anyone in the world--except her father.

Near midnight, she sneaked out of the apartment. She listened to be sure no one else was awake and wandering the halls. Very unladylike, she climbed the stairs to the artist's new apartment and knocked twice on the door.

She didn't know what she would say. If he were home, would he even be awake? Would she be disturbing him as he painted? No, her father said he used pencils. Evelyn wanted to pose for him, to have his hands trace the subtle curves of her breasts and waist, hips and legs. The thought knotted her stomach just as the door opened.

A woman, much older than Evelyn, wrapped in a long silk robe, looked down at her. She towered over Evelyn, long and, unfortunately, quite lovely. "And you are?" she said with a razor tone.

"I must be mistaken," Evelyn said. "I thought an artist lived here."

"Oh, one does," the woman said. One hand rested on the doorknob, ready to pull it shut, the other on her hip. Evelyn expected the woman to start tapping her foot expectantly.

"One does," another voice confirmed. Low, smooth, its owner stepped out of the shadows. He, too, wore a robe, with both his hands in the pockets. The woman stepped aside, chin in the air, with a sudden, annoyed inhalation. "I am Cecil English," he said. "And you?"

"Evelyn Blake," she said.

"It's late for visiting," he said, stepping back and pulling the door more widely open. "Won't you come in from the hall?"

Gingerly, she crossed the threshold of his apartment. Somehow, the existence of the other woman made him safer. Still, her father wouldn't like it. Just inside the doorway, Evelyn hesitated.

The woman had gone into the other room without a sound, shutting the door behind her. The corner of the room had windows on both walls, and she could clearly see the river. Her own apartment faced the other way. She stared a moment at the oily water which reflected street and building lights.

"This view," Cecil said as he closed the door, "is exactly why I'm here."

"You mean to paint it?" Evelyn asked.

He laughed, gently, lightly, not at all condescending as she was used to her father laughing when she said something foolish. "Not at all," he told her. "I'm here to draw."

"People," Evelyn said. "Women." She looked at him. Up close, his eyes exuded even more power, like in photographs of movie stars, and never strayed from her gaze.

Eventually he asked, "To what do I owe the pleasure of this late visit, Ms. Blake?"

"Evelyn, please," she said, giggling.

"Evelyn," he said, nodding.

"I was wondering," she said, looking back to the river. "Might you draw a picture of me?"

"You don't even know if I'm any good," he said.

"Your eyes say you are." She couldn't bare to look at him. How could she have been so foolish? When he didn't answer, she said, "My father says you draw women. I can pay you."

Cecil said nothing. He walked around her, studying her form--her body. Evelyn's stomach twisted, and she realized she was holding her breath. He made her so nervous. A tiny bead of sweat formed over her eye. She wanted to wipe it away, but didn't dare move her hand. Where, exactly, was he looking at as he stared at her back? What did he see? His were the eyes of an artist, and the hands, and she jumped when those hands touched her waist.

"I can draw you," he said, turning her slightly to the left. "Look at me. Don't move." She turned her head and looked over her shoulder. He pushed her short hair from the side of her face. "I can draw you," he said again, "But not in what you're wearing."

The woman filled Matt's dreams. She walked under the moon, though little of its light reached the city. He followed her through a maze of alleys, finally emerging at his new apartment's front door. It was newer, then, shinier and without a neighboring building. She was younger than he first thought, perhaps younger than himself. Silk or velvet, her black dress flowed in and out of the night. She smiled at him once before going inside. His dreams gave her the blue eyes he had painted, as though they'd always belonged to her. They fit perfectly. They revealed a sadness in her, a longing that her lamppost pose had suggested. She had lost something.

He wanted to follow her further, but the dream shifted abruptly so that he was looking down from his apartment window. He saw the river clearly, and the hundreds of city lights shimmering off its rough surface. Another woman stood next to him, one palm on the window and the other on her hip. Her eyes, too, were blue, but these were icy, like steel, and the only emotion exuding from them was anger.

He tried to speak with her, tried to reach out and touch her slender arm.

He woke before dawn, these images strong in his mind. He breakfasted quickly, ran hot water in the shower, and examined the two women in his dream. There shared too many similarities to be two distinct people. She was one woman, at different moments, existing in different emotions. He wanted to draw her and capture those emotions. He wanted to be clean, first. This felt like a special job.

He sketched the eyes a dozen times or more, capturing the similarities between sorrow and anger. They narrowed when angry. They darkened. He started a face around them: wisps of hair, the outline of a nose. The scent of sulfur-no, gunpowder, touched him.

He inhaled deeply, smelled nothing, and sighed. He put down his drawings, opened the windows, and filled his lungs with stale, city air. The night's chill lingered, though the sun shone brightly, directly over him.

He walked down to the river, to a place from which he could see the newer building. He might have looked straight into his apartment once. Hundreds of cars sped along the highway and over the bridges, drowning any river sounds. The odor of exhaust and oil and metal destroyed any lingering scents. He couldn't remember what had disturbed him.

He sat on a park bench and tried to recapture the woman on his drawing pad. He'd only brought the one pencil, with which he hoped to outline her lines and her face, the curves and maybe the eyes. Her image faded, dazzled by the shimmering asphalt and the water beyond it. He drew the scene instead, without the cars: an empty road paralleling a wide, curved river. Roughly, he sketched in the bridges. He turned-- first the page, then his back to the river--and began drawing his apartment building, as it might have appeared before its neighbor had been constructed.

He imagined it as it might have been when built, sometime in the Roaring Twenties, in the heart of a world of jazz and slender cigarette holders, when women still looked like his visitor at the lamppost. He sketched it roughly, his hands and eyes tired, and then packed up to go back.

He nearly stepped into the road before the present came back to him, narrowly missing the path of a white Corvette. He drew back, suddenly frightened. For a moment, it actually had been yesterday.

The old woman stood behind the crack of her door, watching, scowling, as he climbed the steps. "Evening," he said. She narrowed her eyes but said nothing. He paused a moment, nearly wishing for a response, before giving up and resuming his climb.

Evelyn didn't like the way he climbed those stairs. It reminded her of her last ascent, seven decades ago. She'd been young and naive, anxious and nervous. Though she never repeated the climb, she never moved away.

She wore a long black gown that hugged her slim body. She felt like a movie star. She'd stolen it from her mother's wardrobe.

Midnight passed long before Evelyn gathered the courage to sneak out of the apartment a second night. Seemingly heightened senses allowed her to hear her father breathing in bed, inhaling deeply and loudly, pausing a moment to listen for anything out of place, and then slowly exhaling. He paused again before repeating the breath. Evelyn timed her steps to that rhythm. She opened the door as he breathed in--if she heard or imagined the sound, she didn't care--and closed it with an exhalation.

She bounded up the steps two at a time. He'd described precisely what she should wear, to the veiled velvet hat which hugged her head. The dress, tight on her, made her feel more decadent than if she'd stripped for the drawing.

Cecil answered the door himself, smiling, dressed handsomely in a jacket and tie. He, too, seemed more a movie star than an artist. He bowed as he allowed her in, and closed the door behind her.

They spoke briefly, about the dark violet backdrop that exploded through the window, the streets, even the movies. He said her eyes reminded him of an actress, Clara Bow.

"I've drawn a hundred women and more," he said, starting, "so that I might perfectly render you, tonight." They laughed together, but only briefly. "Keep mostly still, $_{standing}$ toward the window but looking back, over your should, at me. Yes, exactly." She stood between him and the window. No sounds came in to interfere.

"I'm glad you came to me last night," Cecil said as he drew, his smooth voice like that of a singer over the rhythmic scratching of his pencils. "I came here to find inspiration.

"You flatter me," she said.

"I speak only the truth," he said. "This city is remarkable, far more exciting than my uncle had suggested, overfilled with every form of life. And to think, I have found the most beautiful of girls in my own building, wishing to have herself immortalized just as I wish to capture her image."

It reminded her, vaguely, of her father's words. "Do you capture my soul?" she asked.

He laughed. "Tilt your head down, keep your eyes on me," he said. "No, drawing does just the opposite. Your soul is already captured, trapped within the confines of your body. Everyone. And here, the artist slowly removes your soul, the top layer at least, with every stroke of the pencil. And when at last the drawing is done, when your energy and beauty have been rendered, not just skillfully but lovingly, then that trapped part of you shall be freed," He tilted his head as he spoke, his eyes darting quickly between the paper and Evelyn's body. She wished, right then, that he had asked to draw her naked, yet blushed with the very thought.

Cecil smiled. "Don't be nervous," he said. "I've done this before."

She smiled to mask her nervousness. She felt him draw her; as his pencil outlined her arms, he might have brushed her skin. As he sketched her face, it was as if he caressed her cheek with the back of his hand. She saw none of what he drew; the easel's back faced her. Still, Evelyn shivered as he shaded the profile of her breasts.

Dawn approached far too swiftly. She feared the night's end. Her father slept downstairs, more alert in his sleep because of the noise she had made. If he found her in her mother's dress...

Evelyn refused to consider it. She glanced through the windows, which revealed a brightening, amethyst sky. It appeared so unlike a city in that moment, as if she'd been transported to another world.

Maybe this sensation, she realized, was her soul being stripped away by Cecil's pencils.

He paused. "Almost done."

She glanced nervously down at the street.

Matt locked the door behind him and sighed deeply. In the morning, another job interview waited. He'd prefer to draw on the streets, collecting coins for his work, except he could never gather enough.

The images from his dream had escaped, and he'd failed to capture them with his pencil. He sat on the couch and stared out the windows. Some of the sky, a charcoal blanket, was visible above the building when he looked straight up. He thought about climbing to the roof, maybe capturing some of the magic that once made this view something fabulous.

"Do you capture my soul?" she asked.

He started, glancing quickly about every visible corner of his apartment. There were no crevices in which to hide. Had he imagined the voice? It sounded like the woman from his dreams, and the woman from the lamppost.

Maybe she stood there now.

He was disappointed to see the lamppost and its empty sphere of light.

"It's getting early," she whispered.

He moved his head slowly, turning to face the center of his room. Over the easel, between the couch and door, was nothing. No one.

He yawned as he entered the bathroom. There wasn't room for a second person. He washed his face, stared at the eyes in his reflection, and gave a short, startled laugh. Her eyes. He rinsed again; his eyes returned to their usual chestnut hue.

He stared a long time. His eyes remained a single shade, steady, the pupils large and the whites more visible than usual. His hands on the sink trembled slightly. Who watched him? What did she want?

These were silly questions. He tried to shake them but they persisted. He'd seen her eyes twice, and they certainly belonged to the woman outside. She hadn't been from here--at least, not from *now*.

Eventually, he tore himself away from the mirror. He gathered his drawings. First the pages of those sad blue eyes. He went to his easel, where he'd left the imagined cityscape, but it wasn't there.

He wasted no time wondering where it had gone; he'd not moved it, of that he was certain. He grabbed his drawing of the woman downstairs, took pencils and a pad, and went to her door.

It stood ajar, waiting for him, with the brass security chain engaged. He knocked.

She came silently to the door, looked him up and down disapprovingly, and said nothing.

"I want to talk with you," he said.

She snorted.

"There's something strange," he said, showing her the drawing of the eyes. "Do you recognize those?"

She stepped back as if struck, looked sharply at him, and said, "You are a contemptuous man."

"How long have you lived here?" he asked. "Decades?"

"Arrogant, disrespectful," she said.

"If I draw someone," he said.

She continued her litany. "Obnoxious, ignorant."

"*If I draw someone,*" he said again, "would you tell me if you recognize her?"

She snorted and shut her door. He caught it, pushed it open as far as the chain allowed, and held out the drawing of her.

She snatched the picture and tore it in half. "You dare," she spat, crumpling the halves and dropping them at his feet. He didn't resist when she slammed the door shut. Head bowed, eyes on the torn drawing, he listened as she engaged tumblers and deadbolts.

The old woman's eyes were sad, like the apparition, and a pallid, filmy blue.

The artist lingered. Evelyn leaned heavily on the door, waiting for him to leave, wishing he had never come. Memories hurt.

"Almost done," he had said.

She looked nervously down at the street. The sky's shade had turned violently bright, as though the sun already peeked over the eastern horizon. The streets and the river reflected it, the streets in solid strokes and the water with a mutable, chalky texture. She could hear her father in bed, turning, repositioning, maybe even sensing something was wrong. He normally slept in on a Saturday, but she imagined today would be different.

"A sense of freedom," Cecil was saying, though she'd missed the beginning. "As soon as it's done."

"It's getting early," she said.

"Almost," he said.

She reached between her breasts, under her bra, where she held a ten-dollar coin. She withdrew it; the gold coin glimmered in the early morning light. It had been a gift, early in the year, for her seventeenth birthday. Today, it had been transformed into a drawing.

"My father said you charge ten dollars."

"That seems excessively high," he told her.

"To free my soul," she said, "I should expect to pay much more."

"From you, I expect nothing for payment, except the joy of having created your image." He smiled, tilting his head to the left. "Another two minutes, at most."

A door slammed somewhere. He didn't react, as if he didn't hear it. Evelyn inhaled sharply. It was her father, discovering Evelyn's room empty, knowing immediately where she had gone. He thundered up the stairs, his footfalls like hammers in the hall. She held her breath, felt her heart's pulse in her throat. Be done, already.

Time suspended. An hour passed before the end of the next moment. Cecil leaned closer to the drawing. Her heart beat. Once. The thunderous footsteps fell silent, their song reaching its crescendo with a sudden shot to the door. It flung open easily. Father stepped in, his face twisted with rage and embarrassment.

Evelyn leapt, though not at all surprised. Cecil merely turned his head. His eyes widened at the pistol in her father's hand.

"Father, no!" she screamed, launching forward. His eyes went from her to the picture to the artist before she'd taken one step. By her second step, he'd pulled the trigger.

Cecil crashed backwards, away from the easel. Evelyn dropped the gold coin, her third step already too late to stop anything.

"You'll not be trashed about while I live," father said, ripping the nearly completed drawing. Tears streamed down her face. When he tore the paper, it was as if he tore a part of her. Her stomach churned. Her heart stopped, constricted too tightly. She reached her father and ripped the burning weapon from his hand. He struck her with the back of his hand.

He'd never struck her before.

Her mother's dress ripped as she fell. Her head reeled. The edges of her vision blackened. For a moment she felt death coming. She tasted blood on her lip. The back of her head cracked against the wood floor.

Her father moved before she'd even hit the ground, crying her name, reaching for her with his loving, fatherly embrace. He picked her up by her shoulders, kneeling on the floor and stroking her hair back. "My poor, naive little girl," he said, closing his eyes. "Sweet Evelyn."

For the first time his touch didn't comfort her. She retreated into herself, cringing as much as she could, but she had no strength and no will. Instead of looking at her father, she looked at the torn drawing. Cecil, bleeding and dying on the floor just beyond her arm's reach, had nearly finished. He'd nearly released her soul.

When the artist finally left, Evelyn opened the door a crack. She looked down at the ground, where she'd thrown the pieces of the drawing. It had been of her, in the present, the only such thing since 1927. He'd taken the pieces with him. Had he, too, captured a piece of her soul?

Matt waited at the window, staring down at the lamppost and listening to the quiet of his apartment. His lights were out. He held a black pencil in one hand. He trembled.

When midnight came and passed, he knew it only by his watch in the dim city ambiance that filtered in through the windows.

By dawn, he'd fallen asleep on the couch. He woke well after noon. He'd missed his interview, but didn't care; he could find a minimum wage job anywhere. This woman, though, who had visited him--had spoken to him--he cared about.

Her eyes, of course, enraptured him. So melancholy, so pleading, as if he--and no one else--could do something to take away that sadness. What if she never came back?

He showered, poured a bowl of cereal, and let his mind wander. He saw his apartment before the paint began peeling, before the floor had been worn thin, before the cracks came to the bathroom and before cigarette smoke stained the ceilings yellow. Mostly, he imagined it before another building obscured his view of the river. Who had looked through these windows and seen that view? Another artist, the old woman downstairs had suggested. When? Forty years ago? Fifty? Or was this back in the twenties, when the blue-eyed woman had been before her sadness, lively and filled with joy? Maybe she had been the artist.

He dumped the soggy cereal down the kitchen sink. He drew the eyes again, and her unseen mouth." He drew a netted veil across those eyes, like the hat worn by the woman at the lamppost. Had she been real? Was any of it?

He didn't care. In the living room, facing the window that once overlooked the river, he started working on another drawing. This time, he meant to draw the woman at the lamppost. He sketched her quickly, not at the lamppost but as if she stood here, between him and the window. He drew the background behind her, the river, the streets, and the midnight sky.

Dusk came before he finished the background. The woman stood before him as he drew, in a long black gown and the veiled hat. She looked at him over her shoulder, so he erased the outline he had already done and started anew. She seemed to tremble as he shaded her waist, and she blushed as he drew her breasts.

"Do you capture my soul?" she asked.

He didn't answer, afraid the sound might chase her image away. Every time he looked up from the picture, he thought she might be gone.

She became more real as he drew, like a woman emerging from mist, while the night darkened outside. He turned on a light--the dim, dirty bulb behind him. He didn't know how much time he had, but didn't want to rush. This was a once-in-a-lifetime picture. Instinctively, he knew he'd never get another chance.

He drew for hours, capturing her essence, her beauty, and the glamour that radiated from her. Matt only hated that every minute brought him one minute closer to completion, when he would be done with the drawing. She glanced down at the street. "It's getting early."

She reached into her dress, between her breasts, and withdrew a gold coin. It glimmered in the early morning light.

"My father said you charge ten dollars," she said.

He hated the light that came through the window. He was almost done, having only her face left to render. His fingers trembled as he touched the paper with pencil. The night had passed swiftly.

"To free my soul," she said, "I should expect to pay much more."

"Nothing at all," he whispered, daring to only while looking directly at her.

Downstairs, a door slammed. It startled the woman, but he ignored it. "Who are you?" he asked.

Someone climbed the stairs. He continued to draw, done with her lips and her nose, left only with the eyes. They were not sad, but frightened. He almost dropped his pencil.

The sound disturbed him. No one else, climbing those stairs, had made so much noise.

Had he? Was that how the old woman always knew to look out her door as he passed? He'd seen no one else in the building, though he knew all of the apartments were occupied.

The footsteps ceased. He finished her eyes, stepped back and compared the picture to the woman. He needed only to add his signature at the bottom for it to be complete.

The door to his apartment; rocked, as if someone pounded it with an ax. The woman looked to the door, crying, "Father, no!"

Matt had to finish. He leaned closer, quickly drawing in his initials. MEL. Done.

The door never opened. He thought for a moment that it would crash open. The sounds ceased completely. The woman stared at the door, eyes wide, smiling. "You've finished?" she asked. "You've freed my soul?"

He showed her the picture. "It's done."

"Evelyn," she said. "My name is Evelyn Blake." She took his hand. Her fingers were soft, smooth and cool, as real and substantial as a cloud. She pressed the gold coin into his palm and softly kissed him. "I have always wanted to kiss those artist lips." Then she stepped back, still holding his hand, and smiled. The sadness had left her eyes. She stepped further back, fading into the dawn light that broke through the windows. She dropped his hand and disappeared completely.

He stared a moment, and then looked down at the gold coin. It seemed to have been minted the day before, a ten-dollar coin with the date 1926.

He slept most of the day, as deeply as he'd ever slept. When he woke, he went out to find out how much the coin was really worth. Surely, it was something more than ten dollars, and he certainly needed the money. When he passed the old woman's apartment, he couldn't help but smile at her.

Evelyn closed her door, engaged all the locks, and leaned heavily against it. Safe within the apartment she'd always called home, she allowed a slow, rare smile on her mouth. She closed her eyes, and whispered, "Those artist lips."

Mending

Cheryl Jessop

Janie sighed and put down her book. It was a good book, or so John had told her, but she had no interest in reading, or in anything else. In the long, empty months, since Steve's death she had found that nothing could occupy her mind for very long.

Why? After all this time that one question still refused to let her be, demanding an answer. Why hadn't he taken more care? Why had he stepped off the curb without looking? Why hadn't the driver seen him in time, or braked, or swerved to avoid him? Why had he left her alone with only memories and pain for companions? Why had her last words to him been unkind and spoken in anger? Why?

She screwed up her eyes to hold back the tears, tears she should have long since learned to control, or so her friends kept telling her. Yet, she didn't want to control them: she wanted to weep until her soul was empty, perhaps then the pain would go away. Steve had been everything she had ever wanted in life and now that he was gone she was at a constant loss, aimless without the anchor he had become.

She pressed her fists against her eyes as the tears well again. She missed Steve so much. She missed his laughing eyes, and the way he would wrap himself around her to keep warm as they lay in bed. She even missed being woken up in the early hours when he would suddenly want to talk bout things that refused to be banished from his mind. Most of all she missed coming home to find him there, ready to soothe away the pressures of the day with his warm smile and gentle touch.

She rose and crossed the room, averting her eyes from the window, knowing that if she looked out and saw the honeysuckle where his ashes lay the tears she had mastered this one time would fall. She turned on the radio and a loud, throbbing noise filled the room. With a grimace of distaste she twisted the dial, searching for something less abrasive, something that would soothe or perhaps even cheer her. A shiver raised the hairs on the back of her neck, and she snatched her hand away from the radio as a song, laden with memories, reached her ears. Her first instinct was to switch it off, but she could not and she listened, her head turning automatically towards the window and the honeysuckle.

It had been Steve's wish to have the song played at his funeral: he had told her during one of their all-night talks, and she had laughed and told him that death was a lifetime away. Now, as she heard it, the grief that still lingered, so close to the surface, threatened to overwhelm her. Each word, each strain of the compelling melody brought so many memories: of Steve laughing as he lifted her high in the air, swinging her round and round until they were both dizzy; of Steve running from the house, angered and hurt at her thoughtless remarks; of Steve lying cold and broken on a slab in the mortuary, and of Steve's coffin as the pall bearers carried it into the church.

As the song ended she had stopped trying to hold back the tears, although she smiled through them as she pictured him singing the words to her, as he often had when they were alone. Then, as she was about to switch off the radio she froze, her hand poised over the switch as the DJ's voice cut into the memories.

"That was especially for Janie, and comes with love and best wishes for a happy birthday, from Steve."

Happy birthday? Yes, it was her birthday! She had forgotten, or at least tried to forget. The cards were left unopened on the table, and the parcel from her parents had been dumped, unkindly, in the cupboard under the stairs so that she wouldn't be forced to remember her last birthday and Steve's childlike excitement as he had watched her open the present he had so carefully wrapped. She remembered it now, and gave a sad half-smile as she lifted her hand to look at the ring she wore on her little finger. It was heavy, antique silver and fashioned in the shape of a unicorn's head, so that she would never forget her dreams, he had told her.

Then, as realization dawned, she shook her head in disbelief. Why was she wondering about her birthday? What she should really be asking is what kind of sick person would do such a thing: to send in a request for her birthday, from Steve? Perhaps there was another Janie and Steve? Yes, that had to be it, surely none of her friends or family would be so insensitive as to think that something so morbid might bring her comfort.

With another heavy sigh she switched off the set and put on her coat. She had to get out of the house, to see and speak to real people instead of her memories. She would go into town and return the book to the library, and then she would ring Tom and ask him to lunch. She had only known Tom for a few weeks, and he was the only one amongst her friends who didn't remind her of Steve. She and Tom would have lunch and they would talk about the weather and the mess the world was in, and for a short while she would pretend that she was fine.

When she returned three hours later her mood was better. Seeing Tom and listening to his bright chatter had chased away the gloom for a while, and for the first time she could remember since Steve's death she had laughed, really laughed. She had almost forgotten what laughing felt like: how it would make her face and her sides ache as she fought to bring it under control, and how it would give her an intense rush of pleasure followed by a feeling of well-being that would last for it would give her an intense rush of pleasure followed by a feeling of well-being that would last for hours. She was still smiling as her hand reached out to switch on the radio, an automatic action borne from years of habit.

The smile disappeared along with the colour in her face as she heard the voice of the DJ announce a special request for Janie, from Steve, who missed her terribly. She felt her stomach tighten, and nausea threatened to overwhelm her as the voice on the radio cheerfully told her not to cry any more, that her tears made Steve sad because he couldn't comfort her. When the voice told her that it was time to find herself some glue she had to sit down and catch her breath.

Steve had once told her that his heart had been broken by a woman who couldn't love. She had taken his hands in hers and stared deep into his soft, brown eyes as she promised solemnly that she would be his glue and that she would mend his heart. No one else knew about that, not even her closest friends, so how could this DJ have possibly found out? She tried to convince herself that it was coincidence once again, that obviously this other couple shared an intimate joke about glue, which was probably a million times removed from her and Steve's. She failed miserably, and as the music began its assault on her emotions she picked up the radio and dashed it to the floor.

This had to be someone's idea of a sick joke. Steve must have told one of their friends at some time, and they had obviously decided to make her life hell with this cruel foolishness. Janie became angry then, white-hot fury replacing her grief. How dare they make light of her tragedy? How dare they soil her memories in this way? She crossed the room and snatched up the telephone, dialling the number of the local station to which the radio had been tuned.

"I want to speak to Nathan Kidd," she replied curtly to the receptionist's cheery greeting.

"I'm sorry?" The voice was suddenly less confident.

"Nathan Kidd, the DJ on the request show. He's on air right now and I want to speak with him."

"I'm sorry," now the receptionist was apologetic, "there is no DJ here by that name. It's Tez Ryan until four o'clock with the chart show, then Danny Stevens until six with the phone-in."

"Look," Janie gripped the receiver, frustration hardening her voice. "I was listening to your station just now and the DJ, who said his name was Nathan Kidd, played a request for me and I want to talk to him. Now will you please put me through?"

"I'm sorry," it was the other's turn to be curt. "I can only repeat that we have no-one by that name here. You have obviously made a mistake. Good-day."

Click. Janie listened to the static on the line for a moment, fighting the urge to throw the phone through the window. Then she shook her head, a groan of despair escaping her lips. What was she doing? She had obviously got the wrong station. The poor woman must have thought her deranged for insisting on speaking to someone she didn't know. Of course this Nathan Kidd didn't work for them, otherwise she would have put her through, or at least fobbed her off with an excuse.

She replaced the receiver and bent to pick up the radio, checking the dial. It was still on the same setting, which was the local station's frequency, so it must have been some other signal cutting in, as it often did on medium wave. She tried switching it back on, but it was dead, without even a crackle of static. When she shook it she heard something rattle inside and she gave a weary sigh. Now she was without a radio, well, a portable one anyway. She switched on the hi-fi, tuning in to the same frequency. She had expected to hear the hushed tones of Nathan Kidd but instead found herself listening to the chirpy, youthful prattle of Tez Ryan as he recited the top twenty singles.

So it *had* been an overlapping transmission, and in which case it could have come from anywhere, which puzzled her all the more. If the request had come from one of her and Steve's so-called friends, surely they would have sent it to the local station, or at least one of the nationals. So it had to be a coincidence, there was no other explanation.

Two days later she was driving Tom to the train station when she heard it again. He was going north for a few days, to visit his parents, and had asked her to give him a lift. She had been only too pleased for the chance to get away from the house for a while, and seeing Tom always left her feeling mellow. She supposed it must have something to do with his talent for talking about nothing in particular and making it sound interesting, as he was doing now. He was going on about his suitcase, and how long it had taken him to pack, and she found herself listening intently as he listed every item, along with its importance, that he had put in the small blue case he held on his lap.

She was particularly fascinated by the fact that he had packed a pair of walking boots. She had always fancied the idea of walking the moors herself, of reaching some high peak to look down on the world around her. But Steve had never been the outdoor type and rather than deprive herself of his company she had pushed the thought to the back of her mind. She glanced down at the ring as Tom went on to tell her how his parents lived near Mam Tor, and how he was looking forward to some serious walking. Never forget her dreams, that was what the ring was supposed to remind her. Perhaps she would buy herself a pair of walking boots.

"This is for Janie," a disturbingly familiar voice interrupted her thoughts. "It comes from Steve with the message, *find the glue*."

Janie brought the car to a halt, her breath coming sharp with panic and sweat beading her upper lip. As the song began she heard Tom's concerned voice.

"Are you all right Janie?" he asked, his blue eyes wide with anxiety. "What's wrong? Why did you stop like that, I nearly dropped my case."

"What can you hear?" she asked sharply, her grey eyes narrowed.

Tom gave her a quizzical look, his fingers fiddling nervously with the handle of the case.

"What do you mean?" he asked, clearly unnerved by her manner. "What's wrong?"

"What can you hear?" she demanded, her voice harsh with desperation. What can you hear?"

"Just the radio, and the engine, look Janie, I don't know what this is about but you're scaring me and I wish you would stop."

"The radio," she hissed, her knuckles white as she gripped the steering wheel, "and what song do you hear on the radio?"

"I, I don't know its name," he said, his voice almost a whisper. He had never seen Janie like this before, so full of anger and grief, and he didn't know how to react. "I think it's by Sting isn't it?"

"Sting?" her voice came out on a shaken whisper. Now Janie was afraid, afraid for her sanity. "I don't hear Sting, I hear The Cranberries!"

Tom reached out to touch her hand as she began to weep, and slowly, falteringly, she began to tell him of Steve, and of the things she had heard over the past few days.

"It's your grief catching up with you," he told her gently.

"But it's real!" she protested bleakly. "The voice of the DJ, the music, it's all so real, how can I be imagining it?"

"The mind can play cruel tricks," Tom assured her. "We all have dreams where we see and hear things that afterwards we remember as being real, well this is just the same except your dreams are coming whilst you are awake."

"So I'm going mad?"

"Not mad," he said softly, "you just need to face up to the fact that Steve has gone and that there is nothing that you can do, or could have done, to change that."

Janie nodded her head. Sometimes, for all his banter, Tom could be wise. She had become obsessed with Steve after his death, let grief dominate her life instead of accepting it as something she must overcome. Perhaps Tom was right: her mind was telling her that enough was enough.

"I'll try," she said, forcing a smile as she put the car in gear and moved back into the traffic flow.

"Why don't you come with me?" he offered. "Walking on those moors will help you put things in perspective, it always does the trick for me."

"Not this time," she said apologetically, not really sure why she felt unable to take up his offer. "I don't have any boots."

"Well make sure you buy some while I'm away," he told her, leaning over to kiss her lightly on the cheek as she brought the car to a halt outside the station gates. "You'll pick me up here next Sunday?"

"Four-thirty," she confirmed, trying desperately not to feel guilty about his gesture of affection.

Tom nodded his dark head, smiling as he closed the car door and waited for her to drive off. She had never really noticed before, but now as she waved goodbye, she realised how warm Tom's smile was, and how it brightened his eyes to the colour of sapphire. Then, as she drove off, guilt attacked her once more, for noticing his looks and she was forced once again to think of Steve.

Whilst Tom's looks were vibrant and startling, Steve's had been quiet, almost fragile. His pale, almost white, blonde hair had fallen in curls to frame his narrow, high-boned face and his skin had been almost translucent, making his soft brown eyes seem enormous and very deep set. He had not been tall, barely her own height, and his physique had been slight, almost skinny. Steve had been someone to be cared for, whereas Tom, with his dark looks and tall, sinewy frame was someone with strength of his own someone to lean on.

She supposed that was what she had been doing with Tom: she had always sought him out when the memories became too much to bear. Being with Tom made her think about now instead of then, wasn't that what she needed? Yet she was always consumed with guilt for seeking comfort in his company, as if she was being unfaithful to Steve's memory. Perhaps that was what these aural hallucinations were telling her: that she wasn't ready to let anyone new into her life yet, that she was somehow hurting Steve by seeking solace in Tom's company.

She was just about to pull into her driveway when the radio invaded her thoughts with another message. This time the dulcet tones of Nathan Kidd announced an address to which requests could be sent. Janie sat for a moment, wondering why, if this was all going on inside her mind, had she invented an address? Was it to make this Nathan Kidd and his show more real? Whatever it was she recognised the address as being part of an old complex of buildings on the edge of the city, a *real* place, although most of it was now disused.

She put the car into gear and drove off in the direction of the address. Now she would find out for sure if she was going mad or if this station and its request show really did exist. Her palms were sweating as she tried to keep her mind on the driving, and she switched off the radio, not wanting to hear any more. As she approached the building complex her heart began thudding and her stomach twisted itself into knots.

The place was deserted, without even one single car in the vast, rubble-strewn car park to suggest that anyone was there. So, she must have imagined it after all, and yet she still got out of the car to take a look around, wanting to make totally sure so that there would not be a single doubt to torment her in the future.

She walked towards the buildings, counting them to find the one in the address she had heard and approached the most dilapidated of them all. There wasn't even a door, and as she entered she wrinkled her nose at the acrid smell that suggested some animal had been using the place as a toilet. There was a longish passageway, at the end of which was a staircase and a room, again without a door. Seeing that the room was empty she began to climb the stairs, taking each step gingerly, afraid that her foot might go through the damp, probably rotting wood. As she climbed she felt the strongest urge to turn around and leave, not from fear of what she might find, but from fear of finding nothing. If the place was as deserted as its state suggested then she would have to face up to the fact that she was losing her mind.

At the top of the stairs were a pair of double doors, remarkably still intact, and she pushed at one of them with great caution, half expecting it to fall from its hinges and land on top of her. It gave, although it was stiff and creaking, and she stepped through into a long corridor. There were doors on either side, and she gave a heavy sigh as she wondered just how long it would take to check out each room. Then something caught her eye and she moved forward, almost running in her eagerness. It was a sign, divided in two and one half was lit, bearing the legend *On Air*.

Beside the sign was a light switch, and she tested it, knowing before she did that there would be no light. This building had been abandoned for years, and a shiver ran the length of her spine as she realised, with unyielding certainty, that there would be no electric supply. So how had the sign been lit? There was only one way to find out, she told herself with a feeling of intense dread: she would have to open the door and look inside the room. She took a deep breath and berated herself for being so craven, then turned the handle and pushed open the door.

As she stepped inside it was like going back in time, to when radio was king and television a dream for the future. The room was soundproofed with the old-fashioned honeycomb type panels and there were great big, thirties style microphones here and there. Boxes and boxes of vinyl records littered the room, along with bits and pieces of extremely outdated recording equipment. At the far side of the room was a turntable, and a high backed chair and Janie could hear someone speaking softly, the voice horribly familiar, reading out a request, although this time it wasn't for her.

"Nathan Kidd!" she threw down the name like a challenge, and the chair moved, swivelling round to face her. Janie felt the colour drain from her face and she didn't know whether the feeling that surged through her was horror or denial. The chair was empty. She shook her head, her eyes wide, staring in total disbelief. This could not be! She moved forwards, closing her eyes for a moment so that when she opened them the owner of the chair and the voice would be revealed, but the picture stayed the same: there was no-one in the room but herself.

So she was crazy after all. She found herself once more holding back tears, although this time they were for herself, for what grief had made her become, and she turned to leave, her step heavy and dejected. It was then, from the corner of her eye, that she caught sight of a figure sitting in the chair. She turned back quickly, as if trying to catch that someone, but, as she suspected, there was still no one there. A trick of the light perhaps, or - more likely - another symptom of her madness. Again she turned to leave, and again, from the corner of her eye, she caught sight of the figure.

This time she did not turn back, but kept her head in that position, so that she could just see the chair on the edge of her vision. This time the figure did not disappear and she was able to study it. It was surprisingly quite solid, instead of the misty, insubstantial figure she thought a ghost must be, and by now she was convinced that Nathan Kidd was indeed a ghost. How else would he be only visible from certain angles. Something struck her as she gazed at the balding, sombrely clad figure of Nathan Kidd, something she hadn't considered until now. Whenever she had heard the request show she had not been listening for it. The first time she had been surfing the channels, looking for something to take her mind off Steve, and the last she had been listening to Tom going on about walking the moors. The only time she had actively searched for the radio station she had been unable to find it. Now, when she looked for Nathan Kidd she was unable to see him, but when she had turned away there he was!

She heard Kidd's throaty chuckle, and the figure in the chair was nodding emphatically.

"Got it in one," the ghostly DJ laughed softly. "I'm only audible to those who do not listen, and visible to those who do not seek me out. That's the way of it with spirits. If we came when looked-for there would be no mystery, no dread."

"So why are you hounding me with those sick requests?" Janie didn't say the words aloud, knowing instinctively that she wouldn't need to.

"They are not sick, but real," Kidd sighed, his voice deep with melancholy. "Steve often gets in touch to send you his love. He wants you to live again Janie, instead of torturing yourself about things beyond your control. He is happy where he is, well he would be if he didn't have your grief to weigh him down."

"So why the request show?" Janie wanted to change the subject, the thought of Steve made unhappy by her grief was something she couldn't bear. "What's in it for you to pirate the air-waves and make people think they're going mad?"

Nathan Kidd sighed and scratched his bald head, his pale green eyes suddenly filled with longing.

"I missed my chance," he said with a sad smile and a shrug of his narrow, black clad shoulders. "When you die, when we all die, we have only so long to find our way to the other world. If we linger too long to watch our loved ones grieve our loss the gateway is closed, and we are trapped between the worlds, belonging to neither."

"You're a lost soul?" Janie's voice came out on a shiver, and she suddenly felt cold all over, goose bumps raising on her bare arms.

"I suppose I am," Kidd nodded, his fingers stroking his grizzled beard as he pondered Janie's words. "I'm stuck here, for eternity, and I'm bored with watching the living messing up their one and only chance, and haunting loses its thrill too quickly: there's only so much satisfaction to be gained from scaring the hell out of some poor sucker in the middle of the night. I had to find something to occupy my time, and time's something I've got plenty of."

We lost souls have one advantage over those that have passed over. We can talk to the living as well as the dead, so some of us find ourselves a medium, becoming their *spirit guide* as they so quaintly put it, and we place them in touch with those in the other world who wish to contact the living."

"But not you," Janie shook her head with a short laugh. This conversation wasn't really happening.

"No," Kidd laughed softly, "not me. I didn't want to involve a middle man, and I'd worked in radio before so I came up with the idea of the request show, a kind of *Medium* wave broadcast." He laughed loudly at his own joke, and Janie couldn't hold back her half-smile. "And I don't do this to make some poor sod think he's going mad either. I really want to help, for Steve's sake more than anything. He should be enjoying the peace of the other world now, happy in the knowledge that you're doing all right without him."

"So I should just forget that I ever loved him, pretend that I don't miss him?" Janie was surprised at the anger in her voice.

"No lass," Kidd shook his head sadly. "He would be heartbroken to think he meant so little, but you've taken your grief to the extreme, let it rule your life and that is not what he wants. His message is clear enough: find yourself some glue, something to help you mend your life. Your time here is so short, much too short to be spent in perpetual self-remorse. Stop using Steve as an excuse to wallow in self pity and get out there and grab yourself a life."

"And if I don't?" Janie felt she already knew the answer.

"Then I'll keep on playing requests for you until you either accept things the way they are, or lose your mind, whichever comes first." The look in Kidd's eyes was suddenly implacable and Janie shivered, knowing full well that the shade meant every word.

She turned away as music began to fill the room, her eyes blurring with tears, although she was smiling. These wouldn't be the last tears she shed for Steve, she knew that, just as she knew she would never forget the depth of love she felt for him, but suddenly she could see beyond the grief, suddenly she could contemplate a future without him.

She left Nathan Kidd without another glance, knowing instinctively that she would never hear his husky voice again. Outside the sky was summer-bright, and she thought of Tom, picturing him striding purposefully to the top of Mam Tor. She didn't know if he would figure in her future, or if he did whether his part would be any more than that of a friend. Perhaps she didn't need any glue, well not in the sense of having someone to help heal her heart. Perhaps the mending had already begun with her acceptance of the need to look forward. One thing she knew for certain: with or without Tom the idea of walking for pleasure held new appeal. As she opened the car door she took one last look at the crumbling building, deciding, as she climbed in and started the engine, that she would go back into town and buy herself a pair of strong boots.

Epitaph

Fara Moore

Call Not Back the Dear Departed
Anchored Safe Where Storms are O'er
On the Borderland We Left Them
Soon to Meet and Part No More

I got the call on a Saturday. John had been moved into intensive care and was failing fast. Could I come? It took a couple of days for me to make arrangements to be away from the business for a few weeks and I wasn't able to get started until Tuesday. The eight-hundred-mile drive was tedious at best. Scattered thunderstorms slowed my progress, sometimes to a crawl. I'd intended to drive straight through, but staring at the back of a tractor-trailer through a rain-spattered windshield was too much of a strain and after five hundred miles I pulled into a motel, exhausted.

Morning dawned clear and I got an early start. Not having to concentrate so much on my driving left my mind free to wander to Anne and what she was going through. We were sisters, but not twins. I was a year older. We were the only two children and had always been close. Anne was the prettiest. Shy and insecure, she reminded me of a fawn. I, on the other hand, had a much stronger personality; a trait that came through in my looks.

Anne and John had been high school sweethearts. By then I'd realized how needy she was and I was terrified that one of the many boys that flocked around her would break her fragile heart. Luckily, John was devoted to her from the start. They'd married before college, working their way through while living in the dingy dorms of married student housing. After graduation John had gotten an entry-level position at a fast growing firm. He was intelligent and dedicated, but also possessed that kind of personality that made most people like him on sight. He'd done well for himself.

Then, three years ago, the happily-ever-after world John and Anne had built started to disintegrate like a sandcastle in an encroaching tide. Unexplained pains and fatigue sent John to the hospital for tests. The results were worse than bad: cancer. Chemotherapy began immediately, but it only provided a temporary respite. When after two years of treatments the disease hadn't gone into remission, John had called it quits. Life was more than simply existing, he said. The treatments only prolonged the agony. He and Anne sold everything they had and moved to a small country town in West Virginia. John had always wanted to live in the country and so that was where he went to die. The last year had been spent living simply. Being with each other was the most important thing.

The exit sign loomed ahead and I pulled myself back to the present. Centerville was about twenty miles from the interstate and I needed all of my wits to negotiate the winding two-lane road that would take me there. The hospital, like the town, *was* small. But that didn't matter to John. After all, he'd gone there to die, not be healed. A nurse gave me directions to the room. I hesitated a moment, then tapped on the door.

"Oh, Jenny, thank God you're here!" Anne rushed to me, arms open, eyes sparkling with tears. I hugged her hard. "Hey, Sis. How're you holding up?" I didn't really need to ask. She looked like hell.

Anne shrugged, tried to smile. "You were always the strong one." This was true. Even as children I'd been the more practical, the more in control. When Anne would come running home distraught about some adolescent problem, I was the one who helped her put things in perspective. As an adult, she'd had John. I wondered how she would cope when he was gone.

I looked over at the wasted figure in the hospital bed for the first time and fought back tears of my own. He was sleeping so I didn't have to think of anything to say. "How is he?"

Anne's tears started anew. "Not well. The pain medication keeps him unconscious most of the time. He . . . he stayed home until he couldn't stand it anymore. I think he wanted to die there but I just wasn't able to take care of him alone. So we came here last week."

The next few days blurred together. Hours spent at John's bedside, trying to keep Anne from falling apart as she watched her husband die. I'd always managed to stay away from death, not because I was uncomfortable with the idea of mortality, but because I never knew what to do or say in an atmosphere that screamed for comfort and understanding.

John slept a lot. In the times when he was awake I made a point of leaving the room so that they could have the small amount of privacy the hospital offered. I was only alone with him once while he was conscious. Anne had gone down to the cafeteria for coffee while I stayed with John. Suddenly I felt a hand on mine.

"Thanks for being here for her," he said. His voice was weak, his eyes barely open.

"You know I'll do whatever I can," I replied, giving his hand a gentle squeeze.

"She wants me to hang on, Jen, and I can't." The agony in his eyes conveyed his meaning in a way words never could. "I try to make it through each day for her sake. But I'm going to have to leave her. I wish it wasn't this way, God knows I do. Jen, help her when I'm gone."

I nodded. The knot in my throat made speaking impossible.

John died the next day, just at sunrise. Anne was hysterical. She refused to leave the body and at one point even climbed up in the bed and tried to shake John back to life. The doctor finally gave her a sedative and I took her home. John had had the foresight to make the funeral plans well in advance, so there wasn't really anything to do.

There was no viewing at the funeral home. Both John and Anne hated the idea of the dead being put on display. The service was quiet and private, with burial at a small country cemetery just down the road from the house they'd shared, the house where Anne now lived alone.

I'd been afraid that she would be uncontrollable at the grave side, but the doctors had put her on strong tranquilizers and she stood there, eyes glazed, face frozen, looking half dead herself. I gave what support I could, though *I* refused to utter any of the *usual condolences* which, even when well meant, sounded inane and empty. The woman's husband was dead. What was there to say?

I'd planned to stay several weeks, until I was sure Anne was going to be all right by herself. I was worried about several things, suicide and a nervous breakdown among them. John had been her world; her life revolved around him like the planets around the sun. Where would she find meaning now that he was gone? She spent a lot of time at the grave. I imagined she was talking to John, though I never went with her to find out. Our family had never been particularly religious and for the first time I wondered if this had been a mistake. Surely Anne had her beliefs about life after death, but I had no idea what they were, and this didn't seem like the time to ask.

After about a week I noticed a definite change in her attitude. She had been quiet and withdrawn since the funeral and while I was there if she needed me, I didn't want to intrude on her grief. People handle loss in their own individual ways after all, and I passed the time reading and watching the big coal trucks race down the narrow road in front of the house. Then one day she started smiling. I'd felt that she would eventually resign herself to John's death, but I'd never expected it to happen so soon, and I certainly didn't expect her to suddenly seem happy. She was still going to the grave every day, but instead of coming home melancholy, she was almost cheerful. She began to talk about her plans for a garden and even went so far as to order spring bulbs.

We were sitting at the kitchen table having coffee one afternoon when she reached out and took my hand. "Thanks for all you've done, Sis. I'd never have made it without you."

"Anne, you don't have to thank me. I'm your sister, I love you."

"I know. But I'm okay now. At first I didn't think I was going to make it. But I am. John's dead, but he's not gone. Not really. Love never dies."

"Of course it doesn't. And John wouldn't want you to be miserable."

She nodded. "You're right. And I won't be. But what I wanted to say was that you have a life too. I know you've got the business on hold, but it can't stay that way forever."

"None of that's important. Not if you need me."

"Knowing you're there helps a lot. But we've both got our own lives and I've got to start getting used to my new one."

My eyes searched her face. "Anne, are you sure about this?"

She insisted that she was and so I left the next day after lunch. I wasn't in a hurry and didn't push myself. When I reached Clarkston, a small city with a selection of decent motels and restaurants, I stopped for the night. After a leisurely dinner and a hot shower I curled up in the king-sized bed and watched a movie on cable. Solitude is something I value and after the stress of the past few weeks it was a relief to be alone. I was relaxed and sleep came easily.

I woke with a start in the wee hours of the morning. There was no sound in the room, nothing to pull me back from the realms of slumber. No, what caused my abrupt return to consciousness was in my own mind. I was worried about Anne. And as sometimes happens when our minds are freed by sleep, I realized what had been nagging at me since I left Centerville. Anne's change had been too sudden. Some part of me had known that something was wrong, but I wasn't able to put my finger on it until now.

I jumped out of bed and threw on some clothes, tossed my stuff in the car and headed back the way I had come. Anne's words went through my mind as I drove - *John's dead, but not gone - Love never dies -*

The sky was turning pink when I pulled into the driveway. I found Anne in the kitchen, making coffee. The table was set for two and John's corpse was seated by the window.

"Hi, Sis," **Anne** said brightly. "Did you forget something?"

I shook my head and stared at John. Anne followed my gaze, a thin smile on her lips. She went about fixing breakfast while I continued to stare at the corpse. Embalming was optional in this rural county and without the formaldehyde to slow its progress, decay was running rampant, especially on the soft tissue of the face. The cheeks were almost eaten away, the movement of the bugs faintly visible through the ragged holes. He wasn't alive, but he wasn't completely dead either. Instead he was lurking in that borderland between the two, held in limbo by Anne's refusal to let him go. He regarded me with eyes clouded over and milky white, but even through the haze I could see the longing there, the same yearning for rest that I'd seen in his eyes that day at the hospital.

I went to Anne and wrapped my arms around her shoulders. "Anne, honey, John can't stay here. It's time for him to move on."

"No!" she cried, trying to push me away. "He wants to stay with me! Love never dies!" Her eyes were bright, but not with tears.

"Yes, he loves you. And he would stay with you if he could. But that time has passed. Anne, if you love him, you've got to let him go."

She looked over at him then and I think she saw him, really saw him as he was. The cry that tore from her throat reminded me of a trapped animal. "Noooo!"

Before I knew it she had dashed out the back door. It wasn't what I expected and it took me a moment to grasp what was happening. By the time I got to the front yard she was already at the road. I saw the coal truck barreling down on her and screamed, knowing it wouldn't do any good but unable to help myself.

I cradled her mangled body as gently as I could. Blood leaked from her lips when she smiled and she managed to say just one word: together. The life in her eyes flickered and died, and I saw peace there for the first time since before John got sick.

They were buried side-by-side in the small cemetery. I didn't linger at the grave; they had moved on I was sure. Some might have called it tragic, but in truth the tragedy was at an end. John was finally free from pain, and Anne would never be alone again.

But None, I Think, Do There Embrace

C. W. J. Joss

He stood pale and naked at the window, vacantly staring out into the dark avenue.

She shifted on her cane and took his cold hand. "Sam." she said, "you can't stand here. If someone saw you – "

She let the words trail off as she peered out at the quiet avenue. Through the bare bones of the rowan trees lining the street, puddles of amber streetlight rippled on rain-slick cobblestones. From a distance came the shush. . shush - shush of motorcars moving swiftly on wet roads. Across the avenue the houses slept. No lights shone at the windows. No one stood on their front lawn with a fist jammed to their mouth and their eyes wide and staring. And no one screamed.

She looked up into her husband's blank face. Would they scream if they saw you? Would they scream, as I did, if they awoke to find you lying beside them dressed in your Sunday best and caked with mud?

She pulled heavy velvet curtains across the window, darkening the room. The only light came from two dim table-lamps with green fringed shades.

'Come and sit down, Sam. We have to talk.' Can you talk? She wondered. The final stroke had stolen his speech.

She tugged his hand and together they moved away from the window.

He walked slowly, his movements spastic. He snapped out his legs and swung his free arm in wild, wide arcs.

Oh, God, he's forgetting how to walk, she thought. How did you make it so far'? Why did no one see you? She imagined him stumbling through dark city streets, people hurrying across the road to keep away from him. Did they think you were drunk or simply daft?

She shuffled slowly beside him, her cane tapping on the floorboards through the 'worn carpet. I'm sending out a distress signal, she thought. I'm sending out a distress signal hoping reality will come and rescue me. But it won't. This is <u>real</u>.

She guided him towards his chair by the fire and folded him into the seat. Lifting her bag of knitting from her seat, she placed it by the fire and sat down with an exaggerated sigh and a forced smile.

He sat with his arms folded in his lap covering his shriveled penis. His face resembled the paper masks their grandchildren made at Halloween. His skin was a gray, pasty color and his mouth hung slack. His eyes bulged in *their* sockets.

She sat quietly searching for where to begin. How could she tell him what he was? How could she tell him he couldn't stay? She couldn't keep him locked in the attic like a mad relation that everyone pretended didn't exist. What would he do when Sally and Jack came to stay? Would he want to play with them as he used to? She pictured them playing ring-a-ring-a-roses. Sally and Jack holding on to Grandpa's cold hands and laughing as they danced in a circle. Ring-a-ring-a-roses, a pocketful of posies. A tissue! A tissue! We all fall down!

She looked across at Sam, sitting quietly in his favorite chair. But sometimes they get up again, don't they? A shiver rippled up her spine and goose bumps broke out on her arms.

This is your husband, she thought. This is the man you've loved for the last fifty-two years. Remember that.

"People have been very kind. I've had lots of cards." She nodded up at the mantelpiece where white cards bordered in black stood either side of the ormolu clock. "And all the ladies in the street have been round with cakes and casseroles. Alan did a good job of organizing everything. You'd have been proud of him. Sally and Jack didn't come. Alan and Jean thought they were too young. And the minister's been very kind, he's – " She snapped her mouth shut. I'm rambling.

Wiping a hand slowly across her face she leant forward in her chair. "Why have you come back, Sam?"

He focused on her, the first time since he'd arrived. A flame of intelligence sparked into life behind his eyes. His jaw worked in slow, lazy circles. His Adam's apple bobbed frantically.

She pattered his knee and smiled. "Take your time."

His head jutted forward then back. Forward. Back. His mouth gulped open and his eyes grew wide. His right arm floundered against the side of the chair, slapping the leather.

Minutes passed. The ormolu clock chimed the half-hour.

She began to cry, watching him struggle to find the words. Pulling a small lace handkerchief from the sleeve of her cardigan, she dabbed at her eyes.

He strained forward in his seat with his mouth open impossibly wide. His gray tongue danced between his shrunken gums.

What did they do with his false teeth? She shook away the inane thought and concentrated on what he was trying to say.

Then a great inrush of air as if from dry, cracked bellows. His mouth clamped shut, trapping the air inside.

She leaned forward. Their faces almost touched.

He opened his mouth. The air wheezed out, stinking of rancid meat. He spoke one strained word. 'Lonely.'

He slumped back in his chair, a large idiot grin spreading across his face.

She patted him on the knee, again. "Well done."

Propping her elbows on her knees, she sank her head in her hands. "I've been lonely, too. It's the first time we've been apart since we were married. I come into a room and expect to see you, and when I don't it breaks my heart. I don't know how I'm going to go on living without you. Alan and Jean say they'll visit, but they've got Sally and Jack to look after. They shouldn't have to worry about an old woman like me."

She wiped away the tears meandering down her face. 'I didn't realize you'd feel lonely. I didn't realize you'd feel anything. But what can I do? What do you want? I can't keep you here. People would find out and they'd cart you off to be prodded and poked by men in white coats.'

She took his pale hands in hers, squeezing them tightly. Looking up into his face she saw the flame of intelligence gutter behind his eyes, as if caught in a cold, dark wind. I have to know what he wants before it dies. I have to know how to make him happy.

"Tell me what you want."

His mouth opened but he closed it, shaking his head as if realized he could never say what needed to be said.

He stood, pulling her to her feet. He led her across the living room and into the dark hallway. His hand fumbled with the locks on the front door.

"Outside? You want to go outside?" He nodded vigorously. "I'll have to get my coat and hat." She picked up her house keys sitting on the table by the door. "And I'll need these."

He shook his head and took the keys from her hand. He dropped them back onto the table.

"But I have to take my keys, otherwise I can't get back in." She picked up the keys again.

He shook his head and snatched the keys from her. He threw them into the living room. The keys clattered against the wall and fell into the fireplace.

"I'll need my keys," she said. "Unless - unless I'm not coming back. A line of poetry from her childhood flashed into her mind: The grave's a fine and private place. But none, I think, do there embrace. Who wrote that? Never mind.

She looked up into his pale, sad face and something in there told her that this was the only way.

She turned and took one final look at the house where they'd spent their lives together. "It wasn't the same after you'd gone. It seemed empty, hollow, and I don't think it would've changed."

She turned back to him and squeezed his hand. "If we're quick we can be gone before the dawn comes."

She opened the front door and together, hand in hand. they left the house.

AUTHORS

Danielle Iserman lives in Norcross, Georgia with her son, Steven. She is an avid enthusiast the paranormal and the Civil War. She has written many award-winning short stories of that era. Her newest work will appear in the upcoming Civil War ghost anthology, *Dead Promises*. When not involved in a writing project, she can be found doing storytelling at major events, including Georgia's Stone Mountain yearly "Tour of Southern Ghosts."

Steve Eller is a former systems analyst who now writes full-time, hidden away in the mountains of North Carolina. He has had sixty stories printed since 1995 in magazines such as "Tales of the Unanticipated," and anthologies *Horrors,* and *365 Scary Stores*, and received honorable mention in Year's *Best Fantasy and Horror in both 1996 and 1997*. He says he makes an honest effort to be happy.

William Churchman raises cattle in rural Kansas where he lives with his family. He's had several short stories published, has a novel with an agent, and is on the verge of completing a second novel. This marks the debut of "For the Love of Claire."

Denise M. Bruchman makes her home in Albany, Oregon. Her novella, "The Lesser of Two Evils" appears in Robert Block's *Psychos,* and her short story "Fates' Exile" appears in *Imagination Fully Dilated*. A compulsive reader, she never knows what will tickle her fancy next.

Daniel Keohane lives in Princeton, Massachusetts with his wife and three children. He is an HWA member and currently works as an independent software consultant, writing part time when not writing software or changing diapers. A newcomer to fiction, "Incineration" is his first published story.

Christine Miller has been writing for a few years and hopes to be able to quit her "night" and devote all her time to writing. She also believes that if her desk isn't cluttered, she isn't working hard enough. Her most recent success is the short story "Friends" to be included in the recently released vampire anthology, *The Kiss of Death* published by The Design Image Group, Inc. She lives with her family in Defiance, Ohio.

Dianne Buckman has two children and a dog. Her work has appeared in the Australian magazine "Spinechiller" and in the U.S. in "Altered Perceptions." Her poetry has appeared in "Micropress Yates" and the "Sunshine Coast Daily" in Australia. She has recently completed a novel, *The Dark Poet* and is working on her second book. This is the debut appearance of "The Last Stone."

Martha Pound Miller is the former executive director of The American Institute for Architects in Arizona and is a native of that state. She moved to Oregon to follow her muse and finds Oregonians cultured, laid back and yes, even web-footed on occasion. She shares her Portland house with Gracie, a feisty Jack Russell terrier. This story, which appeared in the Fall/Winter 1997 issue of *Haunts* magazine, is lovingly dedicated to Martha's grandmother, Martha Bishop Pettijohn.

Gail Sosinsky Wickman has been a newspaper editor, English Composition teacher, corporate newsletter editor, and doughnut seller. She holds a BA in journalism and an MA in English literature. She lives with her husband, Randy, two children, Harrison and Molly and is in the process of building a house in the woods of northwestern Wisconsin.

Lisa Becker's interest in horror began as a kid reading "Creepy" and "Eerie," but it wasn't until she read *The Shining* that she thought how much fun it would write scary stories. She hopes to make people turn on the lights and tuck in their feet at night. She lives with her husband in an isolated schoolhouse. The silence and one hundred fifty years of history provides much inspiration.

Steven Lee Climer wrote "My Dear Companion" for his wife as a way of telling her how he feels about her. His fiction has appeared in a variety of magazines, including *Darkness, Altered Perceptions,* and the anthology *Monsters from Memphis* for which he won the 1998 Darrell Award. He is the author of *Dream Thieves, Blood Red: Book One.*

Trent Zelazny is a native of Santa Fe, New Mexico where he says he was "surrounded by horror." His belief is that the world can be a horrifying and/or humorous place. His hobbies are reading and listening to rock and roll.

Brad Jeske's work has appeared in numerous horror magazines. His radio play, Endless Night was produced last year by Triangle Radio Theatre, and was aired nationally to over fifty radio stations. In addition to radio, his work is also on the Internet at Alexandria Digital Literature (http://www.alexlit.com.) He is currently working on a novel.

Philip Caveney was born in Wales to an R.A.F. officer, and spent much of his childhood travelling the world. His first novel, *The Sins of Rachel Ellis* was published in 1978. His most recent title is *Cursery Rhymes* (with illustrator Bob Seal.) For more information about his work, contact his web site at www.purefiction.com/philipcaveney/

Catherine Nichols lives in New York City with her husband and teenage daughter. She works as a freelance editor and writer. She is currently putting the finishing touches on a collection of spooky stories for children

Laura Capewell is a New Jersey native though she currently lives in suburban Philadelphia. Two years ago at the age of forty-five she decided to follow the road not taken and seriously pursue her love of writing. Since then she has written several short stories and two novels.

Rick Kennett has lives all his forty-three years in Melbourne, Australia where he is that city's longest-serving motorcycle courier. He has had about forty stories published in magazines and anthologies in Australia, the U.S. and the U.K.

Carol MacAllister has placed over thirty-five horror/dark fantasy pieces in various 'zines. She also placed in *Scavenger's Newsletter's Killer Frog* contest and will be included in the *Killer Frog anthology* with "Woebegone." In addition to prose, she is also a poet and artist won many awards with her work. She is currently working on a murder mystery from her old Victorian house on the Atlantic Ocean in New Jersey.

James O. Dukes is a native of Savannah, Georgia where he resides with his wife, Dianne. He is a member of HWA and works in a variety of genres. He recently had a science fiction script produced by Shoestring Radio Theatre based in San Francisco and aired on National Public Radio. "Till Death Do Us Join" was written exclusively for Cemetery Sonata. (For which this editor is quite honored.)

Gayla D. Bassham since she learned to form letters. A native of Arkansas she now makes her home in Michigan where she is a Systems Engineer at Pyramid Solutions in Troy, Michigan. She is married and expecting her first child. The house in "Harold" is loosely based on her great-grandmother's house.

Deborah Markus lives in Santa Monica, California where and her writer husband, Dominick Cancilla, manage an apartment building. Her work has appeared in anthologies The Darkest Thirst and The Kiss of Death. She wishes to thank her son, Markus for all those naps that allowed her to write "Bitter Pills."

Matt Doeden lives in suburban Chicago with his wife, Gina and his pet rats, Kitten and Pepper. He is an editor for Capstone Press, a publisher of children's educational nonfiction. He is also helping to edit the dark fantasy and horror magazine, *Flesh and Blood*. His stories have appeared in many magazines including *Maelstrom Speculative Fiction*.

Phil Locascio grew up in Chicago where he received a degree in Psychology from Northern Illinois University. He works for the Department of Human Services for the State of Illinois and lives with his wife, Jane and five-year-old daughter, Lucy.

Edo Van Belkom is a Bran Stoker award recipient and author of over one hundred thirty stories of fantasy, science fiction and horror. His stories have appeared in numerous magazine and anthologies as well as creating the novels, *Wyrm Wolf*, *Lord Soth* and *Mister Magick*. You can reach him at his web page at www.horrornet.com/belkom.htm.

Calvin K. Bricker regularly writes horror and suspense as well as dabbling in dark fantasy and science fiction. He is currently putting the finishing touches on his first novel and noodling about his second. A member of HWA, he lives with his wife in Pittsburgh, Pennsylvania.

Ray Roberts is a geologist. He lives in the woods with his wife and pets and occasionally writes a short story or article. His short stories have appeared in a number of magazines including *Adventures of the Sword* and *Sorceryl*.

K. D. Wentworth lives in Tulsa with her husband, numerous finches and a one-hundred-twenty-six-pound Akita, and teaches elementary school. Her stories have appeared in *Hitchcock's Mystery Magazine, Realms of Fantasy*, and *Return to the Twilight Zone* among others. Her short story "Burning Bright" was a 1997 Nebula Nominee. She has published three novels with Del Rey. A fourth, *Black/on/Black* is due out from Baen in 1999.

Tina Jens is the executive producer of *Twilight Tales: The Reading Serious,* and editor of the *Twilight Tales* chapbooks. She has published more the thirty stories in horror, fantasy and thriller genres. Recent stories appear in *Horrors*, **365 Scary Stories** and *Monsters from Memphis*. You can visit her web page at www.para.net.com/tina_jens.

Robert Devereaux lives along the foothills of the Rockies, leading a quite contented life with Victoria and enjoying the exuberant writing of nine-year-old daughter Lianna. He is currently finishing a literary romance in the tradition of Segal, Waller, and Sparks. His most recent novel is *Santa Steps Out*.

Liz Holliday's work has appeared in various anthologies and magazines and she has received several "year's best" honorable mentions from Ellen Datlow, Terri Windling and Gardner Dozois. She is the editor of *Odyssey* magazine.

Greg Burnham lives in Canton, Mississippi with his wife, Mandy and children Megan and Peyton. He owns an outpatient healthcare facility which specializes in a variety of health related services. Though healthcare is his profession, story telling is his passion. He believes that the South has a preternatural aura to it and makes it his hobby to seek out the folklore elaborate on it.

Michael C. McPherson is a multi-talented writer whose work has appeared in several magazines and anthologies, including Alfred Hitchcock Mystery Magazine, and the anthologies, Meltdown, and Bizarre Dreams. He is currently working on a screenplay.

Robin Spriggs travels through life with a motley caravan of two dogs, one cat, one woman, and myriad Spirits both ancestral and elemental. When not writing, he acts and does commercials. He has appeared in many films as well as on the stage. His fiction has appeared in numerous magazines and anthologies.

Lisa Silverthorne lives in Indiana. Her fiction has appeared in various publications and anthologies. Her upcoming work can be found in *365 Scary Stories, Prom Night,* and *Sword & Sorceress XVI.*

Terry Campbell is a thirty-three-year-old writer/artist living in Terrell, Texas, a small town about thirty miles east of Dallas. His fiction has appeared in *Blood Muse, 100 Wicked Little Witch Stories,* and *Kiss and Kill: The Hot Blood Series.*

James Van Pelt writes in Western Colorado. His work has appeared in a variety of magazines including *Realms of Fantasy*. Upcoming work is scheduled in *weird Tales* and *bending the Landscape: Horror*. He has also received honorable mention in *Year's Best Fantasy and Horror* anthology.

Carl Hughes is a journalist with a large newspaper in Norfolk, England, and has also worked in radio and TV. His fiction has appeared in a variety of magazines and books in Britain and North America, and he has won many literary competitions. This editor is honored is say that "The Man in Black" was written especially for Cemetery Sonata.

John Urbancik IIII was born on Long Island though he now resides in Orlando, Florida. He has been writing since age ten and completed his first novel in seventh grade. Though he considers that first attempt "horrible," he now has publishing credits in many small press magazines such as *Altered Perceptions* and *Goddess of the Bay.*

Fara Moore grew up reading horror novels and watching "Dark Shadows" though she did not try her hand at writing until a few years ago. She has sold her work to numerous magazines and has a selection in *More Monsters from Memphis.*

Cheryl Jessop lives in a small mining town north of England with her husband and two teenage children. She currently a second year student at Sheffield Haltom University working on her English degree. Though not her first published story, "Mending" is her first U.S. sale.

C.W.J. Joss was raised in and around Scotland. Presently he lives with his wife, Alison in East Lotion, and works as a computer specialist in Edinburgh. He is a member of HWA and has work published in *Weird Tales* and *The Year's Best Fantasy and Horror #10*.